FIRST IMPRESSIONS . . .

As they passed through Kpama the twilight deepened. Rose light poured from the sky. It bathed in pink the mud walls of the houses and the red earth on which they stood and from which they had been fashioned. It cast the mango trees in shades of copper and turned the whitewashed mosques an irreverent flamingo. Calls of the muezzins arched into the flushed vault over the town, summoning the faithful to the *salât al maghrib*, the evening prayer, fourth of the five daily prayers required by Islam. Collections of sandals, like infestations of evening fungi, sprang up outside the various mosques, an indication of the number of worshipping within.

"Where are the women?" Likki wanted to know. She saw only men approaching the whitewashed buildings to pray, their rolled prayer mats carried under their arms like oversized scrolls.

"Women don't pray," said John Lavender.

"Why not?"

"They're polluted."

"Polluted with what?"

"With being women."

"God *damn*! said Likki.

"God *damn*!" echoed Abu. He liked the way she said it.

DOWNFALL PEOPLE

Jo Anne Williams Bennett

SEAL BOOKS
McClelland-Bantam, Inc.
Toronto

This low-priced Seal Book
has been completely reset in a typeface
designed for easy reading, and was printed
from new plates. It contains the complete
text of the original hardcover edition.
NOT ONE WORD HAS BEEN OMITTED.

DOWNFALL PEOPLE

A Seal Book / December 1987

PRINTING HISTORY

McClelland and Stewart edition published October 1986

ISBN 0-7704-42180-6

Seal Books are published by McClelland-Bantam Inc. Its trademark,
consisting of the words "Seal Books" and the portrayal of a seal, is
the property of McClelland-Bantam Inc., 60 St. Clair Avenue East,
Suite 601, Toronto, Ontario M4T 1N5, Canada. This trademark has
been duly registered in the Trademarks Office of Canada. The
trademark, consisting of the words "Bantam Books" and the
portrayal of a rooster, is the property of and is used with the consent
of Bantam Books, Inc., 666 Fifth Avenue, New York, New York
10103. This trademark has been duly registered in the Trademarks
Office of Canada and elsewhere.

PRINTED IN CANADA

COVER PRINTED IN U.S.A.

U   0 9 8 7 6 5 4 3 2 1

To the memory of another Abu
and to all his brothers and sisters
in the shining dark continent of Africa

We call to witness
the sun and its growing brightness,
and the moon when it follows it,
and the day when it reveals its glory,
and the night when it draws a veil over it,
and the heaven and the purpose of its making,
and the earth and the purpose of its spreading out,
and the soul and its perfect proportioning
(He revealed to it the right and wrong of everything),
he indeed prospers who purifies it,
and he is ruined who corrupts it.

*The Quran, the Eternal Revelation vouchsafed to Muhammad,
The Seal of the Prophets*, Chapter 91 (Al-Shams), 2-11.

Arabic text with a new translation by Sir Muhammad Zafrulla Khan
London: 1981. Reprinted by permission of Curzon Press.

PROLOGUE

Abu was among the first to see Fatima's body. He was out with his sling-shot looking for cattle birds when he heard the ugly shouting coming from the public latrine.

The public latrine, or *bomba,* was one of several in the town of Kpama—all of them squat edifices, crumbling concrete pillboxes surrounded by dandruffs of chipped paint. They were strictly gravity-feed operations, flushed by no water, emptying into no sewer. Instead the cumulative excrement of those who could not afford toilets (and who *could* afford them?) moved with glacier-like deliberation down graded trenches inside the building, eventually collecting in cement tanks on either side of the facility, one tank for men and one for women. There it gathered with sickening foulness on the flanks of sanitary progress. Once a month the covers were removed from these tanks and the contents were pumped out into a malodorous Public Works Department lorry, which carried the filth away to the devil knew where. This was always a day for those who lived nearby to visit relatives or make extended shopping expeditions to the market. Even the pigs—in the normal course of their appetites only too pleased to feast on human excrement—even these gross creatures cleared out of the vicinity on pumping day. Only the flies stayed on unperturbed.

The pumping crew comprised the dregs of the community. All the villagers, even the garbage man, turned up their noses at these unfortunates. The despised crew members were hard at work one morning in late April when their hose blocked up in the men's tank. They took the hose out and inspected it—an unpleasant task. Nothing seemed to be wrong. They replaced it in the tank, but it blocked a second time. Muranji, who was already predictably high on

1

guinea-corn beer—he'd stopped off for three pots at Farrah's at 6:00 A.M. on his way to work—went to peer inside the tank. Something was floating in there. Muranji got a stick and prodded it. It revolved slowly in the foetid mush. Muranji saw a face; next thing, he vomited.

Fatima had been missing for four days. Mahmut, her husband, had gone twice to her parents' house demanding his wife back. Fatima's mother, Hawa, had used strong language with Mahmut. If he knew how to look after a wife properly, Hawa had told him, "She would never run off just like that." Everyone had claimed ignorance of Fatima's whereabouts. Everyone had been suspected of lying.

Now Hawa came down to the *bomba* like a biblical curse. She came wailing from her stall in the market, shouting that her daughter had been murdered. She screamed insults at the pumping crew. She slandered her son-in-law and his family. She said she would steal her little granddaughter (Fatima's newborn) away from the house of Mahmut. She would never, never, never let the child be raised by such a flatulent bag of ogres. Hawa threatened Mahmut with reprisals. She threatened his family with sorcery. And then she left Mahmut and his family to their distressful labour, saying that since by custom the corpse belonged to them, they could have the pleasure of removing the reeking filth of the town from the beautiful girl they had murdered. Several people were already retching; the stench was terrific.

Cattle birds and sling-shot forgotten, Abu watched as long as he dared. He was torn between not wanting to miss anything and wanting to be home with the news before Salifu. Abu waited until Fatima's in-laws had rolled her body in a rapidly staining blanket and then left for home.

■

Mother of Issa was alone in the house. She was sitting in the upstairs kitchen plucking a chicken when Abu burst in on her, exclaiming, "Ayyiiieeeeeee, my mother!"

"Unh?" grunted Mother of Issa, who declined to be excitable. She particularly disliked being disturbed by Abu, whom, as a four-year-old, she had rescued eight years earlier from the beatings of strangers. Unlike Salifu,

Arimata and Habiba, the other orphans in the house, Abu had never quite convinced Mother of Issa of his gratitude. He was, perhaps, too mischievous. His abhorrence of physical work (she had taken him in to help out in the house) was too obvious. Poverty and misfortune had left him more exuberant than was seemly.

"They have found this girl, Fatima!" explained Abu.

"Is she home now?"

"The girl is dead."

"Ha?" cried Mother of Issa, looking up dismayed.

"It's true!" said Abu. "And how they found her!"

"Where was she?" Mother of Issa inquired uneasily. She suspected the next piece of news would be more unpleasant still.

"She was floating in the tank of the *bomba.*"

"Ach!" cried Mother of Issa. Blood and tears rushed to her face as if she had been slapped. She took a heavy breath and stared in front of her for a long while. Then she wiped her eyes and handed the chicken up to Abu. "Finish this chicken," she ordered him dully. She rose and walked stiffly to her room like one who is troubled with rheumatism. Shortly afterwards, dressed in red, the colour of mourning, she left for the house of Hawa.

By local custom—an uneasy mix of Muslim and tribal traditions—Fatima would have four funerals spread out over the course of a year. The first of these, held immediately, was to allow people to pay their last respects and then dispose of the corpse as quickly as possible. The second funeral took place one week later, when the women of the deceased's household had had time to prepare vast amounts of food and drink for the hundreds of friends and relations who would gather at their home to mourn and draw comfort from each other's company. The third was a smaller, forty-day memorial service, and the last, a year after the death, was again a large affair, partly a celebration, a throwing off of mourning.

Fatima's first funeral, held the day after her body was found, was an ill-starred occasion. Accusations had been flying and people were out of temper.

Because of her position in the town, Mother of Issa attended as a matter of course, and both Abu and Salifu went along with her for no better reason than that they disliked being left out of anything. They wore their khaki school uniforms because these were the closest thing they had to red mourning. At the gathering, Abu drifted in and out of the neighbourhood of several private conversations. No one paid him the least attention. When he thought he was on top of matters he went home and reported to Mieri, Mother of Issa's youngest child, who was his friend and ally. Salifu stayed on at the funeral to eat more meat than he was entitled to and learned nothing.

Mieri was languishing under the mango tree in the courtyard, suffering from the malaria that afflicted her every rainy season. She was the weakest of Mother of Issa's five children. She was also the last born and the most indulged, since she was the only one still living at home. Abu and Mieri looked after each other; they had their own little scams all worked out. Mieri supplemented Abu's diet with kitchen surplus when she could claim it undetected. Or, if Mother of Issa were making a blouse, Mieri saved scraps of leftover cloth. Or she might pilfer a pencil from the large desk belonging to Kutu, Mother of Issa's husband. In this small and clandestine manner she undid her parents' overall indifference. Abu, in his turn, was Mieri's spy. He was omniscient after a certain adolescent fashion and knew more about what went on in Kpama than any human being had a right to. Occasionally Mother of Issa, or even Kutu, would offhandedly ask Mieri for her opinion on some subject beyond her years. Mieri would always say she needed time to think about it. This was Abu's cue. He would unearth all that could be discovered concerning the matter in hand and report back to Mieri. She in turn would confide in her parents. In this way Mother of Issa had side-stepped several enticing but ultimately unprofitable business entanglements and had benefited substantially from two partnerships formed at the optimal moment. In this way, too, she avoided becoming directly indebted to Abu.

Abu sank onto the bench next to Mieri and waved his hands excitedly while he waited to regain his breath. He had been running hard. His excitement imparted itself to Mieri, and she fidgeted with impatience while she waited for the story to begin.

"Hey!" he began at last. "It is *too* bad! Fatima's mother, she says Mahmut has *murdered* Fatima and put the body in the tank so that no one could find it in there. But Mahmut and his family, *they* say the girl was killed by sorcery and that it was witchcraft that placed her in that tank."

"Who would make magic against Fatima?"

"They say the magic was sent against the husband, Mahmut, but he himself was *too* strong for it, so it went instead to his wife and destroyed her."

"Fatima was not weak," objected Mieri, pondering perhaps her own condition.

"Yes," agreed Abu, "but she had only just brought forth. So at that time, even a strong woman can be weak."

"What will happen to the baby?"

"They are even now at the Ruler's palace fighting over the baby. Mahmut says there is a woman in his house who has lost a child and this woman has come forward to say she can suckle Fatima's baby. But Hawa says no! She says if the baby stays in that family of Mahmut, it will be murdered just like its mother. Hawa says she herself will take the baby away to safety."

"But if Hawa takes the child, how will she feed it?" Hawa was an old woman with tits like two leather wallets. Fatima's baby was not yet five weeks old.

"Hawa says she will give the baby to Ayesha." Abu grinned broadly, for this piece of information was a triumph of surprise. The look on Mieri's face said she was plainly incredulous, although there were reasons why it was a reasonable choice for Hawa to make. Ayesha was Hawa's niece and first cousin to Fatima. The two girls had been raised almost as sisters, alternating for months on end between one another's houses, so it was natural for Ayesha to take an interest in the child. But Ayesha was regarded with (discreet) alarm by certain sections of the community. She was suspected of unmentionable talents. People who ran afoul of her frequently fell ill, and she was said to be familiar with herbs.

Abu explained the choice to Mieri. Hawa had argued only for the child's safety. She had said that the people who murdered Fatima would fear to become involved with Ayesha. On the other hand, if it were true (although Hawa did not believe it), that someone had made sorcery against Mahmut or his family, the baby would still be better off with Ayesha because she knew how to look after herself in these matters.

•

When Mother of Issa returned from the funeral in the late afternoon, she was arm in arm with Ayesha. Ayesha was a dark and striking woman with a telling trace of Fulani in her blood. By tradition an egalitarian people, the Fulani were nomadic pastoralists scattered throughout the West African savannah from Cameroun in the east as far west as Senegal. They were a handsome race, slim, fine-featured and tall, and Ayesha was typical of their number. Thick maned and just under six feet tall, she looked like a midnight warrior in her dark red cloth. By contrast, Mother of Issa was a metaphor of edibility, dumpling plump, her face as dimpled with creases as a warm popover. She was short, a brown pumpkin of a woman, a pudding; but under her smiles she was tougher than elephant hide.

It was Ayesha's opinion that Fatima had committed suicide by climbing into the tank, which was some five feet deep, pulling the cover closed over her head, and then plunging herself into the muck. Mother of Issa was reluctant to contemplate the despair that would lead a human being to such an action.

"It was the sadness that comes after childbirth," affirmed Ayesha, and her lips disappeared in the tightness of her face. In the weeks after the baby's birth Fatima had been full of complaints to which no one in her husband's house had listened. All they would do was tell her not to whine like a kicked dog.

Mother of Issa chafed. Even if Fatima *had* killed herself, as Ayesha suggested, it was obvious that "for this much sorrow there is some sorcery to blame."

If Ayesha had further thoughts she kept them to herself. After a while, to break the thick silence, Mother of Issa said, "Have some beer with me."

Ayesha nodded and Abu was despatched to Farrah's to fill up Mother's green plastic jug with guinea-corn beer. Mother of Issa was Muslim only by marriage and did not scruple to indulge her infidel whim when Kutu wasn't around to scold. Naturally, Abu hurried on his errand, not wanting to miss what the two women had to say to each other. When he returned with the beer they were touching on personal matters.

"What do you hear from your brother?" asked Mother of Issa.

"Ibn Sinna? Nothing," replied Ayesha. "And this time he has taken my husband with him."

"It is a long time then Moomin leaves you alone," commented Mother of Issa. "How will *he* like to find Mahmut's baby daughter in his house when he returns?"

"When he comes, he will tell me," answered Ayesha, and her tone said the subject was firmly closed.

Abu tarried before them overlong with the heavy beer jug. He was itchy with a question of his own. "Yes? What do you want?" grumbled Mother of Issa, who could read the devious expressions on his face.

"How will you feed the baby?" Abu wanted to know. Ayesha's youngest child had been weaned for more than a year. Ayesha would not be able to feed the baby herself.

"I will do as the white women and the big-men's wives," Ayesha answered. "I will feed the baby from a glass breast with a rubber teat at the end." She watched Abu's reaction.

Abu laughed nervously. He was uncomfortable with this information.

Ayesha said, "Maybe you want to come and watch how it is done?"

Abu squirmed. Mother of Issa would berate him for his forwardness, but he dearly wanted to observe this unnatural procedure. Ayesha watched him with cats' eyes, calculating, complacent. "Come tomorrow at noon time," she said.

"Now go away," ordered Mother of Issa crossly, and Abu skipped out in haste and made himself scarce for the rest of the afternoon. Mother of Issa shook her head at him as he left, as one may do who regrets the consequences of a past good deed. "This boy, Abu," she said. "I don't know why we ever took him in. Even as a little child he could always make trouble plenty. Better to live with a nest of thieves than to have this child in the house." To quench the remorse she suffered as a result of her own past kindnesses, she poured out for herself a full calabash of guinea-corn beer. This she took down in one long unbroken swallow—a feat of some note, since the calabash held a good twenty ounces of beer.

"The boy has spirit," said Ayesha.

"Uumph," grunted Mother of Issa, refilling her calabash. She emptied it in another continuous swallow. This time Ayesha refilled the calabash for her.

■

The next noon as he had been bidden, Abu paid a call at Ayesha's house, a large new cement-block building that stood at the edge of the *zongo*. The *zongo* was that section of a West African Muslim town traditionally set aside for strangers—traders, pilgrims, or merchants—who stopped and settled in the area. Although by definition newer than the core area of town, a *zongo* might still be several centuries old. Ayesha's house was located at the newer end of the *zongo*, right at the edge of town. Like most "modern" houses in Kpama, Ayesha's was built on a modified Roman plan: a rough, nearly windowless exterior surrounded the spacious inner court, a tropical atrium onto which most rooms opened directly. Entrance was through a wooden gate, which at night was kept locked against thieves, lepers, wizards, beggars, and other preindustrial hazards.

As he passed through the gate, Abu greeted Ayesha's watchman, a gouty relative who was unemployable elsewhere. The man was lethargic (he was full of intestinal parasites), and as soon as he latched the gate in the evenings, he fell sound asleep. Probably for this reason, Ayesha maintained a bevy of guinea-fowl in her courtyard; these creatures could hear a feather drop and went wild with consternation at the least departure from their normal routine. They made an excellent alarm system. Ayesha also kept a guard dog, a gentle coward, now old and nearly toothless, who had come to her as a gift before her marriage. She had named the dog God Will Provide, but over the years it had become apparent that the dog had taken its name to heart and had, in addition, cast Ayesha in the role of benevolent divinity.

"Good morning, my grandfather," Abu sang out to the watchman as he passed through the wooden gate.

"What? What?" stammered the old man in confusion as he struggled up from one of his light dozes. Then he saw it was only Abu and resettled into his midday stupor. It was a hard life for him, after all. Old men of his years should be waited on hand and foot by reverent progeny.

"Your watchman is just useless," Abu informed Ayesha.

"He is just an old man," said Ayesha. "He has no family. Where else could he go?"

"*I* will be your watchman," suggested Abu. He was always looking out for the extra penny, for advancement, the ambitious intervention of fate.

"Now you are too young," Ayesha told him. "Come back when you are grown and then I will find some work for you."

"Hey! Even now I am a grown man!" Abu stretched himself up as far as his backbone would take him.

"How old are you?"

"Even now I am ninety years."

"Is that it?" Ayesha eyed him. She thought she knew a way to trip him up. "And who was ruler in Kpama when you were born?"

"This woman, Queen Victoria," Abu answered, allowing some of the triumph he felt to show in his smile.

"So you are ninety years old! But are you not small for your age?"

"You know how old men shrink," Abu reminded her.

"But where are your wives and children? How is it you are still in grade Primary Five in school?"

Abu laughed lamely, trapped in chronological inadequacies. "Where is this small baby?" he asked, to change the subject. Wordlessly Ayesha took him to a room at the far end of the courtyard and opened the door. There, lost in the vastness of a double bed, lay a small brown infant. Her long lashes curled up tightly from her closed lids. Her breathing was rapid and gauche in the snuffly manner of newborns, but everything else about her was a perfection of delicacy. She rested one cheek on a tiny closed fist, her head was haloed in a downy brown fuzz. Above her, like a royal canopy, the mosquito netting draped around the bed in elegant folds.

Right then Abu lost his heart. Perhaps it was the baby's minute perfection, or her helplessness, or something in Abu's own motherless past, though the people of Kpama didn't bother their heads with these sorts of explanations. Abu said simply, "She's beautiful."

"I am calling her Comfort."

"Is that the name her father gave her?"

"It is the name *I* am giving her," said Ayesha truculently. Mahmut had endowed his daughter with names full of vengeance: Justice of Allah, Servant of the Wrathful. Ayesha had rescued the child for softer callings.

"Come with me and I'll show you how to fill the glass breast with milk."

Abu declined the offer. "I will just stay here small-small," he said softly, "in case she wakes up." He brushed a fly off the mosquito netting and was content to sit in silence with this new object of his desire.

■

Ayesha's husband, Moomin, was a rich man by local standards, and his house was accordingly well fitted out with the latest thing in Kpama kitchens: a stove that ran off bottled propane, a kerosene-powered refrigerator. There was even linoleum on the floor, though running water was, of course, out of the question.

Ayesha was fishing Comfort's bottle out of a warming pan on her stove when Abu raced into the kitchen. "Comfort is awake!" he announced breathlessly.

And then it was Abu who insisted on feeding the infant. He clucked and fussed and preened like an old biddy hen. He cheered at every swallow. He praised the strength of the baby's fidgety limbs. He greeted each messy burp as if it were the theme song of his favourite rock group. He even volunteered to change the fouled rags that served as her diapers.

Ayesha regarded him with black cats' eyes. "Are you in love?"

Abu overlooked the question. "I want to show Mieri this baby," he said. He said this partly because he had left Mieri sitting alone in an empty courtyard and partly because he wanted her to know right from the start that she had a rival. He knew that Salifu would be envious, too, and this made the expedition even sweeter.

Ayesha agreed and shortly afterwards they left together to show off their new prize. But when they arrived at Kutu's house they found they had been upstaged. Kutu the wanderer had just returned in a brand-new Toyota truck from a long sojourn in the south with his younger wife. Mother of Issa was in grand form, wearing her best cloth and a new gold bracelet. She was thinking of killing a sheep.

"It will be *too* much meat," said Kutu in his low baritone, embarrassed by the vehement bounty of his reception. "One chicken will be plenty."

Mother of Issa was adamant. She gestured towards her oldest son, Issa, who had come north with his father. "This great boy alone can easily eat one whole chicken. Is it not true?" Issa stood fumbling with the awkwardness of the several new inches he had grown in the previous year. He was already taller than his father and would probably pass six-foot-six before he stopped.

Mother of Issa insisted on discussing the dinner for endless minutes as an indirect way to boast of her son's magnificent manhood. Abu grew impatient with what he felt to be an excess of maternal pride. He had, in a manner of speaking, progeny of his own to display. Finally, exasperated, he pushed his way among them all and announced intrusively, "Ayesha has brought the baby." Then he stood like a proud father while Kutu and his household came to inspect and admire. Comfort's black eyes took them in with a wise, unblinking stare.

"Hey! Abu! Is this your new wife?" Mother of Issa had spotted something in Abu's countenance.

"When Moomin returns home," answered Abu, "I will ask him for this small girl child." Infant betrothals were not at all uncommon in Kpama. Parents assiduously sought mates even for suckling babes and newborns. Some children were promised while their mothers still laboured for their births.

"But Moomin is not the child's father," objected Kutu, his

voice clouded with pessimism. "Even though the Ruler of Kpama has agreed that she should be raised in the house of Moomin, it is not Moomin but Mahmut you must ask to have her for your wife. Do you think it is likely that Mahmut will promise this small baby girl to you?" Kutu laughed ruefully; Mahmut was generally thought a miserly soul. "If I know anything about this Mahmut, you will need *too* much money." Salifu grinned at Abu's anticipated failure.

Abu was not one to cower before adversity, however. He puffed out his chest. "As for me," he said, "I will work *too* hard. I will soon become *millionaire!*"

Kutu and his family laughed. Abu gave them a baleful look and walked away with the studied carelessness of a cat that has been caught on the kitchen table, helping itself to paté.

Months passed.

Abu was at Ayesha's all the time. He never failed to discover trinkets and baubles for the youngest woman in his life. When Comfort could sit up unaided, Ayesha often placed her under a rough trellis covered with vines where she could play in the shade and watch the entrance for Abu. As soon as she saw him she would break into body-wriggling laughter. She would drool and coo. Then Abu, to her great delight, would contort his face into hideous grimaces, put his thumbs in his ears, wiggle his fingers, stick out his tongue, and lurch about like a fairy-tale goblin.

Hawa, too, visited her little granddaughter daily. She came to cuddle something soft and to ease her heart by sitting in companionable silence with Ayesha on the bench in the courtyard, while their thoughts dwelled on the baby's mother whom, by custom (because she was dead), they could no longer mention by name. Abu found them thus one afternoon in August. He was full of excitement and burst in upon their meditations like a firecracker. "Kutu's white stranger is coming back!" he cried amid spins of delirium. "Kutu has had a letter!" Abu's cheerfulness acted abrasively on Hawa.

"What stranger is that?" she said crossly.

"This tall man with the yellow hair," Abu told her. "This one Englishman who came here to learn our language."

Ayesha looked up sharply. "John Lavender?" she asked. Something in her voice caused Hawa to stare at her.

Abu said, "Yes. It is this man, John Lavender. He is coming back to Kpama again. He will bring me corol pencips!"

"What?" frowned Ayesha.

"Corol pencips," explained Abu. "These things in many parts, for drawing. Red and blue."

"I don't know," said Ayesha, her mind walking down other paths.

"When John Lavender brings me these things, I will come to you and show them. Then you will see. Corol pencips!"

Over the next weeks, Abu devoted the major portion of his spare time to monitoring activity in the lorry park, checking out each passenger lorry that limped into Kpama from the capital, far to the south.

PART ONE

![chapter ornament] **1**

Likki Liddell arrived in Kpama at the end of August. At loose ends after an unsatisfactory love affair, she had fled from her uninspiring teacher's job at a north Philadelphia junior high school and signed on for two years with the Peace Corps, "just for a change of scene," as she explained apologetically to her friends—for at twenty-five she felt too old to admit how badly things had gone. She pretended, instead, to idealism, and it was true that although she was disaffected with the inequities of her own society she was more than willing to make allowances for those of others. With relief she lost herself in the summer-long acculturation training course on the deserted campus of a New Jersey university, relishing the strangeness of the new customs she was learning: never use your left hand for anything but the toilet, always greet everyone you pass on the street, never refuse an offer of food, etc. Likki also relished her release from the bickering in the apartment she had shared with her older sister, Eunice, as well as the smothering phone calls she had received almost nightly from her widowed mother in the country (there was only a broken pay phone in the New Jersey dormitory). As soon as Likki left Pennsylvania, she felt things had started to go better for her.

She came into Kpama late one afternoon riding side by side in the cab of a grumpy lorry with Kutu's stranger, John Lavender. She had met John a week before in the south, introduced by Peace Corps personnel. (All expatriates in the capital eventually met each other on the wide, well-kept terraces of the outdoor bar of the Victoria Hotel). John, who was still remembered in the capital from his previous sojourn, was presented to Likki as a "seasoned veteran of the north," a sort of modern-day counterpart of the eccentric English explorers of the nineteenth century, and she naturally turned to him for information about her destination. (Would there be electricity? Was the water drinkable? What kind of medical facilities were available?) John supplied detailed and thoughtful answers, as well as pointing out possible problems that had not occurred to her: scorpions in shoes, cayenne in local peanut butter, shortages of washing powder.

Despite his pale—and, in the heat, rather pasty—complexion, Likki felt drawn to him. In the best tradition of Oxford graduates he was intelligent, courteous and an excellent—if opinionated—conversationalist. He flattered Likki's observations and reflections with serious attention and she felt herself expand intellectually in his presence. When she learned that he would soon be going back to Kpama for post-doctoral researches in linguistics, Likki gratefully abandoned the bewildering initiatives of working out her own travel arrangements and allowed herself to follow in the broad wake of John Lavender's assurance and knowledgeability. Behind him she had stood, half spectator, half child, in the tumultuous lorry park of the capital, while he debated with the owners the merits of several vehicles (Likki could see little merit in any of them) and stipulated in advance what seats he and Likki would have and the price they would pay for the journey. Around them on every side surged the urgent, precontractual Hobbesian horde, a bellicose multitude, vibrant and unruly, riding the flood tide of commerce. Looking around at the boisterous crowds of the market and the lorry park, Likki experienced something close to panic and begged to be taken to the north via the civilized comforts of the national bus line— buses newly imported from West Germany as part of that country's "foreign aid" program (Bonn had doled out the money on condition it be spent on German buses). The fact is that after three weeks Likki was already a little disturbed by what she thought she had come to Africa to find— humanity in its pristine condition, free from bondage to machines and schedules and top-heavy bureaucracies; an unfettered humanity, more moral, more cheerful, more open, less sexually inhibited. In fact she had come looking for the Golden Age but still hoped to find the buses comfortable and running on time.

John had scoffed at the mere mention of buses. There was a twice-weekly bus service scheduled for Kpama, he told her, but the vehicles assigned to the route were old, and both buses, the regular and the back-up, were often immobilized for a month or two in Gbiriri, the regional capital of the north. The problem was usually lack of spare parts. Most recently, it seemed, it was tires that were unobtainable, but there was always something you couldn't get—sometimes batteries, sometimes spark-plugs, and, too often, gasoline. For years there had been rumours that a shiny new BMW superbus would be assigned to the line, but when you mentioned this to the residents of Kpama they doubled over laughing. It was like suggesting to the victims of boarding-school cuisine that their cardboard meals would soon be replaced by cordon-bleu cooking.

Meanwhile, all the important trade and transport of Kpama went by lorry. Some of the vehicles plying the routes dated from before World War Two. Many would have qualified as antiques. They wheezed and spluttered and shook like palsied grandparents, but they had a disarming habit of reaching their destinations faster than anything else in the country except the army.

The drivers, who were usually the owners, knew their lorries inside out. They had to. On average they had to perform at least one major overhaul of their engines for every three hundred miles they travelled. And the lorries, with an engaging penchant for rural simplicity, never broke down near a town. Instead they exploded to a halt near villages that had never heard of a screwdriver or, worse yet, along unfriendly stretches of bush where no wind stirred and insects turned the passengers into bloodless pincushions while the driver dismantled his machine with slow deliberation and then put it back together again.

Eccentric veterans that they were, each of these lorries had its own name, which it carried like a flag, blazoned in two-foot-high letters over the roof of its cab. Names that commented on the perfidious nature of the female sex were common: Woman Is Poison. There were also reflections of a more edifying nature: Praise God. Many, however, were little more than the anarchic observations of the common man—People Don't Know, Six Feet at Last—or the resignation of those to whom effective power is denied—So the World Be.

John Lavender eventually secured passage for himself and Likki on a vehicle called Downfall People, one of the ubiquitous, decrepit, bottle-green, passenger lorries with wooden seats and non-existent shocks that carry most of Africa on their backs. Though John and Likki rode in comparative, high-status comfort in the cab of the lorry with the driver, there was little that four inches of foam rubber could do to alleviate the distresses of the road. Nor could the glassless windows shut out the taint of rotting fish that drifted down from baskets riding overhead on the roof of the cab.

At Gbiriri the fish were replaced by three sheep, which bore their lot with neither stoicism nor continence. To Likki, gritting her teeth around an uncomfortably full bladder (toilet facilities were worse than makeshift once they left the capital), the sheep's continual ventings were a double affront.

Over the course of the journey, which lasted three days, John Lavender grew increasingly voluble. As the dense, cathedral-like vegetation of the southern rain forest gradually thinned and dropped in height, John discoursed on the ancient trade in gold that had flourished between the mysterious land of Wangara and the kingdoms of Europe and the Mediterranean. He recounted how, since prehistoric times, the people of the south had brought their gold out of the forest and traded it for salt; of how for something like thirty centuries they had kept secret the source of their yellow ore, so that even today no one was sure exactly where Wangara had been.

As the trees thinned and began to recede before the tall grasses of the savannah, John spun spine-tingling tales of the risky trans-Saharan trade that, up until the Renaissance, had carried to Europe 90 per cent of its gold. He described what was known of the old civilizations of Ghana, Mali, and Songhai that had thrived as the southern "ports" of the trans-Saharan trade routes. And he observed how paradoxical it was that Africa should have financed the wars and royal jealousies of medieval Europe. Of course, after about 1100 A.D., when Muslim influence spread down from

North Africa and increasingly controlled the gold trade, the kings of Europe grew worried and attempted to escape the Islamic stranglehold on their purses by bypassing the Muslim intermediaries. Henry the Navigator sailed south along the West African coast searching for the elusive Wangara, while the Spanish followed the setting sun looking for Eldorado.

By the time Downfall People reached Kpama—small backwater of the once golden trade, now sitting dusty and squat on a small undulation of the savannah plain and as unremarkable as any of a thousand similar African towns— the town appeared to Likki like a New Jerusalem, and she looked around her with excitement and curiosity and a sense of adventure.

There was little in Kpama to elicit such a response. The town squeezed some 13,000 inhabitants into a jumbled area roughly half a mile in diameter. The poorer people lived in adobe dwellings with flat mud roofs upon which they slept in February and March, the months just before the rains came, when it was unbearably hot even for Africans. The wealthier citizens built themselves houses of concrete and roofed them with corrugated iron, which meant that they had to spend the hot part of the year sweating indoors. After the first rainy season the iron roofs began to rust, and a combination of rust stains, mud splatters, and the accelerated deterioration typical of the tropics soon contrived to make the more costly houses look far shabbier than their low-budget neighbours.

The core of the town was centuries old and medieval in layout. Most of the streets were only two or three feet wide and not one of them was straight for more than ten feet at a time. All of them were riddled with gutters and depressions where waste water and urine collected to breed flies, mosquitoes, and a rich medley of suspect odours. The houses, which at first glance seemed to have been thrown down higgledy-piggledy by a fretful child, were actually joined on to one another in vast warren-like collections of compounds. To the uninitiated, the core of the town—old Kpama—was an unfathomable series of labyrinths. Surrounding this gnarled hub were the more recently constructed segments of the town. Roads were wider in these sections and concrete houses more frequent, although they were by no means the rule. Most dwellings, even in the newer sections, were but a single storey high. Here and there, however, a rich man's house could be seen flaunting an upper storey and, near the heart of Kpama, the impressive flutings of the Friday mosque and the Ruler's palace could be seen rising above the flat adobe roofs. Brilliantly whitewashed, elaborately festooned with wooden lintels, these two buildings were magnificent examples of Sudanic architecture. Like majestic white-masted ships they rode above the general scruffiness of the town.

The lorry park in Kpama sat on a small incline. It was only a hill of some five degrees, but it allowed drivers to get off to an easy "roll start." (Hardly one lorry in fifty could start on the key.)

It had rained in Kpama several hours before Downfall People arrived. Wine-brown pools still decked the clay slope where the lorries were beached between journeys. Iridescent oil spills trailed out over the larger puddles like disjointed octopi. As the lorry tilted precariously into the park, it drenched an unwary orange seller with a grievous bath of mud. Oblivious of the woman's protests, the vehicle shuddered slowly to a halt, the sheep on the roof of the cab bleating a last protest. A full fifty feet before the lorry halted, passengers began leaping to their freedom over the back and sides of the truck. Noisily, women collected their baskets, their babies, and the oddly misshapen bundles that had ridden with them between their feet for hundreds of dust-choked miles. A plague of boys besieged the lorry hoping to earn pocket money by carrying home someone's case. They grabbed at any baggage in reach and marched off with it summarily. The women chased after them shouting and waving their fists and beat the boys eagerly when they could catch them.

By contrast the men descended from the lorry with dignity and appeared unconcerned about the fate of their baggage, standing aloof from the angry currents that swirled about the truck, speaking seldom and sombrely—as if discussing matters of religion or state.

•

Surrounded on three sides by adobe shops and wooden stalls, the lorry park joined the market proper through a long driveway near which Downfall People eventually halted. Close by was a typical import shop selling shampoo, soap, batteries, and cheap plastic dolls from Taiwan. A crooked sign over the door announced that the place was called Manhattan East, and Likki was pleased to detect what she interpreted as a local exercise of wit in this regard. She nudged John Lavender to call his attention to the name. "Don't you love it?"

John looked up from his last-minute satchel packing and glanced at the shop. Near the entrance, directly under the sign—which intended emulation rather than the irony Likki imagined—two men stood deep in vigorous discussion. Their long Muslim robes hovered expectantly in the early breeze, the four o'clock stirring of air that came each afternoon to signal the arrival of evening and the temporary fallibility of the sun. John watched the men for a while and then smiled. "I think I know them," he said at last, cheered by the familiar. The hint of superiority in his voice annoyed his companion.

"Oh," said Likki, without interest. She had hardly looked at the two.

"The short one in green, his name is Mahmut."

"He won't win any beauty contests, will he?" said Likki, grudgingly regarding the pair.

"He doesn't need to. He's rich."

"From *that* shop?" The store, a tawdry affair of mean dimensions measuring barely eight feet by ten, was a jumbled collection of worn adobe and discarded lumber, with a ragged tar-paper roof. A kind of commercial slum. It was exactly this that Likki thought made the name so delicious.

"Don't be taken in by appearances," lectured John in the manner of old hand to apprentice. Likki made a face and wrestled her camera into a shoulder bag. Eventually she looked up again. "Who's the other one?" she asked. A tall man in blue with a face like an arrogant angel.

"That's Ibn Sinna," said John. "Rather famous here in Kpama. A trader. A fixer. A lender of money. An adviser to the mighty."

This made Likki stare at the second man longer than she otherwise might have. She noted to herself that he was very good-looking and considered, naively, that this judgement somehow absolved her of racial prejudice.

John, meanwhile, leaned out of the window of the lorry cab to open his door—the inside handle having long since fallen off. He stepped out onto the running board of the truck and stretched in the sun. On the other side of the lorry park a soldier stood with a machine gun slung over his shoulder. He watched John for a while. Then he was joined by two other comrades in arms and, with his companions, made his way towards Manhattan East, sauntering across the central space of the lorry park with proprietary insolence.

When he saw the three soldiers approaching, the tall man in blue spat in the dust and departed, but the little man in green, Mahmut, stayed on. The soldiers walked over to him and seemed to press him with forceful, arrogant questions. Mahmut shook his head and shrugged his shoulders with a show of ignorant humility that was less than convincing even at a distance.

Eventually, the soldiers tired of Mahmut and turned their attention to the lorry, staring at Likki as she emerged to join John Lavender on the running-board of the truck.

Likki, for her part, stared straight back at them. Their importance didn't register. Soldiers at the road blocks. Soldiers on the streets—they were part of her first experience of Kpama and thus seemed to be an integral part of the town, something that belonged to it and had always been there. This was a false impression but a strong one.

John Lavender suddenly straightened, waved, and called out to a boy at the fringes of the swarm. "Salifu! Hey! Salifu." The boy looked up and jumped with recognition and triumph. He had reason to be pleased. It was no small victory over Abu to find John Lavender like this in the lorry park when Abu had been staking the place out for three weeks. "Nasara!" the boy shouted, jubilant. "Nasara! You wait there. I am just coming for you. Hey, Nasara, it's good!"

"What's 'Nasara'?" Likki asked John.

"Sort of creole Arabic for 'white person.' It actually derives from 'Nazarene,'—hence Christian, hence white."

"And who's that boy?"

"Salifu. He's from Kutu's house, where I'll be staying."

Salifu clambered up beside them on the running-board. He was all over John Lavender, like a wiggly hatchling. "Hey, Nasara! You came back!" He grabbed John Lavender's shoulder bags and strapped them round his torso. By this time the driver of Downfall People had started to throw baggage down from the roof of the lorry. "I get your case for you," volunteered Salifu.

"Two red canvas bags and a wooden box," instructed John.

"Is it food in the box?" asked Salifu hopefully.

"Maybe."

Salifu grinned, "For me?"

"Maybe *some* is for you," said John, who was familiar with the ways of Salifu's appetite. To the driver's annoyance, Salifu scrambled up on top of the lorry and quickly located the two red canvas bags. The wooden box, however, eluded him. He was still searching for it when he was joined on the roof by a crestfallen Abu.

"Hey, Abu! Get down!" ordered Salifu. The glory of discovering John Lavender was all Salifu's own, and he declined to share it. He gloated a little, like an overfed crocodile.

"Who is *this* boy?" demanded the driver, annoyed to find a proliferation of youngsters on top of his vehicle. The sheep echoed his dissatisfaction.

"This, our mother, her case is missing," Abu explained to the driver, pointing down towards Likki on the running-board, sending her a supplicating glance. Perhaps, having lost the first round to Salifu, Abu had decided to espouse the female cause.

"Is that woman your mother?" the driver asked sarcastically.

"In fact!" nodded Abu. "And how she laboured for my birth! For two weeks no one stirred in the village. Every chicken was sacrificed to bring me forth and the chief himself sent a cow. How the woman suffered, hey! And now you will not let me bring my own mother her case. It is too bad."

The driver spat heavily over the side of the lorry and wiped his mouth with a red kerchief to hide any expression he might have on it. "Is that it?" he said at last.

Abu grinned. Then he leaned down and said to Likki, "Please, Miss Lady, I go bring your case for you."

"I can get them," she said, wondering how much she would have to pay him.

"Oh, no. I get them fast. Too quick! You can see." Abu thumped himself on the chest.

"I can see your English hasn't improved," said John Lavender—unkindly, Likki thought. (John's own confident, well-modulated tones spoke of six generations of Oxford-educated forbears.)

Abu prattled on, "Oh, Mr. John Lavender, how I study this English. Night and day I don't sleep. Every Friday to the mallams for medicine to make me smart. But Allah gave me no brains for English. At all."

"What *did* he give you brains for, then?"

Abu put his head to one side and didn't reply. Looking up at him where he stood on the roof of the lorry Likki thought his eyes seemed over-bright. "What's your name?" she asked softly.

"As for me, Miss Lady, my name is Abu. Now I go bring your case."

It was easy for him to spot her luggage, for in contrast to everything else on the lorry her bags were firm and new, unscratched, still wearing the soft shell-lustre of imitation leather. While he was up on the roof, Abu also located John Lavender's wooden box. This he commandeered as his personal property, refusing to let Salifu anywhere near it. Abu climbed down from the roof of the lorry with the wooden box on his head. It was a sizeable object, a cube roughly two and a half feet each way, but Abu balanced it with careless ease. When they were ready to go, he went on ahead with his heavy prize, doing silly walks and cutting capers that seriously prejudiced the safety of his burden. The whites, with their medley of shoulder straps, walked directly behind, depending on Abu to thread a path through the people, the lanes, and the houses. Salifu brought up the rear of the procession, herding before him two boys he had requisitioned from the swarm to carry the extra luggage.

More lorries pulled up as they left. More angry women shouted at new swarms of boys. A tip lorry backed precariously through a narrow defile into the marketplace and dumped five tons of oranges into the mud as if they were so much gravel.

■

Likki and John and their young porters filed slowly through the central maze of Kpama's streets, those constricted fissures that twisted between the mud walls of the houses in the old part of town. As they passed, John held forth to Likki on the history and geography of the town in the manner of a tour operator with a particular interest in his subject. The cramped and tortuous dimensions of these streets, he said, were no accident. The town had been purposely constructed to discourage armed attack. No mounted rider could squeeze his way through the labyrinth, nor would he find an accessible exterior window for purposes of surprise. Nearly three generations had passed since the end of the wars and the slave raids, but the houses (actually walled collections of related compounds) still looked inward towards their own fecundity, still brooded on the iniquity of man.

John Lavender delighted in *all* the stories, and he could not be barred from rehearsing them. He knew who had built what—and when. He told how a particular mosque had sprung up magically overnight; how a certain family of princes could never keep their horses alive for longer than a month; how the dwarves had ruined the first Ruler's palace out of spite for a broken xylophone.

Likki, however, was too weary to take much in. The journey to Kpama had been a lesson in the things she took for granted. She had expected discomforts and so did not complain of having to spend two nights of the journey curled up on the front seat of the lorry in cramped but chaste proximity to John Lavender while the driver stretched out with the ignition system on the ground under the cab. But there had been nothing to eat along the way except roadside food that had proven inimical to bowels already saturated with Lomotil. Moreover, the last of their drinking water had been used up early and nothing thirst-quenching had been forthcoming for the rest of the journey except oranges. Worse than anything, however, had been the dirt. Likki craved a bath the way an addict craves her drug. Soap and water to wash the red dust from her clogged pores and allow them to sweat again. She did not have before her, as John Lavender did, the prospect of a warm welcome from old friends to bear up her spirits. Had she been alone she could have wept for an hour.

"Miss Lady," said Abu to Likki, suddenly turning on the path to address her. "You want hot bath. Me, I know it."

"Really," said Likki. Then, noting his incomprehension, she rephrased it. "I want a hot bath very much." She smiled. Hope was everything.

"Good. I fix you." Abu's eyes danced upwards and he giggled at Likki. "Please, Miss Lady, what is this your name?"

"My name is Likki."

"Likki. Yes, it's good!"

"Abu, hurry up," growled Salifu. They were all held up behind him in a line.

Abu heeded him not. He continued to converse with Likki. "Tomorrow I take you to see Comfort," he announced, looking up at her as if to make a detailed appraisal of her appearance: she was somewhat on the tall side, a bit too thin, with grey eyes and long, mousy-brown hair that she tied up from her neck because of the heat. Abu evidently approved of what he saw, however, for he nodded his head and said, "How Comfort like to see one beautiful white lady like you!" And so pleased did he seem with this idea of his that he took off with the wooden box at an unrestrained clip and nearly felled al Hajji Malik at an intersection of passages. Abu's apologies were abject—hajjis were respected as holy men who had made the pilgrimage to Mecca and Malik was a particular friend of Kutu's.

"Who is Comfort?" asked Likki, turning to John Lavender.

John Lavender didn't know.

"Comfort is his baby," grumbled Salifu.

"His baby! How old is he?"

"Six months," answered Salifu.

•

As they passed through Kpama the twilight deepened. Rose light poured from the sky. It bathed in pink the mud walls of the houses and the red earth on which they stood and from which they had been fashioned. It cast the mango trees in shades of copper and turned the whitewashed mosques an irreverent flamingo. Calls of muezzins arched into the flushed vault over the town, summoning the faithful to the *salāt al maghrib*, the evening prayer, fourth of the five daily prayers required by Islam. Collections of sandals, like infestations of evening fungi, sprang up outside the various mosques, an indication of the number of worshippers within.

"Where are the women?" Likki wanted to know. She saw only men approaching the whitewashed buildings to pray, their rolled prayer mats carried under their arms like oversized scrolls.

"Women don't pray," said John Lavender.

"Why not?"

"They're polluted."

"Polluted with what?"

"With being women."

"God *damn!*" said Likki.

"God *damn!*" echoed Abu. He liked the way she said it.

•

At Kutu's, Likki felt herself an inept superfluity despite the fact that she was welcomed enthusiastically as John Lavender's "sister." The family's reunion with John, however, was loud and wild. Kutu said over and over again that it was truly wonderful, his stranger had come back to him again. Mother of Issa said nothing, but hugged John Lavender to her like a grizzly bear, then shouted for the boys to kill a turkey. But for the moment the boys were too busy dancing around their guest, full of questions and gestures and exclamations, full of demands for John Lavender's attention, his affection, and the many presents they had asked for when they last saw him. He had left Kpama three years earlier after completing the field research for his doctorate in linguistics. Unfortunately, even with a D.Phil. from Oxford he had been unable to find a teaching position commensurate with the social standing he felt entitled to and he had had to settle for a part-time job at one of the newer "red-brick" universities. When the possibility of a two-year post-doctoral research grant turned up, John had jumped at the chance.

"You bring me corol pencips?" Abu asked John eagerly.

"Corol pencips?"

"Yes. You know. These things you draw with. Red and blue." Abu grinned at John expectantly.

John Lavender didn't understand, but Likki had a sudden inspiration. "Do you mean *col*oured *pen*cils?" she asked. It was her first reaching out in Kpama, a kind of coming to ground. Aided, perhaps, by an incipient empathy with Abu.

"Yes!" Abu was delighted. "Corol pencips!"

John's mouth was already framing an apology when Likki spoke up. "I have them in *my* suitcase." She had brought some felt-tip pens along with her on a whim. She could part with them on a whim.

John looked at her. "You're off to a bad start," he chided *sotto voce*.

"Why?" She had just brought forth a small victory over confusion and he was denying her.

"A soft touch, that's what you are. Abu will be only too happy to take you for every penny. After that he'll have the hairs off your head. And then he'll sell them."

"So far it's only corol pencips," said Likki, pleased for once to have outwitted her too-competent companion.

•

As he had promised, Abu brought Likki her hot bath. It came to her in a five-gallon bucket, a loofah and calabash disporting themselves upon its surface. Likki had heard about bucket baths, but this would be her first experience. "You scrub with the loofah and rinse with the calabash," John explained.

"I figured that."

Mother of Issa found a bar of scented soap that she had

been hoarding for more than two years in a locked cupboard. Soap was "short" in Kpama and it was a great favour she bestowed, although Likki only realized this much later.

The bathroom to which Likki was directed was a walled-off area about eight feet square inside a small second-storey room. It had a sloping concrete floor with a drain at the far end, rather like a shower stall of monstrous proportions but without any taps. Empty calabashes and buckets stood about on the floor. An oil drum near the entrance was filled with "cold" water (eighty-five degrees Fahrenheit, but still twenty degrees cooler than the temperature of the room).

Likki peeled off her clothing and found that even her underwear was caked with orange dust, both inside and out. Her navel was as full as a miniature flowerpot. At first the water ran down her body in muddy streams and the soap suds turned a brassy apricot. She had to lather her hair four times before it rinsed clear. When she had finally finished washing Likki waited until she was nearly dry and then splashed herself all over one last time with cold, her muscles stretching into the delicious streams of coolness the way a cat leans to a familiar hand. Deliriously wet, she wrapped herself in a large towel and emerged onto the upstairs balcony. The first thing she saw was Ayesha.

"So *this* is John Lavender's wife," said Ayesha, staring at Likki in a way that made her feel as conspicuous as a stripper in a convent.

"I'll just get dressed," said Likki, suddenly conscious of the relative smallness of her breasts. She slipped past Ayesha and headed for the room where she'd left her luggage. "He's not married yet, Ayesha," chided Kutu in his sepulchral voice.

John Lavender emerged from a downstairs bathroom, clad in a towel as Likki had been. Ayesha called down to him. "John Lavender, your *wife* is very beautiful."

"She's not my wife," he laughed, but his voice rang strangely false.

"How is it such a *beautiful* woman has not been able to make you marry her?" Ayesha pronounced the word "beautiful" in a way that distorted the meaning.

"She's not even my girlfriend."

"Then why does she come with you to such a bush place as Kpama?"

"She's just my sister," he replied. "She's come to teach here, at the secondary school." Ayesha slowly walked the length of the balcony trailing a sceptical finger along the balustrade. John continued: "As soon as we've washed and had something to eat, we're going to take her up to the school and get her settled into her own house. I only thought it might be nice for her to get to know Kutu and his family."

"Why explain to me?" said Ayesha indifferently, coming down the stairs. She went to the far end of the courtyard and leaned with studied precision against a large water barrel. There she began to discuss local variations of circumcision (male and female) with Arimata, an eight-year-old who was washing the dishes. John Lavender turned away from her with relief and went to get his clothing. By mistake he walked into the room already occupied by Likki.

Ayesha would not let the mistake pass. "He even shows his nakedness to her and he calls her a teacher," she scoffed.

Mother of Issa chortled maliciously.

Still leaning against the water barrel, which caught her voice and made it echo strangely, Ayesha mused aloud, in Kpamé, on racial characteristics. "I wonder how the whites can find their own women attractive. Skin like the skin of pigs, full of holes and terrible little bristles. Their hair hanging down like the hair of a *juju* doll. Their legs are too short, their buttocks droop. Their whole bodies are just squat, like dwarves. Their breasts are flat and they carry them far down on their chests like the breasts of old grandmothers. Noses like the beaks of vultures. And they do not have lips. I wonder how such a race could even reproduce itself. The men's parts would drop off for the sheer ugliness of the women. Perhaps that is why we hear their genitals are so small." As she spoke Ayesha became animated. Her audience shared many of her opinions if not her desire to paint a venomous caricature. John Lavender, buttoning up his shirt, could not repress a smile. He was a linguist and nearly fluent in Kpamé. Likki understood not a word, though she understood the emotion behind the outburst well enough.

For supper Mother of Issa feasted her stranger on liver kebabs and deep-fried yam. They all ate together in the courtyard, sitting around on low stools and sharing food from the same bowls. For Likki's sake, Mother of Issa served the pepper sauce in a separate bowl instead of pouring it directly over the food. The yam was particularly tasty—like enormous wedge-shaped French fries.

During supper Abu said, with his mouth full of yam, "John Lavender, your woman is not ugly."

"She's not my woman."

"Then who is she for?"

"Not for anyone."

"I'm for *myself*," said Likki in feminist fettle.

"Alone is not good," reflected Abu. "You keep her, John Lavender."

"God *damn*," said Likki.

"Yes! God *damn*," repeated Abu with delight. "Hey! God *damn*. God *damn*. It's good, yes? God *damn*."

■

After supper they took Likki to the secondary school, a self-contained settlement of compounds and buildings spread out along the top of a modestly wooded ridge. It was nearly three miles out of town and Kutu said they should use the family car. This car was a Ford Escort so enfeebled by years of vibrating over corrugated roads that it seemed ready to disintegrate at any moment. John Lavender remarked that he remembered it all too well from his last sojourn in Kpama. Even then he had been nagged by the thought that if he tapped the car gently in some critical spot it would collapse before his eyes into a pyramid of fine metallic dust. To find the vehicle still functioning after a further three years of service astonished him. It seemed indecent to use it—like summoning forth a creature from its deathbed. "Are you sure it still goes?" he wondered.

"It will go!" said Salifu emphatically. He was looking forward to a ride on the rear bumper.

Issa went out to call the driver, whom he found by the courtyard gate losing a game of *owari* to Kutu's watchman. Kutu's watchman was almost as much of a sleeper as Ayesha's, but his somnolence was interspersed with more frequent fits of wakefulness. The watchman compensated for these regrettable incidences of consciousness by directing his attentions to the study of indigenous board-games. *Owari* was the most complex of these, and the watchman was the town's acknowledged master. Everyone lost to Kutu's watchman. People travelled many miles to challenge his supremacy, but unless he became sleepy they invariably left owing him money. The driver was losing with a speed he found embarrassing and was grateful for an excuse to leave the game.

"Two pounds," called the watchman toothlessly as the driver walked away. "Two pounds and one shilling," he repeated, banging his walking-stick in the dust. The sibilants strayed awkwardly among his last remaining molars.

•

The Ford Escort refused to start on the key. Likki was not surprised. She could see ground between her feet; the floor of the car looked as if it had been hit with shrapnel. Only the front doors functioned, the hood was wired shut, the trunk wouldn't close, and the windows were permanently open.

Kutu's family were called out to push. Likki had counted five children in the house. Now, however, six more appeared. Several adults also emerged from the compound. "Who are *they*?" she asked John Lavender.

"Oh, probably relatives from somewhere or other."

"Don't you *know*?" Perhaps he only talked so much of history and folklore to hide a more personal ignorance.

"I don't believe I've ever seen them before."

"But I thought you used to live here?"

"Yes. But they weren't here when I was," he said. Then, seeing that she was upset by his offhand response, he tried to explain that in Kpama a family was considerably larger and more fluid than its Western, nuclear counterpart. Distant cousins might show up (invited or otherwise) for visits of several years. Children might be loaned out to sisters or aunts or grandmothers for most or even all of their childhood. Unrelated strangers might come to stay in the house and, if they remained long enough, they would slowly begin to merge with the other occupants, so that years later only the closest of insiders would recall that the tie between them was of friendship, not of blood. If a man were wealthy or prominent, all sorts of forgotten kinsmen would send their sons and daughters to him to profit from his connections and charisma. Waifs and strays would find a niche inside the door. It didn't really matter who they were or how they came; Kutu's prestige would swell with the size of his household.

"Like a university faculty. Or a government department," said Likki, catching the explanation in an apt analogy. But John looked pained at what he took to be irreverence.

Kutu's great family began to push the car. The boys jostled and shoved for position at the rear bumper so they could leap aboard at the critical moment just after the motor caught. It was hard work. The street near Kutu's house, though unusually wide, was pockmarked and puddled. They pushed for forty-five grunting, sweating, straining yards before the engine finally started. Abu and Salifu jumped onto the bumper, and those left behind sent up a shout, cheering and waving after the departing Escort as if it were the Spirit of St. Louis embarking on its trans-Atlantic voyage.

The driver took things slowly, at first because of the ruts and puddles, and then because of the hog-wallow, a local phenomenon of unpleasant dimensions. There was a lot of mud about and things were slippery; then there was the problem posed by the pigs themselves, who took up nearly all the road. At the wallow, sows of grotesque size congregated daily to escape the heat of the sun in the ooze created by the pooled effluent from several nearby houses. Their innumerable slimy offspring accompanied them, rooting enthusiastically through the mush for another pull at their mothers' caked dugs. Everywhere flies purred lethargically.

"Is that mud wet with what I think it's wet with?" asked Likki.

"Unfortunately, yes," said John, adding as an after-thought, "Muslims don't eat pork."

"I'm not surprised."

Once out on the tarred road, however, the driver could

open up the car. The engine, such as it was, accelerated, and cool evening air rushed in through the open windows. This the two passengers luxuriated in, waving their arms about in the breeze like cormorants learning to fly. Then, at a point just outside the town, the road dipped into a hollow and crossed a small bridge. Here, mist had already collected over a stream and the temperature was cooler by several degrees.

"It's almost *cold*," purred Likki, delighting in a sensation she had nearly forgotten existed.

"Smugglers' Bridge it's called," said John.

"Are there smugglers?"

"I don't know. I don't think so. The bridge is supposed to be haunted."

"It would be nice to live right there, wouldn't it?" said Likki, turning to look through the back window. The car had already started to climb out of the hollow and the breeze was again warmer.

In the front seat the driver shook his head. "There is very bad place, Miss Lady. You don't live there. That place is for Goromo."

"Goromo?" Likki looked at John. He seemed to know all the local stories.

"Some sort of goblin, I suppose. I told you the place was haunted."

"*Ghosts* haunt, not goblins," Likki informed him. She knew a story or two herself.

"What do goblins do, then?"

"They gobble," said Likki, and because she was tired and had seen too many new things, she found her own saying very funny and began to giggle. Her silliness infected John Lavender. He chuckled with surprise at her bad pun and then found it hard to stop laughing. They looked at each other and their merriment broke out anew.

•

The offices of the secondary school were closed when they arrived. The driver cruised the campus looking for the school's night watchman, Come Chop Again, who was a particular friend of his. They found Come Chop Again asleep behind the science building. Like most watchmen he was affable when awakened. "Oh, the new teacher," he said and went to peer in at Likki. It was nearly dark and he turned his flashlight on her for a few seconds. "Very beautiful," he said, wiping the sleep from his mouth with the torn sleeve of his coat. Then he squeezed into the front seat with the luggage and directed the driver to Bungalow 5, which Likki was to share with the biology instructress, Carlotta Reap.

Carlotta Reap, a corpulent, curly haired product of middle America, had been in residence at the school for just over a year. Another Peace Corps volunteer, she was halfway through her second posting in the country. (On her first, a one year fill-in in the eastern, plateau area, she had replaced a volunteer who had left for personal reasons.) Carlotta seemed set in her ways and was well established in Bungalow 5 along with a set of pink calico curtains and a fat, sausage-like, half-beagle mongrel dog named Zulu. Carlotta introduced a note of enigmatic sobriety to the evening of a day Likki was beginning to find bewildering.

"Likki Liddell, welcome to your new home," said Carlotta, casting a withering glance at the boys on the Escort's rear bumper. Salifu squirmed under her gaze. Abu raised his eyebrows and grinned right back at her.

"Hi," said Likki, trying to keep it light. Carlotta Reap was not what she had expected in the way of house company. Still, she was glad to note her roommate's ample dimensions and the fact that she would be prettier by comparison.

Carlotta may have made the same observation, for she frowned as she led the way up the front steps. "Come in, come in," she said. "Don't worry about the bags. I'll call the girls to help." She walked with the impeccable erectness achieved by certain overweight people—without the benefit of corsets. Her hands and arms mimed the gestures of a duchess.

With an indication of grand hospitality Carlotta opened the front screen door to reveal the bungalow's interior: it was standard 1970s West African civil-service institutional—nearly indistinguishable from any other government residence built in the same decade. The walls were hospital green. The floors were covered in grey linoleum tile. The wooden sofa, table, and chairs were of equally anonymous and ubiquitous design—only here they were made of shea-nut wood instead of the mahogany used in the south. The furniture cushions were fashioned of two-and-a-half-inch rubber foam (another standard feature). The local fabric used to cover the cushions provided the sole note of individuality in the bungalow's interior design.

Carlotta sailed in stately fashion to the rear of the bungalow and sent forth a summons through the back screen door. "Fati! Mercy! Binti!" Girl students soon appeared wearing the green school uniform. Carlotta sent them out to the car to bring in the bags. She showed Likki to her new room, the last of three bedrooms along the back hall of the house. The room was monastically bare of furnishings and thickly covered in dust.

"Never mind," said Carlotta. "The girls will clean it for you. If you give them the sheets they'll make up your bed while they're at it."

"Sheets?" It was the last thing Likki had thought to pack. Carlotta said she would lend her a pair. Carlotta then called for more girls and more arrived, like genies of the lamp. She set them all to work and the house resembled a well-run factory by the time she remembered to offer her guests a beer. John declined, saying he was eager to return to Kutu's, but Likki accepted gratefully. Though warm and fizzy, the beer was a great luxury and she measured it slowly, by half glasses, to protract her pleasure. She was only halfway down the bottle when Abu appeared at the front door. "Please, Miss Lady," he said through the screen.

"Oh, Abu, come in," said Likki. She spoke softly, doubtful of Abu's intentions and of Carlotta's reaction.

Carlotta looked out from the kitchen where she was struggling with a leaky faucet. "Who is that boy?"

"It's a boy from Kutu's house."

"Who is Kutu?" grumbled Carlotta, as if it were an imposition to have to ask so many questions. "Well, I don't care," she continued. "As long as you know him. I won't have stray children just walking into my house." Zulu whined his approval of her words. Carlotta returned to her labours, groping under the sink for a wrench, which she applied to the tap with grunts and muffled imprecations.

"Abu, the car has gone already," said Likki.

"Yes, Miss Lady. I stay behind." His body twitched and his face moved, full of something he was having trouble saying.

"What is it, Abu?"

"Please, Miss Lady, I want money."

"Money!" (Well, John had said she was a soft touch.)

"Yes. You see, I need very much, money. I want to work for you."

"Work for me?" He could hardly be more than twelve. Likki was almost sure he was still in school. "What kind of work?"

"Myself, I can do *all* the things," said Abu smiling, relieved to have broached the subject with at least moderate success. "I can do washing. And ironing. And sewing, too. Buttons, mending. Painting. Shopping. I can kill for you, too. And plucking feathers. All things you want. And also cooking and boyfriends."

"We don't want any of that," announced Carlotta from the kitchen doorway where she stood with the wrench in her hand and the left side of her face covered in grease. "I have the girls here to do all those things for me."

Likki managed to ignore the interruption. "What do you need the money for?" she asked Abu.

"I want to marry." He said it very seriously and Likki understood that she was not to smile.

"All right. You can do my ironing for me."

"The girls do all the ironing," said Carlotta.

"Abu can do mine."

"He'll have to bring his own iron. I wouldn't trust him with mine."

"As for me, I have plenty of irons," said Abu, improvising a little jitterbug backwards across the linoleum of the living-room floor. "Tomorrow I come with them—after school." He spun around, twice, made a Kung-fu kick at a shadow on the wall, and bounced out the front door.

As soon as he was gone, Carlotta, still holding the wrench, sat down next to Likki and gave her a little pep-talk.

"May I ask how long you've been in the country?" she began.

"Just over three weeks."

Carlotta said that this was the beginning of her third year in West Africa. She said she understood how these people worked. It wouldn't do to be too soft-hearted. These people would just take advantage. Life was incredibly hard here and the ones who survived were the importunate and the greedy. Everyone had a genuine tale of woe, but you couldn't just go around being a patsy to the entire continent. "You've got to be just as tough as they are," she ended. "And I really respect them." It was the first of many homilies.

2

It was a moonless night, and dark. The sky had begun to
cloud over, cutting out even the minimal light that sifted
down from the stars. Abu could hardly make out the road.
His spirits were high, however, and he hummed softly to
himself, occasionally dancing or skipping a step.

There was a military road-block between the school and
the bridge. This one, because of the relative unimportance
of the road, was tended only by police officers. Just to one
side of the saw-horse obstruction, some four feet past the
ditch, the two police officers had built a fire to cheer
themselves. Constable Obortey was wrapped in a grey
blanket against the damp of the evening, and both he and
Sergeant Awuyu had kerosene lanterns. Abu, because of
certain regrettable encounters in the past, gave them a
wide berth, detouring through the low brush at a distance
of about a hundred yards. He moved silently and kept his
head down. Nearer to Smugglers' Bridge he returned to
the road, but here he did not resume his light-hearted
humming. Instead he moved cautiously and there was
something tentative in his gait. He descended into the
hollow. Thin veils of mist curled above and around him,
obscuring his vision. Inside his thin cotton shirt he
shivered.

Twenty feet before the bridge Abu paused as if to
consider certain matters. Perhaps he was reflecting on
Mother of Issa's warnings. The Goromo, she had said, was a
wicked creature that lived off the flesh of children. It waited
darkly under its bridge for the sound of solitary footsteps.
Then it reached up a strangling claw and snatched its victim
from the world of the living. Its greatest delight was to suck
the bones of little ones, for they were still growing and the
marrow was soft and fat. The Goromo had no spoon. It used

41

the shoulder blade of its victim to scoop out the brains from the skull. On black nights the brave and the foolish could hear the sucking noises it made at these ghoulish labours. Afterwards the Goromo cooked up the flesh of the innocents over a dark fire that gave no light. It stirred these unnatural stews with the shinbones of its prey. For cooking pots it used their emptied skulls.

Abu listened circumspectly. There were faint slurping noises coming from under the bridge. Then a soft splash. Then another. Then silence. In the distance a toad sang.

Abu held his breath. There was another splash from the bridge, this time louder and more distinct. Then came a scratching of gravel—as of stones dislodged in a climb.

Slowly, on tiptoe, Abu retreated. He climbed back out of the hollow and moved along its edge for several hundred yards until he was well upstream of the bridge. Here he again began to cross over.

The first leg of this detour proved uneventful. Near the stream, however, the ground became marshy. It alternately squished and sucked at his feet. The serrated edges of the tall grasses caught at him as he passed. He was making a lot of noise for one who wanted to avoid detection. He bent down and proceeded on all fours, threading his muddy way between hummocks of grass. It was quieter that way, if slower and dirtier.

He was still several feet from the stream when he heard the sound: a breath like a soft, slow whistle. Behind him the grass moved. Abu froze. Squissh, suckk, squissh, suckk. Footsteps. Like an animal reluctant to break cover, Abu tensed but remained still. The footsteps came slowly closer, refusing to change direction. Squissh, suckk, squissh, suckk. They moved as if searching the long grass. A sickening odour came to Abu's nostrils.

He heard again the soft whistling breath. There was a musty smell of rot, and a wheeze, then a flapping as of long robes shaken in the night. Then silence. It was an absolute silence—as if the world had stopped. Not a bird or a frog or an insect sang. There was not one movement in the whole vast night. The very waters of the stream ceased to ripple. Abu could hear nothing but the terrible pounding of his heart.

Slowly he stood up, tensed to flee. Just behind him, a breath rattled deep in a throat. Abu turned towards the sound, and a spectral shape surged out at him from the darkness. He ran.

He ran blindly. Crossing the stream he stumbled badly and nearly drowned himself in a deep pool—like most African children, he had no notion of how to swim—but his forward momentum took him to the far bank before he began to sink. Once up the other side he struck out without plan. In the stream behind he heard the splashing notice of close pursuit, then a roar of fury as a large body hit the pool of deep water.

Abu just kept running. He heard his pursuer's snorts of effort as it scrabbled and clawed its way up the bank. Then it came up behind him again, closer and closer, breathing heavily, still with the soft, whistly note. Abu was out of the hollow now, into low bush. Twigs and leaves lashed him on all sides. The creature seemed nearly upon him; he could hear every sibilant breath of its dark, wet nostrils. He felt the long skinny fingers close on him. They creased painfully across his shoulders and he screamed. He was held fast. For an anguished moment he struggled helplessly, then grabbed each side of his khaki school shirt and ripped it apart in front. He left it there in the jaws of the Goromo and rushed shrieking into town, which he reached in a matter of minutes.

The first person to see him was Ayesha. Abu was still galloping blindly and she had to tackle him to get him to stop. "Abu!" she cried. He moaned and struggled to get free. He was scratched and bloody, his left foot was badly cut, and an ugly bruise was swelling on his back.

"Abu!"

"Let me go. Let me go," he wailed, not even recognizing her. Moomin, Ayesha's husband, was the first to come to her aid. Their neighbours, alert to signs of a promising commotion, were close behind.

Moomin gave Abu an almighty slap on the face. The boy looked up startled, then took a shuddering breath. A neighbour came out of her house with a bucket of water. Another followed behind her, and they doused him again and again as Ayesha held his shaking body firmly. After the fourth bucket Abu began to sob, a convulsive, choking sobbing that left the adults very uneasy.

Al Hajji Moktar left his nocturnal ablutions to see what was going on. As soon as he came into view, Abu struggled free of Ayesha and plunged himself into the folds of the holy man's robes. "Oh, my father, save me," he pleaded, shivering like a creature escaped from an icy hell.

"Bring him into my house," ordered Ayesha, going on ahead to steep herbs. Al Hajji Moktar followed behind her with the trembling body in his arms. Slowly Ayesha's courtyard began to fill with the concerned and the curious and the spiteful.

Once Ayesha's pungent and bitter infusion was manoeuvred down Abu's throat, it quickly took effect. Abu began to talk sense. "I saw the Goromo," he said, and someone gasped. Like one who has escaped the assassin's knife, Abu was now something of a hero. Fame was staring him in the face and he decided to make the most of it. He had a good look at his audience and began his tale.

"Children of Kpama." He addressed the younger people present, for it would have been disrespectful to lecture his elders. "Listen to your mothers. I, myself, heard many times from my own mother's mouth about the Goromo. But, I didn't mind her, and I came to grief. Only Allah Himself has saved me from destruction." Al Hajji Moktar shook his head and the faintest of smiles played over Ayesha's face. Abu continued in the same declamatory style, relating how he had heard the fiendish creature moving about under its bridge, going from pot to pot to stir the gruesome contents; how he had heard the sound of human bones sucked dry. He tried to imitate the strange, whistly breath of the Goromo and several of the elders present nodded their heads and said, "Ah-hah!" in an emphatic way that meant "absolutely" or "yes, indeed." Abu related his fearsome flight from the malodorous and growling Goromo. He described the empty glow of its horrible dark eyes. He showed them the purpling bruise on his back where the spiny fingers had grasped him.

Several adults in his audience had had encounters of

their own with the Goromo in their youth. Together with
Abu they painted a lurid portrait of the cannibalistic ghoul.
Little children whimpered and grandmothers shivered
deliciously by the fire.

It was nearly midnight before Abu was escorted home
like a returning Ulysses. John Lavender was full of interest
and asked Abu particularly detailed questions about the
Goromo, how it smelt and looked and moved and sounded.

"Do you believe him, then, John Lavender?" Ayesha
asked when Abu had gone off to sleep.

"I'm sure *you* don't believe him," said John. It was an old
quarrel with them: his believing and her not believing.

"I thought whites laughed at such things."

"The more time I spend here, the harder it is to be sure."

"I thought you only believed in scientific truth." That's
what they'd been taught at school. She frowned at him.

"There are different kinds of truth," he hedged. ESP and
psychokinesis, for example, would be difficult concepts to
translate into the African idiom as respectable European
ideas.

"Is that what you believe, that the Goromo is a different
kind of truth?" There was something unsettling in Ayesha's
manner.

"What sort of answer do you want?" John wanted to
know. "What are you asking me?"

"As for me, I am only a bush woman. I believe there is
only one truth. It is that one truth I want you to tell me."
There was an edge to her voice, as if she were waiting for
something from him.

"You want me to tell you the truth about the Goromo, is
that it?" he inquired lamely.

"You just say the truth about anything. Anything at all.
You just tell it to me. As long as it is true, I will be glad to
hear it." She was ready to spit at him or to laugh at him and
he knew it.

Unforgivably, he yawned. "The truth is, I am very
sleepy," he said, and it *was* true but it was also dreadfully
inappropriate.

"The truth is you find my company tiresome, isn't it?"

"No, that's not the truth," he pleaded, embarrassed. G

"You are telling lies, John Lavender." Ayesha rose and brushed past him towards the gate. She left without bidding him good night, an intentional slight. Behind her a still fragrance hung on the air—hints of orchid in the mountain forests of the south.

outside, thwarting the weather man's forecast and ruining
the first crop.

3

Ignorant of Abu's tribulations, Likki lay on her freshly
ironed sheets in her freshly cleaned bedroom; but although
she was exhausted, sleep eluded her. With fruitless inevita-
bility her thoughts turned towards the matter she had come
here hoping to forget—her lover of four years, Roger, and
the fact that he had left her. In order to get free of Likki he
had moved his whole family out of the country, but he *had*
gone. All the moralistic and we-only-want-what's-best-for-
you friends who had warned Likki against getting involved
with a married man had been proved correct. But the
attraction between them had been so strong it seemed
futile to withstand it, like struggling against a natural
force—although Roger had taken his time in the beginning.
He'd been going out with her college roommate when Likki
first met him and it was nearly eight months before he
broke off that relationship. She should have understood
that this was typical of Roger's indecisiveness, his de-
viousness, but he explained it as concern for others' feelings
and she took him at his word. From there on it was the
usual story: he loved his two children (particularly his little
daughter), he respected his wife; but his emotions were not
"deeply engaged." He yearned for intimacy. Likki handed
over her whole psyche to him and he took it. He gave back
to her lovemaking like a technicolour dream of her best
imaginings. Yet once he was gone she felt herself short-
changed. Now, Likki found herself in Africa, which she had
searched out as others had the Foreign Legion, to displace
herself as far as possible from Roger and his maddening
capacity for compromise, which she was still too young to
appreciate.

("You're depressed, dear," her mother had said to her last
September while the snowflakes whirled intemperately

outside, thwarting the weather man's fantasies and ruining
the fruit crop.

"Really."

"Why don't you go someplace warm?")

Roger had left her the previous August. Grappled to the
bosom of his family by conscience, habit, and perceived (by
him) economic necessity, he had casually put it forth to
Likki over breakfast one morning that although he much
regretted it, it was, as she was sure to agree, all for the best.
Besides, the teaching position at the University of Helsinki
was only for three years—at least initially. Car, house, and
research facilities all thrown in. What better place to study
boreal forest ecology? Maybe Likki could come and visit in
a year or two? Likki had been calm until he left for work.
Then, the bacon, which had coagulated in an icy knot in her
stomach, insisted on exiting through the same orifice by
which it had entered.

In the August heat, Likki had sat outside near the
overgrown blackberry bushes, communing like an aged
Ophelia with the dark fruits hanging there. Roger, she
realized, had been planning this move for months, months
she had devoted to idle fantasies that he would stay with
her. Stay forever. But she was thankful he hadn't told her
sooner; she was bad at protracted partings. He knew that.
So, after all, his betrayal was an act of love, the love he
always said he didn't feel for her.

•

Likki woke in the bungalow next morning feeling awful.
There was cramp in every inch of her abdomen but the
bathroom, a mere fifteen feet down the hall, seemed a great
and perilous distance away. Standing up was a Herculean
effort and perhaps a pointless accomplishment for, once on
her feet, Likki seemed to hang suspended in the centre of
her room like a distressed sea creature. Navigating across
the room to fetch a robe out of her unpacked suitcase
required a series of complex manoeuvres each of which
demanded a painful effort of concentration. Her slippers
posed a particular problem, floating dimly below her on the
softly pulsing floor.

"I think I'm dying," she said to Carlotta.

"Take a couple of Aralen."

"I haven't got malaria."

"Of course you have malaria."

"How do you know?"

"You haven't been here long enough to have anything else. Did you take your temperature?"

"Yes. It was only ninety-nine point two."

"That's malaria every time. Low fever. Headache. That's how it starts."

"But I have diarrhoea. . . ."

"That's right. And you feel like the last drop of energy has been wrung from your body and all of your friends have died."

Likki capitulated and took the Aralen. She spent the rest of the day on the sofa in the living-room thinking about unpacking but too enervated even to get out of her bathrobe.

In the afternoon, John stopped by to visit and bring the news: Abu had awakened with a high fever. He had shivered through the heat of the day under two woollen blankets. He had begged John to tell Miss Lady what had happened to her new ironing boy.

"He was chased by the Goromo?" Likki was frankly incredulous.

"He's making it up," said Carlotta. "He was probably smoking 'wee' with his friends."

"He's pretty cut up," John defended him. "And he has the most enormous bruise on his back."

"You don't have to see a goblin to get cut up," said Carlotta. "In fact, it's a pretty easy thing to do if you go running through the bush in the dead of night, high as a kite on marijuana." She pronounced it 'Marie-hwaanna,' an idiosyncrasy that was to grow to irritate Likki.

John said he had also come to see if he could take the two women on a personally conducted tour of the town. He looked at Likki as he spoke, but this was out of the question for her. Her head throbbed ominously and she knew it would be tempting fate to venture far from the toilet.

Carlotta also declined. As Girls' Housewarden she felt it necessary to maintain a strong presence on campus, the more so since classes had not yet started and a kind of holiday ambience prevailed. "There's more fooling around right now than any time all year. I couldn't leave the girls alone for a second."

"Why? What do they do?" asked Likki, who was generally unaware of all lusts but her own, which she took very seriously.

"They escape!" said Carlotta. "Turn your eyes for a minute and they're gone. Off! Away into the bush with their boyfriends. The next thing you know it's midnights visits to the herbalist, septic abortions, unwed mothers, the lot! Last year there were twenty-nine abortions—for only fifty-seven girls. *Twenty-nine!* Some of them went *four* times each. Sixteen years old and four abortions. Think about it." She shivered with pleasurable indignation.

■

John Lavender thought about it as he coasted down the hill from the secondary school and decided that it probably wasn't true. More likely, it was one or two abortions and twenty-nine different tattle-tales.

When he came up to the town, John detoured around the periphery instead of striking through the centre directly to Kutu's. He slowed as he passed Ayesha's house as if to see whether she was sitting outside her gate. She was not. Shortly afterwards, John's eye was caught by something fluttering in the bush off on his left. He stopped to get a better look, then left his bike and went on foot to inspect.

A few minutes later he was surging through Ayesha's main gate full of excited animation. Ayesha was sitting in her courtyard with the solitary stillness of a northern icicle. Nevertheless, she gave John Lavender a sparkling smile, a reflection of some other sunlight. "John Lavender, what brings you to this house?"

"I believe I've found Abu's shirt," he announced. He came in proudly, a hero unravelling mysteries.

"Abu's shirt," Ayesha repeated in a flat voice.

"Yes. You know, the one he lost to the Goromo."

"Goromos again?" Behind her an infant cried in a shuttered sleeping room. Ayesha went to rescue the little one from the dark.

"Is that your child?" John Lavender asked when she returned.

"It is not my child."

"Your sister's child?" he asked again, sorting through half-remembered rumours.

"My sister is dead."

"Your cousin?"

"What is my cousin's child to you?"

He was silent, studying her for a moment. "Are you angry with me?" he asked at last.

"How should I be angry with you?" Ayesha returned his question unanswered. She bent over to fasten little Comfort to her back with a piece of patchwork cloth. Then, rising up, she said, "Let us go to see this wonderful shirt you have found." She followed the white man out to the edge of town and into the tall grasses where a torn khaki school shirt hung dejectedly from a low branch in the bush.

"At last you have found the Goromo!" exclaimed Ayesha when she saw the shirt. Her laughter bubbled up.

"So you think the Goromo is all overheated imagination?"

"I see only a shirt on a branch. Where is the Goromo?" Ayesha waved her arms up and down in the air and danced about imitating the spooky sounds children make when they play at being ghosts. "Ooooh, aaaah, ooooohoooo-wweeeeeOOOOO." Comfort, tied to her back, shrieked with the fun of these delectable antics.

"Do you think Abu just *invented* the whole incident?" demanded John with indignation. "Abu is *sick* today because of it."

"John Lavender, you *want* to believe it. You want to believe all the stories. Just like a small boy. I won't spoil your story for you."

※ 4

Abu's fever lasted for seven weeks. Mother of Issa fretted. She sent Abu three times with Kutu to the hospital for injections; she had prayers said for him in the mosque; on the third Friday of his illness she walked all the way to the house of Mallam Yakubu for a jar of Koranic "medicine." (In Kpama, mallams were wise men, learned in Koranic scriptures, who sometimes ministered to mental or physical frailty.) Mother had the cleric write out the most powerful scriptures she could afford in an edible ink on a wooden board. As Mallam Yakubu rinsed the tablet clean, Mother of Issa collected the water in a basin and transferred it to a glass jar. This jar she took home for Abu to drink from. With the sacred word of Allah in his stomach, Abu should have recovered quickly, but he did not. He languished under the mango tree in the courtyard and it was Mieri's turn to be amusing, to report the gossip of the town: to relate how work had stopped on the new administration offices because cement was short and the last shipment from Gbiriri had disappeared across the border on a lorry called No Condition Is Permanent; how Mallam Sidiki had disgraced himself in the eyes of the Faithful by getting caught stealing pigs from a villager; how the army commander in Kpama was being recalled to the south, which seemed to confirm rumours that he had indeed seduced several high-ranking Muslim wives.

Ayesha came almost every evening after supper, bringing with her bitter teas, infusions with medicinal aromas. These Abu drank with reluctance, but their astringence, when he bathed in them, was pleasant to his skin.

When Abu had fallen into the early, fretful sleep of his weakness the others sat round in the courtyard discussing his condition.

"I am worried," said Ayesha.

"He'll be all right," said John Lavender, whose optimism was based primarily on his ignorance of death.

"He is losing too much weight."

"We have tried everything," mourned Kutu in his deep baritone. "No one knows what is troubling the boy."

"But we all know what is troubling him," contradicted Ayesha.

"Yes, it's true," agreed Kutu heavily, reversing his previous statement without embarrassment.

"Have you tried the Earth Priests?"

"No."

"We would be disgraced," sniffed Mother of Issa. She had no desire to risk her standing in the community for the sake of an orphaned waif she had pulled in off the street, a waif with an exasperating talent for discovering trouble wherever he moved. Still, like it or not, he was part of the household, and only madmen and witches were niggardly when it came to the well-being of their own people. Mother of Issa turned to John Lavender. "*You* take Abu to the Earth Priests," she said.

John Lavender looked confused. Mother of Issa explained that it was obvious that Abu's illness was a spiritual trouble, brought on by his encounter with the Goromo. The illness could not be cured by the hospital because it was an affliction of the soul. The mallams were also powerless to cure it because the Goromo, being a pagan creature and understanding no Arabic, would resist the devices of Islam. Only pagans could help Abu, but her husband, Kutu, would lose face terribly if he went to consult with them. Here Mother of Issa stared pointedly at John. John hesitated, but the outcome was never really in doubt. Eventually he agreed to escort Abu to the abode of the pagan healers, though it was left to Kutu to arrange the day. John asked Ayesha to accompany him.

"As for me, I will not come."

"May I ask why not?"

"I do not believe in all this *juju*."

"Oh, why don't you come? You're not afraid, are you?"

"It is against the will of Allah to traffic with such people."

"Are you trying to tell me there's nothing in it?" asked John archly, teasing her.

"It's true. There is nothing there but empty words and lies."

"Then why did you suggest sending Abu to them?"

"Because they are the ones who can help."

"I see," said John. "Only Earth Priests with no power can cure an illness that doesn't exist."

"There can still be some hope for you, John Lavender," said Ayesha. Her voice was soft but she flashed her teeth at him.

He took umbrage. "You laugh at me because you say I believe in stories, but you yourself turn right around and act on something you say you don't believe in. I only sit here and believe. You contradict yourself hand over foot. Where is the wisdom in that?"

"The wisdom is that here we are realists. We believe in what works. You only believe to amuse yourself."

5

Likki found that living with Carlotta Reap had its drawbacks. For one thing, it was difficult for Likki to reconcile Carlotta as she found her in Kpama with what little she knew of her background. Carlotta came from Cleveland, Ohio, where her elderly parents still lived in a discreet and expensive suburb close to their other child, Carlotta's younger, married sister. According to Carlotta, both Edward and Muriel Reap were textbook American liberals. They voted a straight Democratic ticket at every election. They hardly ever attended church. They believed, instead, in tolerance, compassion and the right to make money. They deplored the existence of poverty, injustice and narrowness of mind.

Carlotta, by contrast, was dogmatic and insatiably dominating. She felt that her two years of experience in West Africa had endowed her with a fund of inexhaustible knowledge and expertise and this she wielded like a mallet to beat down her new roommate's observations and discoveries, her sense of fine adventure in a new land. For example, John Lavender had no sooner introduced Likki to the pleasures of the locally brewed guinea-corn beer at Farrah's beerhouse, Crocodile, than Carlotta found time to set her straight on the subject. Guinea-corn beer was an abomination. It was a breeding ground for hepatitis, polio, and God knew what else. The brewsters knew not the first thing about hygiene and Westerners might consider themselves lucky if they escaped with nothing worse than amoebic dysentery. Only loose women frequented the houses where the brew was prepared. Men followed along after them with only one thing on their minds. "You're just asking for trouble," said Carlotta.

For her part, Carlotta found Likki "lacking in character"

and said so on several occasions. She also told Likki she was
"unfocused" and hinted that, for someone who had travelled five thousand miles to teach young minds, Likki was a
bit too fond of male company.

"What's that got to do with teaching?"

"You should show them how to stand on their own two
feet," asserted Carlotta. "Especially the girls."

"I *am* standing on my own two feet," said Likki.

"You're like an overcoat waiting to hang on something."

"You're not jealous are you, Carlotta?" Carlotta never
went out, never partied.

"Jealous of what?"

Predictably, Carlotta objected to any new acquaintances
Likki acquired—particularly the men. Unless, of course,
Carlotta herself had furnished the introduction. Whenever
a visitor of Likki's left the house, Carlotta would pour
herself a cup of coffee and come to perch on the arm of the
sofa, seeming to balance her judgement as she was
balancing her weight. Then with the inexorable conviction
of a guillotine she would point out in unflattering detail the
ways in which the friend was taking advantage of Likki.
Nuhu, the geography teacher, for example, whom Likki
had quickly learn to appreciate as an outstanding conversationalist and drinking companion, and an attractive
escort, was, according to Carlotta, a thoroughgoing scoundrel. He might seem to be solicitous and concerned, but
really all he wanted was the prestige of walking into
Farrah's beerhouse with a white woman. Meanwhile, he
was promiscuously sleeping with the wives of several
members of the teaching staff; he regularly cadged dinners
from the vice-principal's second wife; and the first wife of
the bursar was in and out of his bungalow four times a week
with food. "And you know what *that* means," concluded
Carlotta significantly, for it was an article of faith with her
that food and sex were inextricably conjoined in Kpama.

"That poor old bursar doesn't have much luck with his
women, does he?" Likki suggested wickedly. Only that
morning she had observed the man's second wife sneaking
out of another neighbour's bungalow.

"The bursar is impotent," said Carlotta.

"How do *you* know?" asked Likki. If it were true, she wondered, how had the man acquired his seven laughing children?

"He rents out his wives," said Carlotta.

"What?"

"He's just a married pimp," said Carlotta, her mouth an ugly wrinkle.

"I don't believe it."

"When you've been here as long as I have, you'll understand these people a little better." She rose with a tight smile.

•

Carlotta defined a great portion of her existence in terms of other people's lusts. She was obsessed, for example, with Nuhu's philandering. She said she knew for a fact that he frequently "had sex," as she phrased it, with several sixth-form girls. This was in addition to his extracurricular activities with the wives of fellow staff members. So far, however, Carlotta had no definitive evidence of his lusts. In the attempt to prove Nuhu's fornications, Carlotta devoted many hours to standing by her calico curtains in a darkened room, observing his comings and goings. From this position she was also well placed to observe the activities of her other neighbours. She performed both tasks with equal dedication. She was particularly enthusiastic in her surveillance of her closest neighbour, Mr. Bai, whom she despised because, she said, he had eaten her cat.

It was difficult to understand the headmaster's thinking in appointing such a woman to oversee the moral development of the girls in the school. Carlotta, however, loved the job. She ran a tight clique of seven "best" girls, all of them sixth formers and all slated to graduate the following June. These girls were favoured with coveted oddments from the house and kitchen, scraps of tinned food, butt ends of soap, empty bottles, discarded razor blades, and crumpled pieces of scrap paper. Carlotta further bound them to her with bright promises for the future. She told them that when she left the school for good she would give her sewing machine to Ajara and her high-heeled shoes to

Fati. Mercy would have the cooking pots, Binti a choice of dresses, Ama the dishes, etc., etc.

Behind Carlotta's back, however, or rather right under her nose, at least one of these "best" girls met secretly with the despised Nuhu. A second was in love with the headmaster. A third, Binti, after extracting an oath of secrecy, confided to Likki that she had conceived a great passion for Carlotta's loathed neighbour, Mr. Bai; she stoutly maintained that it was not Mr. Bai but the bursar who had killed and eaten Carlotta's white angora pussycat, Napoleon. Binti also suggested that the remains of Napoleon had constituted an integral part of a bowl of stew that the bursar's junior wife had presented to Carlotta on the occasion of her birthday.

At first such lists of multiple betrayals quite amazed Likki. She was unused to the volume of local gossip. In her first month at the school she heard enough material to satisfy a soap-opera buff for a decade.

"How do they fit it all in?" she asked John Lavender. "They don't have television."

•

Of course, getting around Carlotta was easy, once you knew how her mind worked. A girl caught out of bounds after midnight had only to invent a story that suited Carlotta's prejudices and she would escape all suspicion. The girl might, for example, hint that she had been aroused by the sound of a male voice just outside the dormitory window and had come out to warn Carlotta. If, in addition, the girl could insinuate that the voice had resembled that of the hated Nuhu, her story would almost certainly go unquestioned. The next morning Carlotta would march into the office of the headmaster like an army of occupation and demand that he do something about the abysmal morals of his staff.

Or the girl might say that she had heard a fearful howling and, worried for Zulu's safety, had gone out to look for him. This story played on Carlotta's dislike of Mr. Bai and her very real and well-grounded fear that a protein-deficient neighbour would grab her remaining pet and toss him into a large black pot.

Although Carlotta kept a vigilant watch over Zulu, the lusty mongrel occasionally escaped the barriers of her concern and went courting. Carlotta was ambivalent about these episodes. She would pace the floor, railing at the abominable inefficiency of the three-score students she had commissioned to find her dog. But then, halfway through a tirade, she would work herself up into paeans of praise for the puppies Zulu had sired on the occasion of his last escape. This might spark recollections of similar records of conquest established by the magnificent Napoleon before he became part of Mr. Bai's nefarious repast.

Likki asked her once why she didn't have Zulu fixed. Carlotta was shocked at the suggestion. She said it was immoral. It wasn't right for people, so it wasn't right for pets. After this Likki better understood Carlotta's violent hatred of Mr. Bai. He had not simply eaten her cat; he had committed an act of cannibalism.

Cannibals. In her heart of hearts this was probably what Carlotta really thought of the inhabitants of Africa. However well-educated, sophisticated, and urbane they might appear, she still saw them as little more than flesh-eaters decked out in beads and feathers.

Carlotta, of course, had come to save them by teaching them biology. It was a holy mission of science, not unlike a religious vocation. And, in fact, almost all of Carlotta's visitors were missionaries: Catholics, Baptists, Methodists, and Anglicans. The Anglican minister, Rev. Aston-Tighes, stopped in to see Carlotta at least once a fortnight, frequently inviting her to Sunday dinner, for which his wife, Eleanor, procured taste-alike substitutes for nearly every commodity available on the supermarket shelves of suburban London. Carlotta returned from these dinners oozing complacency as she described how the yam had been made to taste "just like mashed potatoes" and the apple pie had been cleverly concocted from underripe mangoes. Why these gastronomic imitations made Carlotta feel so smug was a mystery, but she was particularly unbearable after returning home from such a meal, so Likki took to spending Sunday afternoons and evenings in town. Inevitably, her footsteps took her to Kutu's house where she joined the others in their concern over Abu's health. She frequently tried to cheer the invalid by promising him a fabulous hourly wage when he recovered to do her ironing.

"I will be there!" said Abu cheerfully one evening. "And soon I will be millionaire."

"You're perky today."

"Tomorrow I will be strong again."

"I'm taking him to see the Earth Priests," explained John without enthusiasm.

"Who?"

John elaborated. The Earth Priests maintained ritual links with the spirits of the land. Unlike most citizens of Kpama, they had not converted to Islam but had remained pagans. "Otherwise they would be abandoning all their spirits," said John.

"Otherwise they would all starve," corrected Ayesha from where she sat bent over one of her mysterious teas.

"Why would they starve?" asked Likki. John, too, looked up with a sudden bite of interest, hoping perhaps for tales of tethered curses, ancestral maledictions, or magical prohibitions delicately overstepped. He should have known better.

"They get all their money from their pagan shrines," said Ayesha. "When you go there to see them you have to pay out plenty."

John sighed. Ayesha had revived their quarrel. "You're an incorrigible materialist," he said to her—in English, of course. (In Kpamé the sentence could hardly be framed, would have emerged as a series of inept and cumbersome expressions.)

Ayesha shrugged her shoulders and turned from him to her malodorous tea. In her experience, whites used oblique and complex language only to mask their aggression or their ignorance. She wanted neither.

"Ayesha, you're sulking," chided John Lavender.

"Is that it?" A disdainful smile played softly at the corners of her mouth. She stirred her infusion with a serenity that was an affront.

John, shielded from Ayesha by Likki's presence at his

side, proceeded to "joke" with the woman and "advise" her in the tones of an older brother. And Likki, relieved for once not to be at the receiving end of someone else's wisdom, laughed too much and too long at everything John said. Yet once or twice she was disturbed by something that lurked in the other woman's eyes, something besides serenity, something sleek and coiled. She whispered in John's ear, "That's enough."

"He can speak!" said Ayesha as if she had overheard the whisper. "I am not a child, not someone without eyes, not someone who needs to be protected. I can see! I can look after myself."

Kutu's square face creased with furrows. "Since you are all guests in my house," he said, "you must not quarrel with each other here." Ayesha's words had been dark and layered, although the whites did not understand. For them, phrases like "I can see" or talk about "protection" were innocent. In Kpama these were the veiled words of sorcerers and they could be deadly.

Later, after Ayesha had left for home, Likki said, "I used to think she lived here."

"No. She lives rather far over in the *zongo*—on the other edge of the town." John gestured in that direction.

"I know that now. Why is she so strange?"

"I don't know," said John Lavender.

"Don't you?"

"I don't *think* so." He hesitated before he answered.

"Then you *do* know," said Likki.

"Oh, come on. There's nothing to know! Absolutely nothing."

"At a guess, I'd say that's just the problem."

"She's much too strange for me," he said. "Besides, I shouldn't want to mess about with a married woman. Not in this town, anyway." With his eyes he invited Likki to join with him in laughing at the absurdity of the idea.

"Her husband seems to be away almost all the time," Likki persisted, not laughing.

"Look here, what are you suggesting? Her husband only needs to come home once to make trouble. Or his brothers might take it upon themselves to discourage misdirected attentions. There's no such thing as privacy in this town. Everyone would know. And think what it would do to my work! I have my reputation to think of."

"You're afraid!" Likki teased, giggling at the thought of John's jeopardized "reputation."

"You're mad!" he answered her crossly.

6

Sima, elder of the Earth Priests, was old. He had seen the seasons pass, not just the back-breaking seasons of planting and harvest, but the deeper cycles, the ones that age the heart. His memories stretched back to the years before white men had come to Kpama. He had been a small boy then, tending Father's Best Cow, hoping that his grandfather would say he could keep the calf for his own when it was born.

In those days the markets had been full of slaves, who told their distress in foreign tongues. When his father and his uncles had gone south to trade their captives for gunpowder, Sima had begged to go with them. "Stay home and take care of your mother and sisters," they told him, and they went off together in the bright morning, some of them mounted on horses. Their gun barrels gleamed with a leaden sheen. Their robes were covered with charms. Charms against magic; charms against bullets; charms against confusion and fear.

Sima still slept in his mother's room, and he was glad of it with his father away. The house echoed emptily with only the children's voices. The women were subdued. It seemed that far more than thirty had gone south, had travelled for the sake of profit and adventure, taking with them all the shouting and the laughter of the house, all the joking, all the quiet, intense discussions that carried on long into the night. Sima snuggled close to his mother's sleeping body and pulled Sil, his little brother, near. Though he did not seem to wake, he was aware that his mother suckled Baby Kyama twice in the course of the night.

On the morning of the third day, his grandfather gave him an old Dane gun and showed him how it worked. "If anything happens," he said, "hide with your brother in the bush."

The raiders came on the fifth day. They were mounted men from the north who swept down on the house like hawks, tearing boys and women screaming from the arms of their families. Sima, only one field away, wept with fear, but remembering his grandfather's words, he grabbed Sil's arm to pull him along, grabbed him so tightly that the blood nearly stopped. He beat Father's Best Cow with a thorn branch to make her move faster. The two boys hid all day in the grove that surrounded one of the shrines. It was the grove where their ancestors had performed initiations.

Their cousin found them there in the evening and brought them home. Parts of the wall surrounding their house had been broken down. The large wooden gates were destroyed. Fires had been started in many rooms and still smouldered under collapsed roofs. In the courtyard, Grandfather breathed with difficulty on a pallet while Grandmother wept softly and chased off the flies from the messy wound in his chest.

Sil found Baby Kyama's body in a charred room and didn't understand why she wouldn't get up. "Don't wake her, Sil, she's asleep," said Sima and went to tell his grandmother. The old woman hugged the two boys to her side and swore terrible, terrible oaths.

Their mother they never saw again.

■

When the men returned from the south they met the news with stony faces. They went to the other houses in Kpama demanding to know why their neighbours, fellow citizens, brothers by blood and marriage, had not come to prevent the abduction and slaughter of their children, their sisters, and their wives.

"It was all over in minutes," they were told by the Ruler. "The raiders had left before we could even reach for our guns." At that time in Kpama the houses had seemed farther apart. Each of the nine large patrilineal clans had settled on a different spur of the hill and there was still open land between them. Even so, Sima's father did not believe the Ruler.

"You are all cowards," he reproached them. "While our children lay dying you crawled to hide." Then he called down on their heads a curse through the agency of the shrine in the grove. "Your power will wither," he told the Ruler, "like the grass dries in the harmattan wind. Within three years your place will be taken by a new force."

It was at that time that great armies began to march across the land. The French came, and the British, followed by a vicious army of Muslim liberation. Then the French returned only to be routed by slave raiders who saw their livelihood vanishing and projected their vengeance onto the local population. At the end of the third year the British returned, and this time they stayed on in Kpama. They deposed the Ruler and put their own man, his cousin, in the palace. They made strange laws. They raised taxes. They outlawed slavery. They put soldiers everywhere in the land. Soldiers prying into private affairs. Soldiers forcing people to build schools and roads. Soldiers lining people up for medical treatment, then marching them south at gunpoint to work in the mines. Soldiers even kidnapped children away to school. Sima himself was spirited off in his tenth year by two officers of the second battalion of the Cumbrian Fusiliers, who shipped him down to Walema, eighty miles south. Sima stayed for seven months in the listless classrooms, eating the bland, pepperless food and sleeping without even a mat on the open verandahs that sheltered both sides of the school. No one in Walema spoke to Sima. No one even knew his language. One night in March he bolted, escaping home through the bush on his own. The soldiers, of course, came after him. Her Majesty's Cumbrian Fusiliers, in their pith helmets and short khaki trousers, tracked him through the bush, but when they got to Kpama, Sima's father told them that his son was dead. Sima, hiding inside the four-foot-high clay balloon that was his father's largest granary, pinched himself with relief.

Now, again, there were soldiers all about, though this time their faces were black. In the intervening years Sima had become rich—in the way that mattered in Kpama: his family was large, his grandchildren numbered more than sixty. Before his own grandfather died on that long-ago day of disaster, he gave Sima the calf that was still within the

belly of Father's Best Cow. Sima watched at the calf's birth.
It was its mother's firstborn and she suffered with it for long
hours, complaining with sad eyes and a rheumy lowing
when the pains were hard. It was a heifer. Sima named it
Lost Mother for the grief in his heart. Father's Best Cow
couldn't stand up for two days after the birth, but Lost
Mother was strong and fertile and began a great herd—as if
to lighten the sorrow of her name.

•

It was late morning. Sima was relaxing by his door on a
striped beach chair, a high-status wood-and-canvas anach-
ronism bequeathed to the elders of Kpama by sixty years of
British rule.

Sima's reflections were interrupted by the approach of his
youngest granddaughter, Ajiki. Sima rubbed her woolly
head when she came to him and thought how like little
Kyama she looked; but perhaps this was memory playing
tricks. "A white man is coming," said Ajiki, and Sima,
having already a good idea of what was up, put on his best
smock and went out to meet his visitors by the gate.

John Lavender was ill at ease. "Welcome," said Sima,
grasping his hand. "What brings you to our house?" In fact,
he knew already; Abu trailed listlessly behind the white
man and all of Kpama knew Abu was ill. And why.

"We have come because of this boy. Seven weeks ago he
encountered the Goromo and since then he has never been
well."

Sima smiled. "A white man speaks to me of the Goromo!"

It was an awkward moment for John Lavender. "We can't
seem to find out what's wrong with the child. I was asked by
Kutu to bring him here. They've tried everything."

"So you have gone everywhere else. Now you come
here."

John Lavender winced, but answered firmly. "I was
asked by Kutu to bring him here."

Sima nodded, then turned to Abu. "Why have you come
with this stranger? Where are your own people?"

"They are dead."

Of course. Sima had forgotten that Abu was an orphan.

As he had been. "I was thinking of Kutu and his wife," he said aloud.

"They wouldn't come here," said John Lavender. "There would be trouble because they are Muslims."

"Many Muslims come here," said Sima. "Although it is true they usually come secretly at night." He bent to examine Abu, looking into his mouth and ears. Under his eyelids. He felt the muscles of his legs and shoulders. "He needs to see the diviners," Sima said when he was finished. "They will find out what is wrong and tell us what we need to bring."

"You don't think it's connected with the Goromo?"

"Perhaps. Or we may find there is some other trouble," said Sima. He led them with casual gait back to his own rooms. The so-called house of the Earth Priests was like a diminutive medieval city, a walled citadel of eleven acres containing hundreds of rooms and courtyards nesting within courtyards. A labyrinthine network of narrow streets and alleyways laced through the warren, linking the various sections and at the same time defining their separateness. Surrounding the whole was an eight-foot wall of sunhardened adobe blocks.

Sima's reception room was cool and windowless. The floor and inside walls of his two-hundred-year-old dwelling had been plastered in the traditional way, with a mixture of white clay, manure, and the blood of oxen, which was used to bind the compound. The result was an unlikely texture: organic, supple, damply dry like the skin of a mushroom, it held neither warmth nor coolness, but promised both. Hides were spread on Sima's floor to accommodate visitors. John brought out some cigarettes so that Sima could smoke while he questioned Abu.

"Why did you walk home alone that night?"

"I needed money. I wanted to ask the white woman for money. For work."

"Why ask that white woman?"

Abu shook his head with things he only dimly understood. He had known all along that she would help him. "It seems she has a kind face," he said.

"And why do you need money?" Sima inquired.

"I want to marry." Abu explained about Comfort.

"Can you not work for Kutu?"

"I am living in Kutu's house. I am eating his food. How can I ask him for money?" And Kutu had laughed when Abu had said he would marry Comfort.

"But Kutu has taken you in as his child. Will he not help you to marry?"

"He says I am too small. When I am old enough, then he will help."

"And when will you be old enough?"

"It may be twelve years. And by then Comfort can already be promised to another."

"And what does Mahmut say to this?"

Abu traced his finger over the tegument of the floor. He considered his answer. "You know Mahmut," he said at last. "If I am a small boy with no family and no money, how can I go to him and say I will marry his daughter? When I tell him I will become rich millionaire, he will just laugh. He will tell everyone. All of Kpama will be hooting at me."

Late in the afternoon Sima took Abu off to the shrine in the grove. The diviners were waiting for them where the path forked out to the bush farms. They had unearthed fresh peanuts in a nearby field and were munching on them to pass the time. "You have kept long," they admonished as the old man and the boy drew near.

"The white man wanted to come with us," explained Sima. "He was *too* curious. He had to be convinced. So, I told him if he came he would get missing."

The diviners grinned. It was a ruse as old as colonialism. When whites became nosy or prying, allusions to the occult often discouraged their curiosity. For although most Europeans scoffed at superstition, many harboured a lingering respect for the dark forces of the continent they had come to subdue.

The foursome walked in single file to the grove, which lay in a hollow. Bush fires were never permitted to reach it, nor were livestock allowed to browse there. The vegetation within was rank and green. The trees reached towering heights by savannah standards, and there were distinct canopies of vegetation layered overhead as in the rain forests of the south. Inside the grove the air was still and leaf-moist, the light dappled and thin. There was a feeling of remoteness, a sense of severed connections.

At the rear of the file Abu shivered. "I think I can meet my ancestors here," he worried.

"Yes," recalled Sima. "One time I left the grove and climbed over the hill only to find that Kpama was gone!"

"So," chuckled Moola, the chief diviner. "You, yourself got to be missing."

"You see! I seemed to be looking at the land before any men had come to it. Strange beasts roamed and the forest was thick all about."

Abu shivered again. Moola noticed and said to him, "You don't mind Sima. He is just trying to frighten you. Probably he was smoking 'wee' and became foolish."

"Hey!" Sima rebuked him. "Did your mother tell you to call your elders foolish?"

Sima *was* Moola's elder, but both men were long past seventy. Moola begged Sima's pardon with a grave face, but his apologies were so elaborate and so abject that they merely enlarged the original insult.

Sima replied in kind. Thus trading sally and retort they progressed to the centre of the grove, where an irregular circle of trampled earth and a large stone plastered with feathers and blood showed they had reached the shrine. A collection of toothy animal skulls stared out from the roots of a nearby kapok tree.

Moola sacrificed a chicken to announce their arrival. It was one of several young pullets Armah, the other diviner, had brought along in a cotton sack. They waited for the chicken to die (propitiously, on its back) before they proceeded to the divination. For this, Moola and Armah each held one fork of a large Y-shaped stick, while Sima fired questions at the shrine's guardian spirits. The shrine had only a two-word vocabulary: two taps of the forked stick for yes and one tap for no. For the first half hour its answers displayed no apparent pattern and it contradicted itself shamefully. Eventually Sima became annoyed and began to scold. He reminded the shrine that a child's life was at stake. He said he was too old to trek three miles into the bush to consult with cranky, close-tongued spirits who behaved like sulky wives in their menses. "Perhaps the shrine is hungry," suggested Moola. *He* was growing hungry. Whatever meat was given to the shrine they would cook and eat themselves before they left.

Armah despatched another pullet, and then another. He poured some gin into a crack in the trunk of the kapok tree and then handed the bottle around. After this matters moved smoothly if not with speed.

■

Abu returned home after sundown, escorted by Armah. It would take a lot to cure him, he said. Then, exhausted, he fell asleep before he had even tasted his supper. Armah was left to elaborate. Abu would have to return the next day with quantities of herbs, soap, oil, new clothing, and twelve red hens, all fat and all laying.

✕ 7

Within a week Abu took up his position as Likki's ironing boy. He was, generally, full of himself. He showed off his new clothes at Bungalow 5 (Carlotta wasn't interested, but sat through it anyway). Three sets he had had to have. All his old clothing had been burned. He particularly regretted the passing of a handsome blue shirt he thought had suited him. He asked if Carlotta wanted to give him a slightly torn madras blouse that lay on her pile of mending. She did not. She gave him an old belt, however, and he really thought he was going places.

Carlotta inspected Abu's ironing with the scathing eye of a Swiss matron. "He's not bad," she said to Likki. "Maybe I'll use him, too."

"You see?" said Abu. It was true. There wasn't a wrinkle anywhere in Likki's wardrobe. While he fussed with the last shirt sleeve, Abu told the two women about his chickens. "*Twelve!*" he emphasized. "All very *fat*. And each one laying eggs every day. But when we get to the shrine we hear that only *one* hen is for killing. The rest are all for *me*." He added that he was keeping them at Ayesha's house. Kutu objected to their noise and excrement.

"So now you have eleven hens."

"Yes. And every day, eggs. Warm brown eggs the colour of your arms." He was looking at Likki's tanned limbs. "Maybe you want to buy eggs from me?"

"Are they fresh?" asked Carlotta, for whom the pursuit of an acceptable breakfast took up a high proportion of her daily energy.

"When you get the egg, the chicken is still crying out in pain."

"How much?"

"Two shillings each." It was an outrageous sum.

"Two eggs for *one* shilling," countered Carlotta.

"One egg for one shilling and a half."

"One shilling each."

"You give me five shillings and I give you four eggs," said Abu after a rapid calculation. Yet every year he failed arithmetic.

"Done," said Carlotta. Both of them were pleased with the price. Carlotta said afterwards that she knew it was too high but she was tired of buying thirty eggs at the market only to discover that half of them were off. Shortly thereafter, Abu bounced out the door with a two-pound advance in his pocket and the heavy charcoal iron in his hand.

Later in the week Abu debated with Likki whether he should open a savings account at the bank in Kpama or invest his money in ground-nuts where he already had a connection. Every year Mother of Issa scoured the local villages to make deals with ground-nut farmers. She dealt in futures. When farmers were willing, she would buy their entire crop while it was still in the ground. After harvest she stored the nuts in large hundredweight sacks in her bedroom and her children's bedrooms (but not, of course, in Kutu's bedroom) until scarcity had driven up the price and she could unload her merchandise in the south for up to eight times what she had paid for it.

Likki said she thought Mother of Issa was a sounder investment than a savings account, although this judgement had much to do with the seedy appearance of the People's National Bank of Kpama. The bank building's worn and fading exterior and glassless windows covered in fence wire inspired little fiduciary confidence.

"Why not buy more chickens?" inquired Carlotta.

"No. If they get sick they can all die, just like that." Fowl epidemics periodically swept through the area with devastating thoroughness.

"Get a sheep, then," suggested Likki. She loved the idea of the soft, miniature lambs, snow white, long-eared as beagles.

"Maybe," mused Abu, but he looked doubtful.

■

It was about this time that Likki and John Lavender began their affair. Likki was feeling lonely and sorry for herself and drifted into it with a kind of half-acknowledged regret. She chose to tell herself that she couldn't expect a great blossoming of passion again so soon, that she might as well take advantage of what was available. Occasionally she even managed to think she was in love. John Lavender spoke in reasonable tones of a "sexual friendship" and felt he was acting liberated. Likki did not bother to correct him.

Inevitably, of course, the arrangement was a disappointment. Despite all those impeccable Oxford-educated forbears, John Lavender did not make love with slow British sentimentality. His style was closer to poor-quality North American, the hit-and-run of highway sidings, of copulations rushed through in old motels in the last twenty minutes of a frantic lunch hour. And John was surprisingly rough—particularly with Likki's breasts, which he either tore at or squeezed flatly against her rib cage as if he could thus transform her into a boy. All the while he pumped away urgently like someone inflating a bicycle tire with a perpetual leak. He worked hard at his lovemaking; perhaps he felt that the glories of intercourse could be satisfactorily quantified in the number of strokes per minute. With it all he was so naively sure of himself that Likki could not bring herself to disillusion him. For one thing she feared her own lovemaking was not above reproach and that he might tell her so. Besides, eventually John provided satisfaction through the sheer volume of his efforts. "Touchdown," she grinned at him after his first success, but he didn't understand. "It's an American expression," she said and refused to elaborate.

John himself found several things to criticize in Likki. For one thing, she was vulgarly curious about other people.

"Ever have any black mistresses?" she queried him once halfway through the night.

"Ynnnnnh?" John was nearly asleep.

"Tell me."

"Tell you what?"

"If you had any black mistresses."

"Mistresses?"

"Yes. You know: women. Black women."

"Oh. Yes."

"And?"

"And what?"

"What was it like?"

"It was like sex," said John stretching, nuzzling her like a colt. He could be tender only after his lovemaking. Beforehand it embarrassed him.

"Was it the same, then?"

"The same?"

"Yes. The same. s.a.m.e. Or was it different?" She wanted him to say it was different.

"Christ!" swore John Lavender, sitting up in bed. "Don't tell me you believe all that garbage, too. Big dicks. Tight cunts. The world's original sensualists. Natural love— whatever that means. What a load of white middle-class crap!" He yawned in weary exasperation.

"I was only asking, you know. Trying to find out so I wouldn't have to believe all that 'white middle-class crap.'"

"It's like Victorians asking if women could have orgasms. It's bullshit."

"Jesus! Can't a girl even be curious without being labelled a racist?"

"Why ask about it? Why not go out and experiment?"

"Why not, indeed?" retorted Likki. She wondered if any of his women had been from Kpama.

■

There were occasions on which John found Likki's reactions inconveniently out of line with local sexual mores—and with his own. He told her she overreacted, as, for example, on the Sunday afternoon when she discovered she was participating in "some kind of Kpama peep-show."

Mother of Issa had prepared a feast that day. She had simmered turkey meat all morning in a great black ten-gallon pot. She thickened the soup with seeds and nuts ground to the finest powder. She added onions, tomatoes, and hot red peppers—all seeded and peeled and puréed in granite mortars. She added salt that came in slabs from Tamanrasset. She added ginger and spoonfuls of local spices that white men had still to name. In short, she produced a culinary masterpiece.

After the meal, full to the point of distress, Likki curled up on John's bed for a nap. In the late afternoon John intruded on her rest abruptly, which is to say she wakened to find him crouched above her at the point of engaging in intercourse with her slumbering person. "Christ!" said Likki when she realized what was up.

"It's not a bad way to wake up, is it?" John commented cheerfully and without any hint of apology. It was exactly this that was most offensive.

"Jesus! I'm not even awake!"

"You don't need to be awake," he said thickly. His eyes were beginning to glaze over. He was less than two minutes from his own touchdown.

"But I'm not even turned on," complained Likki.

"Next time. Get you next time," he said and kissed her broadly and wetly, with his mouth wide and slack, to silence her.

Outside John Lavender's back window, in a narrow alleyway that smelled of urine and cooking oil, Abu and Salifu strained their ears and their imaginations. Ten-year-old Habiba came out from the courtyard several times to take the score. "They go again, I think," said Abu, holding up two fingers and looking very solemn. Habiba returned inside and told eight-year-old Arimata all about it while they squatted together amid scuds of soap bubbles, washing up after Mother of Issa's feast.

Likki mentioned to John that she thought they were being spied on.

"I suspect this is as private as we can get," he told her; he looked smug, for he thought he was serving her very well by anyone's standards.

Later, when John went out to bathe in the upstairs washroom, Likki rose from his bed to light herself a cigarette. She sat at John's writing table inhaling deeply, wordlessly musing. It was hot, well over a hundred degrees Fahrenheit, and the sweat of their exertions was everywhere on her body. Semen slipped stickily down between her thighs. John's odour steamed up to her along with her own aromas. It displeased her that this was so.

Habiba came into the room unexpectedly. "Nasara," she addressed Likki, screwing up her gargoyle face.

"Yes?"

"Our mother want one dish."

"What dish is that?"

"One large blue dish with a lid."

Likki looked around for it half-heartedly, getting her bearings again.

"It is there!" said Habiba pointing up at a Czechoslovakian bowl high on John's bookshelf. Habiba couldn't reach the dish. Likki stirred herself reluctantly. As Likki walked slowly over to the shelf, Habiba saw on the back of her green robe the oval mark of wetness where the cloth had creased up under her crotch. Habiba only partially repressed a snort of triumph. Here was proof stronger than anything they had gleaned in the back alley. Yet it seemed to Habiba untidy of John Lavender to have left something so precious as his semen to spill irresponsibly down a woman's robe. Back in the courtyard with the blue enamel dish, Habiba broadcast her discovery in the loudest possible tones. Exclamation billowed about the household. John caught the tail end of it, but when he emerged from the bathroom wondering what was "so damn funny," the children only stared at him with sober and unknowing faces.

When Likki stepped into the courtyard, she was surrounded. "Nasara, good e-ven-ing!" Abu greeted her with exaggerated regard. At the same time he was trying to edge behind her to see the spot for himself. Habiba had said that it was very large. White men were obviously fertile creatures. Perhaps this explained why there were so many of them, though they took but one wife each.

"What's going on?" demanded Likki.

Abu danced around behind her. He saw it. "Haaiiyyy!" he shouted. "An elephant has copulated!"

Despite linguistic barriers, Likki realized what was wrong. Furious, she retreated back into the inadequate privacy of John's rooms. She felt as if she'd been put up for auction.

"Come along. Don't take it all so seriously. They're only children," John advised with academic detachment.

"Children with their minds in the gutter. In New York they'd be peddling porn. They'd be making porn."

"This isn't New York, it's Africa," John reminded her, neatly summing up Likki's dilemma, for she had come to Kpama to escape from the things she knew.

"Well then, fuck Africa." Likki reached for her clothes and started dressing. She had no intention of trying again to bathe at Kutu's house.

John offered to accompany her up the hill, but his heart wasn't in it. His bicycle was being repaired and it would have meant a six-mile walk for him. Besides he was physically spent.

"I don't mind," said Likki, and it was true, she was glad to be rid of his company. But there were other things she minded. She minded walking home to an unfriendly house. She minded being laughed at. She minded John's large pores and the emotional flatness of their encounters. She minded the way the smell of him lingered on his towels after he had washed. Right now, upstairs in Kutu's washroom, was a red-and-white-striped towel meant for her use that reeked of his acrid musk. Likki wrinkled up her nose. Already she was halfway through Kpama, propelled by the thought of all her dislikes.

8

There were other dubious portents concerning John's and Likki's liaison. The first time they made love at the bungalow, Zulu disappeared. Carlotta had gone off to an ecclesiastical singsong at the Catholic mission leaving Likki and John in charge of Zulu. The dog contemplated the pair on the sofa with doleful eyes. He went to rest his snout on Likki's reassuring lap, but John was fumbling about inexplicably under her skirt and shoved the fat mongrel away.

When the lovers walked hand in hand to the bedroom, Zulu followed at a distance discreet by canine standards and listened by the locked door with his head to one side and the beginnings of an erection. Evidently he was inspired by what he heard for later that evening he escaped.

Carlotta was distraught when she couldn't find him. She opened her crate of medicinal brandy (Remy Martin, the only brand she drank) and bribed the school's head cook for a supply of ice from his freezer. The cook's freezer ran on kerosene and was operational twenty-four hours a day. The bungalow had its own refrigerator, of course, but it was electric and had to rely on the school's diesel generators, which normally functioned only in the evenings, from six o'clock until eleven. "Lights out" was a literal event at the secondary school.

Zulu was gone for four days. Carlotta drank her way through two and a half bottles and was by turns maudlin and irate. Mr. Bai was singled out for acrimonious invective. "He's done it again," Carlotta summed up her anxiety. She kept an intermittent vigil by the curtains in the living-room, paying special attention to every article of food that entered or escaped her neighbour's bungalow. She wanted Binti and Zhohah to go over and spy.

"The dog is not there," said Zhohah, who was weary of

these efforts. She had heard rumours of Zulu's amorous successes in three separate villages.

"How do *you* know?" said Carlotta.

"The man is eating chicken."

"How do *you* know?"

■

Abu brought Zulu home early on a Wednesday afternoon. "I bring your dog again," he said, grinning broadly at Carlotta, for he was sure he was entitled to a substantial reward. He set Zulu down gently on the floor. The dog's left rear leg was in a cast. "I bring the dog to this man, the veterinary officer," explained Abu. "This man says the dog can have been hit by some lorry. The leg is broken in *too* many places."

"Poor doggie," cooed Carlotta. "Nasty people try to run down their supper, did they?"

Zulu whined and licked Carlotta's face. Then he hobbled slowly into the kitchen to inspect the state of his feed bowl. For four days lust had triumphed over appetite, but now he was ravenous. Getting about on three legs, however, was a tricky business for him, he was such an overweight sausage of a hound.

Carlotta fed him Lobster Newburg from a can she'd been saving for Christmas. "He'll be sick!" cried Likki. "It's too rich for him." Carlotta also fed him half a box of Oreos.

The house filled up with well-wishers. The girls abandoned their study hall in order to visit. The bursar's wife came over with beer. A carload of nuns drove up from the Catholic mission, and Eleanor Aston-Tighes stopped by with three "apple" crumbles. Likki was put off by these proceedings. When Abu started back to Kpama she went with him.

"All that fuss about a dog," Likki complained on the way down the hill.

"Anyway," said Abu, "Zulu is not a dog. He is Miss Carlotta's child."

"God *damn*," said Likki, sure that had *she* disappeared for four days, no such celebration would have greeted her return.

"God *damn*," echoed Abu, imitating her delivery. Then he said, "Maybe you want to find John Lavender?"

Likki wasn't sure she did want to find John Lavender. But she said, "Yes, we could do that."

"He can be at Crocodile." Farrah's beerhouse.

"All right. If he's not there I'll share a pot with *you*."

"Eh-eh." It was Abu's nervous laugh. Mother of Issa would delight in beating him if she caught him drinking beer. Her hand would be that much heavier because abstinence was a prescript she so often broke herself.

"I won't tell," said Likki. Abu seldom had more than half a calabash anyway. It was just that he liked being there, sitting with the whites as if he, too, were one of the lords of creation. Besides, Farrah's beerhouse was singular in Kpama—like a hostel at the edge of a younger world. It was an untidy, Elizabethan sort of establishment, a place where ragged farmers in homespun swayed drunkenly on the benches, either arguing or singing, according to their wont; a place where the family cats rubbed shoulders and fleas with every guest and where household chickens obligingly pecked the flies off the edges of the clay beer pots; a place where the blind man came to play old songs on his harp of millet stalks while the children danced in a corner. Farrah, the good brewster herself, could usually be observed sweating over her next brew, a treacle-sweet wort she kept boiling in forty-gallon crocks balanced over vicious fires that crackled and spat into the evening like oriental demons, shooting showers of sparks over the unwary. And the bravura smells of candy and Ovaltine invaded everything, though they could not quite mask earthier emanations— yeast, vinegar, and the intangible oiliness of ethanol.

It was Kpama market day, the last day of the local three- day market week—the market rotated between Kpama, Faangbaani, and Sokpeli. Farrah's beerhouse was full and raucous. Crocodile reverberated with the laughter and discussion of farmers and traders thirsty after a long day's haggling in the sun. John Lavender, however, was nowhere in sight.

"Sit down and have some beer with me, anyway," said Likki, and she found some space for herself and Abu on a quiet bench near the blind man, who was playing soft funeral songs like lullabies.

"How is Comfort?" inquired Likki.

Abu straightened on the bench and nodded his head for emphasis, "She is fine!"

"I'd like to see her one day."

"Yes. We will do it!" He took a proud swallow from his calabash and looked down the tunnel of time. "One day Comfort will be a very fine woman. One day she will be a very *good* person—like you."

Likki, who had not before been described as a good person—at least not to her face—was mildly surprised to find how easy it was to accept this flattery. She looked at Abu appraisingly. When he was older he would be a thoroughgoing scoundrel and women would adore him. They would see the life in him and be drawn to it helplessly.

She sat on at Farrah's for a gentle hour, speaking with Abu as an equal, talking about his orphaned childhood, about the present, about the future that lay before both of them. And when they eventually rose to leave they had fixed something between them, though neither of them would have been capable of saying what it was.

They left Farrah's still ostensibly looking for John Lavender. Abu suggested they visit Last Calabash, the only beerhouse in Kpama to rival Farrah's Crocodile. Farrah herself always disparaged Last Calabash by saying that Wednesday, its brewster, employed scandalous brewing methods. According to Farrah, Wednesday kept the maggot-ridden corpse of a dead rooster in the bottom of her enormous brewing pot. From this inauspicious beginning the process only deteriorated. Old shoes were tossed into the fermenting liquor, it making little difference whether they were soled with leather or rubber. Tobacco was added—from cigarette butts. Filters, too. Then, there were handfuls of "ten-ten's" lifted from the shelves of the hospital pharmacy. There were other items at which Farrah would only hint. She said that Wednesday stirred her pots with odd-looking spoons after midnight when no one was looking. No one but Farrah.

Wednesday maintained that all this was nothing but Farrah's jealousy speaking, because Farrah knew that

Wednesday made better beer. "Farrah doesn't know any-thing. She doesn't know how to malt the grain properly. So how can she get strong beer if the guinea-corn has sprouted too far? And when she makes the beer the water is too hot. If she comes to me here, I will show her how to do it properly."

Farrah declined to learn anything from Wednesday. She refused to go anywhere near her. "She's a witch," said Farrah.

The two women's animosity was proverbial in the town, though most drinkers frequented both houses equally.

Likki followed Abu through a labyrinth of passages to get to Last Calabash, for it was located near the centre of Kpama—an oddity in an ostensibly Muslim town. Never-theless, it was allowed to flourish in the heart of the town, perhaps for the sake of traders and visitors, perhaps for the sake of the police barracks, which was situated close by. It was Likki's first time at Last Calabash. It was smaller than Crocodile, darker, and more crowded. Walking through Wednesday's gate, Likki pulled closer to Abu's side, for she suddenly felt her strangeness, her foreignness, and all the physical appurtenances of her race. It was with grudging relief, therefore, that she spotted John Lavender leaning back against the wall on the far side of the courtyard, deep in discussion with Nuhu.

They looked surprised to see her but made her welcome. Nuhu handed her his brimming calabash.

"My God, that's strong," said Likki after her first swallow.

"Strongest in town, so they say," said John.

"Oh. Don't take it away!" protested Likki as Nuhu reached for his beer again.

Wednesday walked over to them and planted herself before them, hands resting on her hips. She watched them for a long minute before she addressed herself to Likki. "You don't share your beer?" she demanded at last, staring at Nuhu's calabash still in Likki's hands.

Likki was disconcerted. "Share my beer?"

"She wants you to give her some of your beer," explained Nuhu.

"Some of her *own* beer?"

"Yes. She wants to drink from your calabash."

"Why?"

"You don't ask questions. You only give her the calabash. Later I will tell you."

Likki surrendered the calabash, and Wednesday drained it in one long swallow. "Good," she announced and handed Likki back the calabash. "Beautiful woman," she said before she walked away.

"Do you want to tell me what that was all about?"

"She wanted to prove to you that there was no poison in your beer. This is the first time you've come here. Probably she thinks you can have heard stories from Farrah."

"I *have* heard stories from Farrah," said Likki. Abu giggled nervously, for it was he who had translated into English the more gruesome details of Farrah's account of Wednesday's brewing.

John cleared his throat. "What brings you into Kpama in midweek?" he inquired in an offhand way. He wore a curious, dissatisfied expression.

"Don't look so happy to see me."

"I'm sorry," he said. "I was off somewhere else." He tapped his head. "Thinking."

"About?"

"First tell me why you're here."

"Zulu came home—in Abu's arms. Carlotta is having a party. Fifty-seven female students. Eleven missionaries. And several quote, unquote, apple pies. I couldn't handle it. And you?"

"Just having a bit of a discussion with your friend Nuhu. He thinks one of his women is pregnant."

Abu grinned when he heard this. "You have *too* many women," he scolded Nuhu, using the same congratulatory tone he might have used to say, "You have *too* much money." Then he added, "But anyway, this thing is easy to fix." He looked very knowing as he spoke.

Nuhu bridled. "Is that it?" he asked.

"It's true!" said Abu. He looked at John Lavender. "Do I lie?"

John declined to answer. Abu turned and addressed Nuhu again. "You only need some local woman," he said, upon which Nuhu replied testily that this was the crux of his problem. He didn't know any local women—he was not from Kpama. Any woman he approached would treat him like a stranger and pretend she didn't know what he wanted, didn't even understand his problem.

"What do the local women do?" inquired Likki.

"They have herbs," answered Nuhu. Likki thought with disquiet of Ayesha. John, too, was silent. No one spoke for a while. Then, to change the subject, John said, "You know, I've just been hearing the most extraordinary story here this afternoon."

"Which is?" asked Likki.

"It's a story about that woman who died in the cesspool—Fatima. The mother of that baby Ayesha looks after."

"Oh?" There was an edge in Likki's voice. Lately John had found a way to bring Ayesha's name into every conversation. Besides, Likki was bored with this story of post-partum depression. She had heard a dozen versions of it already. Even six months after the event a good scandal or suicide was still an item of discussion in Kpama.

"According to Wednesday's niece, Fatima isn't dead."

"I don't understand," said Likki.

"Wednesday's niece told me that the woman who died in the *bomba* wasn't Fatima."

"How could that be?" Likki wondered. "I thought the whole town saw the body?"

"They saw a four-day-old body, and we *are* in the tropics, you know. Not to mention the fact that the body was covered in excrement."

"Even in the tropics bodies don't disintegrate in four days."

John humped his shoulders at her wilful disbelief. He said to Abu, "What do you think?"

"It was Fatima in the *bomba*," said Abu.

"Did *you* see her *face*?"

Abu shook his head. "Hawa saw her face."

John nodded as if Abu's words had confirmed his own argument. "The way I heard it," he said, "Hawa wanted to get Mahmut into trouble. They have an old quarrel going back a long time. According to Wednesday's niece, there is a rumour that someone in Mahmut's family poisoned Hawa's brother shortly after the end of World War Two. Because of something that happened in the south-east Asian campaign."

"Oh, that's ridiculous," said Likki.

"People in Kpama have long memories. They carry insults around like cankers for generations."

"Are you trying to tell me that Hawa went and stuffed a dead woman into the cesspool so she could blame it on her forty-years-dead brother's possible poisoner's distant relation?"

"Either that or a body turned up in the *bomba* and Hawa made the most of the opportunity."

Likki shook her head, annoyed at John's love of intrigue. "It's too far-fetched. Besides, if the body wasn't Fatima's body, then where *is* Fatima?"

"She's in Chegili."

"Where?"

"Chegili. A village about four miles west of here. It's where Ayesha's family comes from."

"Oh, really," responded Likki, her voice pitched higher than usual. "Ayesha's family."

"She is there!" affirmed Abu suddenly. "Comfort's mother is there."

The three adults turned to face him abruptly. Nuhu said to him, "Is your wife's mother in Chegili?"

"Yes, she is there."

"You see?" said John Lavender with the pride of a scientist who has just proved a new discovery.

But Abu had more to tell them. "She is there. But she is dead. It is her ghost that moves about in Chegili."

Likki said to John Lavender, "You see?" She could have kissed Abu right then.

"Have you see the ghost?" Nuhu asked.

"Ayesha saw the ghost," admitted Abu softly, perhaps sensing tensions in his audience he did not quite understand. "It is Fatima's ghost. It walks like that on the top of the hill and all the children are afraid."

John, ever attracted to folklore of the supernatural, began pumping Abu for more information, not just on Fatima, but on ghosts in general. Likki attempted to dampen his enthusiasm, for it was obvious to her that when Abu didn't know the answers to John's questions he was quick to invent replies that fed his interlocutor's expectations.

John bought a large pot of guinea-corn beer to help along his conversation. Nuhu bought another and began to discourse on love. Likki paid for the third and said how happy she was. The fourth pot was on the house, Wednesday always keeping a weather eye out for thirsty customers who didn't ask for credit. By the time they left for home, the foursome were experiencing that sentiment of communion with their fellow humans that frequently comes to those who over-indulge. To the whites it seemed that they had always lived in Africa, that they belonged in Kpama, that they were born to red-hot pepper and guinea-corn beer. Their lank hair and pallid skins were all some horrible mistake. John lurched back with an inebriated Abu to Kutu's. Likki stumbled homeward in the dark behind Nuhu.

Forty minutes later, giddy with beer and full of mystical love for humanity, Likki wobbled through her own front door. Before her, Carlotta stood with predatory poise. "Where have you been?" she intoned.

"Drinking," said Likki. "With Nuhu," she added with deliberate malice.

"Do you know what time it is?"

"*Should* I know what time it is?"

"It is almost eleven o'clock. The girls' curfew is at eight."

"Carlotta, I'm not a girl."

"How do you think it looks if you come in here three hours late?"

"Late for what?"

"For curfew."

"God *damn*, Carlotta. I'm *not* late. I'm not a student and I don't have a curfew to be late for. Furthermore, I feel no obligation to set an example for your students by letting myself be bullied as if I were still sixteen years old."

It was always a mistake to correct Carlotta. For the next fifteen minutes she pinned Likki down with a lecture on the dread diseases to be contracted by drinking guinea-corn beer and, in particular, by sharing a calabash with "natives."

Likki rose and moved off to the privacy of the bathroom, where she was careful to lock the door. Carlotta followed after her, still lecturing. Likki was sure to get hepatitis, she maintained, drinking in bars with Nuhu. All sorts of people with all sorts of unmentionable ailments, most of them fatal, drank out of the calabashes at these places. The calabashes were never properly washed. They never saw soap from one existence to the next. More people caught hepatitis from drinking in beer bars than anywhere. Did Likki know that West African hepatitis was particularly virulent?

Inside the locked bathroom Likki gargled joyously with Lavoris.

Carlotta was undeterred. Half the people who contracted hepatitis, she said, never recovered. There was no known cure. Carlotta herself had personally known two missionaries and one Peace Corps volunteer who had died of it. She filled out her sermon with detailed information on the death agonies of several heedless Europeans who had not taken her advice but had pursued their addiction to demon rum all the way to the grave.

Likki opened the bathroom door. "Goodnight, Carlotta," she said sweetly. When she reached her own room she locked the door behind her.

Carlotta hovered uncertainly in the hall outside Likki's door, unwilling to terminate her monologue but feeling snubbed by Likki's indifference. Eventually she went to use the bathroom herself. Minutes later she was back in the hall, pounding urgently on Likki's door.

"What is it now?" yawned Likki with exasperation.

"Where's the top to the toothpaste tube?"

"I don't know."

"You used it last," accused Carlotta.

"I guess I lost it."

"It's the beginning of *harmattan*! In this weather the whole tube can dry right out in two days."

"Oh."

"Well, what are we going to cover it with?"

"Use your finger," said Likki and smiled to herself. But afterwards, when an ensemble of snores from the next room assured her that Carlotta and her dog slept deeply, Likki turned over in her bed and wept.

Carlotta Reap could be lonely company.

9

On Thursdays, Likki's teaching load was light, only one nine o'clock class. Afterwards she usually came into town to visit John, or, if he was working in the villages, to browse slowly through the market. Ayesha found her thus one morning in mid-November.

"Nasara Likki, good morning!" Ayesha hailed her cheerfully and with an excess of energy.

"Good morning." Likki gave Ayesha the smile that most people reserve for their dentist.

"Fine morning!" continued Ayesha, grinning broadly. "How is this fine man, your husband?"

"I don't have a husband."

"Oh." Ayesha's face was crumpled in astonishment. "I thought John Lavender was your husband."

"We're not married."

"Oh. Sorry! But he treats you like a husband?"

"No. He doesn't," affirmed Likki. What could the woman want?

"Ah!" Ayesha was reassured. "But that is much better. He treats you like a *boyfriend*. He brings you presents all the time." Ayesha was all cheerful congratulation, innocence itself.

Likki disapproved of the way Kpama women extracted a stream of tribute from any males who were courting them. It was grossly materialistic. It turned love into little more than prostitution. In some cases it was impossible to tell the two apart. "I get no presents from John Lavender," Likki said proudly, yet somehow it seemed an admission of defeat.

"Ohhh. You see?" said Ayesha. "He *does* treat you like a husband. After all, a boyfriend is always kind, always brings gifts to you, always finds you a nice piece of cloth. But a husband is stingy. He gives all the presents to some other woman so he can win her over as well." Now she was all sympathy and consideration.

"White men aren't like that," said Likki, for the moment almost believing it.

"What are white men like?"

"In what way?"

"In any way." She smiled at Likki but her eyes were narrow.

"What do you want to know, Ayesha?"

"What I asked you. I only want to know what I asked you." Ayesha fell into step alongside Likki as if she would accompany her all the way back to the school. They walked together in stiff silence for some time, Likki wondering how to rid herself of her companion.

They were well past the lorry park before Ayesha spoke again, this time in an unexpected voice, tentative, almost deferential. "Nasara Likki . . ."

"Yes?"

"You are going back to the school now?"

"Yes."

"Then come with me to my house. It is not out of your way."

"Why?"

"I want to show you something that is there." She would elaborate no further.

It was a hot day. The harmattan wind had begun to blow in earnest the week before. Nights were chilly, but by mid-afternoon temperatures had climbed to well over 115 degrees Fahrenheit. This wind from the northern desert brought with it all the dust of the Sahara, so that the sun glared down through an ochre haze that subtracted nothing from the incinerating sizzle but rather magnified its effects while at the same time sucking all colour from the land, until the earth was but a dirty brown reproduction of the sky, a reprint one shade darker, in tones of sepia and umber. There was no moisture anywhere in the air. Everything withered. The skin of unshod feet split open in three-inch-long fissures. Lips cracked. Noses bled copiously with the least exertion. The windborne silt of the desert, powdery detritus of Libya and southern Algeria, rubbed like invis-

ible sandpaper upon every surface, making no exceptions
for either life or the works of men. It filled every crevice,
every pore and wrinkle, with a fine, bistre-coloured talc.

Ayesha's courtyard, by contrast, was a miniature oasis.
Clumps of bamboo stood about in the corners; vines
clambered up wires and latticework. A small mango tree
was carefully nurtured at one end. As the two women
entered, a gaggle of fowl parted noisily in front of them:
guinea hens full of unlikely consternations, turkeys like
circus prima donnas, chickens with their startled, spinsterish airs—Abu's eleven among them.

On the far side of the courtyard, opposite the entrance, a
baby played on a mat under a vine-covered trellis. She was
round-limbed, delicate of feature, her long lashes almost as
tightly curled as her hair. She wore mock pearls in her
earlobes and a circlet of red beads at her waist, but was
otherwise unclothed. The cleft of her pudenda, wider at the
top, seemed to mark the upper limits of an exclamation
point, of Aphrodite's dimpled surprise. The baby's nakedness heightened an aura she exuded of constrained sexuali-
ty. Likki found she was disturbed by this in the child and
was puzzled, for Kpama was, after all, full of small children
who didn't wear clothes.

"This is Comfort," said Ayesha, going to the baby and
lifting her in her arms.

"Oh," said Likki, staring at the child. It was easier now to
understand Abu's infatuation. "She's Abu's . . . ?" Likki
hesitated before a selection of words, none of which
seemed appropriate.

"Abu's *wife.*" A reprimand for her timidity.

"Yes. But I wasn't sure. I thought it wasn't completely
settled yet. Something about the child's father."

"The child's father? The child's father murdered her own
poor mother. That is why Comfort is here with us now."
Ayesha looked extremely haughty as she spoke, as though
pleased to correct.

"I heard a rumour Fatima was still alive," said Likki.
Time, now, for a little innocent sleuthing. John Lavender,
of course, would already have questioned Ayesha about
this, but on some subjects he told Likki very little.

"The woman is dead. Her husband drove her into the *bomba* and she killed herself."

"So it was suicide, not murder?"

"Suicide or murder, they are all the same thing."

"Are they?"

"Where is the difference? If you are honest you can come yourself with a knife and kill someone. If you are a coward you can use *juju* and hatred and kill someone slowly with despair until they pick up the knife in their own hand and do the dirty job for you. Either way the end is the same: the person dies. But in the cowardly way the killer more often goes free."

"That still doesn't make them the same."

"They *are* the same. If I kill you with poison or I kill you with *juju* or I kill you with a knife—is not the killing the same?" She did not wait for Likki's reply. "So what is the difference between the knife and *juju*?"

"Maybe the difference is whether you believe in *juju*," said Likki. It was in the way of a concession and Ayesha gave her an ambiguous grin.

"Another thing," continued Ayesha, who had not finished instructing her guest. "Here in Kpama we believe that the cowardly tormentor is guilty as well as the honest killer. But I have heard that in your white man's country only the honest man is punished while the sneaking coward is not reproached. That is what *Abu* tells me." Ayesha stood back as if daring Likki to contradict her, but Likki could think of nothing to say.

"Boo. Boo," drooled little Comfort, as though trying to repeat the cherished name. She dribbled spittle down her chin and belly.

"One day this one will make a fine wife for Abu," said Ayesha, turning towards the child. As she spoke, however, she still watched Likki from narrowed eyes. "Perhaps you think it is cruel to promise one so young?" Ayesha tempted.

"We never do it," answered Likki, avoiding the trap. She had always thought of it as a rather heinous custom. But in this particular instance it seemed to lose so much of its venom. It was easy to imagine they would make a wonderful pair. There was really only one difficulty. "When Comfort's old enough to marry, she may not want Abu."

"Already she loves him."

"Yes. But she might change her mind," hypothesized Likki, having in mind the old Western female prerogative. It was not the thought of the marriage *per se* that was disturbing but the rigidity implied in fixing the match so long ahead of time. The promise of future coercion if desire were to change.

Ayesha, however, read other morals into the dilemma. "Of course she will change her mind! What do you expect? But only after the wedding. It is only after the wedding that you can find out who you have brought into your bed. Until then she will be like every other foolish young girl, eager to marry some man she thinks she loves."

"You must forgive my sister," said an unexpected male voice from behind. "She is inclined to be cynical in these matters." The voice, though the man spoke softly, reverberated in the courtyard like a jungle echo.

Likki turned around to face a tall pillar of blackness. She had seen him before—in the lorry park on the day of her arrival, and once or twice since then. Like Ayesha he had the Fulani stamp upon him; long-limbed, slim of body, his features characteristically fine. His eyes were set in his ebony face like two crystals of midnight obsidian. So dark were they that pupil and iris merged, giving him a look of wide and feral knowing. Ayesha introduced him as her brother, Ibn Sinna.

"My sister has often spoken of you," he said to Likki.

"Of me?" There was something terrible behind his eyes. Something inaccessible. For all their dark depths they rejected her at their surface. She was excluded. This was a relief and at the same time an affront.

"She tells me you are helping Abu," he continued.

"He helps *me*."

"But you pay him?"

"I don't pay him very much."

"When you have nothing at all, every penny is a blessing." Reproach hid in his words.

Ayesha, still holding Comfort, moved between them. "Stay and eat with us," she said to Likki. "My brother can drop you home afterwards in his car." Likki considered the three scorched and dusty miles between herself and the bungalow and accepted. But afterwards she was uneasy, recalling things she had heard about Ayesha. When the food was served Likki was glad to see they were all going to eat from the same bowl, though in another part of her mind she chided herself for allowing Carlotta's paranoia to take root so easily.

After the meal Likki rode back to the secondary school in Ibn Sinna's cream-coloured Mercedes. One of the best-known cars in all of Kpama, it had deep leather seats, push-button everything, and a defunct radio that had once been costly but now produced only static. Despite all these luxuries, Likki and her driver travelled the three miles up to the school in a brutal and stunning silence, a silence that hung upon them like a blight, in which even the hope of small talk eluded them.

When they neared the complex of school buildings, dormitories, and bungalows at the top of the ridge, Ibn Sinna slowed and asked Likki where she stayed.

"Bungalow 5," she murmured, almost inaudibly, unwilling to intrude herself upon the stillness.

"Where?" he asked again. She had ventured too softly into the unfriendly void.

"Bungalow 5," she answered after clearing her throat. "It's right over there next to the girls' dormitories." She wondered if she'd spoken too loudly this time. Her voice seemed to sprawl rudderless through the car.

"I know the place," said Ibn Sinna. "I had thought another woman was living in there."

"I share the house with Carlotta Reap."

"Yes. Miss Reap. So you share the bungalow with her?"

"Yes." Likki spoke defensively. It was as if she were arguing with the man. Something censorious in his tone annoyed her, made her want to counter him, to prove him wrong. But about what?

They spoke no more. Ibn Sinna drove on with an abstracted air, concentrating on the ruts near the head-master's house, almost ignoring his passenger, as if she were a tiresome child he would be glad to be rid of. When he stopped the car, Likki almost leaped from the Mercedes. She neglected to thank Ibn Sinna for the lift.

Carlotta, lying in wait just inside the door, was preening

herself because a Mercedes had stopped in front of the house. "Who was *that*?" she gloated.

"That woman, Ayesha? It was her brother."

"Ibn Sinna?"

"Yes."

"He's good-looking, isn't he?" mused Carlotta. It seemed an odd thing for her to say.

✕ 10

Abu showed up at the bungalow one afternoon full of excitement. He said he wanted to buy a pig. "I know a fine sow I can buy," he told Likki. "A friend has promised to sell me the animal for only eighty pounds."

"A pig!"

"Yes. One very fine pig."

"Why a pig?"

"You know pigs," explained Abu. "Other animals struggle to bring forth one or two offspring each time. But the pig! Twelve or fourteen at once. Sometimes there can even be more! Within one year I can easily become millionaire."

"But can you sell pigs here in Kpama?" It was such a pervasively Muslim town, despite those who reneged in secret.

"I will send them to the south on Kutu's lorries. Down there, the infidels will eat them plenty. They will pay me many thousands of pounds. Then I will buy my cow. And soon I can marry Comfort." He was far ahead, counting his unhatched chickens.

Likki professed scepticism. Abu was adamant. Already he had saved up eleven pounds from selling his eggs and from ironing. He wanted Likki and Carlotta to float him a loan for the remaining sixty-nine pounds.

"You'll never pay us back," lamented Likki, who foresaw that it would be difficult to say no.

"I make two pounds every week." Right there at their bungalow he made it. "Only *now*, you give me money every time. But *then*, you get everything *free*. *Free* eggs every day. *Free* ironing." Free after they gave him sixty-nine pounds.

"Yes, but you have expenses, too," Carlotta pointed out to him. "You have to buy food for your hens, don't you?

Charcoal for the iron? And what happens if the hens suddenly stop laying? They don't go on making eggs forever, you know."

"If the hens stop laying, into the pot with them! I tell them every day: if they don't make eggs plenty, they will feel the knife! Hey! When I speak to them like that, how they tremble."

As Likki had foreseen, it was difficult to say no. She and Carlotta collected seven ten-pound notes from the bank next day and handed them over to Abu, admonishing him to purchase only a young and healthy animal. Not that Abu needed instruction in how to avoid being conned.

John Lavender at one point suggested that Abu call his new beast the Empress, but Abu said she already had a name. As a kind of revenge, perhaps, John started referring to Abu as Parsloe, a joke he was unable to share because no one else in Kpama had read P.G. Wodehouse.

There remained, however, one serious stumbling-block to this picaresque idyll. Kutu, having already refused to accommodate Abu's chickens in his house, would not even consider sheltering a pig. "We are Muslims," he said. "How can we live with swine under our roof?" And though Abu protested that raising pigs was not the same thing as eating them, Kutu replied that it looked bad. People would suspect them of breaking the sumptuary laws.

Mother of Issa put in her two cents. "The animal is not clean."

"I will wash the pig every day," said Abu.

"It is the *inside* of the pig that is not clean," elaborated Mother of Issa. "It will wander to the *bomba* every day and eat faeces there. Is that the way you will dowry your wife?" The indirect reference to Fatima's death silenced Abu.

But the next day he carried his argument up the hill to the secondary school. When he had finished Likki's ironing he sat down on the sofa and tried to look morose.

"What's wrong, Abu?" asked Likki.

"There's something else he wants from us," said Carlotta. Abu shot her a penetrating look.

Abu allowed Likki and Carlotta to extract his story from him—but only slowly. He did not seem to complain, but he let them see how, just at the moment fortune seemed to smile at him, he was blocked at every turn. His was the story of the spirit of free enterprise caught up in the snarls of interfering regulation, the lone individualist shackled with the red tape of mindless bureaucracy. It was a theme that could not fail to appeal to two Americans. Carlotta at once volunteered Zulu's doghouse.

"I keep Zulu in the house anyway," she said.

"Where could I put the fence?" inquired Abu, his plans already far advanced.

"Won't it *smell*?" wondered Likki uneasily.

Abu said that *his* pig would never smell. He would wash her every day. He would clear out her yard each evening after school. He had already arranged for someone to buy the pigshit.

"Who?"

"This woman, Wednesday. She will buy it. For melons it is very good."

"Wednesday from Last Calabash?"

"Yes. That one. She grows very big, very fine melons." He looked at Likki. "You like melons?"

Likki loved melons. Abu asked for another cash advance and said he would bring her a melon next day. When he left the house Carlotta sat down and whistled. "What an operator!" she said.

"I wonder what kind of melons Wednesday grows," mused Likki.

"Whatever they are," said Carlotta, "you can be sure we'll be paying at least twice the going rate."

"Abu wouldn't cheat *us*, would he?" protested Likki. Though, when she thought about it, she wasn't so sure. "Well," she reflected. "We can always check the real price with Wednesday."

"By the time you get to see Wednesday, Abu will already have worked out the *real* price with her. She'll get half again as much as usual and Abu will slap his commission on top of that."

•

Hope of Our Ancestors arrived at the secondary school three days later. Abu did not so much bring the pig with him as allow her to drag him behind. He had fastened a

stout piece of rope to her left rear leg, and as she ran along
he corrected her steering by pulling her rear end around
until her head was pointing in the right direction. The pig
weighed nearly three hundred pounds and was still growing, so it was prudent of Abu to leave to her the problem of
locomotive force, while he took over the helm and concen-
trated his efforts on piloting a course directly to Bungalow
5.

For two days Abu had dug and hammered and wrenched
and pried and fastened behind Carlotta's and Likki's bungalow. The results had been a fairly presentable dwelling—
for a pig. Zulu's erstwhile abode was expanded to accommodate superior bulk. A fence was set up with the bottom
three feet buried underground, to discourage digging for
freedom. The fence was attached to eight strong posts set
even deeper. It would be unfair to say that Abu did not
work exceedingly hard; still, he did have a great deal of
help. Nuhu sweated for hours digging post holes. Mr. Bai
enlarged the doghouse roof. Students came to watch the
proceedings and for each one of them who came Abu was
ready with a shovel (Come Chop Again had inadvertently
forgotten to lock the school's storeroom). Even the girls had
a turn helping out. The headmaster sent over refreshments
on at least one occasion, and the bursar's first wife brought
snacks whenever Nuhu was about.

As Nuhu said (in the hearing of the bursar's first wife),
the story of Comfort and Abu was far too romantic. Two
penniless orphans with all the world between them. Who
could fail to be moved by it? Certainly not the people of
Kpama, who were known for their sentimentality. Anyone
who had ever loved—or hoped to—would give Abu a hand
with the digging.

When the hour came for Abu—desperately trying to
keep pace with the animal—to install his livestock, there
was celebration. Everyone came running out to see the
miraculous beast. Hope of Our Ancestors paid no attention
to the cheering reception she received. She was thinking
about a nice cool roll in the mud. She was thinking about
her dinner. She was thinking about how to get those damn
bits of jingly-jangly metal off the scratchy collar around her
neck.

The bits of jingly metal, as Abu explained, were a series of charms the pig had aquired over the course of the previous two days. Sima, the Earth Priest, her former owner, had fitted her out with fertility charms as a special favour to Abu. Ayesha had sewn health-preserving herbs into the pig's collar. Mother of Issa had gone to Mallan Yakubu for "medicine" to protect the pig against theft.

Even Zulu came out in the late afternoon to watch the enormous expanse of flesh that had come to occupy his former abode. A creature as praised for its blubber as he was ridiculed for his.

When you could see Hope of Our Ancestors' colour, which wasn't often—she preferred a thin covering of wet mud at all times—she proved to be primarily a brown pig with delicate crescents of pink dappling her hindquarters. Abu was religious about administering her daily scrub, but Hope's great delight was to roll about afterwards in the mud she created around her water trough. Otherwise, however, she was clean, and the smell Likki had dreaded never materialized.

As far as pig's manure was concerned, it was definitely a seller's market. Kpama being a predominantly Muslim town, this type of dung was in relatively short supply. Its effectiveness, however, was widely acknowledged. Abu delivered his manure fresh every evening to several customers, among them Farrah. Farrah grew eggplants. She gave Likki several good recipes, which Likki in turn passed on to Carlotta. After that there was a lot of eggplant consumed at Bungalow 5. Even Hope of Our Ancestors ate some, for she got all the leftovers from the kitchen. Carlotta simply tossed them out the kitchen window. Abu perceived in these affairs a fine adjustment of fate: Carlotta and Likki provided land for the pig; the pig provided manure for Wednesday and Farrah and other vegetable growers. These in turn provided eggplant, melons, mint, and other delicacies for Carlotta and Likki, who passed on peelings and wastes to the pig. This completed a circle of relationships almost perfect in its inclusiveness, the more so because, as part of the divine ordering of events, Abu's palm was crossed at several points along the turn of the wheel.

※ 11

Likki saw Ibn Sinna again at the start of the Christmas break. Carlotta had already packed and gone south, leaving the priceless Zulu again in Likki's keeping. Into Likki's care she also entrusted the moral welfare of those girls who could not afford to travel home for the holiday. At least one-third of the students would remain on campus. Before she left, Carlotta delivered to her female charges a well-rehearsed departure speech full of references to the sins of the flesh, venereal disease, moral turpitude, sanctity of life, and diligent application to study.

Carlotta travelled south in the school's large and decrepit lorry. When the antediluvian vehicle finally lurched down the main drive (only five and a half hours late) Likki did a little victory dance in the living-room—behind Carlotta's calico curtains, through which she had been spying. John came up later in the day and the two of them devoted the evening hours to moral turpitude and sins of the flesh. Refreshed by these exercises they rose the next morning at dawn and walked into town to see the annual gathering of *al Id al Kabir*.

This, the great Muslim feast of the year, was a collective commemoration of Abraham's ancient sacrifice, the occasion on which he was ordered to offer his son upon the stone altar. Abraham's relieved substitution of the ram for Isaac was an event re-enacted each year in Kpama. The Friday imam ritually despatched a large male sheep on behalf of the community, and every paterfamilias who could afford to also butchered on the day of the great feast.

As Likki and John made their way through Kpama, clad in sweaters because the harmattan blew strong and the early morning was chill, they were greeted on every side by the bleating of tethered sheep. The knives, already sharpened, rested with deceptive normalcy by the front door of every house as if, when the prayers were finished, they would travel as usual to yam field or market with their owners.

A multitude had already gathered at the outdoor praying field. No mosque could hope to accommodate the numbers of the faithful who turned out for this occasion. Even women had come, though of course they were shunted to the rear of the assembly, far from the pronouncements of their misogynist deity. Men and women alike wore their best clothes, and jewellery that had been handed down for generations. The men almost all had leather shoes and walking-sticks and new (imported) sunglasses still bearing the "passed" sticker. Gold turbans and black Arab robes marked those who had made the pilgrimage to Mecca.

Men who owned horses had decked out their animals in medieval splendour with crimson girths, bridles laced with silver, and saddles draped with cloth of gold. Coverings of rainbow-coloured felt, thickly embroidered and set with sequins, mirrors, and magical charms cased in silver were fitted over the withers and haunches of the animals. The riders, not to be outdone by their mounts, had wound yards of thinnest cloth in turbans around their heads and donned glove-soft boots in leather of many shades. Their bodies they wrapped in layers of bright cotton.

When they all rode out together in the morning light they came in a glory of colour, manes and tails and garments flowing, silver and glass and sequins flashing in the sun. Both horses and men chafed at the restraints that custom imposed on this day of prayer, and occasionally small companies of riders broke away from the main body. In furious billows of colour and speed they raced through the streets of Kpama, singing the old songs of war. Crowds of ecstatic children pursued them, throwing stones; old women, remembering days of battle, ululated, calling for blood.

It was a morning to quicken the pulses, and Likki was not immune to the general ferment. Wildness stirred. War seemed more wonderful than love.

·

Ibn Sinna was among the riders. Unfamiliar in indigo and gold, he looked like a hero of Saracen legend. He reined to a stop and saluted the two whites. At first Likki didn't recognize him. His stallion's nostrils flared with impatience at the halt.

"Will you stay for the prayers?" he asked Likki, seeming to be laughing at her.

"We're not Muslim," John answered him. It vexed Likki that John took over the conversation in this way.

"And the sacrifice—will you stay for that?" How his horse pulled to join its fellows.

"Yes," Likki answered quickly, usurping John's role of spokesperson. Sacrifice: a word at once pagan and biblical. She had no idea what it might connote in Kpama.

Ibn Sinna smiled down disturbingly from his restless mount. "I will send you meat later today," he said. "It is our custom." He gave his horse its head and was pulled back into the maelstrom. Likki looked after him like one who dreams.

"Let's go," John said flatly and started off on his own for the praying field. The muezzin's voice could already be heard warning laggards that ceremonies were about to begin.

The praying field was a twelve-acre expanse of dirt and untidy grass located near the central or Friday mosque. Usually a few goats wandered its perimeter or tugged at its tasteless vegetation. Today, however, it was filled with the faithful, lined up in rows that snaked for hundreds of yards in crooked disorder behind the imam. The Friday imam was a middle-aged man, robed today in white, who led the true believers through the long and intricate cycles of prayer, through the repetitive kneeling, crouching, standing, kneeling, and bowing of the ritual. When the thousands, all together, bent their heads down and touched their foreheads to the earth, the field was transformed into a twelve-acre patchwork quilt, a Brobdingnagian mantle of silk and cotton, sprinkled here and there with the golden parasols of royalty. The Ruler's umbrella was particularly fine, done in crimson and gold brocade, its velvet tassels tugging in the wind.

John and Likki stood on a knoll to one side of the spectacle. Abu came up to them where they watched. "Nasara," he called excitedly to John. He was out of breath from running. "Nasara, you come and see the ram!" He meant the sacrificial beast, imported from Niamey at great expense on the top of al Hajji Musa's lorry, Mother Sweet. Abu led John and Likki around to the side of a house near the praying field. There, guarded by boys from the imam's house, stood the large white ram from Niger, four feet high at the shoulder, his horns curved back like the long grey beards of the elders, his scrotum heavy with the burden of his lusts. When the prayers at the field were finished the ram's turn would come.

"Oh, he's magnificent," said Likki. The ram had an aura of dominion, of irreducible authority. "Will they kill *him*?"

Abu grinned at her. "You will see. They will spill blood plenty!" He drew a forefinger slowly across his throat to show how it would be done. The grin he wore on his face was an amalgam of bloodlust and gluttony. Today the town would wallow in meat; it was the one day everyone would have enough.

Likki experienced a titillating blend of curiosity and pity. She said she would like to stay to watch the end. "I've never seen a sacrifice." She defended her inclinations as a search for new experience.

"You'll be sick," said John Lavender, who had vomited once when Kutu killed a cow. The blood had run out from the animal's throat as from a broken water main—not spurting or gushing as he had expected, but bubbling, roiling out of the neck with a liquid urgency, covering the ground with a broad and sticky puddle into which the crippled animal had sunk, knees first, its eyes wide with surprise at the perfidy of its human masters.

"I want to see it killed," said Likki, now at one with her desires. She looked at John. "You don't have to stay."

"I'll stay."

As the prayers drew to a close, the imam's nephew came to fetch the ram. The beast moved off behind him with surprising docility, as if in expectation of superior fodder. Instead, it met the ceremonial knife, a long and sinister blade held by the imam's brother's son, Sidik. The knife had a telling shine to it along the cutting edge; someone had recently sharpened it, scored it repeatedly on a lump of granite, grating, rasping, filing it down to a point too fine to measure.

As the crowd watched, five young men of the imam's house laid hold of the ram, securing its back and legs. Two others reached for its horns and slowly forced back the great head until the creature's arched neck, long and white, lay open to the blade. Now, too late, the animal sensed its danger and strained against the men who held it. Its eyes rolled wildly.

Sidik slowly measured the blade against the tensing muscles of the ram's curved throat. But without pressure. He drew no blood.

A second time he put the knife in place, then looked around at the crowd, betraying his own reluctance with an uncertain smile.

A third time Sidik readied the blade. Likki, balancing on a fulcrum of lust and horror, felt as though she were suspended in acid. Through a poisoned eternity she waited with the knife edge pressed against her own white throat, feeling the indifferent chill of steel on flesh, wanting the obscenity to start.

The third time, Sidik pressed home the blade. He drew it with slow and horrible calculation deep through the shuddering tissues of life. Then the ram's head slipped sideways, for there was little to hold it firm. The exposed and severed windpipe raggedly gasped and quivered, desperately struggling with its final breath before the lungs were drowned in blood. Likki, bathed in an icy sweat and dizzy with revulsion, could not look away. Blood now ran incontinently onto the sandy ground. It collected in pools and puddles. It splashed. Wanton and red it poured out into the innocent morning, a crimson accusation addressed to the ochre sky.

Not until the limbs ceased their spasmodic twitching and the heart was finally stilled could Likki turn her eyes away from the carnage. When she did, she reached for John Lavender's hand. "Let's go home," she said. Her stomach was shaking. A hard, tight ball of nausea ached in her throat.

"It's something, isn't it?"

She had never before watched anything die.

✕ 12

Late in the afternoon of the same day, Likki lay in bed, furiously unable to sleep. Her return to the school with John had been nightmarish. They had seemed caught in the toils of a cycle of cosmic bloodletting; for after the sacrifice, the great crowd of *al Id al Kabir* had dispersed rapidly from the field, eager to attend to their own domestic butchering. Outside every household in Kpama the ritual murder had been re-enacted. The town reeked of blood; the smell of it hung in the air, astringent and bitter like damp metal drying in the sun. But the people of Kpama had gloried in the slaughter; they were in carnival spirits, singing, dancing, beating their drums. Everyone would eat well today. All over town little children imitated, with exaggerated delight, the death throes of their fathers' fattest sheep, while grandmothers lit fires and laughed and the old men rubbed their gums. A town of ghouls and vultures.

Likki tossed in her bed. Six ounces of Carlotta's Remy Martin had failed to calm her. John had wanted to stay, but the thought of his touch had been loathsome. Now, however, Likki was burning.

Outside, a car pulled up unexpectedly in front of the bungalow and stopped. Likki waited. Seconds later the front door reverberated with knocking. Zulu waddled into the living-room and emitted a perfunctory bark. Glad of a diversion, Likki pulled a caftan over her head and went to investigate. In the doorway, already letting himself in, was Ibn Sinna, looking arrogant and handsome, still in his indigo robes. "I have brought you meat," he said.

"Meat?" Her stomach knotted.

"For us this day is something like Christmas. We carry gifts to each other. But only gifts of meat." He called to someone behind him and a small child came in with a large bowl of red flesh. Likki looked down at it with a confusion bordering on shame. In her mind the blade still teased at the skin of her jugular.

Ibn Sinna studied her expression. "The meat is fresh," he assured her.

Likki continued to stare.

"I killed the animal myself only some four hours ago." He watched her. He probably knew how much whites disliked to hear of the slaughter of animals. Yet they devoured great quantities of meat.

Zulu sniffed at the bowl and whined covetously. Likki remembered her manners and took the bowl from the child. "Thank you," she said, her voice somewhat thick.

"This is my son, Abdul Rahman," said Ibn Sinna.

"Oh." She felt for some reason embarrassed, disquieted. "I didn't know you had a son," she said. She hadn't thought about it one way or the other.

"I have four. And two daughters."

"Oh."

"Two wives," he explained, apparently oblivious to her uneasiness. He was staring about the room, taking in all its particulars as if its dimensions and furnishings held the clue to something deeper he wished to know.

"Would you like to come in?" asked Likki, moving back slowly from the door. She was only being polite. She wanted him to go.

"Yes. I think I can come in," he said, then turned and spoke to his son in Kpamé. The child raced off in the direction of the headmaster's bungalow. "He has gone to play with his friend," explained Ibn Sinna, moving about the room. He spotted the opened bottle of cognac on the table. "You have brandy," he said.

"Would you like some?" Again a reflex. She was sure he wouldn't drink. He was a Muslim.

"Brandy and Coke is good, isn't it?"

"We're out of Coke," apologized Likki. Soft drinks were delivered to Kpama roughly once a month. For two days the town gorged itself on Fanta and then cradled the memory for another four weeks until a fresh instalment arrived.

"I have Fanta and Coke in my car," said Ibn Sinna.

"In your *car*?" Did he travel around prepared for every contingency?

"Why not?"

Before she realized what he was about, he had gone out to his car and returned with a case of mixed soft drinks. "Here, I think you can have this."

Likki was uncertain whether she ought to offer to pay him. When things were short it was a great favour merely to be allowed to buy them even at the inflated price. He read her mind. "I think we can take it that this is part of your present for *al Id al Kabir*," he said.

She wondered at this, but went to get some glasses from the kitchen. She poured out the ·brandy in front of him. And the Coke. It was a fine point of local custom, this preparation of drinks in full view of the visitor; it reduced the likelihood of poisoning. Ibn Sinna drank rapidly, soon emptying his glass. He had another, which he also finished quickly. "I think I can go now," he said rising. Then he paused. "Maybe you would like a lift into town?"

Likki looked up.

"I can drop you at Kutu's," he volunteered.

That spoiled it. Likki was irritated to find he knew of her connection with John. She would have liked a lift, in fact, but not with him, not to be taken to John Lavender's bedroom. She said no.

Halfway out the door Ibn Sinna turned back to her and said, "When the case is finished, you can send word to me. Coke and Fanta I can always get here in Kpama. I will bring more any time." The fixer.

"How will I send word?" she asked reluctantly, unwilling to be further in his debt.

"Why not with Abu?"

"But you'll let me pay for it next time?"

"Oh, why?" he replied in the tone that Kpamans used when they complained of broken machinery, of divorce, of the death of cattle, of the world in dysfunction. And he left before she could think of an answer. His son was already sitting in the car waiting for him, as if he had known in advance just exactly when his father would leave the white woman's house.

Likki guzzled away at her Fanta for well over a week and

even started to give Abu a complimentary Coke when he
had finished his afternoon chores: ironing, eggs, Hope of
Our Ancestors' pen. As a result (and in complete accord-
ance with Carlotta's vehement and urgent predictions—
voiced almost as soon as she returned), the case of soft
drinks was soon depleted.

"I'm afraid we've run out," she told Abu one hot
afternoon.

"Oh, sorry!" he said. He opened his arms wide as if to
offer sympathy. Zulu, in his corner by the door, whined
softly. "I can bring you more," said Abu after a silence.

"More Fanta?"

"Coke, Fanta, everything you like. I get it all for you."

"Where?" she asked hopefully, for some reason eager to
bypass Ibn Sinna.

It was a short-lived hope. "This man who brought you the
case. He has more. He always has plenty."

"Who told you where I get my Coke?"

"Ayesha."

Abu was prompt. The very next evening he arrived at the
school with a case of soft drinks on his head and the charcoal
iron rumbling precariously on top of the bottles.

"Why did you carry all this all the way up here?"
demanded Likki crossly. "It's too heavy for you. *I* could
have carried some of it. Or he could have sent it in his car."

"As for me," said Abu, "I don't mind bringing it." Head
loads, he said, were nothing for him. He could easily
manage eighty pounds. Besides, he knew in advance that
he would be personally responsible for disposing of half his
load and that made his labours sweet. As for Ibn Sinna, the
man was tied up. "He is busy with soldiers," Abu told
Likki.

"Soldiers?!"

"There are many new soldiers in the town. Since last
night they are coming and coming. Some people they want
to ask many, many questions. Even now Ibn Sinna's house
is filled with them."

◆◆ 13

Captain Araoh had come into Kpama in the worst of humours. And, what was worse, the people of Kpama were laughing at him. He had entered the town on Tando Mohammed's lorry, God Said Labour Before Eating, and the townspeople were already drawing lessons from this accident of fortune. It was being said, discreetly of course, that the soldiers would not last long in Kpama, that they would quickly disgrace themselves and be recalled to the south. All because the army transport lorry had blown a tire on the road. There should, of course, have been a spare tire in the back of the lorry, but Captain Araoh had sold the spare in Gbiriri to the brother of a woman he fancied. Without that tire she would never have come to him. And so, after a fashion, he had been well paid (and her brother *had* given him a good price for the tire). But none of this would be helpful when he made out his report to the command post in Walema. Meanwhile, he would have to find a new spare in Kpama to bring in his crippled lorry. If there was a spare in Kpama.

It took Captain Araoh two days to locate a tire. When he finally acquired it, it was nearly bald. Worse yet, it cost him more (50 per cent more) than what he had made from the sale of his good spare in Gbiriri. Still, it would bring in the army transport.

"This is the only tire of its kind in all of Kpama," Mahmut lied as he folded the crisp red notes into his wallet.

"I hope that is true," the army man said, "because I have come to keep an eye upon this town. If I should get to hear that there are other spares in your possession—particularly if they are in better condition than this piece of old rope—I could become very annoyed."

"Oh, my dear Captain Araoh, everyone knows you

cannot cheat the army," Mahmut reassured him unctuously, reflecting perhaps on the safety of the eighteen other tires he had sealed up inside several of his clay granaries.

•

Captain Araoh was a short man, a southerner, and slightly on the plump side. He took himself and his new position very seriously. During his first week in town he paid social calls on all the important families. At Kutu's he discovered Likki. She was sitting in the courtyard talking with John Lavender and Mother of Issa while Mieri searched Abu's head for louse nits. The watchman was asleep, so Araoh walked in unannounced. He stepped through the gate with a spring in his stride, emanating a vitality impressive for one of his size, a pugnacious energy.

"Well, well," he enthused when he saw the group. "I was told this was an *African* house!" Right away it was easy to dislike him. He stared at Likki as if she were up for sale.

"We are all Africans here," intoned Kutu heavily. He rose from his chair and went to rest his arm on John's shoulder. "This is my son," he said in a low bass. It was a warning. "He is one of us." The army wasn't above a little fooling around with expatriates. Hard currency was always short. A few days in jail without their malaria pills and foreigners often remembered that they needed to cash traveller's cheques. Or maybe there would be money sewn into their clothing. Rooms could be searched, too.

Captain Araoh turned to Likki. "Are you his wife?"

"I'm a teacher at the secondary school."

"What is your name, please?"

"Likki Liddell." She repressed an anxious and sudden desire to give herself an alias.

"Likki. That's an unusual name, isn't it?"

"It's Estonian."

"And you are from Estonia?"

"No. My grandmother."

"And have you ever travelled there?"

"No." What could it mean, her travelling there? She knew nothing of Estonia, had never even tried to share her grandmother's memories.

"It's a lovely country. Tallinn. You should go." He paused

as if waiting for a reply. "The people are wonderful there. Wonderful." Again he paused, perhaps expecting her to inquire about his experiences travelling in the Baltic countries. She did not inquire.

"I'll go after the Russians leave," she said.

He smiled. From him it was an unfriendly sign.

"A nationalist?" he said with condescension. "But you may have a long time to wait, you know."

Likki threw back at him his urbane, venomous grin.

Captain Araoh stayed for quite some time at Kutu's, trading small talk with the proprietors of the house. They discussed apparently irrelevant matters: the price of sugar, the quality of discipline in the schools, whether market women were really hoarding soap. When Captain Araoh left at the end of an hour, he seemed pleased with himself. He said he'd give Likki a lift up the hill to her house. It wasn't an offer of assistance. It was an order.

Captain Araoh drove an army-green Peugeot pick-up. "So, my dear Miss Liddell," he said when they were on their way out of town.

"Yes, Captain Araoh."

"Oh. Call me Alistair," he said, grinning as if it were all a great joke, his being an army captain.

"All right, Alistair," said Likki. Her grin was of a slightly different calibre.

"You teach at the school?"

"Yes. History."

"History."

"Um-hmmm."

"Why do you people come all the way to Kpama to teach history?"

"All sorts of reasons," said Likki as she tapped her fingers on the outside of the door: boredom, altruism, naiveté, broken love affairs, nostalgia for the past.

"I presume you are teaching Western history."

"Even some African history."

"When I was in school we were told that Africa had no history. Not to speak of."

"That would have been *before* independence," said Likki. Those without power in the present were always denied their past as well. For the colonies, for blacks, for women, for most ordinary people, it was the masters who wrote the history books that erased the bulk of humanity from its place in the long record of human endeavour.

"Of course," said Captain Alistair Araoh. "Before independence we were nothing."

For a moment Likki almost liked the man, but it was a passing empathy. He had plenty of power now, and he threw his weight about with impunity.

At the secondary school Likki directed Captain Araoh to Bungalow 5. He slowed down as if to admire it. "Not bad," he said. "All cement block?"

"Yes."

"Ah-hah. It's quite big. Is it all just for you?"

"No. I share it." Thank God. She hoped Carlotta was inside.

"Another American, of course?"

"Of course."

He went inside without being asked. He said he was curious to see what standards of accommodation prevailed here in the north. In the south expatriates lived with terrazzo floors and imported carpets. He knew all about the Europeans in the capital, how big they liked their closets, how hot they liked their food, what position they liked their women.

Carlotta met the captain just as he entered the door. She held out her hand to him in the most mannered fashion. "How do you *do*-ooo." Her voice hung onto the final vowel like that of a tired English actress in a bad play.

"Very pleased to meet you." The captain bowed low over Carlotta's proffered hand. For a moment it seemed he might kiss it.

"You are new here in town?" Carlotta minced out her words ingratiatingly.

"Yes. I am now in command of the army post here in Kpama."

"Oh. I *see*. A good man to know, then?"

"Let us hope so, Miss Reap."

Carlotta offered the army man a warm bottled beer, apologizing for the lack of refrigeration. "We're not yet quite as civilized here as we might be," she said. She lit one of the cigarettes she so rarely smoked and placed it in a green plastic filter as though it were an incense stick. The captain made a point of saying that he hadn't seen one of those since he'd left Russia.

"When were you in Russia?" Carlotta inquired. She wasn't nearly as remiss as her roommate about inquiring after the captain's foreign travels.

He informed her that he'd studied for two years at Moscow University. After that the conversation degenerated into a travelogue. Likki was again informed that she simply *must* visit her grandmother's homeland.

"I have this little hang-up about democracy," she said before she realized what she meant. Carlotta shot her a brief, agonized appeal.

Araoh overlooked the remark. "Really, you *must* go," he said. "As a favour to yourself. It's your own history, you know." As if he had broken in on her reflections, he added, "Perhaps, one day, *I'll* be able to show you around there, you never know."

"Who knows?" answered Likki. It was as close to politeness as she could bring herself.

The talk wandered aimlessly, perhaps treacherously, for another fifteen minutes. When the captain left, Carlotta watched through the calico curtains until his pick-up was out of sight. Then she walked over to where she had been sitting and removed the cigarette (her third) from the filter where it was nesting. "So that's the famous Captain Araoh," she said, grinding out the butt.

"Is he famous?"

"Maybe *infamous* is a better word. I heard a little bit about him in the south. He gets sent off to trouble spots."

"Kpama is a trouble spot?"

"Who knows? They say there's lot of smuggling going on up here."

"Then why not send him up to the border?"

"I don't know. But I think I'd stay away from that man if I were you."

"I didn't really have any choice today."

"Next time, then," said Carlotta. "Stay away from him next time."

"Is that what *you* were trying to do? Gushing all over him: 'Oh, it must have been so-o-o-o-o *interesting* for you

n Moscow. So challenging. How did you *stand* the cold?'
Etcetera."

"Likki, I was trying to distract him. It was *you* he was
looking at. The whole time, too."

"Oh, well, that's tough for him. I'm taken." John's smell
was suddenly but a trifle.

"You can be untaken," said Carlotta.

"What does that mean?"

"What it says."

"What the hell, Carlotta. Are you trying to tell me he's
going to get rid of John?"

"Anything is possible," said Carlotta, raising a pompous
finger.

"Carlotta, you are paranoid." Likki was very pleased to
think so, because the army man had unnerved her somewhat. "For you, everything is filled with disaster. You're
paranoid about this whole country. The whole *continent*.
Everything is filled with disease and corruption. Every man
has venereal disease. Every woman has had dozens of
abortions. Every strange dog is carrying rabies. Every
piece of meat you buy is loaded with liver flukes and
trichinae. Every bantam-weight officer you see has only one
thing on his mind: raping white women."

"Everything you've just said is probably true."

"Oh, Christ!"

■

Captain Araoh was back at the bungalow two days later with
a search warrant in his hands. Every house and building at
the school was being picked over like the needle-concealing
haystack. He could make no exceptions, even for his very
good dear friends. But he was prepared to conduct the
investigation himself—to spare the two women embarrassment. "We are looking for cement," he said.

"Cement!?"

"Fifty bags of cement have gone missing from the
construction site at the administration offices."

"What would we do with cement?"

"You might sell it," said Captain Araoh and explained, as
he poked his nose into Carlotta's closet, that because
cement was short it was worth its weight in—well, if not in

gold at least in copper. No construction could take place without it. And as they knew, all cement had to be imported, for there was, regrettably, none to be found in West Africa. Whoever controlled cement controlled the development of the country. Hoarding was therefore the moral equivalent of treason. Unfortunately, there could always be found a certain number of benighted individuals who chose to profit at the expense of the body politic. On the black market cement was worth thirty times its fixed (by the government) price.

"But where would we hide fifty bags of cement?"

Captain Araoh paused and explained gently, as if to a troublesome child, "That is what I am here at the school to find out."

"But we don't have the cement."

"My dear Miss Liddell, that is for *me* to say with authority, not for *you*." With the aid of some junior officers Alistair Araoh satisfied the last whim of his curiosity. He opened every cupboard in the kitchen. He looked inside cereal packets and boxes of sugar. He tapped walls and pulled tiles away from the fittings around the bathtub. He examined every suitcase, opened every drawer, examined many of the papers in their desks.

"God, I hate him. He makes me feel slimy all over," said Likki in a whisper to Carlotta.

"At least he's kept his hands off our knickers," she replied, recollecting a time when a puny runt of a corporal at a roadblock had rifled through her belongings and lingered long over her underwear, fondling her bras and panties as if she were still inside them.

"It's symbolic rape, isn't it?"

"Just hope it stays symbolic."

Captain Araoh reported to them before he left. "I have found nothing, of course, which is as I expected. I hope you will understand and forgive the intrusion?" He didn't wait for them to answer.

✖ 14

John was called away to the south a week later. The message came over the police wireless early in the morning. There was some irregularity with his visa that would have to be cleared up in the capital.

Captain Araoh brought the news to John Lavender himself. He had been in the police station when the wire came through—visiting with his friend, Sergeant Awuyu. The captain told John that there happened to be an army jeep heading south later that same morning. He thought John could squeeze himself aboard if he weren't too particular about his comfort. The jeep would be in the capital by dawn of the next day. Such promptness would be sure to impress officials of the Department of Immigration.

By the time Likki heard about it, John was halfway to Gbiriri. "I've been untaken," she lamented to Carlotta, wondering if there weren't more wisdom in her overweight roommate than she had heretofore credited her with.

"Don't be paranoid," said Carlotta.

"I deserved that, didn't I?"

"Yes, you did."

"What's he after?"

"Probably just your body."

"Why?"

"Status. You're white. You're fairly pretty. You've got long hair. Just walk into any of these guys' rooms here in Kpama. You'll see centrefolds from *Playboy* plastered all over the walls."

"I went to see the Ruler (they'd gone, *en masse*, with the headmaster in the first week of classes), and he didn't have any centrefolds. All he had was a coronation photo of Queen Elizabeth."

"The Ruler is ninety years old. He probably has high blood pressure."

"Carlotta, what am I going to do?" John had been more than her window onto Kpama—though he was that, giving her a welcome in places she could never have ventured on her own. He had also been a wall that separated her from the town and protected her from its unpleasantness. Now the wall had collapsed, taking with it some of Likki's basic assumptions about how an ordinary, law-abiding citizen could expect to be treated. Kpama was suddenly revealed as a place where injustice might be practised with impunity. Where unpleasantness might have no easy correction.

Abu sensed tension in the house that afternoon. "Nasara," he said to Likki. "What is wrong?"

Carlotta took over the explanation. Captain Araoh, she said, was contemplating a seduction and was taking pains to eliminate all competition before homing in on his prey. That, at least, was how she interpreted his behaviour.

Abu thought about this for a while. "If it is true, then the man will come early one morning—bringing food," he told them.

"Why food?" wondered Likki.

"The next time it will be late evening."

"Why?"

"The next time he will try to catch you asleep. He will just start to come like that, at any time he pleases. Just as if the house is for him. And if the house is for him, then you can be for him, too."

"God *damn*."

"Yes. And then soon he will ask you to cook for him. He will bring you some *very* fine meat. He will try to look shy. His eyes will be so-ooooo soft. Everything *too* gentle. 'Show me how white people cook meat.' That is what he will say."

Carlotta smiled with satisfaction. Abu had just given new life to her favourite prejudice. "Abu, you're a scoundrel," she told him and Abu nodded.

Likki was concerned. "How do I get rid of the army?" If there was a formula for success in these matters, Abu would probably know of it.

In any event, Abu's dictum was not exactly reassuring.

"You need a very *strong* boyfriend," he said. "Some very big man."

"I *have* a boyfriend!"

"Is he here?"

"No. Of course not. You know that. That's the whole trouble."

"You *see?*"

•

As if he had been coached by Abu, Captain Araoh showed up on the doorstep of Bungalow 5 two days later at a quarter to six in the morning. He had a ripe pawpaw in one hand and a bottle of brandy in the other.

"Good morning," he sang out jovially as he banged on the door with his fat boot.

Carlotta stumbled into the living-room with her hair in curlers and her face covered in cream. "It's just a little early, isn't it?"

"My dear Miss Reap," the captain addressed her in patronizing tones. "Surely you have lived among us long enough to know that the African day begins at five."

"The day, yes. The drinking, no."

Likki shuffled into the living-room wearing the ugliest robe she could find, her hair unkempt and her face puffy with sleep. By the gleam that shot forth from Captain Araoh's eyes she could tell she wasn't nearly ugly enough.

"Bring some glasses," said Alistair Araoh. Carlotta yawned helplessly, and Likki stood by as if mesmerized, as if witnessing a natural disaster—which may have been what it was for her. The captain was restless and went to get the glasses himself. He took the brandy with him and poured their drinks in the kitchen. He didn't need any help finding his way around, since he had taken their bungalow apart only nine days earlier. He found himself a knife, too, for splitting open the pawpaw. "You know," he said, handing out their drinks, "our ancestors considered the fruit of the papaya tree to be an *aphrodisiac.*" He drawled out the last word with unfettered insinuation, as if he were savouring the pronunciation of the word "cunnilingus." Likki reached for her glass of brandy and had a good pull at it. It went straight to her head.

Carlotta rose and went out to the kitchen to get plates for the pawpaw. On her way back she stumbled against the table and spilled Likki's brandy. "Oh. Sorry!" she said. She looked at Captain Araoh. "How clumsy of me!" The drink had spilled down his clean, pressed, khaki trousers.

He went into the bathroom to sponge himself off. While he was gone, Carlotta switched her glass around with his. "I don't trust him," she whispered to Likki.

"At *this* time of the morning?" Likki whispered back. She had already accepted Carlotta's reading of the situation, though she felt, aggrievedly, that being slipped a mickey was not the sort of thing that was supposed to happen to one in real life. And particularly not before breakfast.

"You may not believe it, but this has all happened to me before," said Carlotta. "In the capital; the guy called himself an admiral."

"I believe you," said Likki.

Captain Araoh returned and urged the women to drink up. "You, too," said Carlotta raising her glass.

Alistair Araoh stayed in Bungalow 5 only until six-thirty, when he complained of feeling dizzy. He wanted to lie down on the bed in the spare room, but Carlotta informed him that it was impossible. She couldn't have that sort of thing going on in the house of the Girls' Housewarden; she took seriously her obligation to set a firm moral example. She held the front door open for Captain Araoh, who departed with wavering step. His face was covered with sweat and he had turned a dismaying shade of grey. He gave Carlotta a very dirty look as he started his jeep. She waved him an innocent goodbye.

The two women waited in some trepidation for Captain Araoh's next move. Likki wondered if they couldn't complain to the headmaster.

"I did," said Carlotta. "He told me to rehearse the word 'no.'"

It was still Abu's considered opinion that Likki's best defence would be a strong boyfriend. The captain was unlikely to make trouble with another man in the picture. Overlooking Likki's scowl, he continued. "If you say no to the army man, everyone will think you are just playing with him—to make it sweeter for him in the end. You see? He will want it more and more. That is what our women do here. And every time the man will come with more and more presents. The longer you make him wait for it, the sweeter it will be for him in the end. You see? His pleasure will be more! Everyone knows this. So, unless you already have another man, there is no one who will believe you that you don't want that army captain."

"What other man do you suggest?"

"What of this man who brings you the Coke?"

"Ibn Sinna?"

"Yes. That one. The man is good. Everyone fears him."

∎

Captain Araoh came again the next week. He came at eight in the evening with three of his junior officers and two crates of bottled Heineken. It was impossible to get rid of the foursome until the last bottle was finished. This took till two in the morning. Likki spent the whole evening trying to pick up the wrong glass. She also smoked way too much and woke up the next morning with a nicotine hangover.

The midnight visit mentioned by Abu also took place as predicted. Captain Araoh arrived in the small hours looking for "burglars." This time Likki lost her temper. She hated being wakened from sleep. She told Captain Araoh, in very straight language, that if he had any designs upon her person he could forget all about it. She wasn't interested.

"My dear Miss Liddell," Alistair Araoh oozed, his voice warm with concern. "You are upset. I can see that you have completely misunderstood my intentions. Please believe me, I have only your comfort and security at heart. I am here only to enforce the law, not to disturb innocent civilians." And he bowed himself out of the room after taking a lingering look at the lace of her negligée.

Likki seethed. She couldn't get back to sleep. "I'm going to report him," she raged to Carlotta.

"To whom?"

✖ 15

The next time Likki saw Alistair Araoh, she was browsing for bargains among the little shops that lined Kpama's marketplace. The captain's driver was speeding recklessly between the market stalls, sending up clouds of red dust and drawing angry complaints from the women traders. Araoh missed seeing Likki, however. She ducked into the obscurity of a windowless "pharmacy" as soon as she spotted his jeep. But the darkness of the shop held problems of its own. Likki was barely inside when a deep voice greeted her from the shadows. "Nasara Likki?"

She jumped, nearly revealing herself to the passing jeep.

"Forgive me. I startled you," said the voice. It echoed uncomfortably through the shop, as though the place were too small for it.

"Who's there?" asked Likki peering into a corner.

A figure moved out towards the light. When her eyes adjusted to the dimness, she saw it was Ibn Sinna, standing there awkwardly as if he did not belong. He was wearing nylon drip-dries and a Los Angeles Dodgers baseball cap. He looked ridiculous; he could have been a weiner salesman from Schenectady, New York.

"You need tablets? Drops?" he asked frowning. "Penicillin? Soap? Batteries? Tetracycline?"

"No. Is this your shop?"

"It is my brother's shop. I am minding it for him today. It seems his wife wants to give birth."

"Oh."

"But what do you want in here?"

"I just . . . I'm hiding," she admitted.

"From the soldiers?"

How did he know? "Did Abu tell you?"

"He said they were disturbing you."

Likki sighed, relieved that she did not have to explain things to him. "If only I could convince that man," she said.

"Abu's advice is good. Get another boyfriend."

Likki began to protest that she deserved to be taken seriously in her own right—boyfriend or not—but Ibn Sinna continued to insist. "It is not only what Abu says. Anyone here in Kpama would tell you that same thing."

"Did Abu tell you who he recommended for the job?"

"No. Who did Abu recommend?"

"You."

The barest trace of embarrassment trailed across his face. Likki was glad to see it there, a little piece of revenge for those cases of Fanta he never let her pay for.

Ibn Sinna turned from Likki and began to close up the shop. "I am just leaving here," he said. "Maybe you would like a lift to your house?"

She hesitated, but it was a long uphill walk to the school. There was also the captain's jeep to be avoided. "That would be nice," she said.

•

The Mercedes was like a blast furnace. It had been parked in the sun for three hours with the windows closed. Ibn Sinna started it up for the sake of its air-conditioning and then retreated with Likki to stand in the shade of a nim tree for a couple of minutes while the car cooled itself off.

Likki was restless. It seemed there was never anything to say to this man. Words floated elusively, hovered before her as in an anxious mirage, but when she reached for them they evaporated, appeared too silly, too trivial to utter. But the silence was also inappropriate, leaden.

Ibn Sinna finally spoke. "I think we can go now."

Inside the car the silence fell on them again. In desperation Likki asked about his baseball cap. He was very proud of it. "My cousin sent it to me from Cincinnati," he told her.

"Cincinnati?"

"He is studying there."

"But it's not a Cincinnati team," said Likki, and she explained about baseball teams and cities. The conversation

yawned with futility but she plodded on because it was
better than the stillness.

Just by Smugglers' Bridge, Ibn Sinna slowed the car.
"There is an old man we just passed," he apologized. "I
should give him a lift to his village."

He looked at Likki as if he were asking her permission.
"Sure, I don't mind," she said, puzzled.

"He will be travelling some miles beyond the school. It
will be out of your way. I can drop you off as we pass."

"Could I come with you?" She had never been down the
Faangbaani road, though it had lured her, dropping down
from the ridge through a tunnel of nim trees, then
stretching out across an open valley to the wooded hill
beyond.

"You want to come along?"

"Yes."

"Why not?" he said, but he frowned as he backed up the
car. In the strong noon light Likki could just make out the
pupils of his eyes, could just barely see the irises about
them. The irises were blue, an unmistakable midnight
blue, as deep as the starlit heavens, and as distant, and as
cold.

The car stopped and an old man got in. It was Moola, the
Earth Priest's chief diviner. Though he carried a walking-
stick, he was a spry old rooster and leapt into the back of
the Mercedes as though he were as ignorant of rheumatism
as a baby. With childish delight he examined the car's knobs
and buttons and levers. He held up his hands to the
streams of air-conditioned coolness. "Hey! My friend! You
are enjoying proper!" he exclaimed. He cackled to himself
in the back and tapped his walking-stick on the floor. He
seemed an arbitrary, incalculable old fellow, and Likki was
dismayed when his attentions fastened upon herself.
"Beautiful. Beautiful. A beautiful woman! Just one thing. I
want to see her face again." Moola croaked away in a
guttural dialect of Kpamé.

"What is he saying?" asked Likki. She had found even the
Kpamé morning greeting impossible to master.

"He wonders if you could turn around," said Ibn Sinna.

Likki turned around. Moola placed his hands over his
heart and fell back into his seat as one stricken. "Oh, oh,

ohhhh," he moaned. "I am dying for the love of this beautiful woman!"

Ibn Sinna smiled.

"What's wrong with him?" inquired Likki.

"Moola says he loves you."

"He doesn't even *know* me!"

"Does he need to know you?" wondered Ibn Sinna. His tone intimated that this was rather a novel approach to human desire.

"Ohhhh. I won't sleep again tonight," Moola continued to complain. "And look at her hair." He reached out a tentative hand.

"It seems he would like to touch your hair," Ibn Sinna told Likki. He appeared to be enjoying her discomfort.

"I don't mind," she said, not quite meaning her words. In her first month of teaching, nearly every girl at the school had come to her, shyly asking to touch her hair. Some of the boys came too, even more shyly, to ask for the same privilege. Nuhu had asked. So had Mother of Issa. Even Kutu had been curious, though he had seemed to follow casually in the wake of his wife. It happened to Carlotta, too, even though she kept her tresses clinically short. Abu, who professed to be wild about white people's hair, was always searching out Likki's hairbrush and asking if he could "groom" her. Carlotta said all he really wanted was the chance to steal a handful of the silken strands to sell in town. They were used in several species of potent local magic.

Likki held out a sample to her admirer. Moola caressed the hair between his calloused fingers as if it were the mane of the Ruler's finest horse. "My heart will never rest again," he said softly. He took his walking-stick and tapped it disconsolately on the floor.

"He really loves you," said Ibn Sinna. "It's not just wanting you, like that. It's the real thing."

For her part Likki considered that Moola was far too old and his passions far too precipitate to be taken seriously. However, she was sensible enough not to say so.

"It was your hair that captured him." In the back seat Moola sighed and sucked at his teeth. He wore the expression of one who is expecting a migraine.

"People always want to touch my hair," said Likki. "I suppose it's because it's different."

"Yes. They want to see if it feels like their own hair."

"Why not?"

"And does it?" he asked her, and she didn't know what he was asking. He might have been asking to touch her hair himself. Or he might have been asking if *she* had fondled the heads of Kpamans and found them different, those soft mats of tight springs. Of course, they *were* different, more cheerful somehow than the lank, melancholy strands of a race that had evolved among the chilly vapours of northern Europe.

"My hair is different," said Likki, noticing as she spoke that Ibn Sinna was beginning to go bald.

"We know that it is different. But does it feel different?"

"You tell me," she said, holding out a strand, leaning slightly towards him with rueful resignation.

He reached out a hand as if to fondle a child, then let the sun-bleached fibres slip softly through his long fingers. He took his time about letting go.

"Is she your wife?" Moola inquired from the rear, in Kpamé, and not without a hint of jealousy.

"No."

"Do you want to sleep with her?"

"Hey! Old man. Are you asking me if we are rivals?"

"As for that," said Moola, "I can defeat you any time. Any. Time. I know women *too* well."

"Is that it?"

"It's true!"

"It's not good. She had too many husbands."

"Oh! Who else?" inquired Moola indignantly.

"That new army captain. He has been disturbing her already."

"Only him? We can easily send him away. Look how long the last one stayed."

"This one is tougher," said Ibn Sinna.

"Hey! Tougher? Should *I* be afraid?"

"Wait and see."

•

They dropped Moola off at the little village of Segou. There had been an outbreak of measles and five of the village's forty-eight children had died in the last three weeks. Nearly twenty more lay ill and some of these had already been rendered deaf or blind. The ancestral shrines of Segou had been unrelentingly silent on the matter. Desperate, the elders of Segou had sent for Moola to see if he could uncover the reason behind the current disaster.

"Isn't measles the reason?" asked Likki, thinking just like a Westerner.

"Measles is *how* the children died. It is not *why* the children died. After all, some thirty children have now come down with measles. So why is it that those five children have died and not some others? Why is it that some die and some recover? Why do some go blind and others recover to see? Why is it that some parents are mourning and others are full of smiles? Who chooses who will die? They have sent for Moola to get answers for these questions. He will go to the shrines of Segou and try to discover what has gone wrong."

"And what sorts of things *do* go wrong?" asked Likki with a mixture of curiosity and admiration. In her own culture the attempt to read God's reasons for the unequal distribution of evil in this world was regarded with superstitious disfavour.

"Moola will try to get the shrines to tell him why Segou has been stricken with this disease. Usually he likes to find an angry ancestor. Or a broken taboo is also good. These things are easy to fix. But if the trouble is witchcraft, then Moola is sad because everyone will begin to fight with one another. People begin to suspect one another. Someone accuses someone else. Then another person accuses the first one. Soon everyone is fighting and making *juju* and the village is spoiled. Then the trouble is much worse than before. So Moola is always very happy not to find any witches."

"You don't sound as if you had a great deal of faith in it. In witchcraft and divination, I mean."

"Why should I have faith in it? I am a Muslim."

Likki received the reprimand in silence. One African is not just like another.

"Do *you* believe in witchcraft?" asked Ibn Sinna accusingly.

"No." At least, at home she hadn't.

"You see? So why should I believe in it? We have gone past all these things."

Likki was uncomfortably aware that she had wanted him to say he believed in witchcraft. And not just Ibn Sinna. She wanted all of Africa to believe in it, to remain in a cradle of savage belief, a state of primitive purity, as a kind of monument to the white man's nostalgia and regret—a place where he might wander for an interlude of archetypal quiet when the chaos of his own busy centuries grew intolerable. She wanted Africa to be a kind of psychic tourist resort; to be taken, pressed firmly into the past, and held there, because in her own time and place she could not be master. These ideas, of course, were not peculiar to Likki but were general throughout her culture; the price of them now was paid by, among others, the undernourished children of Segou, who died needlessly of a preventable disease in a squalid, waterless village because Africa had been equated with the unconscious past and what happens there is not real.

"Isn't there a vaccine for measles?" Likki inquired in a subdued voice.

"Who in Segou has money for a vaccine?"

"I thought that medical care was free."

Ibn Sinna frowned. "You see, it is this way: if the medicine is *here* in the country then it is free. But there is no medicine. There is none of this vaccine in the country. Only if you are a rich man who can order it from abroad. And for that you need foreign exchange, hard currency. But our whole country is short of foreign exchange. Whatever comes into the country is bought with foreign exchange. We need money for building roads, money for buying transport lorries, money for school buildings and hospitals, money for books and paper and pencils. We need money for penicillin, for quinine, for doctors, for antibiotics. Money to dig sewers. Money to clear the parasites out of our drinking water. And then the army, too, eats money. Guns and planes and tanks for the soldiers. Women and cars for the officers. Houses. Airplanes. Money for bombs and bullets. In the end there is nothing left over for the children."

Likki was silent. She could think of nothing to say.

He dropped her off right in front of her door.

"Thank you for the ride." She had remembered to thank him this time.

"Do you need anything? Fanta?"

"We still have a few bottles . . . yes, we *could* use more."

"Maybe I can bring more tomorrow?"

"That would be nice." It would be very nice. She watched him drive off, wondering about the frantic parents of Segou, wondering about Moola with his easily broken heart and his agnostic approach to divination, wondering about the lingering touch of Ibn Sinna's fingers on her hair.

✖ 16

It was three days before Ibn Sinna showed up with the promised soft drinks. "There are times when even I find things are short," he said to Likki's inquiring face.

"Will you let me pay you this time?"

"Oh, why?" Then he relented, "I will show you where you can get the Fanta yourself, at the shop of my friend. Any time he knows you want Fanta he will always keep some for you."

It was a Saturday morning and Likki had no commitments. John was still away in the south and at home Carlotta would be poor company; she spent weekends glued to her calico curtains keeping abreast of campus infidelities.

"I'll come," said Likki and went into her bedroom to get her shoulder bag. When she turned to leave, the man was standing there filling the doorway, with a curious expression on his face. He remained there for a moment, blocking her way, before he turned aside, and Likki had a transient notion, very close to hope, that he might try to kiss her.

In the Mercedes the clamourous silence left Likki giddy with the impossibility of speech. Ibn Sinna finally broke the spell. "Do you want to drive past the soldiers?" He gestured towards a road that led towards army headquarters.

"My God, no." It was the last thing she wanted to do.

"I thought you wanted to fool that army man."

"Oh," said Likki, understanding him now. "You mean he'll think I'm with *you*."

"You *are* with me."

"Really. Okay, let's do it." She felt naughty, suddenly lighthearted.

Ibn Sinna steered to the right at the next intersection.

Near the former post office, which now served as a temporary military command post, he decelerated. The Mercedes purred past the soldiers at a leisurely pace while Ibn Sinna leaned out the window calling and waving to some officers he knew. Likki caught a brief glimpse of Captain Araoh watching them through a screened doorway, his eyes narrow as if focusing on a distant object. She shuddered involuntarily.

"What is wrong?" Ibn Sinna asked, noticing the spasm. One of his hands left the steering wheel, but he merely rested it on his knee. Likki stared, wondering if it had been meant to comfort her.

He parked the Mercedes in the lorry park and led Likki to a small market shop quite near to the "pharmacy" in which she had encountered him two weeks earlier. This shop, too, was dark and windowless. Inside, chewing kola nut, was Sima, the Earth Priest.

"Hey! My friend!" Ibn Sinna greeted him. "But I thought to see your brother here."

"He has gone to a funeral," said Sima. He regarded Likki. "White woman, you are the one keeping Abu's pig?"

"Yes."

"Then it is good."

"I brought her to greet your brother," said Ibn Sinna. "I thought he might have Fanta for her."

"All the time?"

"Why not?"

"I see," said Sima and smiled. "I will tell my brother when he comes."

Likki looked around the shop with eyes slowly adjusting to its dim obscurity. There were handbags and sandals and belts in abundant evidence. There were boxes of high heeled shoes and platform-soled shoes but there wasn't a trace of soft drinks. "Where's the Fanta?" she asked.

"We never keep the Fanta here," said Sima. "Otherwise anyone who walked by could come in here just like that and buy it all at once. You only come here to this shop to order your case. Then, later on, we bring it to you."

She should have guessed as much. As she had come to know Kpama better, she had learned that few things were simple, or self-evident, or exactly as they seemed on the surface in this town. Still, the people who lived here had it all worked out perfectly. Perhaps it was only her strangeness that needed explanation.

"*I* will bring the Fanta to you when it is ready," said Ibn Sinna as they walked back to the car. So, after all, he wasn't bowing out of his part in this. Likki nodded, imagining that she would still be barred from paying. She inquired after the owner of the shop—wouldn't they have to come back another time since she had not yet been introduced to the owner?

"You only needed to know the *place*. You already know the owner."

"Who?"

"The owner is Moola."

"Oh. I see."

"What do you see?"

Likki shook her head and did not answer him.

▪

At home that evening Likki found Carlotta unusually irritating. Carlotta was shamelessly plotting Nuhu's downfall. Within two weeks, she assured Likki, she was certainly going to get him. She looked forward to his capture with relish. The evidence she was accumulating against him would be damning. There would be no way out. He would be fired. Carlotta's eyes were bright. She derived an apparently sensual delight from these endeavours of hers.

"What evidence?" asked Likki. "How will you get him?"

"Uh-uh-uh-uh-uh," scolded Carlotta. "Nothing doing. I know it would be the first thing to slip out of your mouth the next time you went drinking with him. No, no. He doesn't get away that easily."

"Damn right, I'd tell him."

"I don't mind if you warn him, though. He can still save his filthy hide if he'll just leave my girls alone."

Likki took time to wonder what might have been the consequences for Carlotta if she had been made Housewarden for the *boys* instead of the girls. The young men of the school might have been for her like so many Zulus; she could have kept a score card of pregnancies taped to the inside of her desk. Lionized by three hundred virile young men (all of them desperate for passes into town), Carlotta might have blossomed, might have metamorphosed from overfed crone to dimpled darling of the school. "Leave Nuhu alone, Carlotta. He's all right."

"All right! All right? He got Binti pregnant, and the poor girl was made to suffer through one of those horrible backstreet abortions. And Nuhu is all right? If he's so all right, why couldn't he marry her?"

"From the way you talk, she's better off without him."

"But why did she have to go through one of those horrible abortions?"

"It probably wasn't one of those horrible abortions. It was probably more like a calabash of tea and a heavy period afterwards."

"So. You know all about it? You want to tell me where she went for this miraculous tea? Maybe you even know what was *in* the tea?"

For Carlotta abortion could only be knives and scissors. "No, I don't know where, what, or how. But it's probably nothing near as lurid as you're painting it. Besides, Binti is a big girl." Likki remembered Nuhu sitting anxiously in Wednesday's, fingering his calabash, fretting, waiting for news from the herbalist.

"Binti's only sixteen."

"In this town they marry them off at thirteen."

"In this town they marry them off at eleven. They marry them off at one day. They even marry them off before they're born. They've been doing it for centuries. But just because they've always done it doesn't make it right. It doesn't make it right that Binti has to come to me asking for a pass into town to visit her dying auntie, and then walk off alone for *that*. So they've always married at twelve, so they've always married at one day old: it's still ugly." Carlotta did not believe in cultural relativity. Her moral principles were absolute and she applied them universally.

"They don't *marry* them off at one day. They more or less engage them. The girls don't get married until they've reached puberty."

"Christ!" swore Carlotta. "Are you telling me that it's okay to take little girls of twelve and thirteen years old and as soon as they menstruate send them off to the beds of their fathers' arthritic cronies?"

"I didn't say that," complained Likki, experiencing the unpleasant sensation of having been backed into a corner where she had either to lose the argument to opinions she despised or to defend something she didn't believe in.

"Well, what did you say?"

"Just that things are different here."

"I'll say they are."

"Our standards don't necessarily apply."

"Likki, some things are wrong. They're just *wrong*. They're wrong at home and they're wrong here. They're wrong all over." The ultimate heresy for American liberals—but then Carlotta did not consider herself to be one of these.

"Like what, for instance?"

"Like infant betrothal, for instance."

"I don't see that at all. I could make out a very good case for arranged marriage; no unrealistic romantic expectations; everyone knows exactly what they're supposed to be doing, exactly what they're supposed to be contributing to the relationship, what the limits are, and what it's reasonable to hope for. Plus, the in-laws are bound to get along since they're the ones who fixed it up. It's all up front; everything is made explicit. There's no grey area of constant negotiation. At a guess I'd say arranged marriages are at least as successful as the kind we're all so crazy about. The divorce rate is lower here, if that's any indication."

"All right, but there are other things."

"Like what?" Likki asked uneasily, for she was beginning to see what the other things might be and she realized she might have to concede victory to Carlotta.

"Murder? Rape? Wife beating? Child abuse?"

"All right. I agree. There are bad things around and they're bad all over. But Kpama certainly hasn't got a monopoly of crime. There's more of all of that stuff going on at home."

"Well, then, there's female circumcision," continued Carlotta.

"Oh, God, let's not start on that again," said Likki, but start on it they did. It was one of the few topics on which they both held equally vehement and identical opinions. It was also one topic upon which both were equally uninformed. For these reasons it served as an overture of peace between them when other arguments had driven them apart.

"I just don't understand why they do it," mourned Carlotta, lost in a cognitive morass. In her moral universe there was no explanation for the systematic mutilation of the sexual organs and pleasure of half of Africa's women. Except perhaps the devil, although in Carlotta's books the devil was responsible for the increase of pleasure, not its diminution.

"It's all tied up with polygyny and being a virgin at marriage." Likki sought sociological solace in the old, worn arguments. "Any man can satisfy eighty-six wives if none of them knows what she's missing."

"They don't miss it, though," mourned Carlotta.

"Says who?"

"Well, why do they all get pregnant if it isn't any fun for them?"

The discussion was leading back to where it had started, to Nuhu and his unrelenting bachelorhood. Likki was weary of Carlotta's Calvinism. She took shelter in her bedroom. She wanted peace in her life—breakfast coffee without an argument or a lecture, the chance to sit in the living-room without speaking, the right to exist without explanation or justification.

•

Ibn Sinna's car stopped in front of the bungalow again the next day around noon. He wandered casually into the living-room and explained that he had stopped to see if he could take Likki out for a ride—just to fool the soldiers of course.

Carlotta was predictably caustic. "Out of the frying pan and into the fire," she said to Likki while the latter was changing into a cooler dress.

"Remember, you said this one was handsome?"

"I said he was good-looking, not handsome," said Carlotta, who remembered very well. "But that's beside the point. What will John say?" Carlotta clucked with disapproval.

"John's not here." It was the whole reason for the excursion.

"And when he finds out?" The words contained a sermon on fidelity.

"What's there for him to find out?"

"Just look at yourself," said Carlotta. "As soon as you start driving around with an African man you begin to act like an African woman. Soon you'll have a lover on every corner. Soon you'll be taking money for it."

"Oh, Carlotta." Likki rolled her eyes and ran back out into the living-room where Ibn Sinna stood waiting. "And where are we going today?" she asked him overcheerfully—and primarily for Carlotta's benefit.

"My mother has said she would like to greet you," he said.

"Your mother?!" Even for a trip specifically designed to discourage unwanted attentions, this was carrying innocence to the extreme.

"Why not?" Such supreme conceit he squeezed into those words.

■

Ibn Sinna's mother lived in Chegili, four miles west of Kpama. She was a tall, angular woman, lean and utterly asymmetrical, but with a clumsy elegance of manner. Probably as a result of polio, one leg was shorter than the other, so that when she moved she leaned sideways as if tilting at invisible windmills. Nearly every limb departed from her trunk at a different angle from the perpendicular, her elbows were constantly akimbo and even her eyes were crooked. At rest they relaxed into the position that Kpamans referred to as "quarter-to-one." She left people unsettled; it was hard for them to tell whether she was serious or laughing at them behind a polite façade. When she greeted Likki, she bowed so low and pumped her hand so abjectly and for so long that Likki squirmed; but not long afterwards the woman planted herself four inches from Likki's face and demanded a cigarette.

"I want *smoke!*" she said.

Likki fished in her shoulder bag for an open packet and gave her a "555." The old woman was not appeased. She stared long at the twelve cigarettes still in the packet. Likki gave her another seven sticks. Then, eyeing her, the old woman said, "I want *light*."

Likki gave her two books of matches and Ibn Sinna's mother cackled. She made a great display of lighting up one cigarette and putting it to her lips. Then, in a parody of Humphrey Bogart, she frowned and inhaled deeply, letting the smoke issue slowly forth from her mouth and nose. When this performance was over she held the cigarette at arm's length and scrutinized it as if it were a thing of the devil. "Hey!" she cried, and bending with laughter she tilted across the courtyard into her cooking room, all the while addressing the cigarette as if it were a living, sentient being. Several of her grandchildren who were present cheered her on with shouts and giggles. Likki stood by smiling nervously, utterly baffled.

"My mother likes you," said Ibn Sinna to her by way of explanation, but this merely contributed to Likki's confusion, showing her how far from understanding she really was. It was as if, while pursuing her own white rabbit, she had dropped down an underground hole into Kpama, to wander baffled and bewildered and incapable of predicting what might happen next. The man standing next to her was a large part of the puzzle. He must have had some motive for bringing her to Chegili more agreeably selfish than misleading an obdurate army captain, yet he made no move to approach her. Instead he took her around the community of his childhood and its environs, hailing old friends, greeting his myriad "grandmothers," teasing the village children, and pointing out to Likki the features of a landscape intimately known to him—all in the chastest camaraderie.

Likki's brief experience of West African men (much of it gained in those first three weeks in the capital) had led her to expect that she would be asked to bed before she was asked her name. This "custom" was partly a result of polygynous marriage practices: every man in the country wanted to have as many wives as possible and so, at any given time, the entire adult male population of the country considered itself to be eligible. Of course, since women could only have one husband each, the available female population was quickly used up. Paradoxically, one of the spin-offs of polygyny was the enhanced bargaining power of single women. Unattached females were at a premium and could demand, and receive, all sorts of expensive attentions from men who were trying to attract them into their harems. Polygynous marriage being what it was, it was in the women's interests to stay single as long as possible, and even the plainest among them led scores of admirers on a merry and costly chase.

In such a set-up, of course, the men become incorrigible pursuers. They begin to practise their techniques at an early age and carry on with their flatteries and soft looks until they are nearly in the grave. So it was that in the main street of the capital, beggars in rags had followed Likki through the marketplace, wailing hapless love to her retreating back. So it was that merchants sought to lure her with small talk while they asked for five times the going rate on cloth, embroidery, and beads. Soldiers too, their confidence multiplied several times by their uniforms, confronted her with smiles and soft hands outside public buildings. Policemen suggested they might escort her home when she asked directions. Taxi drivers stared at her in their mirrors and plied her with what they imagined were flattering words.

Ibn Sinna alone was chivalrous among them. He alone stood back while all the world about him sought to breed incontinently. With a semblance of regard that was almost distressingly feudal, he insisted on treating Likki like a "lady." And so it was whenever she saw him. He never touched her, nor was conversation ever easy between them. They were often bedevilled by silence.

Likki reflected on her companion's uniqueness as she walked with Ibn Sinna around the perimeter of his village. Eventually, as they approached the southern edge of the village, which was also the top of a small hill, she inquired about Fatima's ghost.

Iba Sinna laughed. "So you want me to show you a ghost?" he asked in a superior way.

"I was really only asking if you'd heard the rumour."

"Where is the person in Kpama who does not hear rumours?"

Likki made a face. What a hopeless man to try to get information from.

"Anyway, I will take you there," volunteered Ibn Sinna after a long moment of silence. "I will take you to see the ghost." His eyebrows arched up as he watched her.

"If you want," answered Likki, refusing to display emotion.

Ibn Sinna led her directly to the top of the hill and paused near the site of a house in the earliest stages of construction. The outlines of future rooms had been traced in the dust. Wooden pegs marked the corners of rooms, and rough twine ran between these, decorated with small scraps of cotton that danced in the light hilltop breeze.

"This is the place?"

"Yes."

"The place where the ghost is supposed to walk?"

"Why not?"

"Someone's building a *house* here!"

"Yes. I am building a house here. With my brothers. It will be for my mother to live in. She will stay with my younger brother, al Hassan, and his wives. The house will be good. All concrete blocks. She will be happy."

"You're going to build right here where the ghost has been?"

"Who has seen the ghost?"

"Abu said Ayesha saw it."

"That is what Abu says. And what did Ayesha say?"

"I don't know. I didn't ask her."

"You see? It is not a good thing to go around believing just like that." How he loved to correct her. How they all seemed to love to correct her.

"I'm sure Abu didn't just invent that story out of his head," said Likki. "There must be other people who say they've seen the ghost."

"Some other people say she has been seen here," he answered.

"But you obviously don't believe it." Or else why would he be building there?

"Do *you* believe it?"

"I don't know," answered Likki. Ghosts were one of the things that might be possible in Kpama.

He took that in, then said, after a pause, "As for me, it is the same. I also don't know."

"But you're still going to build right here?"

"What has my mother to fear from her own sister's child?" he wanted to know.

Likki shook her head. What disjointed arguments it was possible to have with this man. With relief she watched him turn and start back to his mother's.

※17

John returned to Kpama full of complaints. He came in on Yours Is Coming, probably the worst lorry on the capital run, and the journey took five days instead of the usual three. He had the normal traveller's dysentery from eating roadside food, and one of the lorry passengers had given him headlice. But most irritating of all, according to John his trip to the south had been little more than a wild-goose chase. The Department of Immigration had found nothing wrong with his visa although they sat on the document (and his passport, too, of course) for more than a month before returning both to him unaltered.

"It was the army captain," said Likki as they sat in Kutu's courtyard, shelling peanuts. "He wanted you out of the way and me unprotected, so I would have no excuse but to fall into his arms." She told John how she and Carlotta had been harassed night and day for two weeks after he left.

"And then what happened?"

"Then, on Abu's suggestion, I got Ibn Sinna to drive me around in his car. To give Mr. Araoh something to think about. To let him see there was competition." Abu's eyes questioned hers as she spoke and she felt as if she were lying, though there was nothing untruthful in what she said. Only in what she left out—and of that John remained ignorant.

John may have sensed this for he spoke with irritation. "That's a hell of a thing."

"What was I supposed to do? Sit and wait for him to rape me?"

The fact that John had no reasonable answer ready did nothing to improve his mood. Among other things he was in academic dudgeon. A colleague had taken advantage of John's absence from Britain to publish several of John's pet ideas as his own, a fact John had discovered in the periodicals reading room of the capital's university. John sat tight-lipped in the heat and his sweat took on a particularly musky odour.

Later, inside his room he grabbed Likki's wrist—playfully, as he thought—and demanded to know if she were glad to see him again.

Not when you ask me like that, she thought, and a certain revulsion against his mannerisms took hold of her. She prevaricated. "Maybe," she said.

"Maybe? What kind of answer is maybe?"

Likki shrugged her shoulders and walked away from him, turning to face him only when she reached the opposite wall. "Did you bring my book?" She had asked for Proust. In Kpama you read the longest thing you could find, as slowly as possible, and as many times as you could stand it.

"Your book? Is that all you can think of, your book?"

"Did you bring it?"

"No. It wasn't there."

"Did you look?"

"Yes, I looked. But Christ, what are the chances of finding Proust in the capital when you can't even get hold of it in an English public library?"

"Did you bring *any* books?"

"Yes, of course I brought books."

"Don't tell me, let me guess: World War Two memoirs."

"More or less."

"Good grief. You know all the rest of us have to read the damn stuff after you."

"I bought books that I wanted to read. I'm not running a charity for bibliophiles. Besides, you're the historian. I should have thought you'd enjoy that sort of thing."

"God *damn*." Then she paused, letting her heat dissipate. "What about other things? Toothpaste? Soap? Laundry detergent? What about toilet paper?" Everything that was short.

"You're turning into a proper little African aren't you? One look at your man and all you can think of is things, things, things."

Likki took umbrage. "Her man," indeed. She reminded John that there was not one book to be purchased in all of

Kpama except a mimeographed version of the New Testament translated into an unreadable form of Kpamé by the wild men of the Baptist mission. She pointed out that she had read all of her own books three times and most of John's at least twice. The town was chronically short of toilet paper so that all the Barbara Cartlands were disintegrating slowly in the septic tank. In a crisis of these proportions even a Flash Gordon comic book would be welcome. And as for the other items, well, she was tired of brushing her teeth with bicarbonate of soda. It was a horrible thing to put into your mouth first thing in the morning. And she was tired of trying to get her washing clean with local soap.

John softened. "You've had a hard time, too, I guess," he said gently. "Let's go to bed."

It was on her lips to reply that here again was that most typical, most ineradicable illusion of males, the notion that every misunderstanding could be rectified by an upright prick and a pair of orgasms in matching sexes, but she held her tongue and went with him into his bedroom, prostituting herself to their past companionship. She divined that they were coming to the end of things and that there would not be many more times she would come here. Afterwards, she didn't stay for post-coital fondling but lifted from the mattress like a rocket, grabbed her clothing, and dressed with voracious haste.

"What's the matter with you?"

"It's too hot to lie around in bed." It was February, about six weeks before the rains were due. Everywhere it was unbearable, insufferably sticky. The temperature never dropped below ninety, not even at night. The air was saturated with moisture. Likki reached for her shoulder bag.

"Where are you going?" asked John, looking like a deserted child. Likki almost stayed with him then.

"Home to wash."

"You can wash here."

"I *can't* wash here." Not since that awful Sunday. "If I wash here it's a public event. If we were just sitting in here talking, I wouldn't have to wash."

"Don't be ridiculous. Everyone knows we're not just

sitting in here talking. The whole house knows what goes on in here."

"And I guess that's just what I don't like."

"There's always *your* place," John suggested airily, knowing how unpleasant Carlotta could make them feel up there."

"There's Carlotta. Besides, if we did it at the bungalow, the whole school would know. The whole town would know."

"The whole town already knows," said John. Likki knew this was probably true, but she chose to ignore it.

"Then why don't we just go out and fuck in the street?"

"Oh, Likki, be reasonable."

"Be reasonable. Be reasonable. Why is it that whenever a man is losing an argument with a woman he always feels he can win by telling her to be reasonable?"

"All right," said John Lavender in a level tone. "Let's do it your way. Let's go out and do it in the street." He made as if to get out of bed.

"Oh, go to hell!" said Likki and walked out the door.

Mother of Issa stopped Likki at the gate. "Nasara, you are hot!" she said. "I think you are angry with my stranger." Likki made no reply. She was bristling. Mother of Issa continued to prattle; she curled up her face with dimpling sympathy. "What is wrong?" she asked softly, reaching for Likki's hand and patting it gently.

There was no way out of this. Mother of Issa would never let go until she had an answer. "No presents," said Likki, reaching for the explanation that Mother of Issa would most easily appreciate. "He brought no presents at all!"

Mother of Issa nodded gravely. "Not one?"

"Nothing!"

"Hey! The man is *too* bad." And Mother of Issa bent over to let out her warmest Christmas-pudding laugh, full of complacent wonder at the blessings of life, full of scorn for those too selfish and blind to share; a bubbly, brown peal of cosmic glee at the way things were with the world of men. And women. And then she called Abu and told him to walk up the hill with Likki because it would never do to send her away from the house fretting and all alone.

•

This was but the first of several arguments that Likki had with John Lavender. They started over trivial matters: a lost shoe, the temperature of the coffee, how much soap powder to put in the wash. Once they fought about a definition of socialism. It was petty and unbecoming and by mutual (but unspoken) consent they began to avoid one another. Likki continued to come into town, but less frequently, and she stopped less often at Kutu's, though to a certain extent she remained bound to John Lavender because of the fact that they were strangers together in an alien country. Like it or not they were tied to each other for as long as they remained in Kpama. When the sexual attachment slipped, John became, as it were, Likki's brother.

✖18

Mother of Issa kept in touch with her stranger's partially estranged woman by sending little reminders of her affection up the hill with Abu in the late afternoons. One day it would be bush fruits from the villages (these were banned by tradition from the marketplace). A few days later Abu would show up with half a wild guinéa fowl, lightly roasted, delicately smoked over a wood fire. Another time he brought with him the succulent hindquarter of a grass-cutter. Likki reciprocated by sending Abu back home with—at various times—two bars of English lavender soap, some out-of-date magazines, and a saucepan with a curved bottom that was useless on the propane stove in the bungalow but would work perfectly on a charcoal fire.

One afternoon Abu didn't come. Hope of Our Ancestors snuffled plaintively in her pen. She rested her snout on the gate and "mooed." She had grown used to her afternoon bath. She had grown used to her afternoon backscratch. She missed Abu. He knew where all the itchy spots were. When Carlotta threw eggplant and melon rind out of the kitchen window, Hope of Our Ancestors just screwed up her eyes and walked away. Later she refused to eat the supper brought out to her pen.

"She's fat enough, anyway," said Carlotta.

"But where's Abu?"

"He's goofing off. It was bound to happen sooner or later."

"Oh, I don't know. He seemed to love coming up here."

"That's because you let him drink all our Coke."

The next day there was again no sign of Abu. "Maybe he has malaria," suggested Carlotta. It was the time of year for fever. Although little rain had fallen—only a sprinkle to settle the dust—the mosquitoes appeared to have found places to breed and their numbers had increased tenfold since the end of the harmattan. Then there was what felt like the 110 per cent humidity, which wore down everyone's resistance. Many of the students were ill, and even the headmaster was lying abed.

The third evening Abu still failed to show up and Hope still refused to touch her food. She drank a little water, however, and looked wonderfully sad. Likki walked down into Kpama to investigate.

She found Kutu's house in an uproar because of disease. Habiba was down with fever. Mieri and Arimata were showing early signs of it. Salifu was sickly and lethargic with a badly infected foot. Abu had been stricken with measles. This was a particular worry because measles towed deafness and blindness in its wake. Those whose hearts and lungs were affected usually fell merciful prey to malaria and died.

Mother of Issa sat stiff with concern in a corner of the courtyard, almost paralysed with dismay at the presence of so much malevolent fate in her house. If it *was* fate.

Abu lay in a darkened room shivering under a woollen blanket, his temperature soaring. He managed a weak smile of recognition for Likki and asked after his pig.

"She misses you."

Abu fretted. He worried about his manure deliveries, he worried about Likki's eggs. He worried about Hope's daily backscratch. His most particular worry, however, was a rumour he had picked up that Captain Araoh was establishing his headquarters in a house belonging to Mahmut. Abu was certain that this betokened some collusion between unfriendly military and familial powers. If Mahmut now demanded his daughter back, could Ayesha refuse with impunity? Abu's anxiety was driving up his fever, and Mother of Issa had sent for Mallam Yakubu. Likki considered that sending for the doctor might be a better idea but Mother of Issa soon put her right.

"The white man's medicine is useless for this thing," said Mother in corseted tones. "Even the itching is impossible for them to stop." Her constricted voice read sermons concerning the white man's stupidity. Under her breath she muttered libellously about calamine lotion and antibiotic creams.

"Abu looks *awful*," Likki said to John Lavender in the

courtyard. John was measuring out part of the aspirin supply he regularly poured down Abu's throat, despite Mother of Issa and despite Mallam Yakubu.

"It's a very serious disease here," said John in detached, professional tones. "Did you know that measles kills one out of every ten people born in sub-Saharan Africa? And all this misery preventable by one little injection that is good for a lifetime but no one here can afford."

"Do you get pleasure out of facts like that?"

"Come along. Don't worry. Parsloe's far too cunning to let measles carry him off."

On her way home Likki passed through the *zongo* and stopped at Ayesha's to collect the eggs Abu could no longer deliver to her bungalow. She asked if the rumours concerning Mahmut and the captain were true.

"It may be true," said Ayesha ambiguously.

"Is there anything I can say to put Abu's mind at ease?"

"Do you want to put his mind at ease?"

"Of course."

"Why?"

"He's a friend of mine. And he's ill."

"Is he your friend?" asked Ayesha and she turned away before Likki could reply. It was impossible to address her retreating back. Likki walked slowly out of the courtyard, scattering Abu's chickens before her as she went. And they complained of it, fat hens of the devil that they were.

Likki was nearly to Smugglers' Bridge before she realized she had left the eggs behind. It was tempting not to return for them. Ayesha's house was all her own preserve. Most houses in Kpama were brimful of people, overcrowded, ebullient, merry. But Ayesha's house was always unpleasantly empty, pervaded by an uneasy, almost sacerdotal quiet. Moomin was hardly ever in evidence; even Ayesha's children played away from her walls. Only the guinea fowls and Abu's chickens were consistently noisy within her domain. The watchman and the guard dog slumbered almost without ceasing.

To this eerie residence Likki retraced her steps, trying hard to summon an attitude of indifference.

Ayesha had placed the eggs on a bench in the corner of the courtyard, and she gestured toward them triumphantly when Likki returned. "You forgot what you came for," she said, leaning slightly over the bench for emphasis. In this attitude, bent over from the waist, she bore a strong likeness to the old woman in Chegili.

"Are you Ibn Sinna's *full* sister?" Likki blurted out, immediately regretting it. Curiosity had triumphed over discretion. Someone had told Likki—perhaps it was John Lavender—that Ayesha and Ibn Sinna were half siblings, sharing only a father. This piece of genealogical information was difficult to credit when Ayesha stood thus on the tilt.

"Who says I am Ibn Sinna's full sister?"

Likki shook her head repenting her foolishness. Could any reasonable answer be got from this woman? "You looked so much like his mother just then," she explained.

"Do *you* know Ibn Sinna's mother?"

"He took me to see her one day." A sense of betraying secrets. Yet surely Ayesha knew of the expedition to Chegili.

"Why did he take you there?"

"Why *not*?" Two could play at being cryptic.

"Is that it?" Ayesha paused for a moment while she picked up the eggs. As she handed the parcel over to Likki she said, "Our mothers were sisters. *Full* sisters." She studied Likki intently, then said, "Ibn Sinna is thinking of travelling. With my husband, Moomin." She smiled, drew back her lips like a stoat. Her teeth were those of any small carnivore, dainty, well-tooled instruments of precision.

Likki did not answer her.

"Maybe you wanted to know that?" said Ayesha.

"It's none of my business."

"No. It is not."

As Likki left the house she had one glimpse of Comfort, stumbling sleepily from a doorway, hurrying out to hide in the skirts of her adopted mother.

PART TWO

X1

When Abu finally woke from his fevers he rose discomfited for he had travelled in dreams of a nightmare hue and he wanted to know if there were any truth in them. The dreams had all to do with Comfort.

Salifu brought Abu his breakfast and laughed at him because he was dotted over his face and torso with calamine lotion—Mother of Issa having capitulated on this as on most medical matters. Abu looked as if he were about to enter one of the arcane pagan rituals that the good Muslims of Kpama had brought to extinction two generations earlier.

Abu ate his breakfast thoughtfully, a small bowl of fermented millet porridge, grey and glutinous, its rank fullness effectively camouflaged by its unprepossessing exterior. What stranger would approach this substance, what foreigner suspect its richness? Because sugar was, as always, short, Abu had to sweeten his porridge with the grated fruit of the baobab tree, an unsatisfactory substitute because of the volumes required. It took five heaping tablespoons of the grated baobab pod to accomplish the work of one cube of sugar. It had other drawbacks, as well. Abu disliked the way Salifu was standing in the shade of the mango tree confidently stroking another football-sized, spindle-shaped baobab pod. An excellent itching powder could be made from the outer skin of the baobab capsule. All those tiny little hairs. Even after three good washings, microscopic torment would remain in the victim's clothing. It was always a good joke, provided it was played on someone else.

"Salifu, put that thing down."

"I am just keeping it small-small, for our mother," explained Salifu. "She wants sugar."

"Then go and grate some sugar for her."

Salifu just grinned and continued to fondle the pod.

Abu recalled with remorse the occasion on which he had allowed Salifu to shoulder the blame for what had been, after all, a conspiratorial undertaking to infest al Hajji Abdul Raheem's chartreuse undergarments. When Abu went to wash, he took along with him the clothes he meant to wear that day—just to keep an eye on them.

At Ayesha's house, later in the morning, Abu posed the pertinent questions.

"She is gone," said Ayesha, confirming Abu's worst fears. Mahmut had come only the evening before, in the company of Captain Araoh's bodyguard, and had removed his little daughter from the nest she had occupied for nearly a year.

"How will she do for milk?" Abu wanted to know. In his distress he focused on practicalities.

"Mahmut said that he himself can feed her with the white man's rubber tits." Ayesha spat out the words. Her venom may have hidden a secret anxiety that Mahmut, being unschooled in the ways of hygiene, would poison the infant with contaminated water. If so, it was a worry she did not communicate to Abu.

Abu found much to occupy him in the succeeding hours. He spied. He wheedled his way into the houses of Kutu's distant kin and eavesdropped shamelessly on their conversations. He clawed his way up onto the rooftops and peered into courtyards that were closed to him. He enlisted his friends into service. They pried where he could not. The ears of the young were so many ubiquitous vortices through which the secrets of Kpama leaked like water through sand. By late afternoon Abu had all the information he needed, and he went up the hill to visit his pig and to ask the white women's advice. Not that he would heed it, of course; it was more a matter of letting them know whose side they should be on.

"Mahmut has stolen my wife," he told them as he leaned against the back of the sofa with an authoritative air. (It was a mannerism he had copied from a rubber-plantation owner, a man from the Ivory Coast who had once stayed with Kutu and who had made a lasting impression upon Abu as one whose dignity of manner exceeded even that of the Ruler.) As he spoke, Abu swirled the Coke about in his glass just as he had seen Mr. Rochambeau (horse-faced and black as sable) do with his turn-of-the-century Armagnac, an extravagance he had brought with him from Abidjan along with his Chinese concubine and two crates of Iranian figs. Ice cubes—a special welcome-back treat from Carlotta—clinked luxuriously in Abu's glass.

"Mahmut will find he has much trouble to keep the girl from me," Abu continued, frowning. He was speaking like a grey-bearded elder and Likki made a face at Carlotta, but apart from this both women kept marvellously still. Abu gave the two teachers an edited account of all he had gleaned earlier in the day. Edited, because it would never do, for example, to dwell too long on Mahmut's natural right to his daughter's company or his understandable desire not to look foolish in the eyes of the community. Not to mention the morose and lingering passion Mahmut had conceived for Aswayya, al Hajji Umar's bewitching daughter, the indulgence of which (in matrimonial form, of course) depended upon Mahmut's ability to prove that he could "hold all his family together in one place," to quote al Hajji Umar.

According to Abu, Mahmut, driven by an unaccountable hatred of Hawa and Ayesha, had ingratiated himself with the pernicious Captain Araoh. Together these two arch-villains had contrived a plan to realize both their nefarious ends. Mahmut would steal his daughter back into his household and the army captain would strike, through Ayesha, a blow at Ibn Sinna, whom he considered to be the chief obstacle to the attainment of his dreams as far as Likki was concerned.

"Oh, does he just?" said Likki at this juncture, forgetting that she had connived and striven to create exactly this impression in the mind of the military commander. Abu cast a reproachful look in the direction of this interruption and Likki remained respectfully silent throughout the remainder of his communication. Zulu, however, whined frequently, for he had drunk too much leftover ginger-ale earlier in the day and his bladder was uncomfortably full. Everyone overlooked his distress as he sulked and drooled over the floor.

Abu resumed his narrative. It appeared that Mahmut had early recognized the great possibilities that lay with the army and was eager to explore these, because few in Kpama would readily take his side in any dispute with Ayesha. Many people believed, as Hawa did, that Mahmut was directly responsible for Fatima's death, that to silence Fatima's complaints (which Hawa had since augmented and amplified), he had secretly done away with her, hiding her body in a place where he hoped it would decompose beyond recognition before it was found. If this were true, there was little now to be gained by leaving Fatima's daughter in her father's house, for she would be a constant and unwelcome reminder of her mother. Had Comfort been a boy, the situation might have been reckoned differently, for boys were part of a man's true family, his effective contribution to posterity, in a way that wives and daughters were not. Boys remained in their father's houses, eventually bringing their own wives and children to swell the numbers; when girls married they were lost to the families that had raised them.

Even those who believed that Fatima had killed herself felt there must be something amiss with a house and husband that could drive a new mother to such despair, steering her by the force of their contempt into the foetid sewers of the *bomba*. And so by this logic, too, Comfort was better off away from the house of her father.

Because community sentiment was ranged against him, Mahmut had resolved to lodge his claims in the bosom of outside authority. No one was better placed to receive them than Captain Araoh. No sooner had the army officer set foot in Kpama than Mahmut began an assiduous and accomplished wooing. It started with the tire for the transport lorry. It developed rapidly. Within two months Mahmut had made himself indispensable. Without Mahmut the captain could find no batteries. Without Mahmut there were no yams. If the rice were too yellow, Mahmut could replace it. If the sheep were too skinny, Mahmut knew where to find fat ones. When cigarettes were short and the beer ran out, the army captain sent for his Muslim conjurer and the problem was quickly rectified.

Naturally, when he decided he needed a bigger place to

live, Captain Araoh sent for Mahmut. In this matter, as in others, the wily wonderworker was not taken unawares. Six weeks prior to the captain's request, a small army of labourers had moved in on Mahmut's major residence in Kpama, repairing walls, mending cracks, resurfacing, painting, scrubbing and polishing. All the chair cushions were re-covered in expensive cloth imported from Nairobi. New curtains were hung. Cracked louvers were replaced with glass smuggled in from Upper Volta. Mosquito screening, stolen at midnight from the Public Works Department depot, was installed in every window. A stereo system, purchased at great expense in the south, was established with elaborate display in the reception room in close proximity to the sightless eye of the TV set. For several years to come these appliances, like two autistic, electronic beggars from the future (one blind, the other mute), would sit together in helpless idleness, a tribute to the contagion of conspicuous consumption in a town without electricity.

According to Abu, Captain Araoh had said, "I think I could use a bigger house here in Kpama," and Mahmut had quickly volunteered his own.

"But I can't move you out," Alistair Araoh had allegedly protested.

"My house can easily accommodate both of us," Mahmut had rejoined in his most self-effacing manner, suggesting that the captain might at least take a *look* at his house to see if it were the sort of thing he wanted.

Of course, when the captain saw it, it was exactly the sort of place he had in mind. Mahmut had spent six weeks remodelling it to conform to everything he knew of the army captain's inherent likes and dislikes and his acquired models of material display. Mahmut's sumptuous domain clustered around a necklace of inner courts. He had had the two outermost courts remodelled. These were relatively new, of rectangular design, and built of concrete blocks. Further along, deeper within, one came to older structures. Here the ancestral builders had forgone the strict rigidity of right-angled architecture. Instead, the walls relaxed in graduated curves around a well of deep water that had been known to go dry only twice in the last three centuries. The scars of earlier habitations were clearly visible around the well—a line here, a depression there, odd protuberances preserving the spatial memory of ancient kitchens. It was to this older section of his house that Mahmut and his family withdrew when Captain Araoh took possession of the outer two courtyards, their adjacent rooms, and their well, which was markedly inferior.

When Captain Araoh moved in, it was necessary for several members of Mahmut's household to depart. Purveyors of local gossip hinted that Mahmut had used the arrival of the army to pry loose from his train those of his retainers who had become troublesome to him. In Kpama such hangers-on were the attendant burden of riches, and it was seen as a shirking of duty to send the infirm back to their farms or to pack off the childless auntie to a village where she would be mocked by the fertile for the rest of her days.

Some stood up for Mahmut (here Abu scowled), saying that there was not one big-man in Kpama who would not have welcomed the opportunity to disengage from himself some of his leeches, had the chance to do so only arisen. Abu paused and scrutinized the faces of his audience. He wanted them to be sure they knew they were not to sympathize with this point of view. Both Likki and Carlotta strove to look properly contemptuous of any argument that would exonerate the conduct of Mahmut.

Abu persevered with his tale. With the captain established in his very household, it was a simple matter for Mahmut to win his confidence, to pour out his woes in those late-evening conversations when the light from the charcoal fires is dying and darkness loosens the tongue. At first Captain Araoh could not understand that there was indeed a problem. For him it was a clear case: Mahmut had father-right on his side and should simply go to Ayesha's house, pick up his child, and remove her. It took some weeks for Mahmut to impress upon the army captain the difficulties that would arise from such precipitateness. For one thing, Hawa would again become highly vocal. Mahmut didn't want to spell out that his late wife's mother would be ranging up and down the streets of Kpama calling him a murdering devil, but eventually Captain Araoh got the picture.

And there was the problem of reprisals. In her fury, of

course, Hawa might say anything, might even resort to physical attack; but it was Ayesha's coolness that really gave Mahmut pause. She had a locked storeroom with heaven knew what inside. Owls hooted in there after dark. Her fires burned long after midnight and she made foul-smelling teas. She could cure any illness, could call people back from the edge of the grave—just look how she'd succeeded with Abu's measles when everyone else had given him up. But those who can rescue you from the lip of death can also drop you in there again. In short . . .

"A sorceress?" exclaimed Captain Araoh, voicing the drift of Mahmut's insinuations.

"In fact!" agreed Mahmut, well-pleased to have conveyed the message without actually accusing Ayesha himself.

"But such a lovely woman," mourned Alistair Araoh. The Fulani set of Ayesha's dark features had appealed to him, had reminded him with a pang of that beauty in Niger whose husband had been away on a course when he first met her.

Then, displeased to find himself dreaming of a woman no longer accessible (she had died of bilharzia two years later), the captain began to belittle Mahmut. "You are now telling me that all that stands between you and your daughter is two women. And you call yourself a man."

Mahmut pointed out that behind the two women stood some of the strongest men in Kpama. There was Ibn Sinna, Ayesha's brother and Fatima's cousin on the distaff side. Little need be said of him. Alistair Araoh grinned sweetly and ran his tongue across his teeth.

"Kutu, too, would be against it," whined Mahmut. Kutu would support the women because of his friendship with Moomin and because of the ridiculous "betrothal" of one of the orphans in his house to Mahmut's baby girl, a betrothal Kutu would now defend because the honour and credibility of his house had become involved.

Even the Earth Priests would side with Ayesha. Their elders, and Sima in particular, had shown themselves overtly partial to Abu and his precocious romance.

And, of course, there was Moomin.

"Tell me about him," said Captain Araoh. "The man is never at home. Where does he keep himself all the time?"

"He is a trader."

"So. But you, too, are a trader and you are not wandering about the country like that."

"It is said he travels abroad with Ibn Sinna."

"Out of the country?"

"That is what I have heard."

"Interesting," said Araoh. "And do they trade when they are out of the country?" Little matters of import licenses.

Mahmut disappointed him. "I don't know if they have a license to trade."

"I am not asking if they have a license. I am asking if they *trade*. The two matters are distinct."

"As for that, I am not the one to ask," said Mahmut, refusing to drop his enemies cold-bloodedly into the military jaws.

·

Abu brought his story to its conclusion. "So when Mahmut convinced this man, Araoh, that he, Mahmut, cannot go and take his daughter himself, then the soldiers were sent to do the work for him. So, if anyone complains to Mahmut about it, he will just say, 'Go and talk to the soldiers. It is they who have done this thing.'" Abu looked sorrowfully into his empty glass.

Embarrassed by the fact that they had little solace to offer Abu, the two women drew him outside to show off the fatness of his pig. Hope's initial refusal to take food from any hand but Abu's had precipitated a crisis in Bungalow 5 and a rivalry had sprung up between Carlotta and Likki over who could coax the most leftovers down the maw of the giant swine.

Abu had to admit he was pleased with the condition and size of his animal. Her skin had a sumptuous sheen to it, the sleek and well-fed polish of coddled darlings at pet shows. Hope's girth had swelled visibly in Abu's absence—despite the fact that she had been off her food for nearly a week. "She made up for it afterwards," said Carlotta drily, thinking of how much she had "dashed" (bribed) Come Chop Again to borrow the supply department's wheelbarrow so they could fill it with scraps from the school's kitchen. This, while Likki fended off the urgent advances of the cook, who had tried to make all he could out of the slim opportunity that presented itself.

Hope recognized Abu immediately and softly snuffled with pleasure, the heart-shaped end of her nose revolving round and round in her efforts to take in the smell of him again. When she had satisfied her olfactory urges, she presented her backside to the gate and waited for Abu once more to apply the roughened end of his stick to that persistently irritating part of her anatomy, that elusive square centimetre of pork rind that Nuhu had never quite located, lacking as he did a certain precision of empathy. And though Hope of Our Ancestors stood very still while Abu sharpened the point of his stick, still her ridiculous corkscrew of a tail twirled violently with anticipation.

Ibn Sinna's arrival caused an interruption just as Abu had located the focus of ecstasy over Hope's upper right front flank. The pig, disturbed in her most intimate pleasure, walked off with bitter tread to the far side of her pen, from where she glowered at the interloper.

"I have just come to say goodbye," Ibn Sinna said to Likki. He was in drip-dries again.

"Again?" He seemed always to be travelling. And Abu's disclosures had done little to ease her mind.

"I am travelling with Moomin. We leave tonight."

She knew it was pointless to ask where he was going. If he had meant her to know he would already have told her. But, of course, he would *not* tell her. He would not hold himself accountable to her in any way. This attitude he shared with too many other men she had known: the notion that women had no proper claims on men, that they could not command from them either answer or explanation, that women were generally inferior beings who could be indulged when fancy dictated and ignored when they were troublesome. Resisting this ascribed insignificance, Likki questioned him anyway. "Will you be away long?"

He frowned at her before he answered. "As for that, I can't say." It was hardly an answer at all. Then he paused. When he spoke he seemed to have changed the subject.

"Anyway, you may find you have some trouble with your friend."

"My friend, Captain Alistair Araoh?"

"It seems for several days now he is watching Moomin, so he will know I have travelled." To Likki's half-averted face he suggested, "You could stay with my sister?"

"With Ayesha!?" Astonished, Likki faced round and looked him full in the face. She would sooner have visited Captain Araoh. Nevertheless, she blamed her reluctance to move on other motives. "I'm damned if I'm going to change houses just because of the army!"

He nodded as if indulging this whimsical assertion of independence, but then he said, with concern in his voice, "If things become very bad you know you can always leave word at that one shop in the market. Moola will be there every day to help you." Without another word he was gone. Seconds later the Mercedes sent up a cloud of dust from in front of the bungalow. Likki, feeling suddenly forsaken, wandered around to the place from which he had just departed and discovered there, to her dismay, a case of bottled beer nestling at the bottom of the steps.

"God *damn*," she swore softly and stroked Zulu's long, silky ear as if it were a charm.

2

The first week of Ibn Sinna's absence was uneventful. By mutual agreement Likki and Carlotta kept close to home, confining their footsteps to the narrow axis between Bungalow 5 and the classrooms of the school. Carlotta's girls did the necessary shopping for the house, departing in colorful bevies to the market where they flirted with Muslim traders—especially the cloth merchants, with whom one of them would occasionally get lucky.

In the market the girls took the pulse of the town. They gossiped with the orange sellers, haggled with the salt vendors, and heard the bawdiest stories from the woman who sold red onions. From village wives they bought the finest wild mushrooms, vast, succulent fungi tasting of spice. From them they also heard about local miracles: phenomenal cures in Segou, a magical leopard (a black one!) around Dusoko. From the octogenarian herbalist under the nim tree, the girls purchased love philtres, charms against pregnancy, teas to increase their intelligence and seeds to help them see in the dark (so they could study after lights out).

Carlotta and Likki fared well in their self-imposed exile. Nuhu brought round to Likki, to Carlotta's disgust, a daily pot of guinea-corn beer from Farrah's Crocodile, and when Abu came in the afternoons he brought with him gifts from Mother of Issa: small wild cherry-like fruits in bunches like grapes, fresh ginger root, akee apples, and—above all—watermelons. But the present that came on Thursday was the most exquisite—a basket of freshly picked shea-nut fruits, *djuolii*, lying in the nest of their beaded and woven receptacle like so many plum-sized eggs, the fruit as grainy and sweet as crystallized dates, as rich and oily green as avocado.

Life ambled along rather pleasantly until Sunday, when Alistair Araoh turned up on the pretext of wanting to take Carlotta to church. She frequently attended Rev. Aston-Tighes' eleven-o'clock service. The morning was already askew when the captain arrived. Three of the sixth-form girls had gone missing and Carlotta was at a loss to account for them other than by accusing Nuhu of gross and intemperate seduction. Nuhu defended himself vehemently against these charges, hinting that the bursar's first wife might back him up (if only she could do so in private). He was just about to commence broad insinuations against the military when he spotted the army jeep bouncing over the ruts in front of the headmaster's bungalow. "Here come the guilty ones now," said Nuhu, and made himself scarce because he foresaw the direction in which Carlotta would steer the ensuing conversation.

"Good morning, Miss Reap," Captain Araoh hailed Carlotta when he drew near. "And Miss Liddell," he oozed. He was a study this morning in leather and brass, as polished and oiled as an antique Rolls. "I have just stopped by to see if I can offer you a lift to church."

"Not today, I'm afraid," said Carlotta. "Three of my girls are missing."

"Oh. Sorry!" said Captain Araoh, grinning broadly. He had left Jalil, the plumpest of the three, stretching languorously on his rumpled sheets. "Probably they have just dropped down to the market to buy some food. Or *cloth*?" He exchanged a look with his driver, the import of which was not lost on the Girls' Housewarden.

"Let us hope," said Carlotta with emphasis, "that they have not dropped down into some s . . . stranger's bed. To buy food. Or cloth." Carlotta delayed so long on the "s" that Likki really thought she was about to say "soldier."

The captain continued to smile, but turned the talk to other matters. "Where is your friend?" he asked Likki.

"Which friend is that?" she replied, knowing perfectly well whom he meant.

"That tall man with the Mercedes."

"He doesn't tell me where he goes."

"But you know that he has travelled?"

"Of course."

Alistair Araoh's eyes glittered gold. He left his jeep and began to walk slowly round to the back of the bungalow. "A fine *pig!*" he said, stopping by Hope of Our Ancestors' pen with a proprietary air. "I hope you will let me know when you slaughter it." In the army jeep the captain's driver laughed softly to himself.

"It's not our pig," said Likki.

"Oh, yes? And who is it for?"

Likki, regretting she had spoken, declined to answer. "Excuse me," said Captain Araoh, turning to her, "I didn't hear the name."

"It belongs to Abu, Kutu's boy." Carlotta clarified matters for him.

"I see. Thank you." His smile, unctuous and unfailing, grew increasingly sinister as it deepened. He called to his driver, "Sergeant! Is this not one very fine *pig?*"

"*Too* fine!"

The captain came close to Carlotta, almost nuzzling her. "I think you may have one cold beer for my driver?" he suggested.

"Not until I've found my girls," said Carlotta. Her smile now matched his own and was not six inches from it. "I've already reported their absence to the headmaster. If they don't show up soon I will have to notify the police."

"What good are the police?"

"I am responsible for those girls. I have to try every possible means to locate them."

"You could always inform me."

"I just have."

He disliked assertiveness in women any time. "I am sure you may find they have returned here within the hour," he told her with bad grace.

"If they show up here loaded with presents they're in for trouble," said Carlotta in tones meant to discourage the exploitation of schoolgirls by soldiers with full pockets and little sense of responsibility.

"I am sure, Miss Reap, that they are all careful girls who have done nothing wrong," said Alistair Araoh, still very close to Carlotta, still smiling effortlessly. He would take back that piece of indigo batik from Jalil and use it for his next wench.

"Let's hope so," said Carlotta. "I know their families would be most unhappy to learn that their daughters were being ruined by the very men who are supposed to protect them."

The captain's eyes narrowed. "Yes-s," he said with serpentine sibilance as he turned away from her. Then, as he swung up into the jeep, he spoke loudly to his driver. "You know, I am very fond of pork. *Too* fond." And, looking back over his shoulder at the two women, he waved.

"Oh, poor Hope," mourned Likki.

"Maybe he just wants us to sweat."

■

As the captain had predicted, the three missing sixth-form girls were discovered on campus within the hour. Their hands were suspiciously empty for a trio of young ladies who said they had gone to the market to shop for food. Carlotta gave them a sharp lecture on the necessity of getting permission before leaving the school. She also delivered herself of a short sermon on the evils of having soldiers stationed in a community and the need to guard against certain drug-resistant strains of gonorrhoea. Afterwards she put Zulu on a leash and took him for a long walk, as if to put some distance between herself and the events of the morning.

Abu came up to the school while Carlotta was still out walking. He appeared unconcerned about the captain's veiled threats to his prize sow. He said he could easily get protection for Hope from Sima, and two days later brought with him a series of charms and amulets with which he festooned her house, her fence, her gate, and her collar. Anyone who troubled his pig, said Abu, would be inviting the wrath of the shrine in the grove. Lightning would hit him in the first rains, or, if it were the dry season, he might end disgracefully by taking his own life in the bush. His calm certainty of his pig's safety eventually communicated itself to Likki and Carlotta so that they became easy in their minds about Hope.

✖ 3

Likki next saw Ibn Sinna the following Sunday when he came—almost, it seemed, in place of the captain—to take Carlotta to church and drive Likki out to Chegili to visit his mother.

"His mother! Again?" Carlotta was dismayed to have her belief in the venery of African males belied in such an unexceptionable manner.

Carlotta didn't often get to ride in a Mercedes and she dressed for the occasion, taking so long about it that she was nearly late for the service. She wore a ridiculous straw bonnet and her very best blue dress, a fantasy in synthetic flowered silk, which she smoothed over her large thighs all the way to the vicarage.

Although her presence in the car seemed to hamper conversation, when she got out at the church she left behind her only the intemperate silence.

"My mother has long been asking for you," said Ibn Sinna in an effort to break the spell.

"Why?"

"She says she wants to cook monkey for you."

"Monkey!" Likki couldn't eat monkey. It would be like eating a relative—some kind of third cousin in depressed circumstances. She found that Ibn Sinna was grinning hard at her, probably thinking about that bowl of flesh he had brought to the bungalow on the feast of *al Id al Kabir*. Probably his mother hadn't been anywhere near a monkey. Probably she'd been preparing chicken or guinea fowl.

Likki tinkered with the knobs of the car's radio as a way to avoid discussions of meat, but her labours went unrewarded. Only unremitting static issued forth.

"This radio has never worked," apologized Ibn Sinna. "Before I bought the car, it could play any station. But only

one half hour after I drove the car away from the docks, the
radio just finished. Except sometimes, it finds one French
station and tries to play that one."

"A French station." Likki continued to fiddle with the
fine tuning. Ibn Sinna reached out a hand to stop her
manipulations, to end the irritating crackle. Likki started at
his touch. She found herself looking up into his face, into
his ultramarine irises.

"You know you have blue eyes," she said softly, as if in
chastisement.

"I think they are brown."

"No. They're blue. Navy blue."

He laughed at her. "It is your people who have blue
eyes."

"That's what they tell us. You should never believe what
they tell you."

"Is that it?"

"It's true. See for yourself."

He twisted the rear-view mirror, the better to see
himself. While his eyes were averted from the road the
Mercedes jolted over a heavy rut and the elusive French
station suddenly came to life, a wayward transmission from
one of the former French colonies playing a scratched
recording of Ravel's *Pavane*. "Magic fingers," Likki said
wiggling them about. The plaintive melody made the day
seem that much hotter. Ibn Sinna looked reproachfully at
his passenger.

"Is that what your people call music?" he asked her.

"Why not?" *His* favourite reply.

He shook his head. In his world, melancholy was not
something to be fostered.

At Chegili no one was about. Even the goats had shrunk
into shadow to escape from the heat. It was almost March.
The build-up to the rains had begun and the air was dense
with moisture, daily swelling with more as the temperature
climbed into the hundreds. The atmosphere buckled with
its humid burden, lending a quality of mirage to the
landscape. Chegili, clasped to the side of a gentle hill,
wavered in the heat like a reflection of itself in a quiet pond.

Ibn Sinna's mother rested in the shade of a wall along
which several large pots simmered over charcoal fires.

Tendrils of aroma curled promisingly about the courtyard. Even in a reclining position the old woman looked skewed, her limbs splayed without any apparent pattern. When she saw Likki she rose and approached like a disjointed puppet. Without waiting to be invited she plunged her hands into Likki's shoulder bag and removed two packets of cigarettes, three books of matches, and an orange headscarf. Then she showered her benefactress with unintelligible expressions of gratitude and made her sit next to her on her bench through an endless hour during which Ibn Sinna made himself scarce and the heat grew palpably more oppressive.

Time crawled. Likki watched for Ibn Sinna and wondered as she did so if it were an insult to be deserted by her host or if it were a mark of honour thus to be entrusted to his mother's companionship. As dinner neared completion women began to pound cooked yam in heavy wooden mortars, their pestles flying with an insistent contrapuntal rhythm. Similar sounds were coming from all over Chegili. Soon the yam began to lose its mashed-potato mealiness and took on the consistency of bread dough. Sticky and glutinous it adhered to itself in a rubbery mass in the mortar where the pestle strokes now registered with a gluey note and the wad of yam contracted against itself with a slap like that of busy thighs on a hot afternoon.

Ibn Sinna wandered into the courtyard just as the meal was being ladled into bowls. He was making a face as if at some private joke. "So," he said to Likki, "you are now going to eat monkey." He pulled up a small three-legged stool to sit facing her across their dinner, which his niece had placed on the ground between them in a green enamel dish. Two large portions of pounded yam, smooth and rounded like mammoth dumplings, gleamed suggestively under the soup. Chunks of meat dotted the surface.

"Monkey," said Ibn Sinna, picking a piece out of the soup and holding it out to her. "You eat it. It will make you strong."

"Abu told me that only witches ate monkey."

"You shouldn't always listen to what Abu says."

"It was Abu who suggested I drive around with you," she reminded him.

"Is that why you are here?"

"What other reason would I have?"

"Is that it?"

"I certainly wouldn't come here to eat monkey," averred Likki.

"But you said you wanted to know our ways. So now I am here to show you. My own mother has worked hard to prepare your dish and now you say you will not eat. She will be disgraced! Everyone in Chegili will be talking about how the white woman insulted her." He was holding out to Likki something that looked distressingly like an arm.

"You know what you're doing, don't you? You're blackmailing me."

"Is that it?"

He handed her the little arm. Likki took a breath and then nibbled. "I can hardly taste it," she told him. It was drowning in cayenne. A mercy, perhaps.

Other aspects of the meal also demanded fortitude. For example, it was considered childish and rude to chew the pounded yam and so Likki struggled to swallow each bite whole without applying her teeth. Ibn Sinna was aware of her difficulties and watched her efforts with amused disdain. But he said nothing. It was not the way in Kpama to talk at meals, to linger over food, drawing out the conversation in the relaxed pauses between appetite and satiety. In Kpama people ate against the clock and against the other six people sharing their dish. They stuffed as much as they could into their stomachs in the shortest possible time. It could all be over in five minutes, a meal that had taken the better part of a day to prepare—if you included the time spent fetching water and firewood. Likki wondered if they made love with the same inordinate haste. Without thinking, she frowned.

"Is there something wrong?" Ibn Sinna asked.

"What could be wrong?"

∎

Later they walked up the hill again to look at the house Ibn Sinna was building. "It will soon be finished," he told her.

"Already?" It was only a couple of weeks since she had seen the lines marked out on the ground with string. Now, he claimed, little but the roof was lacking. To have raced through construction so quickly seemed almost an impropriety, considering the pace at which most of Kpama proceeded.

Sceptical, Likki followed him to the upper edge of Chegili, where she saw that the house was, indeed, nearly finished. The walls were already between five and six feet high, and only two more layers of concrete blocks would be added. But the house, still standing open to the sky, bore a curious resemblance to a ruin. Chalky smells of drying cement hung in the heat along with the resinous tang of lumber left lying in the sun. Likki felt suddenly playful. On a long-ago summer, near her childhood home forty miles north of Philadelphia, her best friend's father had built his own log cabin—from basement to chimney pot. He had cut the logs himself from the timber that stood in his seven-acre woodland, right in the heart of Pennsylvania's best farmland. And this project, which had lasted the better part of five months, had furnished Likki and Nan with an endlessly changing and versatile playground quite similar to the one in which she now stood. They had been the envy of the township, since Likki was generally recognized as co-proprietor of the establishment by virtue of being Nan's "best friend."

Bright with the memory of the envy of former schoolmates, Likki clambered up onto some scaffolding, where she surprised a tired nanny goat. The creature bolted along the planks and then leapt to the top of a wall, bleating with the indignation of those undeservedly deprived of their rest. Likki chased after it in a half-serious way until she came to grief on an improperly supported timber, which tipped her down six feet into a corner filled with gritty rubbish and nails.

Ibn Sinna waited in silence for a moment to make sure she was not badly injured and then tried with small success to repress a smirk. "Chasing a goat!" he chided and leaned out an arm to help her, for she was penned in behind several large beams.

"I'm perfectly capable of getting up myself," said Likki, refusing his arm as she wished she could refuse other things he had not yet asked her for.

"Is that it?"

"What are you standing there laughing for?"

"Am I laughing? I am only trying to help you."

"You *are* laughing." He was.

"If I had known you were so fond of goat," he said, "my mother could have prepared *that* for you. Instead of monkey."

"Shit!" she said as she pulled free of the beams.

"Are you angry?"

"Of course I'm angry. I don't like it when people laugh at my injuries."

"Where are your injuries?"

Likki looked down at her knees. They smarted and the skin was broken. But really she could boast little more than a few scratches covered in a white talcum of cement. "I just fell into that corner. Anything might have happened to me."

"But nothing has happened."

He saw his lack of sympathy irritated her. "You want me to put on a long face because of something that *might* have happened to you, is that it? But then I would look just as foolish as you do now. After all, something can *always* have happened to you. The car might have turned over on the way to Chegili. Or you might have been hit by lightning yesterday afternoon. So why should I put on a long face all the time because you have managed to escape all these things?"

"I'm not asking for a constant funeral. Just maybe a minute and a half of consideration. It would help if you stopped laughing."

"You run about after a goat like a small girl. Then you fall down just like a small girl. And you weep, also like a small girl. But you yourself are a grown woman and you ask me not to laugh because you haven't hurt yourself?"

"God *damn!*"

"You swear too much," he instructed.

"I'll swear just as much as I please. It's a free country."

"Is this a free country?" Unexpected shadow crept into his voice. The laughter disappeared, taking with it other carefree things.

"That's what we say at home when someone's giving us a hard time." They had slipped into something deeper now.

"And your country, is that free?"

"That's what they tell us."

"Who tells you that?"

"The people who run the country. Who else?"

"Then it's the same as here."

"Except for the army," she reminded him.

"But your country, does it not also have an army?"

"Yes, but it doesn't come marching into my bedroom at three o'clock in the morning." That was the visit she most resented: the intrusive search for burglars when she was in her nightgown, vulnerable, dream-drowsy.

"There are other bedrooms where it marches," said Ibn Sinna. "Most recently, Vietnamese bedrooms. But before that Korean and Japanese bedrooms, German bedrooms. Italian bedrooms."

"That was war," Likki avowed, although it was not a point she would have made outside the confines of the present argument. "There's a difference between war and politics."

"And what is the difference?"

Likki forgot her lines, paused long enough for it to look very much like defeat.

"You see?" said Ibn Sinna triumphantly.

"I don't see anything," said Likki refusing to concede him the victory. Then she remembered. "The difference is bloodshed," she told him.

Ibn Sinna shook his head. "Many places have bloodshed without war."

■

At the house of Ibn Sinna's mother, people were beginning to stir after their afternoon siestas. They regarded Likki's bloodied knees with concern, but any trace of alarm they may have registered on her behalf vanished as soon as they heard about the goat. Ibn Sinna's mother listed more to starboard than ever, and the smaller children began to play at being goats, bleating and leaping about on imaginary walls.

"What did you have to tell them for?" Likki complained.

"It was my own mother who asked me."

"You could have left out the part about the goat." Likki winced. Mother of Ibn Sinna was cleaning out the scratches for her, deftly pursuing gravelly bits of plaster and stone that had worked their way under her skin. Likki had never been good about pain, had always reached for the aspirin bottle at the first sign of a headache.

"You want me to lie to my own mother?"

"That's not a lie. That's leaving something out."

"But everyone knows that leaving something out is the best lie of all."

Likki reflected that within twenty-four hours the entire secondary school would know all about this episode.

Mother of Ibn Sinna continued her ministrations. She had by her feet a jar of the most dubious-looking liquid imaginable—a viscous green juice that might have been pressed from the skins of toadstools. With this she began to bathe Likki's abrasions.

"You don't have to worry," said Ibn Sinna. "My mother was taught by a famous herbalist in Kalembelebiri. She knows everything. She is a midwife in these villages."

Mother of Ibn Sinna nodded emphatically. "Midwife" was one of eleven English nouns she recognized.

"The hospital asked her to go and work for them there, but she wouldn't go." Ibn Sinna was obviously proud of the recognition of his mother's curative prowess by this citadel of Western medicine.

"Why wouldn't she go?"

"She says it is a place of death and wizards. Women fear to go there to give birth. They fear for their children and themselves. They would prefer to come here to Chegili. Anyone who has a difficult time giving birth, they always come here to Chegili."

Likki was silent, wondering what midwifery had to do with her knees, wondering how a woman in labour could hike out to Chegili from Kpama.

"She taught Ayesha everything she knows," continued Ibn Sinna. "Both of them, they can fix anything."

"Can they fix people, too?"

"Who do you want to fix?"

"The army captain."

"I thought we were fixing that army captain now."

"Sure. Until you go travelling again with Moomin. Then he'll be right back at my door."

"Well," remarked Ibn Sinna, "that is because he knows we are not sleeping together. He still hopes for some comfort from you."

"How does he know who I sleep with?"

"Everybody knows."

"God *damn*," said Likki, remembering a similar sort of conversation with John Lavender.

"You swear too much."

•

After the heat of the day, the evening was silky, forgiving, and without haste. The Mercedes crawled back to Kpama at the pace of a weary labourer.

In the shallow valleys a handful of drought-resistant frogs sang like small bells or Christmas chimes, their voices out of place in the vast and heat-wracked savannah. Bats plinked in the trees like pieces of broken machinery. In the car the arguments of the afternoon had died. For once the silence was calm. In the twilight that fell from the sky Ibn Sinna reached out across the seat for Likki's hand and held it fast. He did not let it go until he reached the lorry park in Kpama where he had to change down two gears to avoid hitting a cyclist with a set of kitchen doors balanced on his head.

As though reluctant to approach the end of its journey, the Mercedes lost momentum climbing the hill to the secondary school. It was barely moving by the time it pulled up to the bungalow. Carlotta and John Lavender sat in the doorway engaged in an animated discussion, to the chagrin of the occupants of the car, who glanced at each other in dismay. When the Mercedes halted, Likki sat for some seconds before opening the door. She looked questioningly at Ibn Sinna, full of something she refused to ask him.

"I will come tomorrow," he said softly. He drove away as slowly as he had 'come, lest anyone should think he had more reason now to hurry than before he discharged his passenger.

"Have fun?" Carlotta asked pointedly.

"Fun?"

"Did you enjoy yourself?" John rephrased the question,

noting a certain truculence in the expression of his forme
mistress.

"Well enough," said Likki. The three of them stared a
each other. Likki waited for the other two to move aside s
that she could pass through the doorway.

"Likki, I think we should talk," said John.

"I don't," she replied, shoving her way between them
They had not moved to make way for her.

John rose and followed Likki, as harassing and pa
tronizing as a distracted husband. "Likki, you shouldn't ge
mixed up with a man like that."

"A man like what?"

"A man like Ibn Sinna."

"I'm not 'mixed up' with him." From one point of view
this was nine-tenths of her trouble.

"I don't mean because of his race. I don't mean becaus
he's already married—twice." John couldn't resist that littl
barb. "It's other things. . . . Stories one picks up. He'
dangerous. You'll get in trouble."

"Good! What kind of trouble?"

John found he was wasting his eloquence on the close
door of Likki's bedroom. "Come out of there. I can't talk t
you through this piece of African plywood."

"I'll be out in a little while," said Likki. Tears stood in he
eyes. A fine job she'd made of escaping. Seventeen month
on the run and here she was back at the brink of th
identical problem she had come away to forget, her hear
now beating as fast as any teenager's at the thought of thos
big blue-black eyes. Maybe Carlotta was right. Maybe sh
did lack character. Maybe she was just grabbing at anythin
that floated past to fill the void of Roger's departure. In
year and a half, little in her life had changed except th
scenery.

■

Though conducted under a flag of truce, supper was a
uneasy affair. Carlotta, possibly for purposes of distraction
had gone overboard on the food, copying a recipe o
Eleanor Aston-Tighes' for chicken pot-pie. Thick creamy
gravy bubbled up through little vents in the crust. The pi
looked delectable, but inside most of the chicken wa

underdone. It was local meat and needed two hours in a pressure cooker before it could be chewed. Odd vegetables floated through the sauce. "Try this one," Carlotta kept saying. "It tastes just like lima beans. And this one. This one is just like peas."

Likki forbore to groan, but John was enthusiastic. "Yes, quite!" He speared a cylindrical, orange-coloured nugget and waved it aloft on his fork.

"It's a carrot," Likki told him before he could launch the question.

"*Is* it a carrot?" John asked Carlotta.

"Yes. Imagine, real carrots grown right here in Kpama. Eleanor got the seeds from the Catholic mission."

"How ecumenical," said Likki. The other two frowned at her.

Likki found the pie inedible. As a last resort she reached for the pepper shaker and doused her plate with cayenne.

"Oh, my God!" cried Carlotta at this insult to *haute cuisine*.

"Nothing against your pie," lied Likki. "I just can't eat in this heat without pepper."

"I think you went a little overboard," suggested John.

"This from the man who put Worcestershire sauce on his pancakes?"

"I only did that once," John reminded her.

"You told me you learned it in the Boy Scouts."

"I didn't want you to laugh at my brainstorm."

"I wouldn't have minded so much if you hadn't put it on my pancakes as well."

"What else was there to put on them?"

"Margarine and sugar."

"Sugar was short."

"Okay. Just margarine," said Likki.

"You're kidding."

Likki thought about this. "Yes, you're right. I was kidding." West African margarine was something no Westerner could find palatable. John called it a petroleum by-product, although actually it was made from palm nuts. What alchemy transformed the turtle-soup viscosity of palm oil into a substance resembling lemon curd was something no one seemed to know. No one seemed to know where it was done, either, although rumour had it that it all took place in England, at the docks in Cheapside. That sounded probable. It would have made too much sense to process the oil where it grew.

They neared the end of the supper, and Carlotta got up for some glasses and a bottle. "Have some brandy," she offered, pushing one of her cherished fifths of Remy Martin across the table.

"What's this going to be, the Last Supper?" asked Likki in some dismay. The bottle was a bad sign.

John took this as his cue. "Likki, you have got to end this little pantomime with Ibn Sinna."

"Why?"

"Look, believe me, this isn't sour grapes. Probably he's a super fellow. It's just that he's dangerous," John explained.

"Dangerous to whom?"

"To you."

"What's he going to do to me? Knife me in the car? Poison my water? Abduct me and hold me for ransom?" Now *that* might be nice.

"Don't be silly."

"*I'm* not being silly."

"We have reason to believe that he's trying to overthrow the government."

Likki stared at him open-mouthed for some seconds while the meaning of his words descended on her. And then laughter slowly launched itself deep in her stomach and, catching its stride, rippled upwards out of her throat as if it were a fountain.

"It's not funny, Likki."

"Oh, yes it is."

"*I* don't think it's funny," said Carlotta. "There's nothing funny about a revolution."

"Revolution!" echoed Likki, almost delirious with glee.

John became cross. "I'm not joking," he said.

"I know you're not." For her that was the funniest part. "Who told you all this?" Likki finally asked him.

John looked up warily. "Several people. Why?"

"Just wondering," said Likki. "Several people like Ayesha, for instance?"

"Among others, yes."

"I thought so."

"What's that supposed to mean?"

"It means it isn't true. It means you've been set up."

"You know," said John, "you're obsessed with that woman. You're obsessed with the idea that she hates you."

"She does hate me. And I'm not obsessed."

"The army is watching Ibn Sinna," intoned Carlotta. "All. The. Time." Her voice was ominous. "And they watch him for a *reason*."

"Bullshit. You only believe what you want to believe. What proof have you got?" demanded Likki.

They were silent, facing her.

"You see?"

"Likki, we're not lying."

"I never said you were. I said you were misinformed. Probably misinformed on purpose. But even if I did believe you, what difference would it make?"

"You'd leave him alone," said John. "You'd go easy. Slip out easy."

"I doubt it."

"You would. You know you would," said Carlotta. "If you didn't you'd have the whole army after you."

"I have the whole army after me already. It was to lose the whole army that I turned to Ibn Sinna in the first place."

John tried a softer approach. "It's for your own good. Your own safety. The man is being watched. Washington won't like it."

"What has Washington got to do with it?"

"Just about everything if you hang around with someone who's trying to topple a friendly government," said Carlotta.

"Since when does this country have a friendly government? I suppose that creased little ogre who sits in charge in the capital is the friendly government? A wrinkled prune of a colonel who lets his junior officers ride roughshod over his people?"

"He is an internationally accepted head of state."

"So is Pinochet."

"Are we going to start on that again?"

"We can stop any time you want."

John saw by a narrowing of pupil and an infusion of colour in Likki's eyes that she was now truly angry and he was willing to drop the argument, at least temporarily. But Carlotta had to have her say. "If you won't think of your own safety, think of mine. When that crazy army man comes floating up the road with loaded pistols, who's going to be standing next to you in his sights? Me. And if I know anything at all about men, that one would as soon shoot as fuck." This was strong language for Carlotta.

"I'll move out," volunteered Likki. "Then you won't be compromised."

"Where could you go?" asked John in cynical tones.

"Maybe I'll take up residence at Kutu's," said Likki, just to tease him; but from a secretive expression that crossed his face she divined that she would be unwelcome there. She looked at Carlotta and there, too, she saw something furtive, a fleeting embarrassment that Carlotta strove to conceal. So they were lovers. "How long has *this* been going on?" she demanded.

"That really is none of your business, Likki," John reminded her.

"But *my* affairs are everyone's business. Even Washington's."

"I keep telling you, we're worried about your safety."

"I'm worried about *my* safety." Carlotta adjusted the fine-tuning of his words.

"Then why don't *you* move down to Kutu's?" suggested Likki.

"Don't tell me I should move out because *you* are jealous," said Carlotta, her face ugly with the things she was sure of.

"I'm not jealous," said Likki.

"Why not?" lamented John, but he received no answer.

Minutes later Likki walked with silent and calculated slowness out of the bungalow, trailing clouds of angry vapours behind her like veils of dark silk. Zulu saw them and howled. John just said, "She's in one of her tempers," and wrote it off to jealousy and childish petulance.

•

"Nasara, you are hot!" exclaimed Wednesday when, without even a perfunctory greeting, Likki strode into Last Calabash as though wearing seven-league boots. "Nasara, what is wrong?" Wednesday's voice curled with sympathy. She filled a giant calabash. "Here, I am buying one pot for you," she said, placing a large crock on the earth at Likki's feet. Such generosity perforce loosens the tongue.

"I have quarrelled in my house," said Likki.

"About the man," stated Wednesday.

Likki had been long enough in Kpama not to be surprised that her private affairs were public property. Still, this time, she was mildly curious to know how Wednesday had got hold of the information so quickly. Wednesday told her that John had been there earlier in the day complaining about how she "moved" with Ibn Sinna. "He said if you move everywhere with the man like that you may have trouble."

"He said Ibn Sinna himself is in trouble," said Likki and she watched Wednesday's face for a reaction.

"Ibn Sinna? When Ibn Sinna is in trouble, it is his enemies you want to feel sorry for."

"Maybe John is only jealous."

"He still thinks you are his wife," Wednesday agreed.

"But he has another wife now," said Likki, "the other Nasara woman."

"The fat one?" Wednesday grinned. For her, too, it was ludicrous.

"Yes, the fat one."

"Those two Nasara people," Wednesday told her. "Don't you mind them. At all."

Nuhu arrived at Last Calabash shortly afterwards. In the recoil from her anger, Likki drank with him to excess and, as she had on other occasions, stayed on with him until Wednesday ran out of beer and struggled home behind him after midnight, wondering how he could see so well in the dark.

4

The bungalow was mercifully in darkness when Likki arrived home. Thief-like, she slipped through the door and down the long hallway, pausing only once, outside Carlotta's bedroom, to see if she could distinguish from the sounds of muffled breathing whether one sleeper or two lay within.

It was just after three that the screaming began, a horrible high-pitched squealing from Hope of Our Ancestors' pigsty. The screams were followed by anguished grunts and moans of distress, both in proportion to the pig's great size. By the living-room window Zulu began to howl into the night. Outside there were thumps, thrashings, deep guttural coughs, and then the screaming again.

Likki collided with John and Carlotta in the darkness of the hallway. "Oh, my God. Oh, my God. Where's a light?" shrieked Carlotta. "Oh, poor Hope."

John lit a match. "Get a lantern," he ordered, and Likki stumbled into the kitchen, made clumsy by haste and the unmetabolised beer still in her system. "Hurry," said John. "I've only got one more match after this one."

Zulu, still howling, scratched hopelessly at the back door as if he thought he could dig his way out. Terrible squeals streamed from the pen outside as though a flood of agony had been loosed there. Zulu's remodelled doghouse shook and flapped with unseen struggle. More moans were heard and hurried voices, tersely giving orders.

"Oh, my God, they're killing her! Oh, my God. Hurry!" Carlotta held her chubby arms and rocked herself in the hall. "Oh, my God!"

"Carlotta, shut up and open the door," ordered Likki, who had found the lantern at last. It flickered into life, revealing three faces damp with anxiety. But even with a light, the lock on the back door proved impossible to decipher. It seemed an hour since the screaming had started. With one mind the trio turned and raced out the front, then around the bungalow to Hope of Our Ancestors' pen. There was an ominous stillness as they approached. Zulu, lagging behind with his usual cowardice, whined softly.

When they reached the fence, John held up the lantern and the three of them peered into the darkness. All that was visible was a clump of bloodied straw.

"Oh, my God! She's dead! Oh, my God!" whimpered Carlotta. "They've killed her-rrrr." Her voice hung on the last word until she had made of it the funeral wail of West African women.

"She is not dead," said a voice from the obscurity of the pighouse.

"Nuhu, is that you?" asked Likki anxiously.

"You can come in," said another voice, belonging to Mr. Bai. "The pig is just fine. Very fine. In fact, she is giving birth."

"Giving birth!" said John.

"Oh, come on," said Carlotta.

And Likki said, "Oh, my God."

The three whites stepped tentatively through the gate of Hope's pen as if they were come to an oracle's shrine where only the ritually pure might enter. Nuhu laughed at them. "It's only birth," he said.

"I never saw anything born," said Likki.

As if in response to her words, Hope began to moan again, her abdomen contracting, her legs thrashing spasmodically at the walls of her house.

"Why is she doing that?" Likki asked Nuhu.

"She is in pain."

"I thought only women had pain at birth."

"Who told you that?"

It had been her Sunday-school teacher. "The church told us. They said it was in the Bible."

"This thing is not in any Bible," said Nuhu, who had never read one. "They only told you that to make you sad because you are a woman."

Hope of Our Ancestors began to grunt, throaty, cough-like sounds, as if she were choking. These sounds came closer and closer together, giving the impression of interior acceleration. They ended abruptly as a pinkish missile, bloodied and slippery, shot forth from her loins. Hope sighed, then heaved her labouring bulk around to where she could tend her infant, licking membrane and fluid from its face, chewing the umbilical in an act of final severance. Her nose revolved slowly round and round as she snuffled a tender welcome to this newest creature of the night. The little piglet, with its first lungful of air, greeted Kpama with the high-pitched squeals that had roused Bungalow 5 in alarm.

"Oh, my God, isn't he cute?" gushed Carlotta, with tears welling up in her eyes. Envy of Hope's maternity.

"This is the third one," said Nuhu. When they searched they found two other piglets pressed up together in a corner, sleeping, as it were, in each other's arms.

■

Hope had twelve piglets in all. Carlotta and Likki, weary as any midwives from a midnight delivery, were easily diverted from the classroom lectures next day by students eager for details of the wonderful birth.

There was a celebration. Nuhu and John brought up guinea-corn beer from Farrah's. The bursar's wives cooked food. Mr. Bai searched in his closet and found a bottle of Bacardi. And Mother of Issa, for the first time since Likki had known her, left the confines of Kpama and came in person to greet the newborn creatures. "Twelve," she said solemnly, "like the twelve Apostles," and thus showed off her knowledge of religions other than Islam.

Abu, of course, was beside himself, though he realized that his debt to Sima had multiplied substantially. By anyone's calculations, Hope must already have been pregnant when Abu brought her to live behind Bungalow 5, and Sima was far too canny not to have been aware of this fact. On the other hand—to save face—Abu *had* to pretend that he'd known about it all along, though he hadn't, which involved him in a series of elaborate self-contradictions. He told John Lavender, "See! Already I am a rich man. Soon I am a cattle breeder!"

"Don't count your pigs before they're born," counselled John.

"Party pooper," chided Likki from the safety of her third rum and Coke.

"Soon each pig is seventy pounds!" Abu continued to plot his glory. He meant seventy pounds worth of money, not avoirdupois.

"Sell them first, *then* count your gold," said John, beginning to fall in love with his role as the voice of reason.

"Soon I will get my cow! One very *fine* cow. Mother to hundreds she will be." Liking the sound of his words, Abu repeated them, considering in his own mind whether it would not make a fine name for an animal. "Mother to Hundreds. Mother to Hundreds." She would be a thin, dun-coloured beast with ugly horns and a vicious temper. No leopard would dare come near her. "Hey!" he called aloud. "Mother to Hundreds, you wait there. I am just coming for you!" And Abu allowed himself a discreet prance and a caper, for in his mind his herd was far advanced in number and he was already contemplating a name for his second son. By Comfort, of course.

"Abu, you shouldn't build up your hopes," said John Lavender.

"Oh, leave him alone," Likki scolded when Abu had gone.

"He'll only be crushed, Likki."

"How do you know he'll be crushed? Maybe he'll do it. Maybe he'll do everything he's been dreaming about. Maybe you'll come back here twenty years from now and find that Abu has seven sons and is Ruler of Kpama. You never know, he might even become the head of state." She said the last part deliberately and slowly, to taunt him.

"It's not really very likely, is it? The child is almost completely illiterate."

"He's not illiterate. He's in the fifth form of primary school."

"That's almost the same as being illiterate."

"Well, the Ruler of Kpama is illiterate. So that's hardly a disqualification for office."

"Abu will never be head of state." Rubbing it in.

"He would be a decided improvement on the current model." Fat old Colonel Pruneface.

"Don't be ridiculous, Likki."

"I mean it."

"Likki, can't you ever be serious?"

"See? There you go again. Losing the argument and asking me to be serious."

"But you're not talking seriously. You're being silly, and asking me to give credence to all sorts of ridiculous hypotheses."

When John was cornered he often sought refuge in big words.

"All right." Likki relented slightly. "I'll admit I'm not taking the line of the worldly wise. But I mean what I say. I'm talking to you straight. Really, it's *you* who aren't serious."

"What the hell does *that* mean?"

"You don't take the people here seriously. They're just two-dimensional fictions as far as you're concerned. You come here and breeze through Kpama for a couple of years of so-called research—read: 'paid vacation.' Then you breeze back home to make your academic living by writing about people you'll never see again. People whose economic and political and personal problems you dismiss as unimportant—not serious—even now, while you're standing among them, living with them, face to face with their distress. Ten years from now you won't even remember that there were real human beings in Kpama. Kutu and Mother of Issa, Ayesha, Moomin, Abu—they'll all have been reduced to a series of nasal glides, consonantal elisions, and glottal stops. On a map."

"That's not fair."

"Isn't it? You take all sorts of make-believe about Kpama seriously. Or you *want* to. You want to take the Goromo seriously. You want to take the shrine seriously. But you don't and won't take seriously Abu's fighting hope that he can win. You try to kill it off on the pretext of giving him advice."

"Advice like, 'Don't think about becoming head of state?'" An unpleasant sarcasm teased the edge of his voice.

"Advice like don't count your pigs before they're sold."

"That happens to be *good* advice!"

"It's poisonous!"

He would convince her. "Likki, do you know what Abu's chances really are? Are you familiar with the facts? Do you know how many piglets survive in this area? No? Go and look up the figures at the veterinary office. They certainly are not cheerful. And do you know the cost of getting the pigs to market? The possibility of theft? Of disease wiping out the whole litter overnight? The possibility of having all the piglets stolen even if they can be carried to market?

"And when it comes to cattle! What are Abu's chances of buying a healthy heifer? What man in his right mind would part with a healthy heifer? At *any* price? Only a very close relative would help Abu start a herd. But Abu has no close relatives. He has no family at all. Sure, Kutu took him in—as charity. For religion's sake. Helping the orphan. Kutu expects seventy-times-seven, in the hereafter, for every grain of rice Abu eats in that house. You don't know. You don't live there. Kutu doesn't give a damn what happens to that child. Sure, he'll make certain he doesn't starve, but he'll never set him up in life. Abu is a nobody. He doesn't count as much as your little fingernail. His chances of marrying Comfort are nil. A big fat zero. And all Abu's schemes, and all your schemes, and all Ayesha's schemes—*they* are the real make-believe. They're just a big fairytale."

"Oh, you bastard," said Likki with loathing.

"What's going on?" Carlotta had waddled over to them, sensing that feelings were running high and wanting to know just what kind of feelings they were. "What's going on?"

"I was just saying that Abu should give up some of his pipe-dreams," said John, watering it down considerably.

"You were saying that dreams are a burden," Likki corrected him.

"I was suggesting that he reconcile himself to reality."

"You know what it is, don't you, John? You're *jealous*."

"Just what am I supposed to be jealous of?"

"You're jealous of Abu's world. Of its possibilities—its goblins, and shrines, and sorcerers, and spells." Likki

paused, then added with spiteful glee, "That's why you try
so hard to believe in all that stuff."

"That's not fair!" He said it again.

"You admire all the *silly* things about Kpama, all the
things that aren't important."

"I see," said John, with some annoyance. "And *you*, no
doubt, appreciate the real essence."

"Of course."

John looked as if he were going to say "you bloody little
bitch," but instead he asked what the real essence was.

Likki understood that he was trying to push her into
saying something stupid or extreme but the Bacardi won
out over caution. She told John he was jealous of a world
where people looked the hard things of life right in the face
every day of their lives and still made room for laughter;
jealous of people who owned nothing but who lived with a
drama and an intensity he'd lost when he was three. "And
most of all," she said, drawing to a close, "you are jealous of
Abu, of his so-called fairy-tale hope that he can live out his
dream: become rich and marry the princess of his heart."

"The princess of his heart." John repeated Likki's words
with excruciating condescension and gave her his most
patronizing upper-class smile.

Likki wanted to wound him then, and she let out all that
she had been holding back. "And the thing that really gets
you," she told John, "is that Abu will be able to do it all
without—as part of the bargain—mortgaging his soul to a
career track and his heart to pop psychology. You're jealous
because Abu will live out his life as a boisterous, irrepres-
sible, three-dimensional human being while all you have to
look forward to is forty years of dust off a library shelf and a
cremation that nobody goes to."

The last barb found its mark. John coloured visibly and
Carlotta's jaw dropped. Likki walked away from them with a
wicked sense of satisfaction. At home she would have
needed a lot more Bacardi before she indulged her desire
to hurt someone. But here in Africa she had become used
to a tougher breed of human beings: people not so easily
wounded, people whose sense of self-identity was unassail-
able, people who said *everything* in an argument, who

held nothing back, people who let the most distasteful home truths roll off their backs like water.

Unfortunately, among her own kind this was not the case. There existed instead a domain of restraint, a preserve of private truth into which no one intruded unless they wished to destroy. A citadel, the retreat of a fragile creature—which she had just violated.

∎

Ibn Sinna came later that afternoon. Moola was with him and tapped his walking-stick rapidly when he was shown the newborn piglets. He had a lot to say, in Kpamé, to Ibn Sinna, which the latter only summarized for Likki. "Moola says Abu will soon be a rich man. Then, when he is looking to begin his herd, Moola himself will sell him a fine young heifer. Even now he has a calf in mind, a dun-coloured creature, delivered of the meanest-tempered cow with the longest horns in all of Kpama."

But who among them could know of Abu's dream?

When there was no one to notice, Ibn Sinna bent to Likki and told her she was "hot."

"I seem to find a quarrel in my house every afternoon."

"Then is it not time to leave that house?"

"And go where?"

"I am taking Moola to Kalembelebiri. He wants to go looking there for one black leopard. You can come with us."

Likki hesitated.

"The place is not far. Eight miles—less if you walk. But even if we go by car we will have to walk some part of the way."

Still Likki hesitated, until, from the far side of the bungalow, came Carlotta's didactic, stentorian tones. "Sure, I'll come," said Likki.

∎

At Kpama the Mercedes turned east, past Jebendebiri, Bakprere, Ngmaangmu, and finally Dusoko, where it stopped. Where the road stopped. The villages lay somnolently in the basin of a broad, shallow valley, each of them close to the stream bed from which, even in the dry season, lush groves of riverine trees drew up the moisture that gave them their great size and fullness. Cattle stood ankle-deep in water, muzzles in the stream, or else browsing along the banks. Mists hung in the hollows. In the dusk, across the open fields of harvested guinea corn and millet, the villages reposed like a series of views by Constable, picturesque enough to evoke an ache of nostalgia in the heart of any anglophile.

At Dusoko the three travellers left the Mercedes in the courtyard of a cousin of Ibn Sinna's first wife's father and proceeded, as etiquette required, to greet the chief. He was an alarmingly light individual, a rich shade of *café au lait*, though he swore there wasn't a drop of European blood in his background. Instead he blamed his complexion on a Berber beauty acquired in Khartoum by one of his great-great-grandfathers, a devout Muslim who had made the hazardous pilgrimage to Mecca at the end of the eighteenth century, braving wild beasts and companies of bloodthirsty brigands. The excursion had taken the old fellow the better part of twenty years to complete. Near Alexandria, he had halted to allow his green-eyed concubine to rest at the time of her delivery. While he waited for his son's birth, anxiously pacing the shingle of Aboukir Bay, with the moon just past full, he witnessed the Battle of the Nile—Nelson's victory over the Franch and the terrible explosion of the *L'Orient*. This battle was an event still preserved in the oral traditions of this ancestor's descendants, though with an emphasis that might have surprised those who had taken part in it.

From Dusoko the three travellers followed a footpath that led uphill. Though they climbed only some three hundred feet, there was a noticeable drop in temperature. The path fell off into a small valley, then climbed again. Other paths forked off to right and left at frequent intervals, but though there seemed to be no obvious landmarks, Moola never faltered, never paused at an intersection of tracks. By a huge baobab at the top of the second hill, they rested. "Not far now," the old man said, pointing down into the next valley as if he would show off the clustered roofs of houses; but it was long past sundown and they could see nothing.

When they arrived in Kalembelebiri they again went to greet the chief. In contrast to his counterpart in Dusoko

this man was recklessly dark. And recklessly round—almost
to the point of being spindle-shaped. When he heard that
visitors were coming, he hastily donned his hat, which his
sparse-haired sister found for him. This sister, Gbendlele, a
lean and childless woman, had the air of one who strongly
disapproved of the way the world ran itself.

"Hiiiiiyyyyyy!!!" wailed Gbendlele as the visitors entered
the chief's reception room. "A white woman!" and the old
lady raced from the room because her breasts were not
covered and she knew that whites thought them every bit
as shameful as genitals, although what could be erotic about
her flat leathery dugs, milkless as they had ever been, she
failed to understand. Perhaps the whites had dirty habits.
Perhaps they practised abominations.

She returned to her brother's reception room several
minutes later, fully dressed and with an excess of dignity—
as a cat may do when it has slipped upon the floor. Though
she carried in her hands a bowl of shea-nut fruits for the
visitors, still it was easy to see from her stance that she was
displeased to have been caught with her shirt up. She
retreated to a stool in a far corner of the room and sat near
her usual companion, a deaf boy who always smiled. From
there she scrutinized her brother's guests, particularly
Likki, for it was obvious to Gbendlele that the white
woman wanted Ibn Sinna. And he, cool dog that he was,
pretended not to notice.

The chief of Kalembelebiri, used to having Gbendlele in
the corner, paid no attention to her, but the eyes of his
guests strayed into the gloom at the old woman's end of the
room. They could make out very little, but eventually,
when his eyes had adjusted to the darkness, Ibn Sinna
began to joke with Gbendlele in the bawdy fashion that was
the custom in Kpama. "Grandmother, is it you who will
warm my bed?"

"Make me a hot fire and I will do that for you," she
answered, pretending to shiver as though it were still
harmattan.

"Is that it?"

"You don't worry, tonight your bed will be *hot*!"

"But I won't sleep here tonight."

"Oh? Why not?"

"The white woman will want to go home."

"If the white woman finds you in her bed, that will feel like home to her. Better than home."

"She will find the place here is not fine. She will find she needs a mattress," said Ibn Sinna.

"Hey!" corrected Gbendlele. "You are telling lies. It is a man she needs, not a mattress."

Moola said to the chief, "Where can I get a grandmother like that?"

"You are too old, my friend," lamented the chief of Kalembelebiri.

Moola shook his head and sucked his teeth. Gbendlele changed the subject. She wanted to know what Moola was doing in her village.

"I have come looking for this leopard," he told her.

"The black one?" she asked.

"Yes."

"You will never find it," said Gbendlele.

"Why is that?"

"Only women see it."

The chief told his sister to mind her tongue, but Moola interrupted him, saying that if what Gbendlele said were true, it was a good thing because they heard that the army captain wanted to hunt the cat. Gbendlele scoffed. "The leopard is not there for hunting," she said. "It is only there like a cloud. Can someone go out to hunt the sky?" She shook her wrinkled head. *She* had not brought the world to this pass. She rose stiffly and began to make her way out of the room. As she passed by Likki, Gbendlele laid her claw of a hand on Likki's arm. "Come!" she ordered in English.

"Where?" asked Likki hesitantly.

"Come!" repeated Gbendlele, tugging with a crustacean grip.

Likki rose and went with her, half following, half dragged. She had no idea what was expected of her or to what destination she was being conducted. Unfamiliar with both language and custom, Likki was as anchorless in Gbendlele's world as a two-year-old child.

"You come," Gbendlele repeated, this time in a voice that tried to be reassuring, as if she were coaxing back into the kraal a domestic animal that had strayed to the point of wildness. She grappled Likki's arm and pulled her through a succession of courtyards where lanterns flickered softly in corners and in doorways, shedding little light, serving only to make the night seem darker. Overhead, the stars echoed the sporadic quality of this human illumination—as though the lights of the village were reflected in the sky. In the fourth courtyard Gbendlele halted to scold a flock of doe-eyed children. Then she squeezed sideways through a narrow doorway into a fifth and last courtyard, deserted except for a handful of guinea fowl, who screamed at their approach as if they had seen the pale horseman of the Apocalypse.

In this last court, Gbendlele abruptly turned and confronted Likki. "Want Ibn Sinna?" she asked. Though her grammar was poor and her vocabulary limited, the meaning was clear enough.

There were no end of surprises in Africa, Likki was finding. In this place (wherever it was), cut off from the conventions that had usually governed her life, she had no guideline but the truth. "Yes, I want Ibn Sinna," she said, incapable of predicting what might happen next.

Gbendlele grunted, then opened the door to a large room and began bustling about inside, rearranging the few sticks of furniture that rested in there—two small stools, a low table, a water pot and some calabashes. The doe-eyed children began filing in with brooms, cleaning rags, sleeping mats, and lanterns. One brought a bucket of hot water and a piece of Kalembelebiri soap for Likki to wash with. When Likki had scrubbed herself and was installed cross-legged on a sleeping mat in the centre of the room, Gbendlele left, saying, "Ibn Sinna come." Likki, limbs locked close to her body, wondered if he would know what he was supposed to be coming for, wondered how long he might take, wondered if she might lose courage while she waited, or where she could go if she changed her mind. Wondered if their first lovemaking would be the embarrassed and undistinguished fumbling that first encounters usually are and whether she would be able to say that to him afterwards.

■

In the chief's reception room the talk showed no signs of abating. "Hey! You men!" scolded Gbendlele on her return.

She was hobbling. When she was angry or excited her left foot dragged; it had been broken forty years earlier in a fall from an akee-apple tree. "All men are good for is talk, talk, talk. Africa rides along on the backs of its women while the men sit about in idle conversation."

"We have important matters before us," whined the chief.

"You are talking about the leopard," she accused.

"No. We are talking about the army man," her brother was glad to correct.

"If he wants to come and shoot, let him come. Let him find himself a black leopard. If he can."

"But he is a wicked man," mourned the chief. "What if he *does* find the creature? He would never give *me* the skin." By custom, the skin of any big cat killed in his domain belonged to him.

"Why do you care?" queried Gbendlele. "You are sitting on nine skins now. Will one more skin make you taller? Will it make your village bigger?"

"But a *black* pelt," the chief dreamed covetously.

"As for that, you would not get to keep a black skin long. Soon the Ruler of Kpama would send his man, asking for the skin, and you would have to give it to him. You know you would never manage to keep a thing like that here in this small village."

"It's true," Moola told the chief.

There was a long pause. Then the chief yawned. Gbendlele took this as her cue. "Is it not time to sleep?" she wondered aloud staring at her brother in such a way that he knew his party was at an end. He rose resignedly and left the room. Gbendlele waylaid Ibn Sinna as he passed through the door to follow behind the chief. "Your wife is waiting for you," she told him.

"I have no wife here," he laughed, but his eyes were wary.

"The woman who came here with you, is she not your wife?"

"No. She is not my wife. Where have you put her?"

"She is waiting for you in another room," said Gbendlele noncommittally and, putting out her claw, she led him through the night. In the last courtyard, sensing some collusion, Ibn Sinna hesitated. "Why are you stalling there?" demanded his conductress. "Do you want your woman to sleep alone in a strange village? Hey?"

"She doesn't want to sleep here."

"No? What does she want?"

"She only wants to travel about with me. Now she will surely be waiting to go back to the school."

"She is waiting for *you* in her room."

"Only because you put her there."

"She says she wants you."

"Do you understand her speech?"

"I understand her very well. I see how she talks with her eyes. These things I am too old to be mistaken about. If you don't go to her, she will be disgraced!"

Still he hesitated. Seeing his reluctance Gbendlele poured out on him cascades of vituperation. She abused his manhood, his valour, and his intelligence. She threatened. She insulted. She was obscene. She said she had always wanted to know if white women's genitals were the same colour inside as her own and whether they really were as dry as the streambeds in harmattan. Who else would ever be in a position to tell her? Partly to get away from her anatomical discourse Ibn Sinna opened the door to Likki's room.

Any misunderstandings would have to be cleared up at once. "Nasara Likki," he said. "The old woman says you want me to sleep with you." His tallness filled the doorway.

"Yes." Likki was too embarrassed to invent anything.

He entered slowly and closed the door, then turned and sat on the far side of the room. The light of the lantern hardly reached him.

"Are you sure?" Perhaps he wasn't sure. "There is no bed," he apologized. "No mattress."

"There's a sleeping mat."

He was silent.

"Why are you sitting over there?" she asked him.

"I am feeling shy." A good line; it utterly demolished the last of her own resistance.

To give them both time, Likki said, "What was all that noise about—with the old woman?"

"Gbendlele?"

"Umm."

"She was abusing me." He smiled. "She called me a coward."

"Why?"

"Because I was slow to come in here. She is threatening to watch us all night by means of a small hole she has drilled in the roof. Then, in the morning, if nothing has happened, she will make a report to the village. By noon I will be disgraced in all of Kpama."

"Then you'd better come over here and blow out the lantern."

He came to sit near her on the mat. Outside, Gbendlele, who had been eavesdropping, rattled the door on its latch. "Better blow out the lantern," repeated Likki, almost giggling—at herself, at him, at the old woman's scurrilous matchmaking.

"I want to look at you," said Ibn Sinna, lifting her hand in his, tracing its pale strangeness with his long fingers and a frown in his eyes.

"Have I warmed your bed enough?" Gbendlele wanted to know from the far side of the shuttered window.

"I think the bed is *too* hot."

"Then pour something out to cool it off!"

"What did she say?" asked Likki.

"She is making terrible jokes." He brushed Likki's cheek.

"About us?"

"About us."

"Can you tell me?"

"No." His eyes moved about the room, deerlike, watchful. They were slanted, a trait passed down to him from the red men of prehistory whom his ancestors had supplanted thousands of years earlier. "Have you wanted this?" he finally asked her.

"Yes."

"For a long time?"

She wasn't sure how long she had wanted him. Wasn't sure what a "long time" would be for him. "For a while," she told him.

"Why didn't you tell me?"

She didn't answer immediately. She hadn't known she was meant to tell him, or that she could. She might not have told him even if she had known it was expected of her.

These things were tricky enough at home where you knew all the rules. Even there, it was a quagmire. A morass. The irreducible biological knot. "Why didn't you tell *me*?" Likki finally inquired.

He adjusted the lantern to a low arc of yellow. "You see, it would not be right," he said. "You, a stranger, came to me asking for *help*. Some powerful man was forcing himself on you and troubling you. So how can I then come to trouble you in the same way? It would be bad. You would be ashamed. You might say yes only because I had helped you." He looked at her. "In Kpama we don't kiss," he said.

"So I've heard."

"But your people do it."

"It seems we are famous for it."

"A strange custom. I learned it in Beirut."

"What were you doing in Beirut—besides learning to kiss?"

"I was sent on a course, to study Arabic." He paused. "A French woman taught me."

"Arabic?"

"No. Not Arabic."

"What then?"

He smiled at her but did not answer.

■

Later on he made love to her very badly. He did not spend any time at all on preliminaries, apparently assuming a state of full arousal on her part. Instead, he hoisted himself directly over her, propping his chest two feet up above hers on rigid arms, elbows jammed, veins bulging with exertion. From this detached, superior height he accomplished a series of awkward pelvic push-ups, from which exercise, in very short order, he found his own relief, his face squeezed into an ugly rictus with pleasure.

Likki was too surprised even to protest. She had not imagined it would be over so soon, and she participated with a mixture of stunned amazement and sociological curiosity. (Things were bad indeed for the Third World's women. Poor nutrition, poor water, poor housing, poor health care, and now, to crown it all, poor sex.) There was little in this for a woman—only the minimum contact

required for male satisfaction; it was mating by remote
control, a copulation so ill-adapted to the ends of either
affection or passion that when Ibn Sinna had finished Likki
could willingly have consigned him to the devil—along
with many of her notions of cross-cultural relativity. She
knew, for instance, from John Lavender, that the "missionary" position usually adopted by Westerners was almost
universally deplored by the rest of the world as a brutal and
crushing custom. Could the untouching copulation she had
just experienced *really* be considered an improvement? Or
was it, she wondered, the unenviable consequence of
female circumcision? Had the removal of pliant female
sexual flesh been parallelled by the exclusion of sensual
dalliance between lovers? Or had dalliance perhaps been
the first to go: men revenging themselves on women's
bodies for the secrets they held so well and would never
speak?

There was another possibility, of course. It might be that
it was lingering foreplay and languorous intercourse that
needed justification. Maybe functional, child-producing sex
was really the norm. Maybe youthful, robust societies did
not indulge in drawn-out, sensuous lovemaking. Perhaps
only a society that could produce a nuclear bomb for every
10,000 citizens could also produce books on the multiple
orgasm.

Likki cast an anguished glance back to the long tactile
hours Roger used to tease across the surface of her body.
She sighed, then reached for the man lying next to her, now
an inky abstraction amid the shadows of the room. "Let me
show you how we do it," she suggested to him.

■

Morning came. The village was full of early sounds:
mothers still full of sleep, calling for firewood and water;
babies screaming through their first scalding hot bath of the
day; pots being searched for leftovers; goats playing tag on
the rooftops; hens purring softly to their chicks in the cool
silk shade of the houses.

When Gbendlele brought round the porridge (she had
soaked and pounded and stirred it herself), she could tell
that her plans had met with success. There was a certain

quietness about the pair who had bedded together in the fifth courtyard. Ibn Sinna could not keep from yawning. Even as he progressed through the litany of the morning greeting, he could not keep his tongue from wagging at the sky.

"What's the matter? Haven't you slept well?" demanded Gbendlele with a show of irritation. She was a woman who enjoyed being in charge even if others were discomfited by it.

"In fact, Grandmother, I am weary."

"But I gave you my best sleeping mat."

"There was nothing wrong with the mat."

"I gave you my best room."

"There was nothing wrong with the room."

"I gave you a woman who desired you. Was there something wrong with *her?*"

"No, nothing wrong," he said, but he wore an abstracted expression.

"You are thinking about your wives," said Gbendlele slyly and she made an obscene gesture with her hands. "Well, I can fix that, too, you know." She paused. "But you know already that this problem is easy to mend. Stop in to see me before you leave."

"Herbs?"

"Yes, if you want them. There is other medicine, too."

Ibn Sinna yawned.

"Go back to bed."

He stared.

"Go. Go." She limped out of the courtyard, banging on the shutters as she passed.

Likki appeared in the doorway of the room. She had tied a cloth of purple sunbursts about her body, like a Kpama woman. He knew just which corner to pull to make it drop off her all at once. She looked at him expectantly, hoping without admitting it. Ibn Sinna yawned again.

"Are you sleepy?" she asked, remembering how she had resurrected his desire. He had proved an apt pupil, intrigued with matters of cultural compromise, a student devoid of embarrassment.

"Are you not tired?" he replied.

"Do I have to be tired for you to be tired?"

"Why not?"

"Yes, let's lie down." She saw he would gladly come to her again if she would admit to wanting him.

He laid a damp cloth over the calabash to keep the flies away from their porridge and followed Likki back inside the room. Light seeped in around the door and shutters. Just enough light.

■

It was only in the quiet afterwards that Ibn Sinna's blackness seemed strange to Likki—his body hair, like so many delicate springs snuggling close to his body and the deep-as-space muzzle of his arms, an intergalactic midnight.

"Are you black all over?"

"You have seen me!"

"I haven't!"

"What were you doing?"

"It was dark. And I was busy with other things."

"Is that it?"

"It's true."

"But now it is not so dark."

"No." She touched him, laughing at herself in her mind. She had expected lighter genitals, a pink surprise deep in the heart of darkness.

"Are you black inside, too?" she asked.

"Inside!?"

"Umm."

"Only my skin is black."

"How do you know?" She wanted him to be different everywhere, still hoped to escape something in her own condition.

"Your skin is white. Are you white inside?"

She overlooked the question. "Is your soul black?"

"My soul!" He pushed her playfully. "Yes. I think we can take it that my soul is very black. Yours, too, is now black."

■

"Was it nice?" Carlotta asked as they sat down to an uninspiring lunch of leftover yam and fried canned luncheon meat from Denmark.

"What does that mean?"

"Did you see the leopard?"

"No." Likki had almost forgotten about the leopard. Only when they had started back to Kpama, without Moola, had she questioned Ibn Sinna.

"Moola is after the leopard," he had said. "I will come again to Kalembelebiri when he is ready. To fetch Moola home."

Full of violent softness, she had wondered if he might not take her back there with him, but he hadn't mentioned it. She had dropped some hints that she thought escaped him, but he was busy thinking about his wives.

"So what did you do?" Carlotta wanted to know.

"Nothing much."

"I'll bet." Carlotta paused, then asked in a detached voice, "Was he big?"

"Carlotta!"

"Well, was he?"

"It's none of your business," said Likki and though in reversed circumstances she would also have been curious, still she found the fact that Carlotta had come right out and asked her quite shocking.

"It's just a little informal survey I like to take," said Carlotta undeterred. "Most women say they're *much* bigger. I just wondered if you agreed with that." She regarded Likki hopefully.

"What difference could it possibly make to anything?"

"It would mean that all those sex manuals that say everyone is the same size are wrong." Carlotta would like sex manuals to be wrong.

Likki watched Carlotta as a giant chunk of Danish spam found its way into her mouth. Her jaw moved around the meat like that of an iguana.

"You better be careful," Carlotta admonished after she had swallowed the meat.

✖5

The day was hot and grew heavier as it progressed. By mid-afternoon the sun was a blight upon the land, beating down with a palpable pressure as if it would flatten the landscape to one dead level. Nothing could move. Vultures roosted in the treetops seemingly stupefied with discomfort. Animals breathed and blinked, but that was all. Even the termites had retreated deep underground. It was a world pressed into still life by the heat.

Likki and Carlotta lay in their underwear on the linoleum floor of the extra bedroom—their "office"—correcting test papers. Zulu lay spread-eagled in the same room, shifting every few minutes to a cooler patch of floor.

"I'm going to get a sleeping mat and spend the night on the floor," said Likki. In the humid heat of April a bed was a liability. It collected body heat and returned it, greatly amplified, to the sleeper.

"Get a perm and some brown contact lenses while you're at it."

"I'm only talking about comfort, not going native."

"With you it's all the same," said Carlotta pointedly.

"Go to hell," said Likki. She rather dreaded one of Carlotta's lectures. She didn't want to discuss Ibn Sinna, not right now. Desire, always strongest when memory was most vivid, already strangled her. She wanted the man, dreaded he might be days away into the future.

"You know his wives are like tigers," said Carlotta.

"I don't know one little thing about his wives." His sister was enough.

"Even Ayesha gives them a wide berth."

"They must be sweethearts."

"His last girlfriend wound up in the hospital. The wives nearly blinded her."

"Thanks for the encouragement."

"Just a friendly warning. I don't want to preach."

■

Abu confirmed Carlotta's warnings later in the afternoon. "The women are *too* strong," he said, shaking his head merely with the memory of them. "Any time, if they get to find out this man has another woman, they come together to beat her up. Proper!" He smiled with unmentionable recollections.

"Wonderful," said Likki.

"But, Nasara, you don't have to worry."

"Oh no? Why not?"

"They will never come to bother you. Since you are a white woman and a teacher, they just feel that you are building their name."

"Building their name . . . ?"

"Yes. If their husband is moving with such a powerful woman, it will just bring credit to them. Every time when *I* see them, *I* tell them what a very great woman you are. So they come to feel that a strong woman has become their rival. And they are happy."

"Why are they happy?"

"Because you have raised them up, and still they know there is no chance the man will stay with you."

"God *damn*."

■

Abu had brought Salifu with him to help clean out the pigsty. The logistics of removing dirty straw from under a jealous mother of twelve had proved more than Abu could handle on his own. Salifu was working on a sharecropping basis: he got the piglet of his choice in return for six months' labour. Already he had his eye on a small brown female, the fertility of the feminine gender having been wonderfully brought home to him by the proliferation of so much solid, squealing flesh. But this evening the boys found their labour irksome and departed after collecting only one basket of manure.

The heat, which had been building all day, refused to abate with the decline of the sun. Rather, the air seemed to thicken as light left the sky until the atmosphere was nearly liquid. An anxious oppressiveness hung everywhere, making the smallest exertion unthinkable. Hope's piglets refused to nurse. Zulu was too enervated even to move on to a new patch of floor. Likki, sitting half-dressed on the sofa, told Carlotta that love was utterly hopeless.

The storm began shortly after six. There were the far-off perfunctory rumbles, then the violent dance of distant tropical lightning, neon pink and lurid green, branching into seven or eight unlikely forks as it streaked across the sky. Horizontal fireworks. Impossibly, the air grew even more close. Low purple-grey clouds rolled in overhead.

"This one's gonna be a whopper," said Carlotta.

Likki's heart felt as if it were trying to tunnel under the floor. Zulu was seeking his own security by attempting to bury himself in Carlotta's armpit.

When the storm finally hit, the house shook as if it had been blasted. Trees bent double, and the rain, which sped horizontally before its driving demons, thrust itself emphatically through every seam and crevice in the doors and the louvered windows. Lightning dropped out of the sky around them like a tray of cutlery spilled on a terrazzo floor. Likki told Carlotta she now knew how the knife-thrower's target felt at the circus, halfway through the act.

"Can't you ever be serious?" complained Carlotta.

"I am serious." Between housemates, an incompatibility of humour has decided disadvantages.

Inevitably, the school's electric supply failed. It came on promptly at six o'clock (an unusual occurrence) but by ten past the hour four wires were down by the kitchens and the generator room was flooded.

Carlotta got up to light the lantern. She was groping for matches under the kitchen sink when the front door rattled.

"Is somebody there?"

"It's the wind," Likki told her.

"Are you sure? Open the door and see."

The door rattled again, at insistent intervals, not as something abandoned to the elemental chaos of the storm.

"Open it up and look," ordered Carlotta.

"I'll never get it closed again," said Likki with a reluctance as primordial as the tempest.

"Who do you think it is, the bogeyman?" Carlotta, nononsense bastion of reason, straightened up to scold. She moved towards the door as if she might open it herself.

"I thought it might be a ghost," said Likki; then, before Carlotta could scoff, she added, "Or maybe the bogey-*captain*." This succeeded in stopping Carlotta, who halted apprehensively in the deep gloom of the living-room. She seemed now as hesitant as her roommate, protective of the refuge in which they sheltered while the environment rocked with fury all about them.

Then the door opened of its own accord. Slowly, fractionally, by quarter centimetres, until the wind caught it and flung it violently against the wall, where it flapped helplessly like a loose sail on a shipwreck. The figure standing without was not so much seen as felt. It seemed done up in shrouds. "Who's there?" they called but there was no answer.

"Who's there?" insisted Likki, drawn to the door by the magnet of her own uncertainty. Outside, low lightning welled up from the earth as from a subterranean conflagration and the thunder reverberated interminably. The figure loosened its cowl-like head covering and in the next titanic electrical discharge Likki made out the features of a woman standing by the threshold, not more than two feet away.

"Ayesha!" She was part of the storm, at home with it.

"What do you want?" said Likki, taking in the taut lips and ravenous eyes in the next illumination of the sky.

"Who's there?" Carlotta called out.

No one answered her.

"What do you want?" Likki repeated.

Behind Ayesha the sky wavered in amplitudes of light and piercing strobe-like flashes. Thunder throbbed like artillery.

"What do you *want*?"

Ayesha did not reply; she merely pulled back her lips to reveal her stoat-like teeth, then turned and merged back into the restive atmosphere. Likki slammed the door shut and swore. Likki knew Ayesha had come deliberately to spook her. She had come in the storm to test the mettle of her brother's new mistress—as if there were some sort of family standard that had to be maintained. What business was it of Ayesha's? Likki swore, "Fuck her!" The woman would probably wait now to see if Likki would complain to Ibn Sinna—she would wait in vain.

"Who was it?" asked Carlotta, coming back into the room with a kerosene lantern, now lit.

"Ayesha."

"Is she still out there?"

"She can go to hell."

For once, Carlotta, with uncharacteristic wisdom, held her tongue.

X 6

The storm towed disaster in its wake. In the morning Salifu's chosen piglet was found dead, presumably drowned, in a corner of the run. Hope licked it for hours and would let no one near. At the school, part of the roof had blown off the chemistry labs, breaking glassware that would be difficult to replace as well as bringing into damp proximity substances that were more peaceful when maintained in isolation. And in a wash-out at the approach to Smugglers' Bridge a lorry broke an axle, and fourteen people were sent to the hospital, several seriously injured.

In Mahmut's house, in the old, tangled heart of Kpama, a too-small baby girl had come down with the measles. For weeks the epidemic had raged in the villages around Kpama, and now it seemed to be striking at the heart of the town. Frightened parents blamed it on the army, and Moola was only too happy to affirm that ancestral spirits complied with this judgement.

Hawa, distracted and enraged, paced the sandy street in front of Mahmut's house. Comfort had been for Hawa a resurrection in the face of despair, her only tangible link with her favourite child. Now this link was imperilled and, worse yet, inaccessible to Hawa's ministrations. Hawa was not allowed into the house of Mahmut.

The soldiers standing guard at the entrance eyed her with condescension and distrust as she paced the ground before the main gate over and over again, moaning and wailing in the manner of Kpaman funerals. Some of her friends came and stood at a respectful distance. They made long faces and shook their heads.

"Mother," a young corporal by the gate addressed Hawa. "Our captain has promised that if you are still here at sunset, he will come himself to arrest you and take you prisoner!"

"White man's justice," scoffed Hawa. "His skin is black but his heart has gone against us. He has learned everything he could get his masters to teach him."

"Old woman, you have one more hour," a sergeant warned.

"When that hour is up, then you better watch out."

"Don't threaten me, old woman."

"When the time is right, it is not *I* who will threaten you," Hawa taunted. "My daughter's spirit will avenge itself." But before the sun had disappeared, Hawa's family came and took her home, securing her in the room of an elder of her late husband's clan. There, in the centre of Kpegbabiri, a twelve-acre "house," Hawa held court among several of her other grandchildren who were rounded up from all over the town and sent in to keep an eye on her and to help pass the long, anxious hours of the night.

■

Comfort's recovery from measles was slow and marked by distressing complications. Her eyes were badly affected. For two weeks she could not bear even the smallest glimmer of light and there were many who feared she would go blind. The rash, too, was slow to disappear, while the fever also hung on, settling tenaciously in the baby's lungs. Comfort struggled for breath and was unable to hold food in her stomach. Pound after pound dropped from her tiny frame until there was little left of her but a dusty, grey-brown parchment of skin pulled taut over little bones too well revealed.

Hawa took the case before the Ruler, arguing that Comfort would die if she were not removed from Mahmut's cursed house. Hawa said this so often and to so many people besides the Ruler that the Ruler was eventually constrained to take some action to preserve his own good name. He looked around at the elders of Kpama and asked Sima to investigate the matter for him.

Sima went to call upon Mahmut one Tuesday evening and met with a series of barriers. He had to explain his mission three times, to three separate soldiers, before he reached Mahmut's innermost courtyard. When Sima finally arrived at this recessed citadel, he was greeted with a hauteur that could only make a bad impression on him.

No one, afterwards, was able to say exactly what had transpired between Mahmut and his Ruler's emissary, but Sima left the house in angry haste, having had little more than a glimpse of the ailing child. He reported that sorcery was afoot.

"They are eating her," he said to the Ruler, referring to the ways of those who indulged in the dark arts: sorcerers and wizards attacked from within, devouring the person's inner substance. Eventually the victim collapsed and died. When irate and anxious relatives demanded that an autopsy be performed, the inner organs of the corpse would be found to be shrunken or missing altogether.

Sorcery, however, was difficult to prove—at least while the victim still lived. It was even more difficult to point an accusing finger at the person or persons allegedly responsible for this kind of supernatural aggression. Everyone would deny they were involved and claim ignorance of the dark arts supposedly employed. Then most of them would go home and arrange for protection from their own spiritual enemies. The white man's priests would complain of a new outbreak of superstition and idolatry. The mallams and diviners would grow fat. Comfort's condition would remain unaffected but suspicion would spread through the kingdom. So the Ruler, bowing to the inevitable, did nothing.

Mahmut showed up at the palace some days later, complaining to the Ruler that although Sima was a respected elder of the community, he was not a disinterested party in the dispute that concerned his, Mahmut's, daughter. Mahmut demanded that an impartial investigator be sent to examine Comfort. The Friday imam was chosen as Sima's replacement. Of course, no one expected the Friday imam to go in person to perform the inspection. His position was much too exalted for *that*. Instead he selected as his emissary a certain Mallam Yusuf, an elderly and credulous convert with recidivist tendencies towards gin. Mallam Yusuf took all possible precautions. He came to examine baby Comfort wearing Muslim and Christian rosary beads —three of each sort—hanging from his belt, plus an amulet

of unknown origin and uncertain denomination that some
said had been given to him by his thoroughly pagan
grandmother. Suspicious bulges under his outer clothing
hinted at the presence of unorthodox talismans. In his right
hand he carried his father's own hand-copied version of the
Koran, a sheaf of unbound paper leaves wrapped in a wallet
of pliant sheepskin.

"Is he going to look at a baby or to meet with a *shaitan?*"
demanded Hawa when she saw how the man decked
himself out.

These preparations notwithstanding, nothing was accomplished except talk. Debate in the palace was desultory. It
examined the forms of paternal right versus unspecified
charges of witchcraft. As the Ruler phrased the dilemma to
an official deputation of Hawa's relatives: "You cannot even
say *who* it is who might be sorcerizing the child, yet you
want me to release her to you. And here at the same time is
the child's own father, demanding the right to protect her in
his own house."

Meanwhile, Mahmut slyly circulated the suggestion that
since Hawa was so manifestly full of ill intentions, perhaps
she herself was responsible for the malaise that hung over
his household, trying to frame him by sorcerizing her own
granddaughter. Accusations flew back and forth for days and
no one wearied of it except Captain Araoh. He finally tried
to put a stop to the discussions in the palace because, he
said, they were beginning to interfere with the serenity of
the town. Many people thought "serenity" a strange word
for him to use.

Hawa wanted to know by what authority the captain felt
entitled to rule on the matter, challenging the right of the
army to interfere with non-criminal domestic affairs. The
Ruler was bewildered and confused at the intrusion of the
military into what had always been his private domain.
Hawa had the last word. As she left the palace for the fourth
time that week, she turned at the door to say, softly but
distinctly, "We will *see.*"

A superstitious shudder rippled across the room. People
looked uneasily at both Mahmut and Captain Araoh, for it
was impossible to make out which of them Hawa had
singled out for the threat.

■

Three days later both wells in Mahmut's house went dry. Hawa sat in her doorway spinning cotton and looking smug. When people told her the news she said, "Is that so?" and professed to be surprised.

The sessions at the palace started again. Mahmut said he was certain Hawa had sorcerized his water supply, but this was not a charge that could be brought before the district court. The British had steadfastly maintained that witchcraft did not exist and therefore could not be tried in court. They had said that if it *had* existed it would have been a criminal offence (leading as it almost inevitably did to bodily injury or death); but in the end they banned charges of witchcraft and wizardry from the legal system they bequeathed to their colony.

While the courtly palaver continued, Mahmut enlisted the aid of several powerful Muslim clerics to rid him of the jinn in his two wells—but in vain. The wells remained dry.

Captain Araoh, a more practical-minded man, declined to see witchcraft as the cause. Instead, he interviewed local farmers and sent a series of cables to the regional Meteorology Department and to the national Geological Survey Department. While he was waiting for replies to his queries, he busied himself with examining his soldiers on the parade ground behind the police station. He looked his men over several times and finally selected twelve of the heftiest specimens. These he commissioned for "shovel duty" should the wells fail to hold water after the beginning of the rains.

Hawa said that *she* wouldn't try to stop them. She was just an old woman, what could she do? If anyone wanted to dig in a well, let them go right ahead. The consequences would be on their own heads. And she continued to spin cotton in her doorway, saying that when she had sufficient thread she would take it to have it dyed. After that she would go with it to al Hajji Masuud, who would weave her a fine cloth of green and indigo stripes.

■

It was around this time that Abu began to look extraordinarily innocent. The look of deep unknowing on his face made all who knew him well suspect the worst.

"Abu, what's cooking?" said Carlotta one hot afternoon when the boys came up the hill for manure. (Salifu was back on the clean-up detail after a temporary hiatus. He now had his eye on a pink piglet—another female.)

"Abu is planning something *fine*," answered Salifu, who had no idea what the something fine might be, but was sure it would make folks sit up and take notice. Salifu's jealousy of Abu was solidly based on a grudging admiration for his talents.

"Me?" queried Abu, holding his hands out from his sides as if he would demonstrate his emptiness, his freedom from all collusion. "What would I plan?"

"I don't know," mused Carlotta, "but I bet it's something good."

Odd rumours began to circulate. It was said that Mahmut had lost his favourite shoes outside the mosque where he went every evening for prayers. Some people hinted that Abu had stolen Mahmut's shoes out of spite. Others shook their heads and said, no, Abu had rather found the soft leather sandals and returned them to Mahmut, taking advantage of this opportunity to have a few quiet words in Mahmut's ear. Several people had seen a barefoot Mahmut waving his cane at Abu. At least one said that he had found the two of them closeted together one evening, whispering earnestly, almost laughing. This latter tale was hardly credited.

7

Thunder rumbled in the sky. Once or twice there were clouds at noon, but no rain fell on Kpama. The farmers grumbled. Women complained that the ground was too hard for them to hoe.

The Ruler called for his rainmakers. They tried for three days and shook their heads. They said there was bad *juju* in the town. Moola continued to blame everything on the army.

The Ruler next sent for the mallams. They came in the evening, with small leather pouches filled with sand. They spread the fine white grains out over the leather by the glow of oil lamps and read the future of the town in undulations of the miniature dunes. Allah, they assured the Ruler, was highly displeased with Kpama.

"The Ruler is really rather worried," John told Carlotta and Likki. He had cycled uphill to the bungalow to have dinner and share with the two women the town's anxieties, which had become his own.

"Oh, don't pay any attention," advised Carlotta, a veteran of two rainy seasons. "Four weeks before the rains are due everyone goes hysterical looking up at the sky. They call in the Christians. They call in the Muslims. Then they call in the pagans. When all the priests and all the diviners have had their share of fortune-telling—and when they've all been properly reimbursed—the rains start up. Nobody's been short-changed and everyone is happy. Even Mother Nature."

"But even Moola looks really pinched, somehow. Grey."

"You look grey and pinched yourself, John," said Likki, looking up from her knitting. "Maybe you've got malaria." She was making baby clothes for a cousin who had just produced a daughter. She was giving herself spinsterish airs

213

while she waited for news of Ibn Sinna, who had once again travelled with Moomin.

John sighed. A pall, he said, had settled over Kpama that the two women, separated from the town by three miles of road, could not perceive. But living right in the heart of Kpama, he could feel how the oppressive, anxious heaviness had increased, how the air daily thickened with suspicion, how consternation sat heavily on every brow. Something had moved, he said, something deep underground had shifted. When the surface adapted to meet these subterranean revisions, many settled things would come undone. Carlotta and Likki made light of it, and John left the bungalow early, giving a headache as his excuse.

"And get a blood test!" Carlotta called after him, her face falling into a map of concern. Then she turned to Likki. "I know he has malaria," she scolded, as though her roommate were to blame for John's indisposition.

"He'll never believe *that*. He takes all his pills. And besides, he's a big strong Male."

"We all take all our pills. We all get malaria . . . almost all of us."

"Oh, he's just a little spooked, that's all. It's the weather."

"I'm worried about him," lamented Carlotta.

"What can happen to him? At worst, he'll go on as he is, getting more and more spooked, until he gets really ill and has to admit it's malaria."

"I don't know." Carlotta remained unconvinced. Malaria, in its initial form, was as much a mental as a physical debility: a psychological affliction accompanied by physical enervation and anxious lassitude. It brought with it a deadly lethargy, a longing for perfect stagnation. Carlotta sighed.

Likki experienced a squirm of conscience. "Are you happy with him?" she asked.

"So-so." There was a ring of tinselled tragedy.

"If it makes you feel any better, my relationship with him was nothing much." Likki looked up from the heel of the left bootie as she spoke.

"But you have someone else now."

"Yes," answered Likki slowly and only after a long pause, for she did not know where it would lead, this thing she had begun with Ibn Sinna, did not know how close in he would let her come before he started putting up fences, erecting "No trespassing" signs on his interior territory, and then justifying them by saying this was the way lines were drawn between men and women in his cultural universe. Likki sensed it would matter little to him that her own cultural universe might ordain a different pattern for men and women. The fact that Likki herself might want to imagine a universe in which relations between people were fenceless would probably seem to him like pie in the sky. He would say that the world just wasn't like that, that people were what they were and dreamers would have to accommodate.

8

Likki had an odd encounter during her next visit to Kalembelebiri. The visit started unremarkably enough. As usual, despite all Gbendlele's admonitions, the chief kept Ibn Sinna talking in his rooms late into the evening. Gbendlele waited a while in the reception room and then drew Likki away while the men sat on together, speculating at length as to where Moola could be on his latest trek and why he was not yet back amongst them.

Except for the guinea hens, the fifth courtyard remained deserted, its loneliness both appealing and frightening. The room, however, had undergone certain changes. From a forgotten storeroom in the village, Gbendlele had removed two striped deck-chairs. These she had placed in the deepest recess of the chamber with a small, rough-hewn table between. Like two birds of fine and wild feather, the chairs filled their space awkwardly, aware that they had little in common with humbler tints of earth and wood. A coronation photograph of Queen Elizabeth II now graced the far wall. The rough table held, besides the lantern, just one magazine, a 1971 issue of *Playboy* from which, predictably, the centrefold had been removed.

On this occasion, Likki spent two hours alone in the room waiting for Ibn Sinna and wondering why she had been required to withdraw from the reception room. Was it for honour or insult that she had been led away; was it consideration or thoughtlessness that maintained her in solitude? She daydreamed for a while, then picked up the magazine and perused it listlessly. "Masturbators' Monthly." Even at home it had seemed an adolescent effort. Here in Kalembelebiri the magazine's preoccupations made even less sense.

Kalembelebiri was itself a puzzle—as was Kpama. Likki

216

found herself far from the part of the world in which she easily understood other people's behaviour or their reaction to her own. Here it was necessary—and a considerable strain—to navigate almost totally by intuition; but that, too, was a kind of achievement. An achievement of leaving things behind, of abandoning unnecessary mental baggage.

Three mosquitoes had found their way into the room. Likki caught two of them quite easily, simply by clapping them out of the air. The anopheles is a slow-moving creature. Each time, the crushed remains left disturbing gouts of red on her palms. Someone else's blood. Someone else's malaria? The third insect, more agile than its fellows, zoomed around the lantern and whined behind Likki's ear but never came quite close enough for her to reach it with the rolled magazine. Unimpressed with her efforts, the mosquito continued to circle the room with death concealed in its spittle.

■

At last Ibn Sinna came to her.

"I thought to find you sleeping," he said, regarding the lantern with some remorse.

"It was too dark."

"You have a lantern."

"It was too lonely."

He peeled off his clothing, layer by layer. "You know how it is with these village chiefs . . . out here in the bush they struggle to find a companion. Someone to talk to . . ." He spoke from inside his *agbada*, the first, voluminous, outer covering of his attire. Like a great cocoon it sheltered his shirt and trousers, which in their turn hid more private garments. "He made me taste each year's tobacco—eight years in all. Year by year by year. His sister fills the pots for him each dry season and seals them off with clay." He took off his shirt. There was nothing between them now but cotton briefs, a piece of Western civilization rivalling Coca-Cola's ubiquity—at least among the educated. But here he halted.

"You are still dressed," he reproved.

"So I am." She bent to caprice. "You undress me." A new chapter for his lesson book, but one that plainly gave him pause. He looked about the room as if for succour. "Is that your custom?" he asked at last.

"It happens. I wouldn't exactly call it a custom."

"Here we . . . it would be simple. One pull of the cloth. But with you it could take long."

"That is the point of the exercise."

He shook his head, even though Likki had made it clear that she wanted more in the way of a preamble than he was used to providing.

Outside an owl called. Another answered it. The man came and sat near her on a corner of the mat. "Gbendlele scolded me for keeping so long with her brother. She said you would tire of waiting and your heart would turn away from me."

It was an enquiry he made, like a small boy, like the small child that roamed abroad everywhere in his country; wide-eyed and sedate, a gentle registrar of the world's inequity.

"She was wrong."

"Yes," he said and his eyes—half Chinese boy, half antelope—grew enormous, irisless in the lantern light. The Chinese boy, full of sullen smiles and suspicions that bordered on hatred, she could seduce; but the antelope, round-haunched and nervous, feminine and soulful, she could not. She could only hunt it.

Ibn Sinna covered his eyes with long fingers.

"Why did you do that?" Likki asked, disturbed in her meditations.

"I am feeling shy," he said but he let his fingers drop and did not resist her.

∎

Likki rose early.

She left her lover in the innocence of his dreams, naked on the sleeping mat, vulnerable to all manner of roaming evil. Like a mother, Likki gazed back at him from the doorway, appalled at the tenuous nature of his life. Of all life. So his own mother may have felt when she held him in her arms, a ragged newborn, bow-legged and swollen of head, and whispered to him injunctions to adhere to the stony path of Allah.

The unlikelihood of Ibn Sinna's existence became a

weighty matter for Likki as she trod through the dark, grey dawn, as weighty as the improbability of her own existence or the circumstantial crossing of their ways.

•

Stars still bloomed faintly overhead.

Likki followed an obscure doorway out of the courtyard and soon found herself at the edge of the bush. Vegetation rose abruptly in a thick precipitous veil. A path ran off to the left, away from the village. Likki followed it, remonstrating with herself in a corner of her mind for wandering alone in the wilderness at an untimely hour of the morning.

The path forked. She turned left again, carried now between banks of shrub, down into a gentle hollow where a colony of puff-balls, nourished by the dew, had made an unseasonable appearance. The spore cases nestled suggestively amid the ground cover like a clutch of eggs. Eggs of a sort they were, of course. Reproductive certainly, but asexual. Likki bent to collect some, wondering if they were poisonous. Her great-aunt, sister to the Estonian grandmother, had been an avid collector of wild vegetation. "All North American puff-balls are edible," she used to lecture Likki every August. But this was neither August nor North America. Likki could not even be certain that the fungi in her hands *were* puff-balls. Gbendlele would know if they were edible.

She gathered just under half of the soft ovoid forms, leaving the remainder to get on with their mute, untouching procreation. As she straightened to swaddle her treasures in a fold of the cloth she had wrapped round her body, a warning issued from an archaic centre of her brain. She was being watched. Pretending to a casualness she did not feel, she started back towards the village. A small twig snapped off to the right. Another. Dry leaves rustled over the ground. For some moments silence reigned, followed by a great burst of activity, then a smothered cry, the muffled exclamation of ultimate dismay. Somewhere close by, life had been brought to a close. Indulging a curiosity both metaphysical and morbid, Likki left the path and directed her footsteps into the bush. There she stalked softly, coming to a small clearing that had once been a yam field. There was no sign of any creature. Disappointed, she

turned to go when a stray breeze parted the veil of
vegetation at the far side of the field. On a floor of dappled
shade she caught a brief glimpse of the panther's ebony
muzzle and the gazelle's soft body still twitching under the
sooty paw.

Thought was inappropriate to the occasion. She had a
playful impulse to greet the Beast in the Wood, to say "good
morning" to this embodiment of feline perfection, this
creature of Rousseau's imagination now animated by in-
stinct and appetite. At the same time she felt unwelcome,
like a strange child peering through windows while others
feast. It never occurred to her to be frightened.

She had a second glimpse of the cat, head lifted slightly.
It looked up without malice, almost with invitation. The
next time the curtain lifted the panther had gone and the
gazelle was startlingly skeletal. Likki gazed at it bewildered
for some moments. Still wondering, she faced about and
found Moola a scant four yards behind her.

"You see leopard," he said uneasily, tapping his walking-
stick.

"Yes."

Moola shook his head but did not speak. He led Likki in
silence back to Kalembelebiri and in silence she followed
behind. They seemed to walk forever before they reached
the village.

•

Moola had been out for five days looking for the beast. It
had not been simple. There had been competition, a
boisterous platoon of soldiers lurching about in the bush,
searching for signs, for tracks, for spoor, making so much
noise in the process that they had scared all the game in the
area halfway to Tunis.

The day before, in Faangbaani, Moola had heard the
distant click of rifle fire, like the noise of a worn battery
trying to start up a car. He had waited, but no drum sound
came talking of a kill. Presumably the army captain had
been unsuccessful. Perhaps, as Gbendlele maintained, the
leopard *was* a phantom, a spirit cat. A guardian.

Near Faangbaani Moola had seen a phantom of his own,
the ghost of the woman he might have married, her flesh

still supple and firm as when he had spied on her sixty years earlier, she who had been promised to him. What a beauty she had been, his Warendi, not pretty in the conventional way, but with a quiet radiance, a look of compassionate knowledge—as if, he thought, she could have suckled all of Africa. So might Eve have looked to Adam at the dawn of time.

But then, as so often happened, things had turned down the wrong path. There had been a dispute about the bridewealth cattle and the number of cowries was said to be short by three thousand shells. Negotiations stalled. Then Moola's father abused the name of Warendi's house, calling them villains and thieves, saying they were nothing but foolish and impotent old men. Warendi's family countered this with even more damning indictments. So the woman was lost to Moola, and though he had seen her only once (that one time when he spied through the vent in her mother's cooking room), he had never ceased to regret her loss. If anything, he felt it more keenly with the years, with the accumulating weight of lost possibilities.

Seeing her ghost on the path to Faangbaani was a shock. Moola had stopped the next small boy and made enquiries. Warendi still lived at Faangbaani (the village of her second husband), said the boy, but it was not Warendi that Moola had seen on the path. It was Faalni, her great-grand-daughter. The boy, sensing an old regret, offered to conduct Moola to the woman of his heart, but Moola declined. At eighty-two life holds enough disillusionment.

He was brooding upon these matters as he returned to Kalembelebiri. Morals had fallen off drastically since the coming of the white man. In these modern, corrupted days Moola might easily have taken up a liaison with Warendi—just as Ibn Sinna was doing with his white woman. Nothing like that would have been possible in Moola's youth. Angry relatives would have scorned his passion and abused the object of his desires. The girl's family would have waited in the bush with poisoned arrows and expert aim. The elders would have lectured both of them sternly. Then, in the night, their sorcery would have made him impotent.

So Moola meandered, sifting his thoughts and tapping his stick. Two miles outside of Kalembelebiri he paused.

Something purple flapped in the breeze off to the right of the path. Moola edged towards it cautiously, avoiding twigs that snapped and dry leaves that crackled like fire underfoot.

He was unsure what he expected to find: some soldierly seductions in the bush, perhaps, or the chief's youngest wife with her lover. Of course, cohabitation in the bush was unlawful and ritually polluting, as was adultery. But rules such as these stopped only the meek.

Moola lost sight of the purple behind a thick spinney. Round the other side of the undergrowth he saw it again.

It was Ibn Sinna's woman, in a cloth of purple sunbursts, cradling mushrooms in a corner of her wrap. She stood as if transfixed, staring across an empty yam field. Following the direction of her gaze Moola saw with the next trailing of the breeze the ruined carcass of an antelope, its fleet of ivory masts picked clean. Days must have passed since that disassembled wreckage had carried life through the tall yellow grasses of the savannah, yet the white woman's expression was one of confusion, as though she were amazed to see a dried skeleton there.

Moola understood what had happened. He tapped his walking-stick on the ground. Likki turned around.

"You see leopard," he said uneasily.

"Yes."

He shook his head and led her back to the village in silence. Truth to tell he was a little jealous. An experienced hunter, he had searched many days in vain. But the cat, like happiness, had turned up where it was least expected, where no one was even thinking about it. A talk with Gbendlele was in order.

The old woman was jubilant when she heard the news and she took no pains to hide it. "You see! A spirit cat!"

"What is spiritual about killing an antelope?"

"The leopard never killed an antelope. That was just an old carcass where the panther came to sit."

"Why sit over an old carcass?" Moola wanted to know.

Gbendlele lost patience with him. "You are a stupid old man. The leopard wanted to look at that Nasara woman. But if it were to walk up to her on the path, just like that, with nothing in its mouth, the woman would think only of the animal's hunger. She would be afraid and she would run. Any sensible person would run."

"Maybe," admitted Moola.

"Oh, maybe. Maybe, maybe. Why is it that not one man in the world can bear to be wrong in front of a woman?"

"You have a rough tongue, old woman."

"At least it is my own tongue and I tell the truth with it."

"If you were my wife, I would beat you every day."

"Is that it? But first you would have to catch me."

"Would that be difficult?" Moola asked, staring down at Gbendlele's toothpick legs.

"Hah! You, yourself, are leaning all the time on a stick and you want to tell me now that you can run?"

"The stick is to show that I am an elder." He flourished it proudly. His grandfather had carried it out to greet the first white man to arrive in Kpama.

"Can a human being not become old without a stick?" Gbendlele wanted to know. "How is it I have managed to come to this many wrinkled years without having such a wonderful stick?"

But walking-sticks were sex-linked in Kpama. "It is because you are a *woman*," Moola told her.

"Ohhhhh!" cried Gbendlele, rejoicing at a slip of Moola's tongue. The word for "woman" he had used more properly applied to youth and its attendant fertility; there was an unmistakeable odour of concupiscence to it. Gbendlele had long since passed menopause, becoming for most social purposes virtually sexless. There were at least three euphemisms Moola could have used, any one of which would have been more appropriate.

Moola, locked into an unintended meaning of his word, experienced an unexpected surge of sympathy for the old battle-axe in front of him.

"Is there beer in this village?" he asked hopefully. (God preserve him from Muslim villages.)

"The best beer," Gbendlele answered and straightway led him off to an arboured bench in the southernmost house of Kalembelebiri where they ordered a half-gallon pot and continued, with mutual satisfaction, their vituperative and defamatory exchanges.

•

"So you have seen Gbendlele's leopard?" Mockery traced
Ibn Sinna's voice.

"I saw something." A shade of truculence.

"Was it wise to go off into the bush alone like that?" He
would not admit he'd been worried.

"I just wanted to go for a walk."

"When it was still dark?"

"It wasn't dark."

"The sun was not yet up."

"I wanted to be alone."

"Why do you need to be alone in the bush?" People
would say she was a witch.

"I just wanted to think."

"Can you not *think* in the village?"

"No." Not about him. Not about the strength of her
desire for him and the attendant unrest, that feeling of icy
black treacle that gathered in the pit of her stomach and
made her want to flee.

He relented. "When I woke up you were gone. No one
knew where you were."

"I'll leave a note next time: 'Gone to look for the
leopard.'"

"Moola is now very jealous," he said softly.

"He shouldn't be. Half the village is willing to swear
didn't even see the damn cat. Gbendlele apparently says i
was a ghost."

"If you saw it or not, you will have trouble. So many
people have been looking. When the army man hears you
have spotted it, he will start to bother you again."

"Then I'd better stick close to your side all the time."
This was impossible. They both knew it. The thought o
their separateness gave birth again to desire. When Gbend
lele came to look for them she found their door emphati
cally shut.

•

Captain Araoh was in the village by late afternoon. He
came with a platoon of thirty soldiers. The chief sent ou
Gbendlele as a welcoming deflection while he adjusted the

mall indigo cap his sister had deigned to find for him in the
ottom of his basket of clothing.

Gbendlele measured herself against Captain Araoh and
ooked pleased to see that he was shorter than she was. She
valked out to meet him with her arms folded across her
hrivelled breasts and a look of triumph on her face.

Araoh gave her his best smile, innocent and toothy. "So,
Grandmother, we hear you have seen the leopard here."
Araoh had come to the village prepared for all contingen-
ies. At his side was Arthur, a subaltern fluent in fourteen
anguages.

"Is that so?" said Gbendlele.

"Have you heard nothing about it?"

"I am an old woman. No one tells me anything."

"But it is the old women who hear everything in a
illage."

"I have been away all morning in the bush. Weeding my
arm. Picking mushrooms. Maybe my brother can help
ou," said Gbendlele. She led him into the chief's reception
oom, wondering at the great number of soldiers the
aptain had brought with him. "Have you come to hunt
vith all these people?" What a racket they would make.
There would be no bush meat in their pots for weeks.

"I have not come here to hunt."

"Is that so?" said Gbendlele and, after she had brought
he army man inside, she went to her stool in the corner
vhere she sat with the deaf boy who always smiled and
ogether they peeled the puff-balls.

"I am looking for contraband," the captain told the chief.

"Is that so? We heard you were hunting."

"The activities are not dissimilar."

"What sort of contraband are you looking for?" This was
serious. Across the room the chief tried to catch his sister's
eye.

"Every sort. The government is concerned about smuggling activities in this area. I am under orders to investigate
ow much illegal trafficking is going on and to find out what
ommodities are being handled."

The chief frowned. The last time the army had come
alking like that, they had given themselves *carte blanche*
o turn the village inside out. The soldiers had looted and

pried. They had questioned the village girls at length an
hinted at troublesome coercions. For weeks afterward
fathers had come to him complaining of "spoiled" daugh
ters. Old women had wailed about stolen trinkets. Th
games of the children had become rough and intrusive

"I am not aware of any smuggling taking place in m
village," said the chief. Strictly speaking this was true; a
the smuggling took place at the border, thirty miles to th
north.

Gbendlele spoke up from her corner. "How can you tell
something is smuggled or if it is not?"

"It is my business to recognize contraband."

"But how do you know for certain? For instance, thes
mushrooms here in my lap could have been secretly carrie
across the border . . . ."

"Grandmother, we all know that your mushrooms hav
not sufficient value to make a man break the law."

"What do *you* know? Hey! Not sufficient value! Men wi
kill for these mushrooms!"

"And what is so special about your mushrooms, Grand
mother?" He humoured her.

"They only grow where a lion has walked." In point
fact there was, in the north, a certain fungus that wa
rumoured to spring up in the footsteps of the king of beast
By virtue of this special affiliation to sovereignty, it wa
reputed to do wonders for flagging libido and problems of
similar nature. The puff-balls that Gbendlele was peelin
had nothing to do with the famous toadstool of love, bu
how was Captain Araoh to know that?

"I'll cook some for you," volunteered Gbendlele.

"I don't think so," he answered her.

"Are you afraid?"

"Not of *you*, Grandmother." With scorn in his voice.

"Not afraid of being rude to your elders either, are you?

"No. I am not afraid. Because the elders are no longer i
charge. Now, I am in charge."

"Is that it?" Gbendlele rose to leave before he had tim
to answer her. In her hands she carried the counterfe
fungi. She pushed the deaf boy before her and struck hin
twice across his shoulders with a stick to give relief to he
feelings. Then she walked stiffly through the village drop

ping cautionary words here and there. The villagers, of course, were no amateurs. They all had secret places: caches under the floor, false walls, priest's holes, and the like. And they left just enough contraband lying about (inside granaries, among the staves that supported the roofs, at the bottoms of pots and baskets), so that the village would seem normal to the soldiers. Nearly half the consumer goods in the country entered illegally, and it would have been folly to present the army with a village that was perfectly clean.

·

Moola, meanwhile, was conducting Likki and Ibn Sinna back to the Mercedes in Dusoko—but by a wearying and indirect route because of all the soldiers on patrol. When they climbed into the car, Moola remained outside.

"Are you not coming?" Ibn Sinna asked him.

Moola shook his head.

"I've missed my class," said Likki as they drove away.

"Yes." Ibn Sinna looked at her and she saw that he wished he were capable of wanting her again.

9

The news the following morning was electrifying. Three soldiers had died digging out Mahmut's well. It was a hard thing to take in over scrambled eggs and coffee.

"I don't get it," said Carlotta with a certain air of affront.

The story grew less believable the more detailed it became. The previous evening, Captain Araoh, irritated by the inconvenience that lack of water caused in his headquarters, and perhaps also by the lack of contraband in a certain village, ordered his twelve heavies to descend into the well and dig until they were wet up to their knees. Wells being what they are, there was room for only one shoveller at a time. The first soldier dutifully descended into the well, but after less than three minutes of sending up dirt-filled buckets, he suddenly ceased to function. After the first had failed to respond to shouts, taunts, pleadings, and the threats of his military superiors, a second soldier went down into the well to learn why his comrade kept so quiet. This second soldier fell silent as soon as he reached the bottom. Fearing the worst, Mahmut's sister began a funeral wail there and then, but she was ordered to be silent by Sergeant Awilobe, who sent a third "volunteer" into the well to reconnoitre. The third man also fell silent. No further volunteers were forthcoming.

Sima, sitting at home in front of his door on his favourite striped deck-chair, looked pleased with himself and said that the earth had claimed her own. He was sent for within the hour, but he declined to come immediately. It was late in the day, he said. Preparations had to be made. Divinations had to be performed. Certain troublesome spirits would have to be contacted and appeased.

Likki said to Carlotta, "Some *juju*, no?" intending to tease; but Carlotta was touchy on the subject.

"*Juju* had nothing to do with it," she said in the self-righteous tones of those whose beliefs have been seriously challenged. "It's a simple case, really." She paused, waiting to be questioned. Likki just looked. "Poison gas," said Carlotta. It was a conclusion she had arrived at after hours of brooding.

"Where would anybody in Kpama get poison gas?"

"Where there's a will, there's a way. Mahmut certainly has enough enemies. So does Captain Araoh. It would have to be something heavy. Something that would sit in the bottom of the well until it was disturbed. Maybe even carbon dioxide. The first man would go down, use up all the available oxygen, and die. The next two would be asphyxiated as soon as they got to the bottom."

"Could be," said Likki. She wondered if Sima were in danger.

"If he decides to go down into that well today, he'd better hold his breath," warned Carlotta.

■

Around noon Sima went down into the well. There was a lot of fanfare, a lot of paraphernalia. Prayers were said. Burning paper (containing cryptic spells) and incense were dropped into the well. Long incantations were pronounced by Moola and other elders. At the end of it all a rope ladder was laid over the lip of the well to hang down far into the inner fearfulness, and then Sima descended with measured pace, singing children's songs to those who waited up above in the sunlight.

When he had dropped into the interior of things, Sima fell silent. Those who waited above began to fear. Moola stopped his murmurings long enough to remonstrate, "Hey! Sima! Why don't you sing?"

There was no answer. The elders wagged their heads and many pairs of eyes turned angrily upon the rooms of Captain Araoh. But then Sima's voice was heard again from the depths. "You can pull up this rope," he said. They pulled. At the end of their efforts they extracted the corpse of Private Serajé. The women in the house began to moan and weep. A second time the rope went down, to return with the body of Private Avipaoh. A third time it brought up Corporal Baranjaah.

Sima climbed up the rope ladder and stood in the courtyard brushing his arms with the air of one who has emptied a battlefield single-handed. Or an unpleasant chamber pot. For a long time he waited to be thanked by Captain Araoh, but no one came to speak with him. When he left for home he said, "We have not seen the end of this."

At this point even Carlotta had to face up to certain difficulties in providing a natural (as opposed to a supernatural) interpretation of events. For if the scientific criteria of simplicity and elegance were applied to the facts in hand, then surely witchcraft provided the simplest and the most elegant explanation.

"I'm stumped," admitted Carlotta. "I've got to admit that I'm stumped. How can three men go down into a well, one after the other, and all of them die down there? And then a fourth man goes down and is perfectly all right? He stays down there for forty-five minutes trussing up corpses so they can be hauled back up into the world again—to be returned underground within hours, of course—and he emerges fit as a fiddle. Not even short of breath. I'm stumped." She looked expectantly at her roommate.

"Don't ask me," protested Likki. She had no answers either, but unlike Carlotta she was undisturbed by their absence. Next to the force of the events themselves, explanations seemed trivial. Death had intruded. The demand for causes was irrelevant, irreverent, almost grotesque. She could imagine how somewhere far in the south, three mothers would be approached as they leaned in their evening doorways, full of confident relaxation, and at first they would refuse to hear what the visitor at the gate had come to tell them. Wearing grins that parodied gladness, they would appeal in their disbelief to the second soldier, the one who lagged behind. This one, embarrassed by his mission, would lift up his eyes only long enough to whisper, "Please, Auntie, it is true." To their chagrin the women would find themselves pitying the second soldier's gentleness, his expression of dismay, the solicitude of his averted eyes. They would remember other eyes, eyes that had teased and made them laugh, eyes they had nursed through terrible illnesses. Boys' eyes. Babies' eyes. Then the soldiers would leave and the women would turn away and no one could comfort them. But Carlotta wanted proof that sorcery didn't exist. That was all that mattered to her in the death of three men in a well.

10

Ibn Sinna and Likki got into the habit of making regular visits to Kalembelebiri. There was no place in Kpama where they could shelter anonymously—no hotel, no motel, not even a government rest house left over from the days of British rule.

The rainy season had finally started in earnest. The skies were overcast most of the day. The nights were as dark as mythic imaginings. But the Mercedes continued to make regular excursions to Dusoko, and the two travellers continued to climb the lanternless path to Kalembelebiri, as though their feet had learned to see in the dark, to feel out the contours and direction of the track and to sense stones and other protuberances before coming to grief on them.

So they rode out together one evening, bathed in the green glow of the Mercedes' speedometer, which cast a dusty, unreal semblance of illumination over the front seat of the car.

"What's this?" Likki asked, patting a long cylinder that rested on the floor between herself and the driver. She could only just make it out, a dull gleam. "Why have you got a pipe in here?"

"It is not a pipe."

"What is it then?"

"A shotgun."

"Oh." Unwelcome things John Lavender had said about Ibn Sinna's subversive activities came back to her. She fingered the object gingerly, feeling it out with purblind fingers. "I thought shotguns had two barrels."

"This is a single-barrelled shotgun. It is hard to find a double-barrelled gun in Kpama."

"Is it loaded?"

"Yes."

"Why?"

He did not reply.

"Do you want me to stop asking questions?"

"Since I know you are always asking questions, why should you stop asking questions now?"

"Maybe because you won't answer them."

He waited a while. "You are upset?"

"Let's just say I'm not used to riding around with a loaded gun in the car."

"It is for game."

"Oh, come on!"

"You yourself saw a leopard. You know there are animals about."

"There have always been animals about. Why start carrying this thing around now?"

"I have the gun with me because I am travelling."

This was the first she had heard of it, although she was not surprised. Ibn Sinna came and went according to his own inner rhythms and felt little need to explain his actions to anyone—least of all to her. Not only because she was a woman, but also because she was not related to him. The closeness she looked for in a lover was something she was beginning to understand he would never give her. It would go only to his family of birth; not even his wives would share in it. Still, Likki hazarded a probe. "Going someplace dangerous, it seems?"

"It would be more dangerous without the gun."

A long pause stretched through the car.

"Don't go," Likki wanted to say. And he would answer, "Why not?" What reason could she give? "Because I'm in love with you"? Was love a reason to hold back from the business of life? Or death? Sometimes it seemed so.

"Don't go." She said it.

"Why not?"

"I'll worry." A lame distillation of unquiet distress.

He did not immediately reply. He was thinking of how he had parted from his wives. Their uneasy protestations. Their dismay at the sight of firearms. Wrapping him in their affections to hold him back.

Likki, too, was far away. Inevitably, with Roger. ("Don't

go." Wrapping her fingers inextricably around and through his beloved green sweater so full of his smell and that of his tobacco.

"Don't go. You can't go." It was unthinkable that he should really leave her.

"I have to go.")

Ibn Sinna spoke from the present. "Women are all alike," he reflected.

"Men too."

"Is that it?"

"Yes."

By the side of the road up ahead, a light showed. Ibn Sinna slowed the car and dimmed the headlights. Before they shut off altogether Likki made out the figure holding the lantern. It was Gbendlele. The old woman moved off into the bush with her lantern and they followed behind her in the car, blindly; they could see nothing in the darkness but the lamp and the folds of their guide's green cloth.

Several hundred yards into the bush Gbendlele paused and turned to face them. Ibn Sinna switched off the engine. Leaving the car buried in a woven clump of trees and vines, they proceeded to the village on foot.

"Do you want to tell me what all that was about?" asked Likki when they had come to the familiar path that led from Dusoko up to Kalembelebiri.

"Later."

But later he told her very little except that it would be a help to him if she returned to Kpama not the next day, Wednesday, but the day after.

"I have *four* classes to teach tomorrow!"

"I know," he answered softly. "I am asking you as a favour."

"It's my *work*!"

"I know. This thing, too, is my work."

"You're using me," she accused, beginning to perceive that the real question was whether she was willing to trust to his reading of a situation he would not reveal to her.

He paused. "Yes," he said, admitting it slowly. "You don't have to stay. I can't make you stay here. But it would help.

Maybe you could say you were taken with fever. Everyone in the village would swear to that for you."

"If I'm going to start lying for you I deserve a better explanation than that."

"It is better not to know."

"Maybe. But in the meantime my imagination is over-worked." And by now painting some lurid pictures.

"That can be. But imagination is not facts. Unless you are foolish, only the facts can harm you."

Facts could hurt other people, too. Was that what appealed to her—not just the secretiveness, but the danger? "No," she said at last. "I don't think I want any part of this."

"But already you are here. What will you do?"

Likki refused this sweet trap. "I can walk home," she said. "I don't like blackmail."

The child in him looked out at her then, registering her chagrin and her disquiet but holding out little comfort. After a while Ibn Sinna spoke: "Nasara Likki, this thing is very important. Please say you will stay here. It will help." He reached out his hand. His eyes implored her acquiescence, at the same time filling with a need for her body. But it was not this that turned her toward him again. It was rather a certain stiffness that she sensed in him. An inner chill. Fear. Because of this, she at length said yes, but by then she, too, was beginning to be afraid. Ibn Sinna looked down as if he were ashamed.

Their lovemaking that night was sharp as any snatched at the edge of uncertainties; a telescoping of a decade's pleasure into a matter of an urgent hour. It was the love of wartime or perilous adultery.

When Likki woke in the morning Ibn Sinna was already several hours into his secret journey. She spent an es-tranged and vacant Wednesday in the village. Gbendlele made great efforts to tempt her guest's enjoyment.

She secured a large calabash of fresh cow's milk from her brother's Fulani herdsman for Likki's morning Nescafé. She prepared smoked fish and steamed corn dough for break-fast. She made soft, sweet, yeast-raised millet cakes. Moola came by at eight and together they took Likki to Chilka's where a hard core of bibulous invalids (all the healthy ones had already left for their fields) pledged her health and her love life over half a dozen shared pots. In the afternoon Likki was kept busy rolling yarn and shelling peanuts. It was only at the end of the day that she found sufficient time and privacy to examine the vacuum of her lover's absence, the nub of unquiet misgivings that he had left in his wake. Time for reflection, however, was soon curtailed. In the middle of undressing, Likki became aware of two small sleepy forms standing at the threshold of her room. Schoolgirls.

"What do you want?"

"Please, miss. Gbendlele say, 'Go sleep white lady.'" It was a fine point of native courtesy. In Africa no one sleeps alone.

✳11

Carlotta Reap was outraged.

"You've lost all sense of responsibility. It's disgusting! Two *days* of classes you've missed."

When Likki had asked Ibn Sinna how she could return from Kalembelebiri (she had assumed, correctly, that the Mercedes no longer fitted into her travel plans), he had suggested she take the market lorry that ran in several times on Thursday, Kpama market day, the end of the three-day market week. But on market day the market lorry from Dusoko had blown a tire and there were no spares. Likki had waited in the sun all morning and through lunchtime for Enemies Are Not God, a substitute vehicle with an enigmatic name and only two forward gears. It had stuttered into Kpama at ten past three in the afternoon.

"Why didn't you just stay away until Monday and make a week of it?" continued Carlotta.

"Why are you so hot and bothered?" demanded Likki. "It wasn't any extra work for you, was it?"

"I don't like having to cover up for you."

"Nobody asked you to cover up. All you had to do was tell the truth: you didn't know what happened."

Carlotta sniffed, then carried on, "And just what did you tell the headmaster?"

"I told him I was sick."

"That was original."

"I wasn't trying to be creative. Any lie will do in a pinch." Her day in Kalembelebiri had been unsettling, had left her edgy, resentful, and feeling burdened with things she could not share.

Only Abu was sympathetic. "Nasara, you don't worry," he counselled over his chore-time Coke. "It will all come out all right."

"I wonder."

He put his face close to hers and winked. "Me, myself," he said, "I know everything. I know it can all work out right. The man himself is safe. You don't worry." Platitudes.

"What do you know about it, Abu?"

"Myself, I know *too* much."

"Like what, for instance?"

He moved closer. "Like Mr. Moomin has also travelled with a gun."

Abu had other news that evening, as well. To begin with, he told them that five of Captain Araoh's best soldiers had been hospitalized for severe nausea and dizziness. The doctor, suspecting poisoning, had demanded samples of water from Mahmut's two wells.

"*Both* wells are working now?" asked Carlotta.

"Since two days," affirmed Abu. It appeared that Sima had not only removed three dead bodies from the outer well, but had also lifted whatever obstructions, natural or supernatural, were in place to prevent water from collecting in the underground cisterns.

"Sima probably poisoned the wells while he was down there pulling out bodies," said Carlotta in tones that said she nearly approved of this course of action.

"Nasara!" said Abu, shocked. "Sima is a good man. He doesn't go about spreading *juju* like that."

"I thought *juju* was magic," said Carlotta in confusion.

"*Juju* is anything that works," Likki informed her. Carlotta scowled for she disliked being instructed in any matter on which she already held an opinion.

Abu's last item of information was more sombre because more personal: John Lavender was ill with diarrhoea, confined by necessity to his rooms, and in very low spirits.

"Oh, let's go visit him. Let's go cheer him up," suggested Likki as much to distract herself as Carlotta.

Carlotta hesitated, hating to be thought "forward," to be chasing a man.

"Oh, come on," chided Likki. Two visitors at once was bound to seem innocent—at least to Carlotta. The idea of a *ménage à trois*, for instance, would never occur to her. Even for lusts as coarse as Zulu's it was unimaginable.

They took Zulu with them, for he stood by the door

looking plaintive and abandoned as they left. Carlotta dug up his leash and double-checked the fastenings. She would take no chances in a town where she considered no canine to be safe as long as one cooking pot remained meatless.

At Kutu's they found John drunk on Lomotil and weak with the diarrhoea it hadn't cured.

"It's malaria." Carlotta delivered the verdict.

"Yes!" affirmed Abu. "It is fever! Every time I tell him. Every time he doesn't want to hear me again."

"I. Have. Not. Got. Malaria," rasped John, but then he had to leave them for another round on the toilet. His seventeenth of the day. They could almost hear him clenching his teeth while the spasms crashed through his lower abdomen. Once he choked on his own spittle as the pains came through, and his coughs were like muffled screams.

Afterwards, back in the living-room, damp with sweat, he was told, "You better go see the doctor."

"It's not malaria, though," he begged of Likki. "You'll admit that much at least?" This from a pale, clammy face, misty with exertion.

"You better hope it *is* malaria," Likki advised.

"Good heavens, why?"

"Everything else it could be is worse."

John paused. "You know," he said, "you Americans are obsessed with illness. It's only some intestinal flu. I'll be over it within twenty-four hours."

"How are you fixed for toilet paper?" Carlotta asked, ever practical. With dysentery, toilet paper, always chronically short, wouldn't last long. A roll a day.

"I'm afraid I'm up to Wodehouse. The Agatha Christies are finished." Three weeks earlier Carlotta had given him a set of detective books to help him preserve his "serious" reading material intact. It was a consideration of unflagging interest to see where different people drew the line between what reading matter they could and could not use to wipe their asses. Some individuals would cheerfully sacrifice Plato in the name of personal hygiene while others were smitten with guilt at even the thought of using the absurd propaganda pamphlets put out by the government printing office. Africans simply used the fingers of their left hands, too earthy and simple a procedure for Westerners, who on the whole preferred to shit on their own literature.

John asked Likki for a cigarette.

"You're not smoking?!" cried Carlotta, aghast.

"Why not?"

"It's the worst possible thing for malaria."

"I have not got . . ."

"Yes, we know that," Carlotta interrupted him. "But it's also the worst possible thing for dysentery."

Despite Carlotta's protests, Likki handed over the rest of her pack to John. As John said, there was precious little else currently available to him in the way of pleasure.

Likki herself was running low on cigarettes and she left Carlotta with John while she walked over to the shop in the market to see if Moola had had any luck getting hold of her brand. Abu went along with her.

"The man is not well," he said as they passed out of Kutu's gate. His voice was sharp.

"No, he's not well."

"Comfort, too, is not fine," continued Abu, his voice now quite scratchy with anxiety. "She is long since past one year. This time she should be moving everywhere. But she only lies in one place, breathing so." He took several rapid, shallow breaths, swelling his abdomen with a jerk at each one.

"It's probably malaria, no?"

"Already Mahmut has sent for this man, the doctor. Already he goes there and he says he doesn't know anything again. Not measles, he says. Not malaria. Then he goes away and leaves no medicine. No drops. Nothing." Abu was lost in caverns of distress.

"What do you think it is, Abu?"

He averted his eyes and would not answer.

"Don't worry. Everything will soon be all right." The standard local catchphrase for disaster, when no one could think of a comforting truth.

"Nasara Likki, you know how it is. More than half our babies die." It was not a statistic in which to seek solace, a cruel thing to know so well at twelve.

"Comfort won't die."

Abu drew a shirt sleeve across his eyes, then left Likki's

side and plunged ahead to clear a way for her through the clogged avenues of the market place.

■

Moola was not in. Sima was tending shop. He smiled when he saw his visitors. "Cigarettes or Fanta?"

"Both."

"Yes, I think we can do both. Is it '555' for you?"

"Yes." Likki looked around. What an unlikely nook of the world this shop was. Not a shoe had moved since her visit with Ibn Sinna. Every handbag swung from the ceiling on the identical piece of string from which it had dangled three months earlier. "Do you ever sell any of these shoes?" she asked.

"We don't want to sell shoes. Why would we sell shoes?"

"But why have them here? What happens if someone comes along and insists on buying a pair?"

"Then we just put up the price until it is *too* high. We tell the person, 'One hundred pounds.' So the person goes next door to al Hajji Rashiid and is happy to find the shoes for only seventy. So Rashiid, too, is very happy to have us here." Probably al Hajji Rashiid had supplied them with all their shoes.

"Jesus."

"Is it something you don't understand?"

"Why hide? Why not just sell Fanta? Why bother with the shoes at all?"

"Because in these times Fanta is short, isn't it? Cigarettes, too, are short. Bottled beer is short. And anything that is short, we in Kpama will never get to see enough of it. Every place, every town along the road, someone will always come to steal away Kpama's share. The government takes its dash, its . . . rake-off. The army, too, takes its dash. Years ago the British took their dash, and before that we had a caravan tax that we had to pay to the Ruler and the bigger robbers along the route. So the mighty are always willing to grow fat. Then the trader, too, puts aside for himself, and there are plenty of other thieves. When at last the lorry comes to Kpama, it is already nearly empty. But here, in this shop, we try to make sure that Kpama finds some of its share again." Robin Hood.

Sima located some cigarettes for Likki, but not very many. Only four packs. He apologized. "You see how it is, we have to have some packets for every person who comes here. And even for us the supply is now short."

"Never mind, I smoke too much anyway."

"One thing, please. I would like to keep this boy Abu. He can stay with me here some short time," said Sima.

"Why not?" said Likki. He probably needed him to help out in the shop.

Back at Kutu's house Carlotta asked sharply, "Where's Abu?"

"He stayed with Sima."

"What for?" She seemed annoyed.

"I don't know. I guess he wanted another pair of hands to lift boxes or something."

Mother of Issa insisted on giving supper to Likki and Carlotta, feeling perhaps that because they were white (from the same tribe as her stranger?) their one meal would establish a kind of metaphysical compensation for all those that had been missed by John Lavender.

When they departed for home the sun was long down. The moon, a day or two past fullness, rose calmly in the sky, and the children of Kpama began to gather in great flocks in open places. They came to the market, to the wide streets, to the squares outside their large houses. They came to sing and to dance and to play their fathers' drums. Or their uncles' drums. Or the drums they had made themselves from empty margarine tins.

The moonlight hardly touched their inky figures. It gave out only the faintest hint of their forms: a shoulder etched in silver, the pale glint of a curved cheekbone. Mostly the children were invisible, gentle obscurities that slipped through the darkness, elfin wraiths on their way to convocations, to faerie revels ruled by the moon.

But though the children were nearly invisible, their voices were reassuringly near. And the sound of their singing and their laughter seemed to lift up from the sand and gravel and mud of Kpama and reach out over the town like an umbrella, a shield of innocence against the night.

"I wish I lived in town," said Likki when their footsteps had carried them almost to the edge of it. Carlotta did not demur. Even Zulu seemed reluctant to leave behind the celebrations of the little people. He made out that his leg was bothering him (the one he had broken on the occasion of his last disappearance) and the women, wanting something to mother, were well content to carry him up the hill.

❊ 12

Carlotta and Likki were roused at dawn the next day by a violent pounding on the back screen door.

"My God, what's all the fuss?" grumbled Likki as she unlatched the screen to admit Nuhu. It was a morning still falsely grey.

"That baby, Comfort, she is just gone missing."

"Why tell us?" grumbled Carlotta, too sleepy even to yawn.

"Because your army friend will soon be here. He is just crazy looking for that baby."

"Not again," protested Carlotta, staring at Likki as if it were *her* fault.

"Tell us about Comfort," insisted Likki. There was something disturbing here, something that teased at the edge of consciousness.

"They say she has just gone missing. When the women came in the night to tend to her, they couldn't find her again."

"You mean she was sleeping *alone*?"

"They put her in a room with two women. But Comfort was sleeping there early in the night. So when the women, too, went to sleep in that room, they got to find that it was empty. Then they shouted for everyone to come with lanterns. So, the whole household was walking about, looking for that baby. But they couldn't find her again."

"How could she just crawl off like that?"

"She never crawled to any place. Someone has come to take her in the night."

"But *who*?" asked Likki, and then began to imagine who.

"No one knows who can have taken her. But anyway, even if someone did know, it is not likely that they come forward to say so, isn't it?"

"I bet the captain is mad as a hornet," said Carlotta, smiling.

"The man himself has said that he will find the girl even if there is not one house left standing in all of Kpama. Already he has visited Moomin's house and started a quarrel there. He found nothing, of course. The baby would never be there. Even if Ayesha herself were to steal this baby away, would she be so foolish as to bring it to her own house? You see how it is? Ayesha even said this to the army man. But the man says he has no time to listen to the foolish talk of women. Then, he ordered his soldiers to shoot all the birds in that house of Moomin. He said it was not clean to have these birds walking about in the courtyard just like that. So even now they are all dead. Not one guinea hen is calling in there. And all Abu's chickens are dead."

"They killed all the birds?" Carlotta was shocked.

"It's true. And when Ayesha complained of it, the man told her, 'Where is your husband?' Moomin has travelled and Ayesha was alone in that house. So what could she say?"

"And how did Abu take the news?" asked Likki.

"It is said that Abu is struggling hard to make a long face and put some tears on it."

"Oh, my God!" said Carlotta as possibilities dawned for her.

Likki's thoughts strayed back to the "shoe shop" in the market. "And Sima," she inquired. "What was his reaction?"

"As for Sima, they can't find him again. And the army man is *too* angry because just since last night he suspects Sima of trying to kill him."

"What?"

"It seems someone has seen fit to send this army captain one present in a very *fine* box. So this man, Captain Araoh, he got one junior officer to open that fine box for him. As soon as that man removed the lid, out jumped a cat and bit the man. So now they are sending that man across the border for vaccine because that cat had rabies."

"Somebody sent Araoh a rabid cat?"

"It's true."

"Too bad he didn't open his own box."

Nuhu grinned. The tribulations and frustrations of a resented army are a constant source of pleasure to the civilian population.

"Do they think Sima sent the rabid cat?"

"That is what they believe."

"That's crazy," said Carlotta.

"Maybe, but the army can soon be coming up here," warned Nuhu. "If you want to keep something from this man, then now is a good time to put it away. You see?"

Captain Araoh turned up at the bungalow an hour later with his urbane and implacable grin. Once inside, he tore through the house like a shredding machine. If his last search had been symbolic rape, this one was metaphorical homicide. Drawers and closets were emptied, their contents stripped and dropped onto the floor in a heap. Any article of value—an opal ring of Carlotta's (she was, unbelievably, a Libra), a pair of Likki's earrings, a gold chain, John's Nikon 35 mm—all these were tossed into a blue laundry bag held by Sergeant Awilobe. "They can be claimed next month from headquarters—if they are not contraband," Captain Araoh informed them.

Beds were stripped and mattresses ripped open in several places, releasing kapok fibres that floated through the house for weeks afterwards like vagrant dandelion puffs. Kitchen cupboards were turned out in a similar fashion, their contents emptied together in a large enamel basin on the floor. No attempt was made to keep sugar or flour separate from salt, coffee, raisins, or dried peas.

In the living room, the cushions of the sofa and chairs were divested of their fabric coverings. Zulu, who up to this point had only been watching, now recollected latent talents buried in his past. He lowered his head and approached the soldiers, growling as ominously as he dared.

The grin on Captain Araoh's face merely broadened; it spread in an impossible arc across most of his lower face. "A fine hunting dog," he said. "Very *fine*! I only hope it is not vicious. You know rabies is plentiful in this area. It would distress me to have to shoot this animal."

The captain next turned his attention upon the women

themselves. "You will also have to be searched," he told them, and the revelation was obviously sweet to him.

"For what?" demanded Likki. The man had come in ostensibly looking for Comfort. But Comfort was fourteen months old. It was impossible that she could be hidden under the clothes they wore on their bodies.

"I am searching for con-tra-band." He drooled over the word in a way that made it sound obscene. After he spoke he was silent for a while, as if to give them time to wonder how thorough he would be in his search of their persons. He walked over to an armchair and seated himself ostentatiously, surveying the two women all the time. When he spoke again it appeared he had changed the direction of his thoughts. "Miss Liddell," he said unctuously. "Where is your tall friend?"

"Nuhu?" she inquired. Carlotta scowled at her temerity.

"No, I am referring to Ibn Sinna Abdul Rashiid Ibrahim Tarawor."

"I haven't seen him today."

"No. I am aware of that. The day has hardly begun. But yesterday, perhaps?"

"No. I wasn't around here yesterday."

"Yes. I know. You were in one of the villages, weren't you? I didn't realize at the time. Had I known I might have called on you."

"That would have been nice."

"Yes. Wouldn't it? I was in Faangbaani."

"What a pity we missed you."

"We?"

"We were in Kalembelebiri."

"Of course." He paused. "You travelled there with Ibn Sinna?"

"Who else?"

"Why?"

"It was too far to walk," said Likki. She wondered if this were the exercise for which her absent lover had tutored her ignorance.

"I see." Again he paused. "But you missed some classes Wednesday."

"Four classes."

"I see. Why was that?"

"I was ill."

"In the village?"

"Yes. Where else?"

"Why did Ibn Sinna not drive you home? Since you were so ill? Why did you come back to Kpama on this broken market lorry, Enemies?" He knew a lot about her movements.

"Ibn Sinna had to leave. He said he had business."

"What kind of business?"

"He didn't say."

"Please forgive me, Miss Liddell, but you are lying."

"What?"

"The man was never there with you."

"Yes, he was."

"I want to know why you went to this village on your own."

"I didn't go on my own."

"I have had reports from Dusoko. The man's car was never seen there this time."

So that was it. Araoh must have spies all over. "Believe what you want. I went with Ibn Sinna in his car Tuesday night. Ask Carlotta. She waved goodbye to us."

Carlotta hadn't waved. She'd stood, hands on hips, with her lips curled down in disapproval. Then, she had tossed her hand at them as though shaking off a departing jackal.

"Ibn Sinna never went to Kalembelebiri," insisted Captain Araoh.

"Then why ask me about it? Why not ask in the village? They'll tell you what happened."

"I am not a foolish man, Miss Liddell. Every person in Kalembelebiri tells the same lie. That does not mean that I believe it."

"If you don't believe the villagers, then you don't believe me."

"That is true. And I have a word of advice for you," he said, rising from his chair, leaving behind all pretence of goodwill. "And the advice is not to become involved in things which are not your concern, things which are no business of yours. You have picked up with some unsavoury characters. I do not hesitate to tell you that we have grave suspicions concerning the loyalty of some of your new-found friends. I advise you to put some distance between yourself and them before you are cut down in an untimely harvest." He was standing very close to them now. They could smell the beery staleness of his breath. "Now you will please go into the bedroom so that we can search you."

Neither woman moved.

"I see you are not enthusiastic," said Captain Araoh and motioned for his second in command. "Sergeant Awilobe," he addressed him. "These two ladies need to be persuaded of the seriousness of my intentions. Please take them into the bedroom and search them for me."

Sergeant Awilobe looked embarrassed. "You should please go now," he begged.

"I'm not going anywhere," said Likki.

"Oh, my dear Miss Liddell, you *will* go," said the captain, and he removed from his holster the pistol he always carried there. He turned the gun over in his hand and ran his fingers lightly down the barrel as if he were inspecting it for flaws. Then he pointed the gun at Likki. He adjusted the hammer with a preliminary click. "Now, ladies, let us please proceed about our business."

Carlotta wavered. Likki said, "This is illegal. A woman has to search us."

"Oh, I don't think so. Besides I have no women on my staff. Unfortunately. Please move."

They stalled.

"Miss Liddell. Miss Reap. May I repeat: you *will* be searched." He called again to Sergeant Awilobe, a short, well-muscled southerner, also armed with a pistol. With this escort they were marched into the spare room.

It was an unpleasant business. The inspection went down as far as underwear. It was fortunate for Likki that she was wearing a bra. Usually she managed without one, but in the week before her period her breasts were always tender and the only comfort she could offer was to cradle them in the antique garment of custom. Carlotta was not so lucky, for though she wore a bra that was more armament than corset, still she was mortified to have her rolls of belly fat so visibly on display. Outside, a chorus of windy soldiers had congregated to observe what they could through the marginal opacity of the louvered windows. They hooted at

Carlotta's bulk. Sergeant Awilobe leaned against the wall throughout the operation with his gun aimed straight at Carlotta. He looked tense. In fact, the sergeant, whose ideal of beauty was a perfectly spherical woman, felt his genitals tighten alarmingly as Carlotta disrobed, and he thought with anxious anticipation of the voluminous charms of the bead-seller at the entrance to Kpama's marketplace.

Captain Araoh stared appraisingly at the uncovered bodies of the two women. His expression was one of unabashed enjoyment. One way or another, now he *had* seen them. Power had reaped satisfaction. As his eyes followed her divestiture, Likki felt the shame of his glance trace over her skin, and she began to hate him with the collective fury of her entire sex. Araoh noted this with relish.

When they had finished undressing, the captain searched through their cast-off clothing. He did this very thoroughly, suggestively, and slowly. When he had finished, he walked around them several times. He was close—close enough to caress—and his fingers moved lasciviously. Likki felt tendrils of loathing prickle the skin of her stomach and thighs. But although several long minutes passed before he let them dress, Araoh never once touched their bodies.

"I'm lodging a formal protest with my embassy," Likki announced when she was once more arrayed with decency.

"Why not?" answered Captain Araoh, with his provoking grin, which was now augmented by his knowledge of her and his dominance. He left the bungalow and drove off in the first army jeep, leaving his sergeant to follow behind in the second.

Before he left, Sergeant Awilobe pushed a crumpled piece of paper into Carlotta's hand, but Carlotta, far more upset than Likki, hardly noticed what he did. She sat staring straight ahead and only later opened her palm to wonder at its contents: a five-pound note.

"What's this?" she bleated. She had thought he had left her a notice, some kind of official warning.

"Five pounds!" exclaimed Likki. "It must be love. Maybe it broke his heart to see the captain break yours?" She was trying to tease Carlotta out of a pale-blueness of face, a numbed withdrawal of spirit. "You could be the woman of his dreams."

"I can't keep his money," protested Carlotta.

"Carlotta, you have to keep it. You know you do." According to the etiquette of the country, hard cash was as acceptable a gift as flowers or expensive boxes of chocolate. Just as certain an indication of refinement as slim volumes of poetry.

⋈ 13

The army's house-to-house search continued. Extensive
roadblocks were set up. All over Kpama people talked and
wagged their heads and said no good would come of it. The
army had let a personal dispute become a matter of military
honour. Things could only get worse.

That evening, after dark, but before the moon had risen,
Ibn Sinna soundlessly appeared at the door of Bungalow 5.

"Where's your car? Why didn't you come in your car?"
scolded Carlotta, who was alone in the living-room when he
arrived. Her voice was shrill with paranoia.

"I have left the car behind. This time they are stopping
cars everywhere. Searching them, taking them apart. Even
removing tires and keeping them."

Likki came slowly into the room, biting her lower lip.
Though she would have blessed his presence and protection earlier in the day, now it was difficult not to think of
him as the enemy merely by virtue of his sex. "Hello," she
said. The word hung inadequately in the space between
them.

"I am back."

"So I see."

"I came without the car. I wanted to bring your Fanta but
I couldn't. Sima said you were short."

"It doesn't matter." He stood there folded in his long blue
robes like a dark angel. "It doesn't matter."

"Sima said you had trouble here this morning."

With a shaking voice Carlotta told him all about the
trouble. Nothing could deter her from the recitation—her
fourth of the day. It was a kind of exorcism for her, and even
Zulu paid respectful attention while she spoke.

When she had finished, Ibn Sinna said, "It is not a good

hing when the army governs the country. Foolish men go
bout, just disturbing people, and everyone is afraid."

"He took my ring, too," said Carlotta, wiping her cheeks
vith pudgy fingers.

"Carlotta, why don't you have a little brandy?" suggested
Likki.

"I'm down to my last bottle," Carlotta mourned.

"If you want more brandy, I will bring some for you,"
volunteered Ibn Sinna. The fixer.

"*Real* brandy? Or that awful Six Drums stuff?" Carlotta
made a face at the memory of the expensive paint-thinner
hat was bottled in the capital.

"You like French?"

"Remy Martin is what I drink."

"Any kind. I can get any kind for you. Remy Martin.
Hennessy. Courvoisier. Martell. Or Armagnac, too. Whatever you want." He knew a lot about it for someone who
vas supposed to be teetotal.

"How soon?" Carlotta inquired.

"There is some in town now. I think tomorrow is soon
enough for you?"

"You bet." She smiled for perhaps the first time since
morning and waddled out to Hope of Our Ancestors' shed
to remove her last bottle from behind a loose board in the
corner where, on Nuhu's advice, she had hidden it at dawn.

"You're upset," Ibn Sinna said to Likki when Carlotta was
out of the room.

"Yes." She was shaking, though whether with rage, grief,
or fear she knew not.

"We can go to the village. It will be good for you to leave
this house."

"Tonight?"

"Why not?"

"You said you didn't bring the car."

"But anyway the walk is not far. Some four miles through
the bush, and the path is good."

"But what about Carlotta?"

"What is wrong with her?"

"She won't want to stay here alone tonight. She's
spooked."

"Her girls can come and sleep in the house with her."

"Oh . . . I don't know." Likki wasn't sure she wanted t
go anywhere with Ibn Sinna. Her desire for him ha
withered. Her heart was like a piece of old parchment

He saw that the morning's troubles were reaching ahea
into the future, spoiling the innocence of things to come
'Now you hate the army man, will you also begin to hat
me?" he asked.

Likki was silent.

"You see how it is, don't you? Without even touchin
you, that army man has accomplished everything he hope
for. All day you have been sitting here thinking only abou
him. And now when I come to see you, you want me t
leave."

She looked down.

"Is it true?"

"It's true."

"Then it is better to go to Kalembelebiri. Far from thi
house it will be easier not to think of him. If you want yo
can sleep with Gbendlele. As for me, I will stay with th
chief and let him talk himself out through the night."

She nodded glumly while he moulded her future. It wa
not in her power to resist him then.

Carlotta came back into the room with her bottle an
three unmatched glasses. These she placed in a row on th
table and poured out too much brandy for everyone. Ib
Sinna protested that he was a Muslim.

"I won't tell," said Carlotta, for whom it was an article
private faith that all Muslims broke this proscription
their religion. The imam, she had said on more than on
occasion, kept vodka in the tea kettle that he used for hi
ritual ablutions before prayers. When people thought h
was rinsing out his mouth, he was really having a pull at hi
soul's sweetest perdition.

Carlotta belted her brandy. Unabashed, she poure
herself another. And then another. She said she wanted
get drunk, and she did. She became loquacious. Sh
disburdened herself of the insults of the morning. Ho
could the guardians of the people so despicably overrid
the canons of decency? How could the army so blatantl
ignore the responsibility with which it had been entrusted

How could the people of the country endure such a state of affairs?

"It is not the people of this country who keep the army in charge," Ibn Sinna replied at one point.

"Who, then?" asked Carlotta, trying to remember an aphorism about people getting the government they deserve.

"It is other countries, the money and the guns that come from other countries, which keep the army in charge here."

"Ohhhh," said Carlotta. She had heard this argument before, from Likki, and she stared at her roommate as if *she* had made him say it, had whispered the words to him, cueing the stage-frightened actor. "Just tell me one thing," said Carlotta. "How?"

"How?"

"Yes. How do other countries keep the army in charge here?"

"The explanation of this thing is not simple."

"Of course not." Carlotta settled back in her chair with the look of one who has just won at chess despite drinking far too much port after dinner.

Ibn Sinna frowned. "It has to do with many things," he said at last. "It has to do with other nations setting the prices of our own country's goods far too low on world markets. It has to do with the ties put on our foreign aid. It has to do with big corporations who do business here but manage never to pay any taxes. It has to do with the World Bank telling us what to do with our politics before they allow us to get ever deeper in debt to them." He began to develop his theme with some vehemence. Carlotta watched him with an increasingly out-of-focus expression. Zulu had crawled onto her lap to comfort her. She nuzzled him, played with his silky ears, and eventually appeared to forget that she was having a conversation. After some time she rose clumsily and excused herself saying she was sleepy.

When she had gone off to bed Ibn Sinna said, "Your sister is an innocent."

"Innocent? Carlotta has the dirtiest mind in Kpama."

"Yes, but she is an innocent. She believes that the world is filled with good people so that if we were all to sit down together and talk, we could finally come to agree on everything. Every baby would be fat. Every grandmother would smile."

"And you don't believe that?" Likki imagined that she believed it herself, though she had never thought it through.

"Yes. I believe that most people are good-hearted. But there are just enough greedy ones to spoil it for the rest. When these few become so greedy, the others become frightened and then they all begin to act like fools."

After they had checked on Carlotta, who was snoring half-dressed on her bed, and after they had removed all traces of alcoholic indulgence from the living-room, Likki called in the sixth-form clique to maintain a protective vigil in the bungalow. The girls were glad enough to do it. A little surreptitious pilfering in the kitchen. A series of fragrant baths with special thanks to Balmain for the scented oil. A ceiling fan that ran until the electricity went off at eleven. Magazines to look at. Cards. Games. It was like sending a bunch of eight-year-olds to Macy's at Christmastime.

Likki and Ibn Sinna left on foot for Kalembelebiri as soon as the moon came up. It was a shrunken orb, collapsed on one side like the cells that sickled in the blood of the people below. It gave out at first only a thin, disinterested light that did not penetrate to the ground, but merely marked the footpath as a systematic parting amid the random vegetation of the bush. Ibn Sinna carried a flashlight, but he did not use it, saying they would more easily get lost if they depended on it. Also, it was rumoured that batteries would soon be short.

Night sounds were muted, as if the bush were holding its breath, listening for unfriendly footsteps. Likki followed her guide as silently as she could, unwilling to intrude on the nocturnal meditations of the savannah. Once she tripped and gasped for breath and then apologized. But otherwise her heavy spirits lightened as she left the school. The morning's infamies receded. Suddenly it seemed a great adventure to stumble through the bush in the dead of night with the tall man before her and intrusive iniquity left behind.

After an hour or so Ibn Sinna paused at the top of a long,

sloping ridge. "Do you want to rest a while?" he asked. A wide valley spread out before them, dusty-white in the moonlight, like a chalk world. In the far distance, pricks of firelight sparkled red and orange, intruding slightly on the pale repose of the moon. Drums throbbed softly. "That will be Kalembelebiri," he said.

"It's nice right here," said Likki.

"Do you want to stay here?"

"Oh, *could* I stay?"

"I could make you a bush hut," he hypothesized, referring to a rough structure used by hunters, or by farmers when they tended distant fields.

"If you made me a bush hut I would stay."

"How long would you stay in a bush hut?"

"Ten years." She just gave it out as the first thing that entered her mind and was surprised, after she said it, to discover how close it felt to the truth. But he was disturbed and shook his head. "It won't last ten years," he said.

"The hut?"

"The hut, too, will not last."

"You mean you and I."

"Yes. There is only so much, then it is gone."

"Is that why you don't come around more often?" Each day without him seemed too long, although she never said this to him. She was ashamed to reveal her need. It would be giving him too much.

"It is used up too fast, then it is gone. It doesn't last," said Ibn Sinna. When his second wife had grown fat with child, her moods had slowly gone ugly. By the time she delivered and turned back to him again, the thing between them had been broken. Worse than broken. He had been younger then and it had been easy to blame her for something that neither of them controlled, any more than he controlled the look of malignant satisfaction in his first wife's eyes when she saw how their passion had failed them. "It doesn't last," he repeated.

"Never?" Likki's cynicism did not stretch as far as her lover's. Nor did she espouse theories of limited good.

"Some old ones here say that it can last. But usually we blame that on *juju*. Certain women are clever at finding magic like that to keep a man. And often such a man has only one wife."

"And the women? What keeps the women?"

He looked at her before he answered. "I know what you want to say," he said. "You want to say that it is injustice that keeps the women."

"It *is* injustice."

"*How* is it injustice?"

"Women here have nowhere to go except to a man. If not a father, then a husband. Or at least a lover. Otherwise they starve. Or *worse*." Back to the morning again.

"But the man, too, has nowhere to go."

Likki sensed he was speaking now of himself and not of his culture, and she let the argument die.

✖ 14

It was approaching midnight when they came to the village. Even so, Kalembelebiri seemed to be in an oddly festive mood: children danced and sang around its moonlit perimeter. They had their fathers' drums and their uncles' drums. Someone even had a xylophone. Fires blazed brightly for so late in the night. Adults were moving about with unusual animation, talking and laughing loudly.

Someone must have been watching the path, because Gbendlele came out to meet the two travellers a good quarter of a mile before they reached the village. She spoke rapidly with Ibn Sinna in Kpamé for several minutes and shook her head emphatically saying "No!" a number of times. Eventually, giving every evidence of reluctance, the old woman turned and led the way into the village.

"Doesn't she want us?" Likki asked.

"She is upset. It seems someone else has come to stay in your room."

"Who?"

"Some niece of hers."

"We can stay somewhere else can't we?" It was unlike Gbendlele to allow something like this to disturb her. It was so un-Kpaman to fret about inanimate things like rooms.

Ibn Sinna continued. "Gbendlele says you can stay on with the deaf boy in her room. As for me, she is sending me out to her bush hut."

"Her bush hut!"

"You see."

■

In the chief's reception room Gbendlele brought them a late supper of smoked grasscutter, a bowl of rice and beans, and a large pot of new frothy beer. After they ate, talk

carried on intensely and at length. Gbendlele was peculiarly emphatic whenever she spoke. Likki, understanding so
little of the language, had to glean impressions from the
manner of delivery, and there was something discernibly
conspiratorial in the tone of conversation this evening.
Everyone, Likki was certain, knew a great deal more than
she. She was equally certain that she would either be left in
ignorance or deliberately misled.

"We are discussing Comfort's disappearance," Ibn Sinna
explained during a pause.

"I thought you might be."

"Many people think she has been carried across the
river." He meant into the next country.

"Do you want to know what *I* think?" asked Likki.

"What is that?"

"I think Abu kidnapped Comfort and brought her out
here to Kalembelebiri."

"You think Comfort is in this village?" He smiled as if
indulging a child.

"I think she's in our room."

Ibn Sinna shook his head. Gbendlele noted the gesture
and questioned him sharply. When she had received his
answer, she scrutinized Likki intently. Then, after a pause,
she rose. "You come," she ordered. Likki obeyed and Ibn
Sinna, too, followed behind, his face a mask of suppressed
amusement. The old woman took them by a devious route
to the fifth courtyard. The guinea fowls, erstwhile proprietors of this establishment, were this evening huddled into a
corner of the court, where they stood dishevelled and
forlorn, as if all their prerogatives as well as all their
territory had been usurped by busy humans. Gbendlele
now slowed and faced Likki. "Go!" she said, pushing her
towards the end of the court where, in the doorway of
Likki's room, a lantern softly gleamed. Inside the room the
light of other lanterns glowed. Likki walked to the threshold and halted. Within, several elderly women wearing
serious expressions tended a young one moaning and
sweating on the mat. One of the old women kneeled close
to the reclining figure on the floor and massaged oil into her
swollen stomach.

Likki drew back. She had no experience of childbirth and

was uneasy in its presence. Ibn Sinna, she discovered, was laughing.

"You might have told me," she accused him.

"You would never have believed," he said. "This way you will believe it more."

Likki frowned.

"Is it something you don't understand?"

"Why put the woman in *our* room?"

"You know this our place is empty. No one sleeps here. So the woman can make plenty of noise and not be afraid to wake the village. And this woman, it seems, always has much trouble. Even my mother has been sent for. Tomorrow she will be coming here."

●

Midnight found Likki and Ibn Sinna sitting at the edge of the village on a bench in the moonlight like an old married couple. It was an evening for sybarites. The air was warm and voluptuous, moist as if off tropical seas. It carried with it earth scent and blossom and the song of frogs in stagnant pools. The moonlight, like an equatorial snowfall, lent an obliging softness to all that was pointed and hard.

"I could sit here forever," said Likki.

Ibn Sinna snorted. "Hey!" he exclaimed. "The white man is truly wonderful! You yourself, every fine place you come to you want to stop there again."

"Why not?"

"You would soon tire of living in Kalembelebiri."

"Oh, I don't know. If I knew the language better I'd probably love it out here."

"You would soon find the place is not lively. Soon, every day, you would come to me to complain there was nothing for you to do."

"Oh. *You* would be here too?"

"Why not?"

"Then how could I be bored?"

"Is that it?"

"Maybe," she hedged. The morning seemed farther away now. "Would you have your wives living out here too?"

"No. I would leave them behind in Kpama." His voice thickened with dawning hopes. "Should you not be going

to find the deaf boy to bring you to Gbendlele's room?" h
asked pointedly.

"Oh, I don't want to go to Gbendlele's room," Likki tol
him as if correcting someone who is frequently mistaker

"Why is that?"

"Oh, Moola told me she snores."

"How does Moola know that?"

"I didn't ask him."

"I see." She was not veering away from him as emphatic
ally as she had done earlier. "Then maybe you will like t
come with me to see my bush hut?"

"I thought it was Gbendlele's bush hut."

"Yes."

"Is it far?" She feigned weary reluctance.

"No, not far. It is just to the other side of one small hil
You come." He rose to lead the way with a kerosen
lantern.

The hut was, in fact, a good half mile from the village
Nestled among large boulders and covered with creepin
vines, it was well camouflaged in the moonlight, a habita
tion only remotely connected with human beings. "So th
is a bush hut," commented Likki with something else les
than full admiration.

"Was it not you yourself who told me this evening tha
you would happily live in such a place ten years?"

"I hadn't seen one when I said that," said Likki. "Are yo
sure there aren't any snakes inside?"

He opened the door and swung the lantern inside. "N
snakes," he informed her. "I think it is a very good place fo
you."

"Why is that?" she asked peering inside. By the lanter
light the room looked almost cosy.

"Out this far you don't need to worry; there is no one t
hear you." It had become his joke with her, her nois
lovemaking.

"So I can let it out tonight?" she asked.

"Have you been holding something back?" He moved th
lantern urgently about the room. Even by village standard
the accommodation was spartan. Still, if nearly bare, th
room was clean. And it was redolent of herbs and spice. Ib
Sinna pulled Likki to his side. He sniffed ostentatiously

"You see! Already Gbendlele knew you would sleep here
with me. She has put *juju* down all over to make me love
you."

"Is it going to work?"

"She has done it as a joke. Already I have told her you are
bad for me."

"Oh? Why am I bad for you?"

"You make me want to forget my other women."

■

Later in the night it rained. Not with violent winds and
thunder, but with a steady relentless determination so that
by morning the ground was drenched through and the
footpath back to the school was a four-mile exercise in mud.

Likki and Ibn Sinna left the hut early, pausing in the
village only long enough for one hot cup of coffee to warm
them against the damp. Gbendlele was proud of her tin of
instant Nescafé, which she had been rationing out for
special occasions over the last two years. No one liked to
tell her that it had gone just a little bit stale. Likki and Ibn
Sinna marched homeward through an adhesive dampness
that repressed all attempts at conversation. The track was
too soggy and slow for speech. When they were still a good
distance from the school, Ibn Sinna parted from Likki,
saying he did not want to be seen near the road. His caution
made Likki vigilant and she, too, approached the road with
hesitation. Soldiers were on patrol from the school down to
the police roadblock. Likki detoured widely. She veered off
through the bush in the direction of Segou and parallelled
the road for almost three-quarters of a mile before she
crossed it and slipped into the bush on the other side.
There she continued in fits and starts until she reached
Bungalow 5, just after seven, wet through and shivering.

"Don't tell me where you've been. Let me guess," said
Carlotta, who was annoyed that her guests of the previous
evening had abandoned her as soon as she had passed out.
She didn't say "passed out." She said "slipped off to sleep."

Likki put it to her that the seven sixth-form girls who had
slept with her in the bungalow should have been sufficient
to protect Carlotta from any untoward circumstance.

"Yeah, but they must have been in the bathtub all night

long. The Balmain is finished. And what about all the Oreos? Who told them they could eat up all our Oreos? For all I know they could have had a gang-bang with Nuhu on the sofa all night. And Zulu looks sick."

"Carlotta, how about a little brandy to warm up the insides?" Likki's lips were very nearly blue and her teeth clattered in irregular spasms.

"Sure, here, have some. We might as well finish the last of the bottle. You'll need it. I've got bad news."

"Already?"

"Yes. You came home too late. The army's already called this morning. Your absence was noted."

"Shit."

"I told them you had gone for a walk."

"In all this rain?"

"That's what Sergeant Awilobe said. But I told him you were English."

Carlotta paused. When next she spoke her tone had changed. "He brought me a pawpaw. Sergeant Awilobe. He brought me an enormous pawpaw." She preened. No one before had ever prized her for her plumpness. Carlotta looked as if she believed the sergeant had a true line on her inner self.

"Carlotta . . ."

"*He* was the soul of politeness. *I* was the soul of decorum," Carlotta bridled. But when the two women looked at each other they laughed because for a moment they saw themselves from a great distance off, saw how they both were tangled in meshes of untidy and, by the standards of home, probably unacceptable relationships. Yet here they sat like two old sailors in a harbour café, drinking brandy at seven-fifteen in the morning, one hoping to cure a hangover, the other to prevent pneumonia acquired in the course of a dubious adultery. It is also possible that Sergeant Awilobe, having lent a more human face to the workings of a thoroughly despised organization, had done something to make the overcast morning bright.

"Do you know what I think?" said Likki when the brandy had warmed some of her fears.

"Do you think at all?" pondered Carlotta. She inclined to philosophy only after her breakfast.

"I think Comfort is in Kalembelebiri."

Carlotta frowned.

"Really," Likki insisted, as if she had been contradicted.

"Why? Did they say so?"

"No. Of course not. But they wouldn't, would they?"

"So, why?"

"We couldn't stay in our usual room last night. We had to stay in a bush hut half a mile out of the village." Likki drew a sharp breath of remembrance.

"*I* see," said Carlotta.

"What do you see?"

Carlotta saw an expression of aching sensuality on the face of her roommate. She said, "So you think Comfort is in your room?"

"Not exactly," answered Likki, and she confessed the existence of the woman in labour.

"So what makes you think Comfort is in Kalembelebiri?"

"Just a feeling. I don't know. Maybe the woman *wasn't* in labour. I'm just not convinced somehow."

"Don't be paranoid." Carlotta mocked Likki's earlier refrain to herself.

Likki overlooked the remark. "And I bet you any amount of money it was Abu that smuggled her out there."

"Probably—if it's true."

"I have half a mind to ask him."

"Leave him alone, Likki. You'll just get him in trouble. Besides, it's better not to know."

"That's what everybody keeps saying."

✖15

Abu himself showed up later that morning. It was well before noon when he came. He was greatly agitated. "Please, miss," he said to Carlotta. He was terribly out of breath. "You come. The man is *too* sick."

"John?"

"Please, Nasara, you come. He is *too* hot."

With one accord the two women rose and followed Abu back into town. Both of them had classes scheduled for the afternoon and both abandoned these without the faintest prick of conscience, or even an explanation.

They encountered three roadblocks on their way into Kpama: the army on the road just outside the school, the police barricade near Smugglers' Bridge, and the army again on the edge of town. The men at each of these barriers delighted to detain them with trivial questions, and it was nearly two hours before they reached Kutu's. Coming up to the gates they hailed Kutu's watchman: "What news?"

Anxiety had made the old man wakeful. "It's not good," he told them, but then he yawned, wagging his toothless gums at the sky.

Inside, Salifu ran up to greet them. "Nasara, he vomits everything again. No water. Not any thing." John was prostrate in bed in an advanced state of dehydration, begging for water in a tremulous, four-year-old whine. Mieri stood by him wringing her hands. Likki stared at her shamelessly; she had never before seen anyone actually do this. "Has he had any water?" demanded Carlotta.

"Nasara, even we put lemon juice inside the water but every time he lose everything again."

"Since when?"

"Since morning time. Fifteen, maybe twenty times he

loses everything." Mieri wiped her eyes as she gave her explanation. Habiba looked up anxiously from where she sat at the head of the bed, wiping the heat from John's brow, sponging the fever from his body, soothing him with platitudes. "Don't worry. Everything will soon be fine." Her voice was quintessentially calm. Her eyes, however, when she turned them on the visitors, were full of alarm.

"Okay, let's try it again. Water and lemon juice, just a spoonful at a time." Likki held the teaspoon to John's lips. They were cracked, and blood had collected in the crevices. His body burned, unable to cool itself. He was desperate for liquid, sucked it greedily from the spoon, then asked for more. Mieri moved to comply, but Likki held her back. "Take it easy. Just a little at a time." She averted her head from John so that he could not see her face. With her lips she framed the words, "We've got to get him to the hospital." Carlotta nodded. But they waited there a while by the bed, hoping to calm their patient, hoping, perhaps, for a miracle. Every five minutes by the clock, they allowed John one more teaspoon of water. After the fifth teaspoon he vomited.

Ugly spasms shook his frame, and his stomach contracted uncontrollably, ejecting the priceless fluid they had given him, spewing forth mucous and bile. And when everything inside had been cast out, still he retched, choking and coughing as if his lungs, too, would issue forth from his mouth. He writhed helplessly, while tears of exertion spilled from his eyes and beads of sweat stood out on his forehead. More precious water wasted. Cold fingers closed on the stomachs of his nurses.

When finally John stopped gagging, he was seized with trembling. He looked up at them and something grey moved deep in his eyes.

"I think you've got malaria, John," said Carlotta.

For that one sentence, thought Likki, she might forgive Carlotta everything.

■

Getting John to the hospital would be no easy matter. Mother of Issa had gone to ground. She was hiding in her room upstairs, sitting in a dark corner, seeing no one. She

would not speak or weep. There was illness in her house.
Bad illness. Issa, her pride, had been stricken. Kutu, too,
lay abed in Gbiriri; she had heard the news the night before
from one of his labourers. And now her stranger. All the
men of her house. Something unfriendly menaced. She
would sit like a stone with her anxiety in a darkened corner
of her room until it was over. But she had the keys to the
car, and they would need them to take John to the hospital.

"Please, Salifu, I *have* to see her," begged Likki. She
wanted him to go in to Mother of Issa with a message.

"She will never come out of her room unless Issa and
Kutu is better. Or if . . . there is nothing else."

"She doesn't have to come out. You can go in."

"As for me," averred Salifu, "I won't go into that room."
He might sooner fit his neck to a guillotine.

"Can I go in?"

"Anyway you can try," said Salifu. He said it without
conviction.

"Nasara," Abu advised her, "you go *in*. When you are
inside, then you *cry*. Any time you cry you can get the
keys. When you cry you can get everything."

Likki went in and she cried. She would once have considered such behaviour reprehensible. Now it was merely
necessary—and surprisingly easy. A simple matter of crin-
kling up the face and letting the inner sense of defeat
inundate the spirit.

•

Abu, meanwhile, going out to find the driver, discovered
him sleeping with the watchman's daughter and had to avail
himself of a rather elaborate subterfuge—a harmless garter
snake dropped in through a hole in the back shutter—to
pry the man out from her bed.

There was further difficulty. John was reluctant to go. To
be admitted to the hospital in Kpama was to submit to
bodily frailty in the most ignominious fashion and to subject
one's well-being to institutional chaos. For example: the
hospital buildings had been designed along a Western plan
that made no allowances for the caprices of medical care in
the local idiom. The kitchens of the hospital had long since
ceased to function on a regular basis, so that patients had to

crawl out to the gates to purchase local "fast food" from the daily congregation of vendors, or more likely the patient's family would have to be accommodated along with him on the ward—either on or under the bed. The family then made itself responsible for the patient's daily sustenance. This arrangement had a deleterious effect on vegetation in the neighbourhood, and there was a dearth of firewood for a radius of half a mile in every direction from the hospital. The locust-bean trees the British had planted to provide dappled shade for the hospital verandahs had long since disappeared under somebody's soup. Only a baobab, considered sacred to a pagan spirit, had survived.

Another difficulty was laundry. The hospital took no responsibility for changing linen between patients. Everyone with any foresight brought their own sheets along with them. If a sheet remained on an empty bed, chances were it had been left there because someone had died on it. The sheet was more likely to be taken out and burned than to be recycled to the hospital's linen stores. No one ever looked forward to a hospital stay. The general feeling was that folk mostly went there to die. In a vicious circle, dislike of the hospital made people postpone seeking medical aid until all else (herbs, *juju*, diviners, mallams, and wild men in the bush) had failed—increasing the likelihood that Western cures would also prove inadequate.

The doctor—there was only one for an establishment of a hundred beds—saved his daily share of lives, but these exploits were mainly confined to the operable crises of appendicitis and obstructed labour. Hardly a day went by when the poor man did not perform at least two "Caesars" and as many appendectomies. His average of six operations per diem was filled out by ectopic pregnancies, monstrous cysts, splinters in the eye, and complications stemming from broken bones. After his early morning surgical stint (it had to be *early* morning, before the patients' relatives had time to feed them porridge or fermented corn dough in total disregard of anaesthetic procedure), the doctor devoted the remainder of his mornings to reviewing the thornier diagnostic puzzles that came to the outpatient clinic.

The outpatient clinic was always crowded. Legions of the

infirm converged upon it daily from up to seventy miles away. For most, this was the closest Western-trained doctor. How they made the trip to Kpama was fearsome to contemplate, for few of them could afford to come by lorry. The waiting line was hundreds of yards long. It wound with resigned gravity down the porches and verandahs of the hospital, a torpid and joyless serpent awaiting the next misery. Two-thirds of those who queued were mothers with ailing children.

The nurse in charge of admissions was a stout, emphatic woman, an affirmation of vitality in this unwholesome citadel. She questioned every person who came to the hospital and divided the ailing into three streams: those who needed chloroquine or penicillin were sent to the treatment clinic; those with unusual symptoms and those who were locally well-to-do were sent to be examined by the doctor. Some, the dying and those too weak to stand, were immediately dispatched to the wards.

"Miss Likki," beamed the nurse as the white woman approached her desk. Behind Likki, Carlotta helped Kutu's driver support John's sagging weight.

"Miriam." Likki was relieved to see a familiar face. Miriam taught health classes twice a week at the school. "Our brother is ill."

"Oh, sorry! What is wrong with him?"

"We think it's malaria."

Miriam rose to inspect, feeling pulse and forehead, looking in John's eyes. She did this because they were respected members of the community. She did it to convince them of her thoroughness. In fact, she could spot a malaria victim from a distance of eighty feet.

"I think it can be fever," she said. "Can he walk?"

"He can hardly stand up."

"He should go to the wards." John shivered. It sounded like a sentence of execution.

A male nurse was summoned to prick John's finger and examine the drop on a slide. He found the parasites there, disporting themselves amongst the wreckage they had made of his red blood cells. "Sixty per cent haemoglobin," said the nurse when he returned fifteen minutes later. "Eight point four grams."

"Don't say it," ordered John in a voice lacking all authority.

Carlotta said it anyway. "I told you so."

He pulled his lips back into what would once have been a smile.

•

It was long past dark when Likki and Carlotta left the men's ward. John was sleeping on a bed freshly made up with sheets borrowed at the last minute from the watchman's daughter, who had forgiven Abu's ill-timed interruption. John's bottom had been pricked as full of holes as a porcupine in mating season. A glucose drip delivered merciful fluid into the vein of his right arm.

As they turned along the hospital verandah, Carlotta thought she saw something move outside John's window. "What's that?" she gibbered. She was startled, jumpy from the long day.

"Nasara?" a familiar voice assailed them from the dark.

"Abu?"

"Yes."

"Abu, what are you doing out there?"

"I come to help Nasara John."

"How can you help him out there?"

Abu walked towards them where they stood under a light on the covered walkway. In his hand he carried a small black pouch. He looked uncomfortable, embarrassed, almost sly.

"What's that?" Carlotta wanted to know in a thready voice that spoke of tautly stretched nerves. It had been a bad day to begin with a hangover.

"This is medicine," said Abu. "Our Mother bring from one Mallam Yakubu."

"For John?"

"No!" he chided their ignorance. "No, it is not for Nasara John. It is for sorcerers." But Abu knew that they probably did not believe in sorcerers. Whites were skittish about certain troublesome areas. He explained, "You see, this hospital, many sick peoples I know are in here. So the sorcerers who are eating them are thick all about. But with this medicine we keep them away."

"Abu, no one is eating people here."

"Nasara, you listen." Abu gestured at the night. Bats plinked like metal harps. Night insects chirred on their winged errands. Mosquitoes whined.

"Listen to what?" said Carlotta, ever sceptical.

"You wait!" ordered Abu. He paused with his head at an angle. "There!" he exclaimed. A hoarse sound scratched in the baobab tree close by.

"What was that?"

"That is *owl*. And when the sorcerers travel at night to eat our people, they travel as owls." The sound repeated itself, rasping like a rusty hinge. Likki found the noise unnerving, a sinister finger stretching the fabric of the night. Carlotta shivered. "You see!" Abu continued. "When these sorcerers come like that, they eat the person inside so no one will know until they die. Then, when the person is *too* sick, his family will bring him here. So the sorcerers, too, will follow, to finish their meal and kill them all. That is why you find *so* many owls here and the place is *too* bad."

Carlotta shook her head with the weight of so much intended malevolence. Abu, apparently misinterpreting the movement as outright disbelief, felt the need to convince. "Nasara," he said. "My own father himself, lying in this place, he saw *so* many wizards. Every night he sees them, they come inside every night. Wizards and sorcerers and witches. All this thing. And the people inside scream and fight, but the wizards chop them all and they all die. If not I was such a small boy then, I could carry my father away. But no one wants to listen to me and I am too small, so he dies in this place."

"Oh, shit," said Likki reaching for Abu's thin shoulders. Carlotta pretended to blow her nose.

✗16

It was Abu who raised the subject of Comfort with Likki. "Nasara," he addressed her, standing stiffly erect before her, only his fingers expressing the squirming embarrassment he felt.

"What is it?" He looked as if he had come for another loan. Some madcap money-making scheme he would be sure to tell her could never fail.

"Miss Lady . . ." Very formal now. What could be afoot?

"Yes?"

"Miss Lady. I not take that baby Comfort away." He let out a long, tensely held breath when he finished his sentence.

"I see," said Likki. "Someone's been telling tales."

Abu seemed not to understand. He made a noise something like "rRnnhch?"

"Did someone tell you I said you took Comfort?" Likki rephrased.

Abu looked down and stiffened. "It's true."

"Was it Ibn Sinna?"

"Yes, Miss Lady. . . . No! He told Ayesha and she told it to Mother of Issa."

"And you were listening by the door?"

"Eh . . . eh."

There was a pause. Then Likki said, "So you didn't take Comfort away from her father's house?"

"Nasara, I not take any babies."

"So Comfort is *not* at Kalembelebiri?"

"Yes," he said relaxing now. "That baby of Gbendlele is another baby.

"Oh, I *see*," said Likki. This was the first she'd heard about Gbendlele's baby, but it wouldn't do to look ignorant. You could never get information out of people unless you

acted as if you knew it all already. She waited expectantly
for what might come next.

"Yes, you see it is since long time that Gbendlele wants a
child. All these years she is childless. And without children
there is no laughter in the house. And then, too, after some
few years the baby girl will grow and can help Gbendlele
small-small. Gbendlele is getting old now, and she wants to
look for her future."

Likki hazarded a probe. "Well, I didn't actually see
Gbendlele's baby out there, so that's why I thought it was
Comfort."

"Ah-hah! You think Gbendlele is hiding the baby from
you because of some secret. You think she is afraid to show
you the baby because you might tell somebody."

"Something like that," replied Likki, wondering whose
baby it was that Gbendlele had.

Abu answered her thoughts. "Nasara, you listen; this
Gbendlele's baby, this baby's mother is dead. Listen,
Nasara, one woman died in the lorry park last week. We
don't know her. We don't know anything. She has no
papers, no addresses. No markings." He meant tribal
markings. "Nothing. But she had one baby girl that we
don't know where to send home. So Gbendlele says she
wants that baby."

"And they just gave it to her?"

"Why not? That baby girl with the mother dead, she has
no family. If they then come to give her to someone who
wants her, then it's better, isn't it? The baby has a family
again."

"Sure," murmured Likki, growing more puzzled as the
story progressed. For instance, *she* hadn't heard anything
about a woman dying in the lorry park.

"Nasara," Abu pointed out, "up here at this school you
don't hear everything. The town is far. And then there was
plenty of trouble to keep you busy too, isn't it?"

"I didn't even know Gbendlele *had* a baby. Any baby."

Abu looked disturbed at this, as if he realized now that he
had given away more than was called for. "Gbendlele is
keeping that baby a secret," he said at last in a subdued
voice.

"Why is that?"

"She is afraid the army will think that baby she is keeping is really Mahmut's child and try to take the baby away." He paused for a moment of introspection. "And that baby, too, is very *fine!*" He smiled.

"Hey! Abu! Another wife already?"

Under his dark skin, Abu appeared to blush. "Why should *I* not have two?" he defended. "All these big-men want to take many wives, more and more and more. Even Ibn Sinna is chasing a new one."

"A new wife?" Likki felt an unpleasant numbness start at her throat and work downwards towards her bowels.

"It's true, Nasara. All the time he is chasing along behind al Hajji Umar's daughter, Aswayya, and all the time calling Mahmut names because Mahmut wants that same woman, too." Abu frowned. He may well have been aware of what sort of Pandora's box he was opening up now, for he said, "Nasara, don't tell the man you know."

"Of course I'll tell him I know." Likki was already wrapping up this knowledge into a thick black cord that she meant to knot about her lover's throat.

"Nasara, if he finds I told you, he will beat me."

"Then why *did* you tell me?"

"Nasara, I am your friend. Every time I tell you the truth."

Likki was momentarily disinclined to argue this point. Abu meanwhile was screwing up his face and forcing tears of anxiety into his eyes.

"I'll pretend I heard it at Farrah's, okay?"

"Eh . . . eh."

■

Carlotta, when she heard the news of Ibn Sinna's infidelity from her vexed and furious roommate, was unimpressed. "What are you so upset about? It doesn't mean anything here—it's like he was buying another car. It's not like at home. At home, if your boyfriend gets married it's a disaster. But here, he's already married. *Twice!* What difference can one more wife make to you?"

"Jesus Christ!" swore Likki. "It's bad enough to be a wife supplanted by a mistress. But a mistress supplanted by a wife!" It was a misfortune for which no amount of pre-field acculturation training could have prepared her.

"You're taking it all too seriously," instructed Carlotta.

"Carlotta, go to hell."

"Have you seen the girl?"

"No."

"She's only about fourteen. Brain of a toadstool." Carlotta could be comforting in her own dismissive way.

"Is she pretty?"

"Luscious. Like a tree-ripened mango." Grinding it in.

"Shit." Likki knew the type: fruity, full-fleshed, sensuous; eyes like limpid pools; an irresistible pear-shaped perfection begging to be plucked in time.

"By the time she's twenty she'll be a worn-out old bag," continued Carlotta. "So all you have to do is hang in there for another six years."

"Thanks a lot."

Carlotta continued. "Apparently the girl hasn't got a brain in her head. It's a miracle she can even speak."

"She doesn't have to speak. She only has to open her legs."

"Ah, but she's managed *not* to do that. Just enough brains to keep them all in suspense."

"How do you know all this?"

"The bursar's wives were complaining to me. Nuhu is one of the mango's admirers. Apparently she carries water to her father's house every afternoon and drives the whole town mad with lust."

"Oh, Christ."

"But so far nobody's even touched her." Carlotta pressed her lips together in a prim smile of admiration for chastity preserved in the face of overwhelming odds.

"I'd like to touch her," said Likki with malicious vehemence.

"Oh, Likki."

"I'd like to touch her with a disfiguring disease. Smallpox perhaps. Or maybe leprosy. That would be nice, too. Slow and drawn out."

"Do you know what you sound like?"

"A shrew?" suggested Likki.

"You sound like a Kpama woman."

"So?"

"So what happened to all your nice liberal middle-class ideals?"

"Bull. Shit. Carlotta."

"Aren't you just a little bit ashamed?"

"No." She wasn't, either. She was experiencing a state of uninhibited malice and was surprised at how exhilarating it felt.

"Likki, she's only a kid."

"The hell she's a kid."

"She's only a little bit older than Abu."

"Abu? Abu isn't any kid. Abu is ancient. Abu was well over a hundred years old the day he was born. He's a monster. He's hatching five new plots every minute. He's probably turning me over on every single one of them, too." Likki paused for a moment of reflection. Had Carlotta spoken like this to her five months earlier, Likki would have sworn she was paranoid.

"Well, then, maybe Abu was lying to you about Asway-ya." Carlotta held out the olive branch. "Probably it isn't true."

"Oh, it's true all right." Abu's revelation had all the scratchy unpalatability of truth. Likki was faced with a situation she had no immediate idea how to counter. Everything that troubled her about Ibn Sinna now took arms under the flag of jealousy.

In this frame of mind, Likki found the afternoon excursion to visit John Lavender at the hospital understandably irksome. Carlotta, perhaps because of her budding flirtation with Sergeant Awilobe, was also unenthusiastic.

John, for his part, contributed little to the pleasure of their visit. In his bed in an alcove at the end of the ward, he was irritable and self-pitying. He drank down the Coke they brought him and wondered out loud why the Oreos had been left behind.

"We had the girls in two nights ago and they finished them all up," Carlotta told him, staring accusingly at Likki.

"This book isn't any good either," John complained, continuing his criticisms as if she had not spoken. He held up in his hand a worn Penguin classic. "I need toilet paper, not Dickens."

"Dickens is all there is until we get some newspapers."

"Isn't there any junk left on my shelves?"

"It's only *Barnaby Rudge*," Likki pointed out. "Six hundred pliable pages. Not their author's best, certainly. We wouldn't do it to *David Copperfield*."

"Not even to the pages with Uriah Heep?"

"You mean you think we should go in for a new form of censorship?"

"Yes, the truly expurgated edition."

It was a poor joke, but they laughed, making what they could of it for the sake of his illness. But afterwards, when they had left him, they owned to each other that they were none too sure of his progress.

"I don't think John is really any better," opined Carlotta.

"He's better than when we brought him in."

"Is he? He just seems to be standing still somehow."

Likki made a face. If John were really ill they would have to think about him constructively and that would be an additional item on an already crowded agenda.

"He's so *thin*," continued Carlotta.

"He said the hospital food was off," Likki replied. John had not told them that he'd stopped eating altogether. "Maybe he thinks there's *juju* in the food," reflected Likki, now coming fairly close to the mark, as she was soon to discover. The next day, when the two women again braved the heat in another joyless expedition to the hospital, they found their patient's condition considerably worse. John lay feverish and fretful on his bed with an unwholesome pallor to his skin. He looked as if he'd just come out of deep-freeze on an intergalactic space flight. His eyes were glassy, restless, and untrusting.

"I must leave the hospital," he said shakily.

Likki felt his forehead. Fire. Under her fingertips his pulse ran thin and thready. "You're in no condition to go anywhere," she told him.

"They're poisoning us," he said. "It's in the food. And the water."

"Don't be ridiculous," said Likki. John's fears irked her, touching a nub of unquiet resonance deep in her own consciousness. The people of Kpama were, after all, not quite "civilized," not twentieth-century civilized, anyway.

Renaissance civilized, yes. They could poison and did poison and might poison again at any time, without remorse, and without detection.

"Three people died last night on the ward." He trembled as he recounted the events: the choking, gasping struggle for breath that failed, the tortured moans of those who made hard work of letting go. And all the while the murmurs of fear that swept through the ward among those who still hoped for life. Cries of owls. Screams. Ghostly visions. "You'll take me," he pleaded, grasping Likki's hand too tightly.

"You'll go when you're better."

"I won't *get* better here. I simply must leave here. Please!"

The two women looked at each other across his bed. "We'll have a talk with the doctor," decided Carlotta out loud.

John coughed. "What doctor? We never see any doctor."

Likki stayed behind while Carlotta went out to look for Dr. Kaweyu. "We'll take you back home if we can," she assured the patient, hoping it wouldn't come to that.

"To the bungalow."

"You want to come to the bungalow?"

"Yes." He brightened.

"Why not to Kutu's? You live there."

"Oh. I would so much rather stay with you," he said. "Only until I'm recovered, of course. I wouldn't dream of imposing."

Of course not. One more try. "I still don't see why you don't want to go home to Kutu's."

"It's Mother of Issa. Or rather her *teas*. I swear whatever she uses is making me worse. But I could never say that to her, could I?"

Likki made no reply.

"No. Of course not. Better to avoid the whole issue," John continued. His eyes, feverish and bright, roamed round the room evasively. He was hiding something. A secretive, canny expression came over his face. "Do you believe in *juju*?" he asked.

"Oh, Christ! You're not going to tell me you're being magically attacked?"

"Well, not just me personally. The whole place is full of it." He looked up at her wisely as he spoke, like a wizard confiding spells.

"You sound like Abu."

"Yes, I know. I had rather a long talk with Abu concerning all this." John smiled. "*He* brings me Mother's tea. And medicine to put outside my window at night. Every night. I rest it there on the window-sill every night. You see, Abu knows. He told me. This place is very bad. Abu thinks I should leave it as soon as possible."

"When the doctor says you can leave, we'll get you out of here."

"To your bungalow."

"Yes, to our bungalow," lied Likki.

"Yes. Good. Much better." He paused while his eyes flicked round the room. "You know that army captain is rather spooked," he remarked, now pursuing a new train of thought. "He's had the mallams here all morning driving off the ghouls."

Likki frowned.

"You don't believe me, do you?"

"I don't want to believe you."

"Oh, it's true enough. Our dear Alistair Araoh has been having *dreams*. Very nasty dreams. He dreams he's stalking game in the bush and then he sees the leopard. Up goes the gun! He pulls the trigger! But all he hears is a dull click. The rifle isn't loaded. He's frantically trying to shove in a bullet when the panther springs."

"Who told you all that?"

"The other patients."

"How do they know what Captain Araoh dreams about?"

"*Everybody* knows. He's been to the diviners three times. He has other nightmares, too. Every night. Whenever he falls asleep a long black finger creeps out of the darkness and curls around his throat. He sees it coming. A three-foot-long, horrible, ugly, evil-smelling claw. And he tries to run away, but he can't move. He's stuck there. Then, when it chokes him, he wakes up screaming and he can't get back to sleep. A long, evil finger of a claw. Like a crab—a monstrous, over-sized crab. Alaskan king!" John laughed.

"It's just his guilty conscience."

John laughed again, with unfriendly satisfaction. "Not quite. It's Sima and Moola. You see, they're out to get him. It's because of the wells. And the ghost. And the leopard. And other things, too, of course. They know what they're doing. Whatever they use, there won't be any trace of it. Arrow poison or something like that, something that will have destabilized before it can be sent to a laboratory to be analysed. Or they'll make it look like suicide. Or lightning. Whatever. Those two are true professionals; no suspicion will attach to them no matter how hard the army searches. That's why Araoh is terrified. And that's why I must leave this hospital. There's too much going on here! You see that, don't you? Everyone's plotting murder. I have to get out."

"John, have you been eating properly?" Likki asked. John's dinner lay untouched on the table by his bed.

"I don't eat here. Are you mad? I've been telling you for fifteen minutes. The food is poisoned. All of it. All poisoned. Everything that comes in here is tampered with."

"But not by Sima?"

"Yes, by Sima. That's what I've been trying to tell you. He wants Araoh. Wants him badly."

"Captain Araoh isn't staying at the hospital. He doesn't eat here."

"Oh, but he *does* eat here. His soldiers are here, you know? The ones Sima poisoned through the well water. They're all here, and Araoh comes to visit them every day. He eats with them. He's even ordered the hospital kitchens to start cooking again. But Sima has got his spies in the kitchen. The poison is strong. Araoh would probably only need to take one bite."

"Do you know what you sound like?"

"You think I'm crazy, don't you? That's just what I thought when they first told me. But it's true. You can taste it in all the hospital food." He paused. "If you know how it tastes."

"Who told you how it tastes?"

"The other patients. They know. They don't eat either."

"They don't eat because they're too ill. You're ill because you don't eat."

"But I'm still alive. And they're dead." He grinned and his eyes, when he looked at her, were those of a mind profoundly darkened. Likki shivered in the heat. Saying, "I'll just go out to find Carlotta," she excused herself from his presence, abandoning his troubled ramblings with relief and hurrying towards the door at the end of the ward as if it were the threshold of sanity. She opened it. Behind the screen, camouflaged in the shade of the verandah, stood Captain Alistair Araoh.

"Miss Liddell," he oozed. "What an unexpected pleasure."

"The same, I'm sure," Likki replied, certain that the meeting was planned. He had been waiting for her, checking his snares.

"Now that I see you here, I wonder if I might trouble you for a little information."

"Why not?" What information would he want? Comfort? She smiled at him and made her face a mask of innocence.

"It is pleasant to find you so co-operative," he remarked, but suspicion gathered behind his smile. He paused for a moment to take a bearing on his quarry. When he spoke again, he was right on track. "You have been out to Kalembelebiri?"

"Yes?"

"Is that baby there?"

"Comfort?"

"What other baby am I looking for? Is she there?"

"I don't know. I suppose she might be there."

"Miss Liddell, that is hardly an answer. Even I know that the baby *might* be there. She *might* be anywhere. What I am asking you now is if you have seen that baby in that village."

"No, I haven't seen her there. On the other hand, it's not very likely they would show her to me, is it?"

"That is debatable, Miss Liddell."

Likki waited silently for more. The pause grew awkward. Then Araoh said, "Perhaps you noticed something unusual in the village? Something different. A change in routine?"

She hesitated as if for reflection, remembering the village's unwonted air of festivity, the woman in labour. "No. Nothing," she lied with an exhilarating sense of accomplishment.

17

Likki walked home alone that evening. Dr. Kaweyu (bless him!) had told Carlotta he would not even contemplate releasing John Lavender for at least another five days. John's case was curious, fitting no common pattern. His symptoms were proving intransigent and he needed to be kept under observation.

As Likki and Carlotta left the hospital precincts, just outside the main gate, where they stopped to buy fried plantain and ginger, they had a serendipitous encounter with Sergeant Awilobe, who made haste to improve upon accident by inviting the two women out for a drive. He suggested a picnic near the old government rest house by the river, and afterwards, he said, he would show them the crocodiles at Gbigga—enormous, half-tame creatures, which would walk up to visiting automobiles to beg for food with awesome, two-metre grins.

Likki took pity on her roommate. Carlotta, bashful with desire, could hardly collect herself sufficiently to accept the offer. "I'm afraid I can't come," Likki told the sergeant. "I have exams to mark. But I'm sure Carlotta would love to see the crocodiles."

"Oh, yes," Carlotta managed to squeak out, though she could not bring herself to look at Sergeant Awilobe when she spoke.

"Keep the doors shut," Likki called after the departing army pick-up. Carlotta's bulk would keep five of the giant lizards slumbering with satiety for more than a week. An uncharitable thought, but then Likki had to thread her way up the hill to the bungalow on her own. On the road ahead she could already make out the silhouettes of police officers patrolling the first roadblock. Beyond were two more checkpoints: the army near the school and a police barricade by the bridge.

Likki paused, then headed off into the heavy bush at the side of the road. She had some well-developed opinions on the nocturnal African landscape, opinions that were noticeably stronger when she travelled on her own. There were snakes in the bush, and yard-long centipedes; toads with poisonous stings; scorpions; every kind of creepy-crawly you could think of. An array of Hallowe'en monsters left over from the Pleistocene era. But the army was also repellent. Even if the soldiers never touched you there was not enough soap in Kpama to wash away their dirty and complacent glances. So this evening Likki chose the perils of the bush because the things she imagined were less frightful than those she was sure of.

She came up to the bungalow from an odd angle and noticed a suspicious pink glow emanating from the hall. Had Carlotta forgotten to turn off the light again? Had it been on since the previous evening? They wouldn't have noticed, of course, with the power turned off all day. Was someone inside?

"Anybody home?" she called from the back door.

A familiar voice answered from inside. It was Ibn Sinna. Likki's apprehensions lost ground before another, more angry emotion.

"So it's you," she said coming into the living-room where he stood removing bottles from the cardboard box. He frowned at the edge in her voice. He said he had come to deliver Carlotta's brandy. He apologized for its inadequacies: it was Martell, there was no Remy Martin in Kpama. None in the north, he said, watching her all the time, trying to read in her face the new note he had heard in her words.

"Is that why you came? For the brandy?"

"No." He smiled at her, playing for time while he attempted to define the change in her tone. "I came because there can be trouble tonight. Already we know the army man has been asking you questions. Sima told me that he had captured you at the hospital and tried to make you talk. Now, tonight, another soldier is dead—one who was drinking from the well. The army man is hot. He is running about like an angry tiger, searching for her cub. He is going through people's houses. He is going through people's rooms, through their baskets and granaries. He is searching again. Anyway, it's better you are not alone."

"Oh, really. Are you going to stay here all the time?"

"Likki!" It was a reprimand for the kind of question of which women are so fond. And for her coldness.

"From what you say, I am in danger all the time. So why pick tonight to come and protect me?"

"There was the brandy," he reminded her.

"Yes, of course." He could always find a reason for doing whatever he did. And what he did was always exactly what he wanted to do. He always came to her because of his own need. The timing was always of his choosing. It was his way ever to drift in when she least expected him, always to refuse to be pinned down as to the next place and time. She had, for a long time now, given up trying to work out the rights and wrongs of it; there was, in any case, little that could be applied in the way of moral leverage. He accepted so few of her standards. But she was angry now and her own standards were the only context in which she made sense to herself. "What about your family?" she demanded. "Don't they need protection? Or is it only me who's helpless?"

"My family is safe. My brother is there with them. Here, you are just two women alone. Tonight, just one woman." So he phrased his concern for her. Ibn Sinna looked at Likki. "I don't think you are worried about my family," he said to Likki. "I think there is some other problem, isn't it?"

"What other problem could there be?"

"I don't know."

"Oh, I'm sure you don't."

"I don't know. You should tell me."

"All right," she said grimly, but she avoided telling him. Instead she circled around the main issue. She told him that the problem was his unscheduled coming and going, his self-appropriated freedom. Likki envied this in him; she would have liked to be that way herself, but she could not see exactly how it was managed. So she pretended that this capacity of his was immoral. Predictably, Ibn Sinna was only confused.

"You want to say I should not be moving about, is that it?" he asked in tones of well-dramatised amazement.

"Why should you be able to roll about wherever you want when I can't even move?"

"Is there something to keep you from moving about?"

"There's plenty. There's my job. Then there's *your* police. And *your* army. And if that weren't enough, there's a whole library full of social conventions telling me *where* a woman can't go and *when* a woman can't go and *why* she won't be welcome and *how* she'll be asking for trouble. And that she ought to know better and behave herself."

"And I am responsible for all these rules you find in your library?"

"You profit from them. They make your life easy."

"But I didn't make them."

"You didn't try to change them, either."

"Why should I come to change the rules? Our rules here in Kpama have worked for centuries."

"They've worked for men, yes."

"Hey! Is it my fault you are a woman?"

"I don't suppose it is." She wished it were his fault. It would be so much easier to confront him with his prejudices if he could be held personally responsible for the general imbalance in human affairs. "It's not my fault, either," she reminded him.

"Would you rather be a man?" he inquired with condescension.

"If you weren't all such a pack of jackals, yes, I would. Of course I would. It's all laid on for men. The whole show. The power. The money. And the women, too, of course. Women are something else that's laid on, and not just metaphorically. Don't ask what women get, though, because all they get is the shit."

Ibn Sinna listened to this and much more, still watching to spy out its source. Eventually, Likki sent out a signal of the real trouble. "And then, when they're all worn out, they get to watch from the sidelines while their husbands chase around after other tight young things with zippered cunts."

"What have you been hearing?" he asked, too quickly.

"Me? What would I hear? I live all the way up here on

his hill three miles out of town. What would I ever hear
vay up here?"

"What was it?" He spoke more slowly now.

"What was what? I haven't heard a thing. If there's
something you don't want me to hear, don't you worry. I
won't ever hear it up here."

"Has someone been talking to you?"

"Lots of people talk to me." They eyed each other across
the room like mongoose and cobra. In the space between
Likki's anger and Ibn Sinna's indignation that a woman
could imagine that the way he ran his life was any of her
business, the rounded form of Aswayya, al Hajji Umar's
daughter, took shape almost as tangibly as if she had been
conjured.

"You're jealous!" he exclaimed at last. He spoke with a
sense of victory, of triumph over Likki because of her
inappropriate reaction and because he had at last disclosed
her secret, an empty secret that had no force in it that could
move him.

"It's time for you to leave now," she said.

Victory made him generous, however, and he sought
reconciliation. "Likki," he cajoled. "There's nothing for you
to be jealous of."

"Go!"

He approached her with the magnanimity of success.
"Please tell me why you are jealous."

"Get out."

"Please." He spoke very softly now. Along with the other
emotions Likki saw in his eyes, she recognized a growing
desire for her body. Her intensity had roused him and she
could see the will to dominate her wrestling visibly with a
gentler but equally urgent need to break her hatred and
transform it into cries of ecstasy. She would not pleasure
him today.

Carlotta's old pocket knife lay open on the table and Likki
lifted it in her hand. "Don't come any closer or I'll carve
your face into a chequerboard," she threatened and looked
forward to seeing him hesitate.

Ibn Sinna was not deterred. All boys in Kpama wrestled
with knives. With a quick dart of his hand he grabbed hold
of her wrist. But he was not quick enough; Likki had read

his intention and had already launched herself toward
him. Her momentum carried her close enough to carve
long mark down his cheek with the blade even as he hel
her and tried to force her away.

The cut surprised them both. Likki dropped the knif
and Ibn Sinna let go of her. He touched his bloodied chee
and examined his crimsoned fingers. "Is that it?"

Likki, her heart beating like a captured bird's, waite
tensely for reprisals.

"You think I am going to hit you?"

She puckered her mouth and spat on the floor.

He would not make advances to one so unwilling t
forgive. Turning abruptly he left her with long strides, hi
robes sweeping behind him like winter. When he had gon
Likki sought consolation by making inroads on Carlotta
brandy.

●

Carlotta herself did not come home until early the next day
when she bounced through the door of Likki's jaundice
morning with swollen and ill-concealed joy.

"Sergeant Awilobe wants to marry me," she announce
right away.

"Uoooomlph!" In surprise, Likki swallowed too much h
coffee. It stabilized scaldingly halfway down her oesoph
agus.

"I really love him, Likki," said Carlotta softly, thickl

"Carlotta, you only just met him last week." Somewher
in Likki's adolescence her mother had denied Likki
feelings with the same flat words.

"I don't see what time has got to do with it."

"You're not thinking of saying yes, I hope."

"Why not?"

"Why not? It's madness, that's why not. You've only sle
with him once."

"Five," Carlotta corrected, holding up the pudgy finger
of her right hand. "We did it five times."

"Carlotta, you hardly *know* the man."

"This is different, Likki," said Carlotta mistily. "I neve
knew it could be like this."

"Oh, my God."

"He really loves me." Carlotta looked as if she were going o cry.

"Oh, Christ!"

"I can tell he does."

"I'll bet."

"You don't believe me, do you?"

"No. I mean I don't believe you know what you're doing. Lither you or Sergeant Awilobe."

"Peter," Carlotta corrected. She spoke the name softly, as f she were still in bed with him stroking his inky stomach.)r as if she were in church.

"His name is Peter?"

"Mmmmmmmmmmmmmmmm."

Likki tapped her knees with the palms of her hands. It vas hard to know whether to laugh or to scold. "Carlotta, low many men have told you they love you?"

"Peter is the only one." Her face was radiant.

"And you *believe* him?"

"Why not?" Carlotta paused. "That's *your* trouble, Likki. bet people tell you all the time and I bet you *never* •elieve them." There were several grains of truth in this nd Likki did not reply. Carlotta did not press home the oint. Instead she mused thoughtfully, "We'd have the utest kids. Little brown chocolate drops." She turned oulful sheep's eyes on her imaginary brood.

Likki waited a moment, then asked, "Was he big?"

"Likki!"

"*Was* he?"

Carlotta looked affronted, as if she were going to say, Don't pry," but then she caught Likki's eye and blushed.

✳18

The day came on thick and oppressive. It was the kind of day in which people move about in a stupor waiting for something to happen, something that will break the spell of the heat and animate them again. Likki also waited, in a private vigil, for a certain cream-coloured Mercedes to pull up in front of the bungalow and bring with it either a reconciliation or a more satisfactory continuation of the quarrel.

Instead sombre news came up in the late morning. The last of the poisoned soldiers had died in the hospital after numberless slow hours of agony. In addition, it was rumoured that the army was advancing on Kalembelebiri, that the chief had already been taken prisoner, and that Captain Araoh had every confidence that Comfort would soon be found and taken into protective custody. Within minutes of receiving the news, Likki began lacing up her walking shoes—under a storm of protest from Carlotta.

"You can't go out there! It'll look like you're involved."

"I *am* involved."

"There could be all kinds of trouble out there."

"Of course there'll be all kinds of trouble out there."

"You think Ibn Sinna might be out there, don't you?" said Carlotta with unwelcome precision.

"Go to hell, Carlotta." Likki was beginning to feel frightened about the quarrel, appalled that she had physically attacked someone.

"Just don't fall afoul of the law," continued Carlotta.

"The law? Or the army?"

"There isn't any difference, is there?"

"There ought to be." Likki scowled. This was the main trouble. Captain Araoh's authority in no way derived from the moral consensus of the community in which he exercised it. Thus, even according to Carlotta's reactionary schemes of social justice, this called his position into question.

"I'll be careful," Likki promised.

"Sure," said Carlotta, almost sadly.

Likki hesitated, then asked, "Do *you* want to come?"

Carlotta didn't answer right away. "No," she said at last.

"Are you sure?"

"I'm sure." Seeing that Likki still hovered unconvinced, she added, "I'm sure. I'm sure. Go on. Get out of here if you're going."

■

The difficult part of getting to Kalembelebiri was finding the right footpath. The opening to it was unmarked, a modest parting in the tall grasses at the side of the road, a parting that could only be searched for in the intervals between the soldiers' sporadic patrolling. Once set on the right path, however, there were few forking intersections to tempt the traveller aside, and the few there were had been only thinly trodden—with the exception of one very obvious path, which veered off acutely towards Segou.

Though it was late afternoon, the sky was overbright. It reflected back far too much sunlight, as if, over the next bank of hills, the restless ocean tugged, catching the light of the sun in the flux of a million mirrors and throwing it back again over the weary land. The relentless glare cancelled out all shadow.

Likki came down over the last ridge and was surprised by her first glimpse of the village. She had expected perhaps a bright conflagration to match her mood, a fiery chaos. She did not find it. Kalembelebiri looked almost normal. With its neat round-cornered walls it loomed ahead like a smallish mud fort, something an ambitious child might build on the sands between ebb and flow. It had an emphatic way of sitting to one side of its little valley as if it would defy anyone to say it did not belong there. In fact, there was little in the aspect of the village to dismay the casual viewer unless it was a small plume of smoke, rising from the furthest quarter, that might easily have been a smouldering stack of grass or other vegetation. The really discomforting element was negative. A subtraction rather than an intrusion. The village was eerily still. It was deserted.

Likki slowed her steps by the outer walls and called out a few feeble hellos. She received no answer. Every room into which she peered looked as if its inhabitants had only just stepped out for a minute. Soup simmered over charcoal fires. A weaver's threads lay carefully spread out next to his loom, as if he had laid them down while he went for a drink of water. In the chief's reception room the old man's pipe and walking-stick and slippers lay casually strewn about on the mat next to his pile of chiefly lion skins. And Gbendlele's kitchen next door displayed all the disorder of a meal still in preparation. A fish stew was beginning to burn dry within arm's reach of the deaf boy's stool. A mangy cat purred near the stool, waiting perhaps for the fire under the stew to die out. It gave Likki a look of feline consternation.

"I don't know, puss," Likki answered it, and the sound of her own voice startled the stillness. "I don't know," she repeated, but in a whisper.

She retraced her steps through the chief's reception room. By his outer door she thought she saw something dark and wet glistening on the threshold. On inspection this proved to be a bird dropping, but for a moment Likki saw it as blood. She could imagine the old chief standing there, his fat arms wide at his sides, protesting the intrusions of the detested army. And then some reckless soldier, impatient of delays, firing and bringing him to ground, along with his endless, tedious stories, his overweening fondness for tobacco, his lusts, his little hatreds, and his undeniably generous heart. "God damn," said Likki, again startled by the dry sound of her voice.

In some trepidation, she started towards the fifth courtyard. The smoke seemed to be coming from there. The familiar intervening courtyards slipped by her now in a parody of their former wholesomeness. Without their customary occupants, they menaced. Vacant doorways and windows grinned skeletally as she passed. She had imagined all this differently. She had imagined pandemonium, distress on familiar faces. Solitude was one thing she was not .prepared for.

She came at last to her own part of the village. A disordered fire smouldered in the centre of the courtyard. Nearby, the once raucous guinea fowls lay dead together on a heap of ashes, their necks inelegantly twisted, the smell of the scorched feathers nauseating.

Likki's heart suddenly leapt. Through the smoke she had seen someone lying on a mat near the doorway to her room. It looked like a woman sleeping. "Hello?" called Likki, drawing closer. Oh, but someone had spoiled the doorway. All round one side of the entrance someone had chipped away ragged chunks of adobe the size of eggs. It would be difficult to mend, even with the best mud from Ngmaangmu. Gbendlele would be furious.

The sleeping woman did not waken. She lay reclining to one side, an arm stretched casually above her head as though she had just turned over in her sleep.

"Hello?" Likki called again. She halted several yards from the reclining figure. Despite the smoke a bottle-green fly crawled at the corner of the woman's eye. Fear rustled. Likki watched the figure's abdomen intently. Yes, she was sure she could see the rise and fall of the miraculous tide of breath. But then she misdoubted her perception. She moved closer. Six feet from the mat Likki recognized the sleeper. "Ayesha!" There was no response. With unwelcome, icy certainty Likki acknowledged that the woman was dead. She spun around to leave, to flee, to think about getting help, and then she saw them through the smoke: five soldiers in starched khaki and, in front of them, approaching her, their crisp, impeccable commander.

"You!"

"Miss Liddell, how pleasant we meet again so soon." He bowed deeply in a parody of greeting.

"Are you responsible for this?"

"The woman?"

"The woman. The village. Everything." As she spoke she was suddenly sure that it was Captain Araoh himself who had flung Ayesha down on the dirt of the courtyard, like an uprooted water plant, a lily tossed carelessly on the bank to wilt and dry in the sun.

Death had left behind such insignificant signatures; a few dark holes in breast and shoulder, for some reason almost bloodless. It was eerie, the lack of blood, almost as if the man had witched her.

"*You* killed her, didn't you?"

"It was a most unfortunate accident." He minced out his words with staccato precision.

Likki looked down at Ayesha. She felt no grief, for they had not been close, except in some ill-defined antagonism. She felt only outrage and intense defeat.

"You murderer," she said at last.

"Excuse me, Miss Liddell, but I am no murderer. This woman was killed in the exercise of duty. She was killed because she broke the law."

"The law? What law?"

"She kidnapped the baby and brought it out here to hide. When we came to reclaim the child, this woman foolishly tried to stop us and lead us astray. She threatened my soldiers with a knife. She even threatened to kill the child! It was necessary to use force against her."

"You shot a woman because she was looking after a baby?"

"She was breaking the law."

"Is there a law that says you can't look after a baby?"

"There is a law against threatening an agent of authority with a deadly weapon. There is another law against the obstruction of justice."

"I suppose that's what you brought here, justice?"

"Justice is what I always bring."

"Then God help Africa."

"Miss Liddell, you need not upset yourself about Africa. Africa is not your business. Africa is *my* business. You are an outsider here. And please, I beg you, do not deceive yourself that your so-called finer feelings are not understood. I know that you stand there and you hate me because you think that when you see me in this army uniform you are looking at the betrayal of Africa. But, I ask you, what Africa is it that I am betraying? Am I betraying Kalembelebiri? A village with no water supply and no sewage, a village with an infant mortality rate of sixty per cent or more? A village where no one has enough to eat? A hamlet of drunken farmers with sores on their feet that never heal? This is not the true Africa here. It is nothing more than senseless and unproductive poverty. It is suffering without any object."

"Then why not leave it alone if it's so hopeless?"

"Leave it alone? Oh, yes. Leave it alone to infect the country all about with stagnation and poverty and reverence for the past. Probably you think I should be the one to help preserve the old ways, is that so? But let me tell you, our old ways brought us nothing. Nothing. But *now*, when we are struggling to enter the twenty-first century alongside the other nations of the earth, suddenly there are *so* many people who are concerned about preserving the old ways. The old ways and the supposed true Africa. So many people who find much to criticize in the emergence of military governments. But what sorts of governments did we have under the colonial powers? Were they not military governments of the worst possible sort? What sort of government *should* we have? Councils of elders from every village in the country, congregating annually to sit on goatskins in the squares of the capital?"

Likki was silent. It was obvious Araoh had rehearsed this speech in his head many times.

"You have nothing to say?"

"It still looks like murder to me."

"Ah, you are a missionary! You mean to tell us what is right. Just once! And then after that you expect us to behave like angels. You people are too kind, really. Much too kind to us. You want us to have everything. Modern factories, universal health care. Buses that run on time. And, of course, let us not forget democracy. Above all we must have a freely elected democratic government. Oh yes. But I ask you, Miss Liddell, where is the ground base for this democracy you are so fond of? Do you see it here in Kalembelebiri?"

"All I see are pistols."

"Very witty, Miss Liddell. Very witty indeed." He drew close to her. He smelled of smoke and of strong animal excitement. From the killing? Likki felt her gorge rise, and for the first time wondered about her own safety. He moved closer still. "And how do you suggest we keep this country from tearing itself to pieces? This country with nothing to hold it together except a set of artificial boundaries agreed upon in Europe ninety years ago. How else do we keep it together if not with guns?"

Again Likki was silent, hating him.

With uncongenial calculation he raised his pistol until it was level with her breast and held it there between them, not quite pointing at her heart, while he delivered himself of the rest of his lecture. "And let me tell you what is happening while we fight to hold this country together. Yes. While we struggle, your so-called democratic businessmen come over here and seduce our ministers with bribes they would never dare to contemplate offering at home. Then, from the boardrooms of their fat corporations they accuse us of the corruption we have learned at their hands. They congratulate each other on how much money they save on taxes by not paying taxes in *this* country; and on how much money they will save in wages by paying our best workers one-tenth of their own minimum wage. And still they find time to wonder why we do not have a wonderful democracy like theirs. I tell you, Africa is not yet callous enough to have a democracy like that."

"And Ayesha, was she such an enemy of your brave new world?"

"She was in the way."

"And the baby? What happens if the baby gets in the way?"

"You have not been listening to me. Otherwise you would have understood that my anger is directed against the past, not the future." He paused, his soliloquizing energy spent. When he spoke again, it was to suggest, in his most pointed, unctuous tones, that even though it was nearly dark, Likki would do well to make her own way back to the school. Immediately.

Likki left, but she did not go directly home. Instead, acting on a whim, she turned off down the half-mile path that led to Gbendlele's bush hut. She went with a vague hope of finding someone there, a living person to undo the spell of an empty village and a dead enemy. She felt at that moment like a child of Cain, as if in some intangible way, *she* were responsible for a woman's mortal wounds and the desolation of an entire village. Responsible because she had feared and disliked Ayesha, and had fought with Ayesha's brother and drawn his blood. Responsible because she had wanted Ibn Sinna on her own terms but had found too many excuses for never telling him what these were, as if he should know by telepathy or osmosis. As if, if he loved her, he would be able to read her mind. And now, irrationally, she felt that her blood guilt and fear and selfishness and her loathing of Captain Araoh had spilled out over Kalembelebiri and wrought disaster.

Likki had trouble locating Gbendlele's bush hut. Built of mud and grown over with creepers, the structure appeared, even close up, to be little more than a haphazard extension of a large nearby outcropping of red laterite—part of another ragged boulder decked with scrub. When she finally located the hut it seemed to have subtly changed, to have grown smaller. She hesitated some time before opening the door, then warily peered into the gloom.

A voice surprised her from the dark. "Nasara! How are you?" It was Abu greeting her from the obscurity.

"Abu?"

"Nasara!"

"My God, what are *you* doing out here?" He surely belonged in Kpama.

He diverted her question in a half-whisper. "We are all run away from the village. Every peoples is now hiding on their farm. You see, Nasara, this escaping is an old trick. Our grandfathers use it since Mohammed's time. They just empty the town. When the raiders come, you just run. You don't grab for anything. You just take your life and put it in the care of your feet. When the soldiers come to find the place is empty like that, they don't like it. They feel very bad. They start to think about sorcery. Then they go away again because no one is there. Because they are scared."

"Where's Gbendlele? And the chief?"

"Nasara, the chief, they take him. He doesn't have any time to run. Anyway, he is *too* fat! So they catch him. But Gbendlele is okay. She is fine. Hey! How Gbendlele can move! Such an old woman, too."

"But where is she?"

"Anyway, I don't know. I thought to find her here. Maybe she is gone to Segou."

"Abu, they shot Ayesha. She's dead."

He had not known this and he began to weep. He remembered that Ayesha had been valiant, and he praised her. "This woman, Ayesha, she was holding the soldiers there to give us time! When that army devil sees Ayesha—hah!—then he is sure he has Comfort in his fist. So he takes his time like that with her. Like a cat. And while he is making that palaver with Ayesha, the whole village is escaping into the bush."

"But he got the baby."

"Yes, it's true." He brightened. "But the baby he has is not Comfort. The baby he has is Gbendlele's baby."

"And what happens when he finds out he has the wrong baby?"

Abu shook his head. "Nasara. We don't like it. That man—it's not good."

✖19

Captain Araoh was displeased. He had rescued a sickly, spindly infant from the clutches of her kidnappers and returned her to her father's house only to be greeted with the news that the child was not Comfort.

"What baby is this?" Mahmut's sister, Warikietu, inquired. When Araoh told her it was Comfort she laughed. She found a hundred small marks of difference: a blemish here, an injury there, a mole on the upper right buttock. Even the tribal marks were different. Unlike this child, Comfort had but one slight cicatrice—across her left cheekbone. But this little one carried a sunburst of twelve short lines radiating outwards from her navel. "This is not our child," Warikietu informed Captain Araoh. "I do not think this is even a child from Kpama. We are Muslims! We do not have marks like these." She handed the baby back to him again.

Mahmut also rejected the child. He commented that the baby did bear some slight resemblance to his daughter— particularly in her thinness and the lustreless pallor of her skin—but he, too, was quick to notice a score of dissimilarities.

Alistair Aroah understood that he had been made to look a fool. He understood that the impetuousness and the efficiency of his methods had been turned against him. He had been caught in a snare cunningly contrived out of the stuff of his own character. This little victory would be sweet to his enemies. Well, there was one thing at least he could do to curtail their enjoyment. He called for his squad of heavies and gave them deep orders for the night.

■

The men went after midnight and in stealth. They went with the small rain that fell in the dark hours, the soft rain that drummed on roofs and muffled the noise of their footsteps. They took knives and guns and evil intentions and accomplished their work before anyone could prevent them.

Likki woke from a bad dream in the middle of the night. She had been calling to Roger across a swimming-pool full of corpses. Somewhere in the centre of the foetid, stench-ridden, concrete container, someone still moved, still moaned, still faintly called for help. Likki sat up in bed. Unpleasant ripples of noise teased at the edge of consciousness. If her dream had been less gruesome, she might have caught at the edge of it and let it pull her back into sleep, but she remembered the smell of the corpses and she let herself waken instead.

The noise outside was inappropriate. Furtive footsteps. Whispered speech. Speech of which only the sibilants survived the rain's disguise. Likki rose and groped through the dark towards Carlotta's room, reluctant to light her lantern.

Carlotta woke with a startled yelp, which Likki tried to smother. "Carlotta, something's wrong."

"What?"

"I don't know."

The sounds grew.

Carlotta heard them too: an ill-concealed tramp of footsteps heavily shod. Sounds of protest inadequately muffled.

"What is it, Likki?"

It was then that the squeals erupted, followed by an angry bellow and grunts of surprise from human beings. Carlotta lit her lantern with shaking hands. She already knew what was happening. "Oh, my God. Oh, my God! Likki! Oh, my God, this is it!" She raced in her lace nightie towards the screen door at the back and pushed her way outside into the night. A shot was fired. A warning whine—as if from a mammoth mosquito of unimaginable velocity—breezed by just inches in front of her nose. "Oh, my God!" she said, jumping back, toppling both herself and

Likki, who was just behind her, into the mud by the door of the house.

"Put out the lantern," ordered Likki.

Carlotta extinguished the flame and the two women crept stealthily back inside the door.

Thin light seeped through the cracks of Hope of Our Ancestors' house. Inside there was dreadful movement of shadows and ugly noise. "I've got one!" said a lecherous voice as a small squeal of agony rose up and quickly died. It was followed by another and another. Hope's screams of maternal rage were as old and as broken as the universe. "The mother! The mother!" someone shouted. "Watch out for the teeth!" Then a triumphant, "That is it!" as Hope gave out a mortal groan. The light in the pighouse was extinguished, the door opened, and the furtive shapes of men disappeared into the night.

Numb with shock, the women held onto each other as they stood in the doorway of the bungalow.

Soon, other lanterns began to make their way towards Bungalow 5. The bursar was first to arrive with Come Chop Again. Then the headmaster, and Nuhu and the bursar's wives. Some girls from the dormitory; other staff members. People stood around in the rain looking at each other. No one spoke. No one wanted to be the first inside the pighouse.

Finally, Nuhu walked in with his lantern, and Mr. Bai followed behind. The bodies of the pigs lay cast about like inflatable rubber toys at the end of the summer. All twelve throats had been cut. The amount of blood in the shed was unforgivable. Hope's legs continued to twitch spasmodically. Her dead eyes still held their final look of thick despair.

Nuhu cried, "Why?"

His eyes met those of Mr. Bai. Hardly two months earlier these two had celebrated joyful mysteries in this same place. "Why!" repeated Nuhu. "They didn't even take away the meat."

"Did you see them?" the headmaster asked.

Likki shook her head. She stared at Hope's whitening eyes and said, "Poor Abu."

"The thing is, what do we do now?" said the bursar.

Everyone was distraught. Hundreds of pounds of fresh meat lay there before people who almost never had enough of it, people who were not the least bit sentimental about their animals. It had always been known that the pigs' ultimate destination was the butcher's knife. But the animals had also been a source of pride and affection at the school. It would be hard for those gathered together behind Bungalow 5 to consume any part of their carcasses with a contented or a thankful heart. No one would want to profit from the ugly slaughter of Abu's dream.

"Miss Carlotta!" A plaintive voice pierced the group's indecision. It was Mr. Bai with further horrors. He had found Zulu.

The dog lay panting by a fence post, his stomach ripped open, probably by the same knives that had killed the animals he had tried to defend. His eyes were glassy with shock. On the ground beside him his intestines spread out in a blue and glistening pile.

"Please, miss, he can't live," said Mr. Bai, gripping Carlotta's arm. He carried in his other hand a long-forgotten shotgun.

"No!" said Carlotta and she stared down at her fat pet as if she would order him one more time to pull himself together. Huge bubbles were forming in the animal's exposed guts, swelling the intestinal walls to monstrous proportions. The dog whined feebly and tried to lick Carlotta's ankle. His tongue was like parchment.

Mr. Bai spoke again. "Please, miss. He can't live." Mr. Bai cocked the gun. Someone reached out to pull Carlotta away.

Carlotta fought free. "I have to say goodbye," she insisted. She knelt down on the ravaged earth and patted Zulu gently on his head. "Good doggie," she said. His tail moved faintly. With his dry tongue he licked her grieving hand. "Good doggie." Carlotta looked up at Mr. Bai. "I can't do it," she said. She meant she couldn't say goodbye.

"He knows," said Nuhu. "The dog knows. It is only *you*."

"Goodbye, Zulu," said Carlotta. She kissed him softly between the eyes, on his snout. Then she looked up at Mr. Bai and said, "Okay."

She turned away as her neighbour fired the shot.

The headmaster had the steward awakened so he could start up the electric generators. Some light was needed to pierce the heavy blackness, even if it were only the light of Thomas Edison.

Carlotta withdrew to her bedroom and wouldn't come out. She refused to look at Zulu's body. She wanted nothing to do with his corpse. Mr. Bai sat desolately on the sofa in the living-room.

Likki finally took matters into her own hands and went to give her roommate a scolding. "Christ, Carlotta, you could at least have a drink with that poor man. He's out there in the hall feeling like a murderer. He thinks you hate him."

"Oh, I didn't know. Tell him to come in."

Mr. Bai proved to be a blessing. A calm and quiet man, he had brought along his bottle of Bacardi. The house slowly filled with the regretful and the bewildered and the thirsty. By four o'clock in the morning the gathering began to resemble an Irish wake—which was what Kpamans made of most funerals anyway.

•

Likki left at first light to go to the house of Ibn Sinna. More than she disliked seeking him out, more than she regretted being the first to bridge their quarrel, more than she hesitated at the thought of meeting his wives on their own ground—more than all of this she dreaded maintaining her separation. For while she might quarrel with him terribly in times of good fortune, now that unpleasant fates seemed to be closing around her, Likki was suddenly very sure of where she stood with this man. Suddenly she understood that when he had taken her to bed he had acted with a seriousness she had not fully appreciated, that he had accepted a responsibility for her safety and well-being that went far beyond the obligations of bi-weekly copulation. Without announcing it, he had quietly become for her what everyone reckoned most necessary in Kpama—he had become her "family." And if, as a lover, he was infuriating and disappointing, still now he would be there for her as solidly as the ground under her feet.

The entrance to Ibn Sinna's house was open wide. Likki stepped cautiously through the gate. A young bullock stood hobbled and tethered in the courtyard along with several sheep, which all began to bleat pitifully on her arrival. These animals were presumably meant for Ayesha's funeral. Large covered basins of fermenting porridge and corn meal were visible through a dark kitchen doorway. They would also be used for the mortuary feast.

Likki stood solitary in the courtyard for some minutes and then a round-faced woman appeared in the doorway.

"Yes?" she inquired.

Then, as she took in the details of Likki's appearance, in particular the objectionable colour of her skin, the woman's eyes narrowed and her face grew treacherous. "Why are *you* here?" she demanded. Never removing her hostile gaze from Likki's face, she pitched her voice to the far end of the courtyard. "Hey, my *husband*. Your white whore has come here to look for you."

A door opened and another woman stared out at Likki. The woman was very black and would have been very beautiful had she not distorted the strong lines of her face with a pinched and miserly expression. "What do you want here?" she spat. "Get out!"

"I want to see Ibn Sinna."

"Who are you?"

"Who are *you*?" asked Likki.

"Why do you come into this house before the sun is even up disturbing everyone? And then not even tell us your name?"

"I am looking for someone who lives here. What right do you have to shout at me?"

"I have the right! I live in this house."

"Then, since you live here, you can tell me where to find Ibn Sinna."

"Even if I know where this man is, why will I tell you?"

"I have news for him."

"So do all the people. Everyone has news for him. The whole town is full of news for him. But the man is not here."

"I don't believe you."

"It's true. He has gone out to see one of his other whores."

"It's easy to see why he might want a whore—after

meeting you," said Likki, smiling easily. She was beginning to enjoy herself.

"You get out, you slut!" The round-faced woman came forward waving a stick. "This house is in mourning."

"I'm not moving," said Likki, looking around for a place to sit. "If you won't call your husband for me I'll just have to sit here and wait until he comes." She deposited herself defiantly on a bench in the centre of the courtyard and sat erectly, expectantly. In a room behind her an infant wailed its reproach at the morning.

The two wives drew together some distance away, uncertain of the wisdom of calling her bluff. Then, at last, another door opened and Ibn Sinna emerged wearing on his face an expression of surprise and rueful affection. He barked something at his wives in Kpamé, but they shouted back at him so fiercely he could not pull away from them long enough to greet his visitor properly. The three of them raged amongst each other until Likki could no longer contain her bad news. Walking over to them where they stood arguing, she announced that men had come in the night and slaughtered Abu's pigs. She shouted her message out over their argument and it was a kind of victory to throw the news at them.

Stunned faces turned to her for explanation. "Abu's pigs. All of them. They killed every one of them." She remembered Zulu. "And the dog, too. We had to kill the dog. Mr. Bai did it."

Ibn Sinna reached for her. "Who killed them?"

Likki brushed free of his arms. "Men came in the night, killed all the pigs, and left Zulu dying by the fence post. Mr. Bai had to kill him."

"Did you see the men?"

"No. How could we see them? They were shooting at us."

Ibn Sinna frowned and thought this over. Then he asked, "Did they speak English?"

As soon as he had asked, she understood what he meant: the men were not from Kpama. Their only common language was the one used in their organization. "Yes," she said. "They spoke English. So they were soldiers?"

"Yes. It will be soldiers."

She repeated Nuhu's question. "Why?"

"They suspect Abu has much to do with Comfort's disappearance. They suspect Sima of killing their soldiers through the well. They suspect everyone is against them in this matter of Comfort and so they become suspicious and cruel. The pigs are a way to revenge themselves on all of us."

"Their suspicions give them a right to go killing livestock at midnight?"

"Why not? They have done it to others. They will do it again. Of course, if you ask them, they will say they are not the ones."

"So there's nothing we can do?"

"Just now, I think, we can go to the Ruler and inform him. There will be a meeting at the palace anyway— because of my sister."

"What can the Ruler do?"

"This time, I am afraid, he may find he has little power."

"Oh, Christ." The worst thing had been the trusting look in Zulu's eyes. "I feel like I want to *kill* somebody."

"Someone will already have thought of that," replied Ibn Sinna.

An ambiguous counsel.

20

The Ruler had called a meeting for late morning, to invite public discussion of recent events. On their way to attend, Likki and Carlotta made a perfunctory halt at the hospital to fill John in on the news. No one had visited him the day before, and they expected to find him spiteful and sarcastic. But he was not; if anything he was gleeful, and his fever appeared to have receded.

"So many stories!" he chirped, rubbing his thin hands together. He appeared to know all the news already.

"Not all the stories are true, though." Likki wanted to restrain him, afraid he would start talking about *juju* again.

"Oh, *my* stories are true."

"Are they?"

"Oh, yes. Of course." He grinned. "For instance," he grimaced and turned abruptly to Carlotta, leaning close to her face, "I have a story that *you* are in love!"

Carlotta drew back from him and frowned.

He turned to Likki. "And I have another story that *you* tried to kill Ibn Sinna."

"Is that so?"

"And I have dozens of stories about Araoh: how he lost another soldier, and how he didn't find Comfort, and how he killed off Abu's pigs out of spite."

He said this last with such an air of I-told-you-so that Likki wanted to hurt him right back. "Araoh killed Ayesha, too," she reminded John.

John shot her a look close to hatred. "Your friend, the fat chief of Kalembelebiri, was put in jail, wasn't he? I wonder what will happen to him?" He was pleased to chastise her with worry.

"He's out," said Likki. One story John hadn't heard. "They let him go this morning."

"Did they just?" grinned John. "Who told you *that*?"

"I *saw* him, riding past the school this morning." Riding on a horse, a poor creature not much bigger than the chief himself. He had looked dejected, straddling his little mount.

"Back to his deserted village, then?"

"I guess," said Likki in a tone she struggled to keep polite. She found John infuriating this morning.

"I wonder why they let him go," mused John. Likki did not respond. "I said, 'I wonder why they let him go.'"

"I heard you the first time."

"You didn't answer."

"It wasn't a question." Irritation showed in Likki's voice.

"We're a little touchy this morning, aren't we?"

Likki stared at him, then turned and walked out of the ward. Carlotta began to follow her, then paused and tried to make peace. She leaned over John apologetically and said, "Don't mind Likki. She's a little tired. We hardly had any sleep last night."

"You don't have to explain. Don't forget, *I* know Likki. She's extremely emotional. You can't reason with her at all."

Out on the hospital verandah, Carlotta said to Likki, "Isn't he *awful*, today?"

"I think he needs an exorcist, not a doctor."

•

The Ruler of Kpama had a large reception room in his palace, but by the middle of the morning it was full. Everyone remotely connected with the events of the night before—that is to say, everyone remotely connected with Abu and his pigs—was there. Nevertheless, many of those present had quarrelled with each other, and angry looks between them were frequent. The town elders occupied solemn benches around the periphery of the room. Outside, a crowd of curious and outraged citizenry filled up the palace courtyard. Many were carrying bows.

It was hot, with the tooth-chipping heat that comes in the early rains when the midday sun is like a sledge-hammer. People grumbled. Flies crawled at the corners of their eyes. Everyone was tired of waiting. They understood that

Captain Araoh was pointedly making them wait in all possible discomfort, and they resented it.

It was nearly noon before the army jeep pulled up outside. Despite the throng, Captain Araoh and his attendants walked briskly into the reception room. Araoh went over and greeted the Ruler of Kpama, though he refused to make the low bow required by custom. He withdrew to the high-status comfort of a striped deck-chair, where he perched like a gadfly in uniform.

The Ruler's linguist stood up and began to outline, in Kpamé, the events that had led to this gathering. Araoh, ever prepared, had Arthur, his universal translator, again at his side. Likki and Carlotta, sitting in the back behind a wooden pillar, relied upon Nuhu to interpret the proceedings. When matters went slowly Nuhu gave the two women a word-for-word, whispered translation. Long-winded and loquacious speakers, however, he merely paraphrased. Unfortunately, when things really got exciting, or when several people were trying to speak at once, Nuhu tended to get wrapped up in the arguments and forget Likki and Carlotta altogether. Likki prodded him several times and Carlotta once tweaked his ear viciously.

When the Ruler's linguist rose to speak Nuhu made a face. "You watch," he said. "For over one hour now we will hear nothing but ancient history."

The linguist started his recitation. On their sundry perches the elders let their eyelids droop in anticipation of what was coming. The linguist commenced with the foundation of the town, some five hundred years earlier, by a dark and mighty warrior prince. He spoke of wandering Muslim pilgrims ensnared *en route* to Mecca by Kpama's boundless charms—and also by the rather more bounded attractions of the warrior prince's daughters. He told how the miraculous magic of the Earth Priests had driven off plagues of insects and wild beasts, famines and terrible floods. It was long past noon before he arrived at the genealogies pertinent to the present litigation. All those concerned had to have their ancestry traced: Sima's genealogy, Abu's genealogy, Kutu's, Moomin's, and Ibn Sinna's— all back to the twelfth and thirteenth generation. A long iteration of begats. The linguist would have liked to include

Carlotta's and Likka's genealogies as well, but Carlotta hadn't been able to remember back any further than her grandparents, and Likki had been shaky on her grandmothers' maiden names. The Ruler's linguist had decided to overlook their ancestry. Two-generations-deep genealogies were unseemly. People might think that their ancestors had been slaves.

"What time will it be before he comes to the point?" Likki asked Nuhu.

"It will be long past dinner time," Nuhu advised. His words conveyed an admiration of tactics. Everyone knew that tongues were sharpest when appetites were strong and hunger rolled around in people's stomachs. The dilatory ramblings of the linguist were very much to the point. If the linguist took too long to say too little, those who followed would say far too much in the shortest possible time. Tempers would flare and afterwards everyone would think they had a good reason for doing whatever they did.

Some of the elders pretended to doze, though these were usually the very ones who were listening most carefully, watching to catch out the linguist in mistakes or libellous omissions. Every so often the linguist would pronounce a name that acted like a morning alarm on his geriatric audience: ". . . and the son of Bakari was Musa the Red who drove off the Mande invaders and reclaimed the goldfields across the river." At "Musa the Red," the old men would fidget. Some would nod and say, "Ah-hah!" And some, those who were descended in a direct male line from this rufous ancestor, would feel obliged to tap their walkingsticks and proclaim the glory of their grandfather. "Hey! This Musa! A very strong man. How people feared him! My grandfather's father."

The linguist finally came to the present. "Now we get to find," he said, "that the harmony of this our town is spoiled. It is broken, just like that! And we ask ourselves, how has this come to be? And we get to find out that all of the trouble in this town today has come because of one small girl. One very small girl-child." His voice held tones of incredulity. Could Kpama go to ruin because of a female? The audience stirred.

"Now the facts are these, and I will only bring you the facts. First: a woman was found dead in the *bomba* . . ."

"She was murdered!" Hawa stood to scream it from the back of the room. "Mahmut himself killed my daughter. With his own hands he took her life. And until blood money is paid for my daughter, death will visit this town." The closest bench of elders pulled Hawa down and ordered her to be silent.

The linguist ignored the interruption. "Next, it was agreed before us here in this court that the woman's baby child, Servant of the Wrathful by name, but who is now called Comfort, should be given into the care of her grandmother, Hawa. Is this not so?" Around the room a hundred heads nodded approval. "And then Hawa, being old, gave the child into the care of her sister's daughter, Ayesha. And Ayesha was to keep the child while it was small. She was to keep the child until it was weaned. She was to keep the child for two years. Was this not so?" Again approval was universally given.

"But then," continued the linguist, "some few months ago, the soldiers went, just like that, and removed the child from that house of Ayesha and took her to the house of her father, Mahmut. And now we would like to know how it is that the army can just go about doing things like that without first coming here to this palace to consult with us."

Captain Araoh rose. "I am the military commander of this town," he said through the offices of his translator. "When I act it is with the authority of the national government, which takes precedence over local jurisdiction."

The Ruler demurred. "But surely this is a matter of civil law and ought to have been settled—and stayed settled—through the workings of this court, particularly in view of the long-term consequences this child's adoption has had for the town. This matter would have been better served had it remained the preserve either of the traditional court of Kpama here in this room, or of the district courts in the region."

"The national government is greater than the courts. It has authority over them," Araoh informed the Ruler.

Moomin stood up to challenge from the back of the room, and behind his words was the weight of his mourning. "If the government is greater than the courts, then there *is* no law."

"There *is* law," Araoh answered him. "There is the law of the government."

"But the government is only one man," said Moomin, his voice full of travail. "So if one man is the law, then the law is the will of one man. But this is a blasphemy and an abomination against Allah."

"You are making religion come into it," accused Alistair Araoh. "Religion has no place in this discussion."

Ibn Sinna rose up to defend his friend, and his face as he spoke belonged to the Middle Ages. "It is you yourself who have made religion come into it," he said. "You are saying that the will of one man can be the law. And we are saying that the only law that is from one will is the law that comes from Allah, and that is a greater law than those made by armies."

Captain Araoh favoured Ibn Sinna with a designing stare. "My friend," he said in the quietest of voices, "your disregard for the *law* of this country is well known. But perhaps it may not be long now before you will pass before *all* the laws of which you speak: first the laws of this country, and then afterwards the laws of Allah."

Ibn Sinna did not reply, but gazed down at Alistair Araoh as if from the battlements of a storied keep, as if he were the dark seneschal of Kpama. And then he laughed at him.

"My friend," said the army captain. "We shall see who laughs best from all of this. We shall *see*."

Sima tried to turn their quarrel. He stood with one hand resting on the shoulder of Abu. "How is it," he asked the assembly, "that the weight of all these matters has come to rest upon this small boy? Why has a child been made to suffer so that grown men can call each other names in front of a chief? Why does an orphan pay the price for the actions of the mighty?"

"Old man, I do not understand your words," said Captain Araoh Everyone was pretty sure he understood them perfectly.

"This child, until last night, was the owner of twelve fine pigs. A sow with a strong litter—only one had died. But because of your jealousies, because of your annoyance at a baby's disappearance from her father's house—a place she had no business being—because your own actions made you look foolish, you went in the dark night and killed the child's hope. You destroyed his hard work of over a year. It is *compensation* that we should be discussing at this meeting, not a definition of law."

"Are you accusing me of tampering with local livestock?" Araoh inquired with the untouchable condescension of the powerful.

"It was your soldiers who did the work."

"Do you have proof of that? Who has seen my soldiers play at being butchers?"

"The voices of your soldiers were heard," said Sima. "The footprints of their heavy boots were found in the mud."

"Since when is it necessary to be a soldier to wear boots in the mud? I am asking if anyone has *seen* my soldiers playing at butchers, and I am sure no one will rise to accuse them. I can assure you that all my men are innocent. They were, every one of them, in their barracks last night—or on guard duty. I am sure that they are all willing to swear to that." By the entrance to the reception room Araoh's heavies bobbed their heads obligingly. "You see?" he said, his voice sweet with assurance. "I am sure you will agree you are mistaken."

Sima had not finished. "Unless compensation is made to this child, there can be trouble. The pig was under the protection of the shrine in the grove. Spirits are not easily taken in by lies."

"Old man!" Araoh addressed him. "Is this what your precious legal system comes to, that you are now ready to stand there and threaten me with *juju*? I want you to know that you may not have long to practise your *juju*. You may be arrested at any time. You are under grave suspicion of having committed murder."

"I have murdered no one."

"No one!? Are my soldiers no one? I am sure you know very well that both my wells were poisoned and five of my soldiers died drinking the water. Not to mention the matter of a certain cat sent to me as a gift."

"I know nothing of any cat. But as for the wells, you know that if you send your soldiers to drink from a well of death, then their fates must be on your own conscience." After all, who in their right mind would use a well that had recently held three corpses?

"The well was *poisoned*," insisted Araoh. In fact, nothing concrete had been found in the water, but in any case he suspected arrow poisons: complex organic compounds whose presence could not be detected by any means available in Kpama. Samples had been sent to the capital, but by the time they arrived the compounds would probably have deteriorated into less objectionable substances. The charge he was making would be impossible to prove, even if it were true.

"It is you yourself who poisoned the well," Sima said. "You have strutted through Kpama thinking only of your own belly, never considering the welfare of the people. You have disregarded our customs and led our daughters astray. You have disturbed people in their homes evening and morning. You have wakened us in the night to search for contraband. You have taken our fattest yams from the market to eat them yourself. You have killed our fowls. You have slaughtered our pigs. And now you are wondering how your well came to be poisoned. It is the poison of your own heart that has found its way into that well. It is the revenge of the Guardians of Kpama for the wrongs you have done our people."

The captain, fed up with talk of supernatural bogeymen, turned to address the wider audience. "Are we cave men or human beings?" he demanded. "Do we have to make ourselves the laughing-stock of the world? Or can we behave like people who live in the twentieth century? It is now almost five centuries since the white men came to West Africa. It is almost one century since they came here to Kpama. It is only some few years before we begin the third millennium after Christ, but here in Kpama we are conducting ourselves like creatures from the Stone Age. How can we send our ambassadors to stand and address the assembly of the United Nations of this planet while the elders of our country are throwing around accusations of witchcraft, threatening each other with *juju*, calling upon the protection of holy shrines and relying on ignorance and superstition to get their way? Why don't we just dress our mbassador in feathers? Why don't we pay our government ministers in beads and cowrie shells? Why don't we admit we are just cannibals and wizards?"

It was Ibn Sinna who answered him. "You want to stand here and say we are not human beings here in Kpama, is that it? But I ask you now, who *is* a human being? The white men, who you say are laughing at us, are *they* human beings? They carried off our wives and our brothers and our children in their ships and they killed them with disease and overwork. Is that what human beings do? And the whites who came in the last century, were they human beings? They forced us at gunpoint to dig our gold out of our own ground and hand it over to them. Then they laughed at our poverty. Is that how human beings behave? And now, as you say, we are at the gates of a new millennium. But every day we read that white children go hungry while their governments make bombs. Is that how human beings should be? Even these whites themselves are wondering if they can survive the technology of their own malice and yet you say we should worry that they might be laughing at us. I say it is no great thing to hold up our heads in their assemblies and announce, 'I am a human being like you,' because these people are *not* human beings. They are just crazy people, full of greed and immaturity."

"We are not addressing the same issue," said Alistair Araoh.

"We are! You are standing there asking for progress. You want us all to become modern men. Then everyone in the world will be like the whites. And I am saying that there is no progress at all in following the devil down to hell."

"Is that why you travel abroad to buy guns?" asked Araoh. "To keep us from following the devil to hell?" His smile grew broader, more sinister.

The elders were now all very much awake. Likki, despite the heat, went cold when Nuhu translated these words.

"Why do you speak of guns?" interrupted the Ruler.

"I have had reports of this area," Araoh said, beaming at them all. "Of course, the information is classified." Here he paused so that his next words would register a threat. Then he continued, slowly. He spoke of looking for contraband in

"one *last* place." He hinted that his patience was runnin
thin. The consequences for the town would be severe
Sima should disappear again or if Moomin or Ibn Sinn
were to travel. The *real* Comfort must be found an
returned to her father's house or a suitable explanation
her whereabouts brought to him. He wanted action on th
matter within twenty-four hours or he would have to sta
thinking about reprisals. As he spoke, his smile was fixe
and implacable, like the rigid grin on a jack-o'-lantern.

The talk carried on for another forty-five minutes. Th
Ruler finally ended it when a stray breeze from his inne
courtyard told him his dinner was burning. Ayesha's deat
had not even been mentioned.

What was left of the day was taken up with Ayesha's obsequies, which became, perforce, a rallying point for those in opposition to the army.

Outside Moomin's house the soldiers had stationed themselves by the gate in sizeable numbers, perhaps in the hope that their presence would scare off mourners. If so, they were disappointed. Despite their stares, no one loitered on the way into the house. A few mourners even abused the soldiers to their faces as they passed through the military gauntlet.

Hawa, in particular, shouted as soon as she saw the soldiers. She waved her fists and accused them of every heinous crime she could think of: sodomy, incest, cannibalism. And, after she had gone off into Ayesha's room to take a last look at the corpse, she returned to stand just inside Moomin's gate, where she began to wail like a mother who has lost every child.

Meanwhile a trail of old women in long red cloths paced the central portion of Moomin's courtyard like a chorus of the Furies, keening the obligatory lament, their dirge containing all the weariness, futility, and rage of mortal creatures who know they are ultimately condemned. They seemed at home with their role, old women long past the vigour of their years, well acquainted with death, but not resigned.

Likki, who came in rather late along with Abu, put out her hand to steady herself on his shoulder. On a bench outside their mother's room, Ayesha's three children sat with forlorn, frightened faces, swinging their feet in the dust. Seeing them, Likki shed tears.

She remained at the house of Moomin for only about twenty minutes, after which the assembled mourners

departed with Ayesha's body to the cemetery. In a lor
procession the bereaved set forth to the burial field, full
prayers and laments and discordant music. There wa
nothing gracious in the spectacle they made, only a chaot
cacophony as unwelcome as the death itself.

■

The atmosphere at the bungalow that evening was heav
and listless. Out of habit Carlotta stood by her post at th
calico curtains. It was a vigil Zulu had often shared wit
her. Though the loss of his companionship was accentuate
by this ritual, it was also partially assuaged by it. It wa
nearly dark when Carlotta spotted the army jeep bouncin
over the ruts by the headmaster's house.

"Oh, God! Here they come again." There was n
mistaking the "they."

"I'm leaving now," said Likki, rising from the sofa. The
might still be time to disappear from the bungalow.

"Wait, it's not Araoh."

"The hell it isn't." It was almost night. It would be easy
vanish out the back door.

"It's the sergeant!" Some of the slackness seemed to li
from Carlotta's frame. "And Ibn Sinna," she added, as
wondering to see them paired.

The jeep stopped by the front door. "Miss Reap!" th
sergeant called out excitedly as he clambered up the fro
steps two at a time. He was wearing a broad smile an
carrying a shoe-box in his hands.

"Sergeant Awilobe, please come in," said Carlotta with
voice that had regained its customary command. And a hi
of extra warmth.

"I have brought you one small gift," said the sergea
shyly, like a four-year-old proffering a bouquet of wiltin
wildflowers. In the sergeant's hands the shoe-box assumed
life of its own. It rocked suggestively. "This is for you," h
said, holding out the box to Carlotta. "Everyone's hea
is sad for you." Behind him in the doorway Ibn Sinr
stood with stiffly folded arms, as one whose patience wa
stretched with trivialities. Likki made a point of not lookin
at the bandage on his cheek.

Carlotta reached for the box, but she was slow to open it. Perhaps she was thinking of rabid cats. While she hesitated, the lid pushed up of its own accord and slipped off to one side. Inside the box was something small and warm that Zulu had accomplished on the occasion of his last escape. A pint-sized, velvet-spotted likeness of a half-beagle, half-mongrel sausage of a dog. A puppy. Its parentage was unmistakable. As soon as it spotted Carlotta, it wagged its ridiculous tail and drooled. It tried to chew on her finger. Likki frowned. It was too soon for this.

Carlotta also hesitated. She endeavoured to remain aloof. She was in mourning. They were all in mourning. Levity was out of the question. Besides, it would have been a betrayal of her regard for the deceased Zulu to indulge in wild displays of affection. Still, the little fellow *was* cute. "Hello there," she said and got a wet puppy kiss. She drew back and said sternly, "But he is *not* Zulu." She looked to the sergeant to acknowledge the correctness of her words. "No one could ever take the place of Zulu."

"Of course not, Miss Reap," agreed Sergeant Awilobe. "No one would ever suggest such a thing." He wrinkled up his brow. "But this poor little animal needs a home. He has nowhere. Not any place at all. And I knew that your house was, regrettably, empty, so I brought him here. As a last resort."

"No home?" deplored Carlotta.

"He would just be out there all alone. Fending for himself in the bush."

"Poor *doggie*."

"What will you call him?"

Sergeant Awilobe had Carlotta pretty well figured out. Perhaps, after all, it really was love on his part. When, after a discreet half hour and three rum and Cokes, he invited her again to the rest house by the river, for a "changing of scenes," Carlotta accepted without embarrassment.

"Say hi to the crocodiles," Likki called out as they left.

When they had gone, Ibn Sinna turned to Likki. "So," he said. He sounded weary, flayed. Under its bandage his cheek looked swollen. Likki wondered if the cut were ugly.

"So?" she said.

He kept very still, watching her; still as a hunter. At last he took a deep breath and reached straight for the frayed threads of their quarrel. "It seems last time we were fighting about some other woman, isn't it?"

"Al Hajji Umar's daughter."

He compressed his lips. "Is the girl not very beautiful?" he asked, as if offering fresh grounds for the resumption of hostilities.

"Why ask me?"

"Should I rather say she is ugly?"

"Why talk about her at all?"

"Because she is making trouble between us."

It was Likki's turn to take a deep breath and let it out slowly. "I heard you wanted to marry the girl," she said at last.

"Who told you that?"

"I'd rather not say."

"I know where you heard it."

"You do?"

"It was Abu who told you."

"*Was* it?" She had made promises to Abu.

"Abu has been making trouble for me because of this woman."

"Because of al Hajji Umar's daughter?"

"Yes."

"Why? Don't tell me Abu wants to marry her, too?"

"Abu has been going around telling stories. He has been telling stories to my wives. He has been telling stories to you."

"And why would Abu do that?"

"Abu is trying to fix things so that Mahmut can marry the girl."

It was an absurd accusation. "Why would Abu do that? My God, *how* would he do it? Abu doesn't have any influence over al Hajji Umar—or over Mahmut, either, for that matter."

"Abu has been busy around this town making things difficult for any man who wants this girl, Aswayya—any man except Mahmut. And at the same time someone has recently started a rumour that the girl is now very eager to

lose her virginity to one Muslim trader and seller of love
philtres in the market called Yahyah. This rumour, too, can
have been started by Abu. The result of these two things
together is that the father is now very eager to get the girl
married while she is still a virgin; but it seems that only
Mahmut can see his way clear to collect her in time."

"In time to save her from Yahyah?" Yes, Abu might have
stooped to this. The plan had many of the earmarks of one
of his contrivings.

"Yes. In time to save her from Yahyah."

"And were you thinking of marrying her?"

"Small-small."

"Small-small?" Unhappiness was gathering behind her
eyes.

"If it would be easy to marry her, then I would take her.
Because it is true that the girl is beautiful. And it is true
that I want to marry again. But it is not true that I want to
marry again now. Now the time is bad. It is *too* soon. But if
the girl and her father say they will agree to wait,
then . . . but still it would not be true that another wife
would push you away from me. You can see how it is."

"No. I can't."

"Look. If I have only two wives, they can just become
friends and then together they can turn against me. And
they have been doing that for these last weeks. But if I have
three women in the house, then one is always left out. Two
make a treaty but one is still pushed to the side. So that one
will be kind to me again. Then, when the other two see how
the third one is always smiling and cooking for me every
night, they will quickly become jealous and fight. They will
begin to hate each other again. Once that happens, then I
am once more king in the house."

"That's a hell of a way to run a family."

"It is politics. In the end, everything is politics."

"And just where do I fit in to all these politics?"

"You know you have no part in the politics. You are rather
for love."

"What are your wives for?"

"Wives? Wives are for children. Wives are for family.
Wives are for farming, for cooking, for the house. Wives are

for marriage. Marriage is not for love. It is only your people who confuse the two."

Likki favoured him with an expression of stormy confusion. She knew Ibn Sinna could not be held personally to blame for the institution of polygyny. In fact, by the terms of reference that prevailed in his world, he had treated her admirably. But she was beginning to understand that his world and its definitions would not be sufficient for her. She wanted more, wanted the man himself, the inner nub of him, the soul he would never share with her. And because it would never occur to him to give her that, and because she did not know how to ask, she was left like a lost child, reaching for the prize she could not name or describe.

"If I marry again, it is only my wives who have reason to complain," he continued. "Between us nothing would change."

"How could *nothing* change?"

"What is there to change? You are not my wife and I come to see you. If I married again you would still not be my wife and still I would come here to see you."

"Are you *sure*?"

"Maybe you think I should marry *you*."

"That would be cute, wouldn't it? Ibn Sinna's junior wife, a white woman, pounding millet in the courtyard at five-thirty in the morning. I might become a kind of tourist attraction."

He considered her words as if mentally he were trying to spear the meaning behind them and examine it, once he knew what it was. "If I were still a young man," he said at last, "with no family and no other wives, and if I came to you and asked you to stay with me, to be my *only* wife—as your people do it—would you stay?" This was closer to the heart of the matter. Likki wrestled with the question and when she answered him, she told the truth.

"I don't know," she said.

It hurt him. "You see?" he said with carefree pretence, but his voice was flat.

She felt ashamed. She wanted to push him into the same dishonourable corner. "If I said yes, *would* you marry me?"

"Yes!"

"Bullshit!"

"You don't believe me?" he asked sadly.

"No."

"That is because you are only here to amuse yourself. And yet you want to say that I am playing with you."

"You *are* playing with me," said Likki.

"Oh! How?"

"You have three women—three that I know of. Or rather four that I know of. I have *one* man. I don't even have one man. I have a piece of one man."

"But with all of my women I am serious. And you cannot even be serious about one!" Was that really how he saw her? Frivolous?

"You mean *I* won't marry *you*, is that it?"

"You yourself have said it!"

"Is marriage the only way of being serious? Christ! Maybe if I could have fourteen husbands, I could be serious about all of them all the time, too. Just like you."

He got a gleam in his eye and said, "God *damn*."

In spite of herself Likki grinned. She hated him right then for making her smile.

He relented. "Likki, I am not coming to marry some girl today or tomorrow. Now I am only looking around small-small. It is after you go from Kpama I may want to find some new joy in my life again."

"What about the new joy in my life after I leave here?"

"There are plenty of men in your country. I am sure you will find one. Or fourteen."

"And you just close the door on me when I go?"

"If you are not here, what good are you for me?"

"*Something* must be left."

"Something is left but it is useless. What good does it do to pull a long face? It is better to forget."

She sighed. "I suppose you don't ever write letters?" She asked this bleakly, looking forward to a future where he might hold back from communication, severing the lines utterly.

"Can you put these things into letters?" he asked, drawing his hands along her body to demonstrate what could not be communicated by means of the written word.

He made her weep for the time when he would be gor
When she would be gone. They made love that night wi
the restrained tenderness of everything that divided ther

Outside it had begun to rain. Birds called through t
drizzle. "Owls," said Ibn Sinna, just before he slept.

By their door the puppy listened and sniffed, w
curious, and may have dreamed of escape.

✖ 22

"Wake up." In the predawn, Ibn Sinna roughly pulled Likki out of sleep.

"What?" Her mouth was dry and wide for oxygen, like a stranded fish.

"Come," he urged, tugging her out of bed. "There is something for you to hear."

Behind Ibn Sinna, Likki stumbled down the hall of the bungalow, giddy and still swaying with sleep, and then, in the back doorway, she saw Abu. Wondering, she tried to understand what it was that he had come to tell her.

"Captain Araoh is dead."

She tossed her head as though shaking it free of water.

"He is dead," repeated Abu.

"How?" she asked when she had wakened sufficiently to take in this news. Someone must have murdered him.

"They found him hanging from a tree in the grove." Abu paused. "Do you want to come and see it?"

Likki hesitated, then looked at Ibn Sinna. She felt there was no surprise in this for him. "Sure. I'll come." But it was the living she was concerned to scrutinize more than the dead.

The two of them dressed hurriedly and left, following behind Abu on an obscure footpath that led to the grove. The morning through which they followed him was pearl-grey and innocent.

Everything was haze and mist and shadow. Nothing in the landscape held substance except the crooked track under their feet, and even that was partially obscured by swirling vapours. Though they walked only about forty minutes until they arrived at their destination, it seemed as if hours had passed.

The trees of the grove, when they finally came up to

them, appeared detached from the earth, as if they were
dark raft of vegetation floating on a sea of cloud. Among th
lower vapours the hazy forms of soldiers could be made ou
fending off the interior mysteries, cordoning off the grove
Their spiky bayonets were at grisly odds with the softness
the dawn.

A knot of civilians had already gathered at a safe remov
from the soldiers, whose uneasiness in the face of some
thing they could not easily explain rendered them con
siderably more dangerous than usual. The civilians stoo
about on a small knoll and Ibn Sinna immediately made h
way over to them. There were many familiar faces amon
the group—Moola, Sima, Kutu, Mother of Issa, Mahmu
Gbendlele, Hawa, many elders unnamed but remen
bered. Nearby, a collection of hajjis in full ceremonial dres
hovered, their long black robes giving the air of a convoca
tion of ravens. It was Sima who voiced the general feeling
satisfaction. "This time is ours," he said, nodding toward
the grove. He spoke in English, as if expressly for Likk
benefit. When Likki looked to Ibn Sinna for explanation h
turned from her, saying, "It is over now." His face wore
closed expression, and she saw she would learn little mor
from him about this.

The "facts" of the case, when they became known
explained little. Early the previous evening, Captain Arao
had ordered his second platoon to arm themselves wit
pickaxes and shovels and proceed with him to the grove
He told them they were looking for guns in "one last place
Disassembled firearms in wooden crates. Contraband.

The digging details were well fitted out with pressur
lamps and lanterns and battery-operated floodlights. The
also kept alive the comforting mechanical beams of the
jeeps and lorries. Nevertheless, the men were disturbed
Though they were mostly Christians or Muslims (som
were both), they felt it was unseemly to disembowel th
ceremonial ground of pagans. It was graveyard work.

For several hours Captain Araoh had acted as oversee
bustling energetically from group to group, inspirin
confidence, action, and also resentment. Then he ha
disappeared. At first everyone had assumed he was wit
another digging detail. Then members of different group

got together and made each other uneasy about his absence. The men left the grove and began to circle the periphery, calling, listening, keeping close to one another. At first light they took courage and threaded their way in among the trees. There, in the centre of the grove, they found their commanding officer bloated and already stiff, suspended over the bloodied stone.

The doctor, after a preliminary examination, said that the man had been dead for several hours. Later he had the body removed to the hospital for an autopsy, and afterwards it was whispered about the town (and also, inevitably, by John Lavender) that Captain Araoh's body had contained no liver and that his heart had shrivelled down to the size of half a kola nut.

But standing on the knoll outside the grove in the early morning, Likki suspected forces more tangible, if no less sinister, than witchcraft, and she asked her lover the question she knew he would not answer.

"Who killed him?"

"If someone has killed this man, then it is the man himself who has done it." She was meant to infer suicide.

Ibn Sinna saw the disbelief on her face and accepted it without qualm. "So," he said, and it was as though he had come to the end of a long story.

"I want to know who killed him."

"If that is what you want, then he killed himself."

"Try again."

"I can see you do not believe me. Still, it is true. It is also true that I am glad he is dead. As you yourself are glad."

Likki was honest enough not to protest.

"You are only angry now because you have no one to point your finger at and say, 'There is the guilty person.' The truth is that we are all guilty because all of us have desired his death. Now he is dead you should let it finish and forget about him. He may have killed himself, or any person here may have helped him along. We are all able to do it. Even you are able to do it."

Likki turned away as the sun pierced through the mists, whitening them to a blinding purity.

✖ 23

Tensely, Kpama waited for reprisals.

The army's immediate reaction to the loss of its leader was a wary retreat into barracks accompanied by anxious hourly radiophone messages to the capital reporting nascent insurrection in the northern provinces.

In the meantime most of Kpama's residents smelled trouble coming and began moving out to their bush farms or their ancestral hamlets, along with their families, their livestock, and their valuables. Rumours began to circulate concerning a convoy of transport lorries carrying three hundred fresh troops into Gbiriri, all of them intended for Kpama's chastisement.

Abu came to the bungalow on the morning of the second day after Araoh's death to give counsel and to ask for help.

"Miss Lady, I want to stop here small-small," he said. Kutu had moved out. He had gone off in his biggest lorry with his family, his hangers-on, twenty-three baskets of household effects, seven turkeys, two dogs, the cat, and the ever-somnolent watchman. The house was boarded and hammered shut. Muslim clerics had been busy for the previous thirty-six hours devising theological schemes to make it thief-proof.

"Where did they all go?"

"They don't say anything. They only go away from Kpama. Kutu has many houses. When the trouble is past he will be glad to send them all back again."

"But why didn't you go with them?"

"Myself, I have work to do in Kpama."

He fidgeted slightly under Likki's gaze. Now, she thought, we'll hear of some other pot put on the boil.

"What kind of work?"

"Miss Lady." Abu paused, but after consideration he

apparently decided there was no way his request could be made palatable. "Miss Lady, I need money," he said in a small, almost apologetic voice. His words must have sounded familiar to him, for he added, with a sheepish grin, "Again. Eh-eh."

"Another marriage?" inquired Likki, remembering the same conversation.

"Nasara, no! It is still for Comfort. Only now I need money to get her away from the soldiers. You see how it is. I need dollars."

"Dollars!"

"Yes, Nasara, this time the soldiers don't want our own money again. They only want foreign exchange. I know you have dollars. Everything is already arranged. Only you give me the money and Comfort is safe."

"How much?"

Again he paused as if to calculate the expenses of the bribery involved. "One hundred and sixty dollars," he intoned, rather in the manner of a mathematician arriving at a new formula.

"Jesus Christ!" It was exactly the sum she had been hiding under the lining of her suitcase—for emergencies. Eight crisp twenty-dollar bills. "I don't have that much," lied Likki.

"Nasara, I know you have it."

"You *know* I have it?"

"Yes." Another prescient hesitation. "Sima told me," he explained, though it explained nothing.

"I see."

"You don't believe me?"

"Certainly not."

"But you will give me the dollars?"

"I might."

Abu untensed his shoulders. In Likki's last response he had detected the signal for which he had been waiting, the signal that she had her price. "Yes, Nasara, it's good. You give me the dollars and I will get you anything you want."

"Um-hmmm?"

"Nasara, what do you want?" He spun out for her his most charming smile.

"I want to know what's going on."

Abu's face was a masterpiece of empty surprise. "Is there something you don't know?"

"Abu, I know you too well. You say you need money. Dollars, no less. You say you need one hundred and sixty dollars . . ."

"Two hundred is better, but I can manage with less."

". . . You said a little while ago you needed one hundred and sixty dollars to get Comfort to safety."

"It's true. Everything is arranged."

"Where is she?"

He stared at her round-mouthed. "Nasara, it's better you don't know."

"Of course it is. But if you don't tell me where she is you won't get the money." If she still had it, of course. Abu wasn't above a little pilfering in a just cause.

"Nasara . . ." he begged.

"Tell me all about it, Abu, and then we'll make our deal."

He seemed actually pleased to be thus forced into confession. Like a veteran performer he relaxed in anticipation of the astonishment and delight his words would bring to his audience.

"Nasara," he began deliciously, "you see it is this way. There is only one baby."

"Only one." Likki nodded, still mystified.

"Yes, Gbendlele never had a baby. All that time the other baby she had was really Comfort. But you see," Abu explained, "that army man, he thinks he is *too* smart. Too clever for us all. In fact! He finds Comfort and he captures her. But *we* are smarter than him. We say, 'This baby is *not* Comfort.' We tell him, 'This is not our baby,' again. Then everybody is saying, 'Look at that smart army man who gets fooled by a baby.' The whole town is hooting at him. He begins to think about himself, about being too smart like that, and he begins to be afraid. Once he is afraid he begins to act stupid and then he is ours."

"So there never was a woman who died in the lorry park?"

"Nasara, that is only some story we told to fool people!"

"I see."

"It was good. Hey! Everybody believed us!"

"Who is us?"

"Us" turned out to be Abu and Comfort's father, Mahmut. Abu said that he had gone to Mahmut about Comfort shortly after the wells in Mahmut's house had gone dry. At that time Mahmut was less concerned about his daughter's welfare than about the uncanny fact that his ancient wells had become waterless overnight. He feared he was being sorcerised. Abu had pointed out to him how much community resentment against him (and, therefore, sorcery) would be diminished if Mahmut would only hand Comfort back to those who had been selected to care for her in the first place. To this, of course, Mahmut had two objections. First, Comfort's whereabouts had become a matter of principle with Araoh, and the army commander would never willingly surrender the child to Ayesha—or allow Mahmut to do so. Therefore the baby would have to be stolen. Second, of course, there was the matter of al Hajji Umar's daughter. She would not come to Mahmut if he relinquished Comfort. Here Abu grinned and said, "But I told Mahmut, 'You give me Comfort and I will give you Aswayya.' So we agreed on that."

"And how did you make al Hajji Umar agree to give his daughter to Mahmut?"

"Nasara, I started too many stories. Soon the man is certain he has to marry her *fast*."

"I see. You made up the rumours about Yahyah and Aswayya, and you arranged to chase the other suitors away? So then the field was clear for Mahmut."

"Eh-eh. . . . It's true, Nasara. And then we stole Comfort away to Kalembelebiri."

"And in return, Mahmut lied when Araoh brought him the baby for identification?"

"It's true. We fooled the army, proper!"

"And how did you get Mahmut's sister to lie?"

"Nasara, she didn't lie. We put new marks on the baby, so when Mahmut's sister saw all those marks around the navel, she knew that the child could never be a Muslim child. So she told Araoh, 'This is not our baby.' And she believed what she said."

"And where is Comfort now?"

"She is in the hospital. But they don't watch her too much because they think she is that other baby. They think she is Gbendlele's baby."

"And how do you propose to get her out of there?"

He gave her a searching look—as if he were no longer sure his judgement of her intelligence had been correct. "Nasara!" he complained. "The money will get her out. One hundred and sixty dollars. On the black market it will make that man a millionaire, the one who is watching her."

"I see."

"Nasara, I need to do it today. This very afternoon. Because soon the new soldiers will come from Gbiriri and everything will be hard for me again."

"You want the money now."

"The dollars."

"Are you going to pay me back or is this a gift from me to you at your request?"

"I will always pay you back," said Abu. "I promise you."

Likki went into her bedroom and retrieved the money from her suitcase, ripping the lining to get at it.

Abu received the money sombrely from her hand. He did not thank her for it but instead nodded, or rather bowed from the waist, like an oriental warrior. Then he rolled the bills into a tight cylinder and inserted them into the amulet bag he wore about his neck. Still, having achieved what he came for, Abu made no move to leave, but remained awkwardly in the living-room.

"Abu, is there something else?"

"Nasara John. You should bring him here today. The hospital is not good for him now."

"Oh, God." That was all she needed. Even Carlotta would rebel. Their last meeting with John had been so unpleasant that neither of them had been to see him since. John, with his whining irritability and his superstitious paranoia. "Why can't he stay where he is?" Best place for him if he were ill. Particularly now that Kutu had left town and there would be no other logical place for him to go but to the bungalow.

"Nasara, he is talking too much. All the time he hears stories but then he tells them again."

Likki sighed. She understood the trouble. Because he was white, most people gossiped freely to each other (in Kpamé) in John's presence, forgetting how easily, how expertly, he could eavesdrop. Curiously, although he was the soul of discretion in English, anything he picked up in Kpamé he treated as a scientific "finding" that had to be submitted to every person he met for examination and verification. As Abu was now hinting, some of this knowledge was dangerous.

"Any particular story?" asked Likki. John, ever credulous, collected rumours as easily as flypaper catches bugs. Every stray tale in Kpama eventually came to him and stuck. Which one was causing trouble?

"It is one story about Comfort's mother."

"What is he saying? That Mahmut murdered her?"

"Nasara, it's not true. She killed herself in that *bomba*."

"Ayesha once told me it was the same thing, murder and suicide."

"Yes, it's true," said Abu. "You don't kill yourself for being happy but rather because someone hates you."

■

In the late afternoon Carlotta and Likki travelled down to the hospital in the school pick-up to bring John Lavender back to the bungalow. As they passed through the hospital gates they spotted Abu chatting hopefully with the woman who sold deep-fried bean cakes near the dispensary. On his head Abu balanced a very large basket of what looked like clothing and personal effects.

"What's he up to?" asked Carlotta. Something in his stance had alerted her suspicions.

"Looks like he's moving out of town, doesn't it?"

"Why would he do that?"

"Kutu's left town and the house is boarded up." Likki could tell Carlotta only half the truth because Peter Awilobe would hear everything Carlotta heard.

Abu saw them then, and waved. Likki felt that the gesture was only for her, and that only she could read the triumph in his smile. Then he turned and headed off down the footpath that led to Chegili, balancing his burden as carelessly as he dared, for he knew it would never do for him to look cautious.

"He's up to something, I know it," opined Carlotta. "He's always up to something."

⬛ 24

John, in the bungalow, was a deep trial to his hostesses. Propped up among the floral sheets of the bed in the spare bedroom, John looked as pink and fresh and lovable as a newborn mouse. At the same time he was as demanding and self-centred as a hypochondriacal great-aunt, and within eighteen hours of his arrival both women cordially hated him.

"How's Ibn Sinna?" he asked Likki knowingly.

"I don't know. I haven't seen him."

"I'm not surprised."

"What's that supposed to mean?"

John just shook his head. Then he asked, "What about Mahmut?"

"What about him?"

"No need to be so curt!"

"What would I hear, or want to hear, about Mahmut?"

"Well, you might perhaps hear *something*, since Mahmut and Ibn Sinna have been plotting together for more than six months to embarrass the army in Kpama."

Of all the unlikely stories. "Ibn Sinna and Mahmut!"

"You think about it, Likki. Why, we even saw them together in the lorry park the day we arrived in Kpama."

"Yes. I remember. They were arguing."

"They were having a discussion. And as soon as the soldiers started walking their way, Ibn Sinna departed in haste."

"John you are so full of shit," complained Likki.

So then, to prove to her the superior state of his knowledge of Kpama, John favoured Likki with the story for which she had been silently waiting, relying on John's verbal incontinence to give her what she dared not ask for outright. Had she done so he would, in his present condition, have clammed up out of suspicion, contrariness, or the sheer pleasure of denying her.

According to John, Mahmut's role *vis-à-vis* Captain Araoh had been an act from start to finish. Mahmut had been using Araoh all along as a means to revenge himself on a junior officer, Lieutenant Apim, an extraordinarily handsome young man with whom, it was rumoured, Mahmut's wife had had an adulterous liaison. When Fatima became pregnant, Mahmut was understandably suspicious. Fatima's protracted labour (a fifty-two-hour marathon, which nearly killed both her and the child) was considered in Kpama to be more or less proof of infidelity, although it had to be admitted that even in the agony of unending travail Fatima had vehemently maintained her innocence.

After delivery, however, she had gone into a decline. Some people said it was because she had sworn falsely in her labour. Others, Hawa for instance, said Mahmut was poisoning her out of jealousy. Meanwhile, Mahmut was planning to revenge himself on Lieutenant Apim. To do so he first befriended the new army commander in Kpama and, by the subterfuge of fitting out quarters for Captain Araoh and his staff, lured Lieutenant Apim into his household. Within the intimacy of a shared courtyard, murder was easy to accomplish.

"When? How?" demanded Carlotta, who was enjoying this recital.

"Apim was one of the five soldiers that allegedly died from drinking water from the well."

"And the other four?"

"Camouflage," announced John Lavender and smiled at the disbelieving disgust on the faces of his audience. "Their only purpose was to disguise the real victim of attack. I was there in the hospital when they died, you know. And Apim was the last one to go. Mahmut made sure he put him out slowly. Apim got to watch the other four struggle in agony for two days. Then it was his turn. I heard him. He shrieked like a banshee for seventeen hours."

"Ugh!" Likki shivered in distaste.

Surprisingly, it was Carlotta's turn to be sceptical. "I don't believe a word of it. Five men died, so now it's murder. Last week it was witchcraft. Next week we'll probably hear it was suicide. You know, *nobody* in Africa ever dies a *natural* death. Such a thing isn't even understood in a place like Kpama. Every death is always somebody else's fault: *juju*, poison, witchcraft, ground glass, whatever. So now this death is Mahmut's fault. The whole thing is ridiculous."

"I don't know," pondered Likki. The story had a cohesiveness that made it credible—too credible, perhaps. "Where does Captain Araoh fit into all this?" she asked John. "You said Mahmut's whole thing with him was an act."

"Araoh? Nothing was supposed to happen to Araoh at all. He was just a means of getting at Apim. Of course, other people had it in for him. And he may have started to get suspicious."

"So who killed him?"

"According to the town it was witchcraft—or the shrine."

"Oh, come on."

"That, my dear Likki, is the verdict of Kpama. The man *was* unnerved you know. He lost three men digging out the well and then another five died in screaming slow motion at the hospital. He began to have nightmares. I *told* you about them. Maybe he was drinking too much. Maybe he was afraid. Eight men dead—eight men very close to him—and no one to point a finger at. Then, when he raided Kalembelebiri, the village wasn't there! Poof! It was empty. He killed Ayesha and a ghost started walking. He brought his prize baby back to Kpama and discovered he had the wrong child. He slaughtered Abu's pigs and then found out they were under the protection of the most powerful local shrine. That's a heavy platter for an African, even if he imagines he's a thoroughly modern man."

"So you're saying it was suicide?"

"Well, by Western definitions, probably, yes. But, you know, after the autopsy the doctor said he had no liver."

"Jesus Christ, John. Everybody has a liver."

"You don't have to believe me. Ask the doctor."

"Ugh!" She regarded John's credulousness as a loathsome concoction of mysticism and immaturity. There was something in his own world that so offended him that he took on the beliefs of another without scrutiny or question.

It was Carlotta who told Likki that she should think about getting John out of Kpama. Carlotta had gone to see Dr.

Kaweyu concerning John's course of medication, and he had told her it was likely the hospital would be closed down temporarily for purposes of military investigation. John, he said, needed to be under close medical supervision. He was still very weak. More to the point, no one was sure exactly what, besides malaria, had been wrong with him; nor could anyone say that he might not have a relapse. He would be far better off in the south. "By the way," said Carlotta, when she was finished with these communiqués, "I asked Dr. Kaweyu about Araoh's liver."

"Oh, God, don't tell me," groaned Likki.

"He said he couldn't find it."

"Oh, shit. Only in Africa."

"He said there was a little piece of something that might have been the liver still left attached to a blood vessel."

"Tell John all about it. It'll make him so happy."

"But what do you think could have *happened* to it?"

"I don't know, Carlotta. I can't even imagine."

✖25

After Araoh's death Likki was troubled in her mind about Ibn Sinna. On that mist-white morning, Ibn Sinna had moved among his fellows like a master of ceremonies, a successful director receiving accolades at the close of a virtuoso performance.

He had admitted nothing, of course. He said the army captain's end had been a surprise to him. Likki did not believe this. Even if her lover had not drawn the noose himself, other hands, well known to him, had fingered the lethal knot, acting possibly on his orders. Ibn Sinna was at the centre of troubling matters and his calmness there, his assumption of virture, was an affront to Likki's sense of sin.

So it was with relief that she faced the prospect of travelling south with John Lavender. And yet at the same time she was also disturbed, for it seemed she was about to undertake something much more definite than a temporary journey to the capital.

Abu was plainly distressed at the prospect of her departure. "Miss Lady, you don't go." He spoke disconsolately from the corner of Likki's bed as she packed a small ration of clothes. Her other possessions she had stowed away carefully in boxes.

"I'm only taking John to the capital. He's too weak to travel on his own."

"Nasara, I know you are thinking you will not come back."

"I'll be back," she said, but it was true that the lorry that might return her to Kpama hid behind a locked door in her imagination.

"It's because of Ibn Sinna, is it not so?"

"Only partly."

"Miss Lady, he never killed that man."

"I know. He was here with me when it happened." In many ways that was the worst part. He must have known it was Araoh's last hour and yet he had made love to her with such bittersweetness it was hard to believe the two of them had not invented passion that night.

"Miss Lady, that army man was just a useless man," continued Abu.

"Then why not leave him alone?"

"Did he leave *us* alone?"

"What good did it do to kill him? You wait, things will only go worse now for Kpama."

"Nasara, we never killed that man. His death was for himself."

"Abu, there is no way I will ever believe it was suicide. For starters, it would have been physically impossible for him to tie himself up where he was found." He had been dangling from a branch forty feet up a tree with a trunk as smooth as a telephone pole. And there were many other trees in the grove with limbs more accessible to the anxious and depressed.

"We don't say he killed himself. We say that in the end it was the shrine that took him. Because of my pigs. Because of Fatima, because of Ayesha, because of Comfort."

"Go tell it to John. He likes that sort of thing."

Abu sighed. He toyed with the buckle of a shiny red leather belt. "Why is it Nasara John believes and you do not?"

"John believes everything. He probably believes in the Tooth Fairy."

"And not you?"

"Why should I believe?"

He fidgeted. "It is because we lied to you about Comfort."

"Only partly."

"Nasara," Abu explained seriously. "We couldn't tell you everything at once. If we tell you everything at once you would worry too much. You would think, 'What if the army comes asking me questions?' You see? Just being ignorant you are happy."

"No, I'm not."

■

An hour or so later, Likki had much the same conversation with Ibn Sinna, who had come to drive her and John to Faangbaani; the lorry park in Kpama had been placed under such strict military scrutiny that for all practical purposes it had ceased to function.

Ibn Sinna was no more comforting than Abu. He told her, "You think just because you have a question, that you also deserve an answer. But for us, it is not our way. Here you have to earn your answers. You have to prove you are ready to carry them. Even then, the answers you get may not go deep. Did you get all the answers you wanted in your own country?"

"I guess I never really asked for them. I thought I understood."

"And here you don't understand?"

"No."

"For both your people and mine, is this not said to be the beginning of wisdom? Knowing that you do not understand. Perhaps I should congratulate you, now." His eyes sparkled into hers.

"Go to hell," she complained, not to his words as much as to the condescension with which he delivered them.

Abu rode with them to Faangbaani in the back seat of the Mercedes, prattling all the way about the calf Moola was about to give him. It was a short journey, not more than thirty-five minutes despite the condition of the roads. Faangbaani itself was glutted with traffic and people. It teemed with émigrés from Kpama, and its small lorry park was strained to dysfunction with trying to handle the erstwhile commerce of Kpama. The sole petrol dealer in Faangbaani was by way of becoming an overnight millionaire; but even so, gasoline was short and twenty lorries sat idly waiting for the next clandestine delivery.

Only one of these lorries, its tank newly filled at crushing expense, was taking on passengers for the capital. And so it was that John and Likki found themselves once more climbing aboard Downfall People.

"Leaving as we came," cheered John, finding some obscure symbolism in the fact.

"Not quite," demurred Likki.

"Oh, come along. Why so gloomy?" He clambered feebly into the cab of the lorry and established his space, spreading out his maps and cameras with still-trembling fingers. He also attempted to re-establish his relationship with the driver, who was not at all certain he remembered John. He said that, after all, he carried many, many whites. How could he be expected to remember every one of them? Besides, they all looked alike to him.

John fretted because Likki hung back. "You'd better take your seat," he chided. "Someone else may come along and steal it away from you."

"I'll be there in time. You save it for me."

John scowled petulantly.

Likki walked over to Ibn Sinna. "Will you keep long?" he asked her, like an African child.

"I don't know," she answered, half wishing that at this late moment he might try to detain her. She wanted from him now the magic phrase that would keep her from leaving, the words that would unravel his connections with the guilty recent past, the words that would untie him from his culture as she had become untied from her own. But he was still living in his world. How could she unfasten him? Why should she? "I'll probably only stay a week or two. Long enough for the movies, for swimming pools, for cocktails and the hit parade. Long enough to reacquaint herself with the cheap bits of her own civilization that floated like debris over the surface of the capital. Long enough to play with them until they palled and offended."

When Downfall People pulled away from the lorry park Likki felt as if she were being erased. She leaned forlornly out the window to wave, but no one was looking her way. Ibn Sinna was already engrossed in conversation with a cloth trader from Niamey, and Abu was standing with suspicious innocence next to a large pile of oranges. Likki was just an eddy in the current of their lives, a brief turbulence, a swift pull to one side and then, with a short correction, they were back on course. It felt like dying to leave them, but they did not even seem to notice.

And then, a mile or so south of Faangbaani, the road began to smile warmly in the sun and Likki felt a lightening in her stomach, a deep, almost unpleasant irritation, to be moving faster and faster. She looked with excitement to the far edge of the horizon.

"All right!" she applauded when the driver changed into top gear and the tires sang boldly, if thinly, over the corrugated road sending village children and lazy goats leaping to safety from the path of the roaring diesel monster.

John looked up from his map with something close to distaste. "Abu said you're not going back to Kpama," he accused.

"Did he just?"

"*Are* you going back?"

Likki shrugged her shoulders. "Wait and see."

"Don't you *know*?"

"Why should I know?" Why should she tell him if she did?

✖ EPILOGUE

"How is this fine woman, your wife?" inquired Ibn Sinna in the Mercedes on the way back to Kpama.

"She is fine! Gbendlele is keeping her again."

"And the father?"

"Everything is settled with the father." Abu squirmed under Ibn Sinna's gaze.

"And soon he will have his new wife, Aswayya."

"Yes." A horrible pause. Then Abu insinuated, "But you know, this girl, Aswayya, I hear she is just some useless girl. She doesn't know anything. No cooking, no farming, she doesn't even trade. And the way the flesh hangs on her now—in five years she will be *too* ugly."

"So you have done me a favour?"

"You have two wives already. I have none."

"You are young for a wife, is that not so?"

"Not young to want one."

"How did you get her out of the hospital?"

"I dashed the guard, proper!"

"How much did he want?"

"Seventy-five dollars. I gave him fifty."

"And the rest?"

"Is there more?"

"I heard you took more than one hundred and fifty from Miss Lady."

"It was a loan!" protested Abu. "She didn't ask what I do with it!"

"Is that it?"

"It's true!" lied Abu.

"And the other hundred?"

"I am buying cattle. That way, some day I can pay back Miss Lady. I am buying heifers from Moola."

"Then it seems Nasara Likki will have to wait some time for her money, is it not so?"

Abu crinkled up his face. "Is she coming back?"

Ibn Sinna did not answer right away but drove on for nearly half a mile before he replied, "As for me, I don't know if she will be back."

This sounded like no to Abu, who stared at the road ahead with overbright eyes.

Ibn Sinna smiled at his unshed tears. "It seems you love this woman."

"She was good to me. Every time."

"Hey! You have *too* many women."

"She was *your* woman," accused Abu. "And every time you quarrelled with her."

"That is because we are human beings, isn't it?" Again Ibn Sinna fell silent.

Then, a few bends further on he said, "Maybe that is why she will come back—to finish that quarrel with me. But what can we do? We can only leave things in the hands of Allah."

ABOUT THE AUTHOR

Born and raised in Brooklyn, New York, JO ANNE
WILLIAMS BENNETT holds a doctorate in social
anthropology from Cambridge University. She has
spent two years in West Africa where she gathered
material for her dissertation on Muslim education
and absorbed many of the impressions that en-
abled her to write the novel that won her the Seal
First Novel Award for 1986.

A Canadian landed immigrant since 1980, she
lives in Ottawa with her husband and three
children. She is currently conducting research into
syllabic literacy among the Cree-speaking people
of northern Ontario.